FALLING INTO FOREVER

AVERY MAXWELL

That's What She Said Publishing,Inc.

www.AveryMaxwellBooks.com

ISBN: 979-8-88643-931-1 (ebook)

ISBN: 979-8-88643-932-8 (paperback)

102123

This book is for anyone who has ever lived in the shadows—I see you, and you're perfect.
Don't let anyone tell you otherwise.
Needing someone to be your strength does not mean that you're weak—it means that you're real.

AUTHOR NOTE

Dear Reader,

Saylor's story shows how she handles anxiety and depression after a major loss. As someone who has suffered with anxiety most of my life, this is a story that's near and dear to my heart.

But here's the thing, depression and anxiety is not one size fits all. They hit us all differently, even if common themes carry over from one person to the next. So while I dug into my own history, as well as listened closely to the stories and examples given to me by sensitivity readers, Saylor's story is not a blanket depiction of either anxiety or depression.

To say that she encompasses all would be dangerous, and I won't do that. Her story is just that—a story created from a compilation of stories to develop her character.

If your battle with mental health doesn't look like Saylor's, that's okay. It's not meant to. We can all have different experiences while supporting each other and helping to break down the stigma still attached to all areas of mental health.

This is Saylor's story. I hope it resonates with some and opens eyes for others.

Kindness & Luv,

Avery

If you or someone you know are struggling with anxiety and/or depression, please know you are not alone, and someone cares—I care.

If you need help taking the first step, please reach out:

https://www.samhsa.gov/mental-health

And if you need a friend, please join us in my reader group:

https://geni.us/AverysLUVclub

PLAYLIST

FALLING INTO FOREVER

This is Saylor's playlist—she'd call it her musical journey from darkness to light.

1. Growing Sideways, Noah Kahan
2. Begin Again, Colbie Caillat
3. Turbulence, P!nk
4. Fake Happy, Paramore
5. Heavy, Linkin Park
6. What Have I Done, Dermot Kennedy
7. Give You Love, Forest Blakk
8. Renegade, Big Red Machine
9. Outnumbered, Dermot Kennedy
10. Call Your Mom, Noah Kahan
11. The Middle, Jimmy Eat World
12. Demons, Imagine Dragons
13. Say You Won't Let Go, James Arthur
14. Foolish, Forest Blakk
15. No Complaints, Noah Kahan
16. this is me trying, Taylor Swift
17. Unwell, Matchbox Twenty

18. Fall Into Me, Forest Blakk
19. My Mind & Me, Selena Gomez
20. Wrecked, Imagine Dragons
21. Head Above Water, Avril Lavigne
22. The Reason, Hoobastank
23. Better Days, Dermot Kennedy
24. I Remember, Forest Blakk
25. Flaws, Calum Scott
26. Not Today, Imagine Dragons
27. Whatever It Takes, Lifehouse
28. Just Give Me a Reason, P!nk
29. Glass, Thompson Square
30. Come Home, OneRepublic
31. Imagine, Ben Platt
32. Never Really Over, Katy Perry
33. Good In Me, Andy Grammer
34. What About Us, P!nk
35. Change My Mind, One Direction
36. Come a Little Closer, Dierks Bentley
37. Home, Edith Whiskers
38. Want You Back, HAIM
39. Come Back…Be Here, Taylor Swift
40. Want It Again, Thomas Rhett
41. Thank God I Do, Lauren Daigle
42. Saved My Life, Andy Grammer

PROLOGUE

SAYLOR

Twelve Years Ago

"There's no way she does it."

"What does he even see in her?"

"She had a panic attack in algebra last week. What's wrong with her? I mean, it's math class." She laughs while anger and hurt well in my chest.

Strong hands wrap around my biceps and keep me planted on this platform high above the ground, but he can't silence my mouth.

Turning my head, I glare at the mean girls who torment my days. "My grandfather died, you stupid twits. I know the concept of empathy is beyond your comprehension, but try. I don't wish my pain on anyone."

Dante presses himself tightly to my back, silencing me, and making us one.

"Don't listen to them. Listen to me," he whispers in my ear. I catch the scent of his minty toothpaste as he leans in, reminding me that he has me up way too freaking early in the morning for this crap.

1

The treetops sway with a strong breeze that has me regretting everything this guy has talked me into over the last two years. Why the hell did he think signing us up for a ropes course would be a good idea?

Dante tightens his arms around me while my heart slows to a steady rhythm that matches his, and the noisy chatter blurs to a dull roar.

This is why I go along with his stupid ideas. He's the only one who can calm the chaos that swirls through me. I'm not sure when the darkness found me, but at sixteen, I'm painfully aware that I don't see the world as my peers do.

"You can do this, Sayls. I believe in you," he says so only I can hear, kissing the back of my head so softly I could have imagined it, but then he retreats and takes all his warmth and calmness with him.

My palms are sweaty, and it's hard to swallow as the ropes course master checks my harness. He's speaking in tongues as he goes over safety measures for the millionth time. If my entire body wasn't shaking like it's buried somewhere in the tundra, I might be able to listen to him, but I only catch his lips moving and an annoying buzzing in my ears.

Oh, God. I'm so dizzy. This was a terrible idea. I can picture the news article now—"Teenage Girl Falls to Her Death." They probably wouldn't even give me a name, and I'd be forever known as "teenage girl." I'll end up as one of those cheesy made-for-TV movies, with a B-list actress who cries all the time.

"She's so weird." The girl's words pierce my wayward thoughts and break me out of my wild imagination.

Sometimes it's easier to live in the make-believe.

"And what is she wearing?"

"It's a trust fall, Saylor," Dante yells from below. Geez!

How the hell did he move so fast? "Let go, Sayls. I'll catch you. I'll always catch you."

I make the mistake of looking down and almost throw up. But then, his eyes draw me in. I shouldn't be able to pick out that endless blue color from this height, but it's all I can focus on—he's speaking the truth.

"Trust me," he says with a cocky grin that even I'm not immune to.

I do. I trust him more than anyone else in my life. With him, I don't have to pretend I'm something I'm not. With him, I don't have to be anything other than me.

And with a painfully long exhale, I let go of my fear, fall back into nothingness, and trust that my best friend will catch me.

The rope snaps taut, jerking my body from its freefall, and suddenly I'm floating above the ground. Dante was right —I could do it—and while I want to find that annoying, I can't quite reach that level of sass. Not when the clouds are perfect little marshmallows reminding me of campfires and picnics. The sounds of chatter and the wilderness sync to create a lullaby for my anxiety.

Calm.

"You did it," Dante yells, always my fixer. Begrudgingly, I allow happiness to settle over my expression.

I turn my head and find his gaze like we've been tied together with an invisible string that will always connect us. I'm as certain about that as I am that mean girls are the sharts of humanity.

I don't know what force put him in my path when he moved here two years ago, but I hope he'll always see me the way he does now—as someone worth loving.

The ropes master releases my line through the carabiner attached to his harness while Dante stands next to him. I honestly wasn't sure those contraptions would hold me, but Dante promised it would, and he always keeps his promises.

His smile shows off perfectly white teeth that never needed braces. He's not like any other seventeen-year-old I've ever met. My grandmother would have called him an old soul because he sees more than most and has an innate need to fix everything and everyone. It's that annoying people-pleasing gene. Ainsley has it too.

Maybe that's what drew him to me, my brokenness. He thinks he'll fix me. He believes he can fix the whole freaking world, and part of me almost hopes he can.

He's more handsome than any movie star and has a heart too good for my bitter one. Dante Thompson is Hollywood style meets Prince William. He's the perfect hero, with a strong jawline and eyes that can charm even the most poisonous snakes.

And then he's there, behind me, while I'm still picturing him as the lead in a romantic comedy. His hands hook under my armpits and stop the inevitable crash as he lowers me to the net with a hug that makes everything okay.

Leaning down, his lips hit just below my ear when he says, "I've always got you, Saylor."

I open my mouth to fire back a snarky remark I haven't thought of yet, but Dante quiets the snark I can't seem to control. He cuts me off with a gentle kiss. I'll never get used to the butterflies he creates.

My heart trembles in my chest. Somehow, my soulmate found me before I had a chance to feel lost.

CHAPTER 1

DANTE

Twelve years later

"*I*'m not selling, Trent. Not now, not next week, and definitely not to Playmore Inc. Do you have any idea how unethical the Playmore brothers are?"

His fist clenches on his thigh as he fidgets in his chair, but I turn my head to the wall of windows. The LA smog is as thick as ever. Leave it to my brother to bring that cloyingly suffocating air into my office with him.

"Marcus Playmore was the only one keeping that company from being truly bereft of morals, and now that he's left, it's gotten even shadier. I won't do that to my company or my employees."

Lena was right, and I've avoided acknowledging it for too long. Guilt, the dirty motherfucker, steals my breath as my mind springs into action. What facility can I get Trent into this time? What damage has he already done? What will Lena and Poppy need while he's away?

My heart aches for Lena. She deserves so much more, and

Trent has never treated her well. Poppy is the happy result of their union, and that kid stole my heart with her first breath.

Even as my thoughts run rampant with what I can do to stop this from happening to him again, one question plagues me. "Why are you pushing this?"

As I stare into a face that reminds me of my own, it's clear—he's using again, and I missed all the signs. *Or you didn't want to believe them*, my traitorous conscience says bitterly.

Trent always had an excuse. He explained the bloodshot eyes and shaky hands as lack of sleep—the mood swings and erratic behavior, a change in meds.

And I was the idiot who believed him.

My gaze immediately falls to the photos on the corner of my desk.

Saylor and me.

Trent and me.

Poppy.

I allow myself one moment to linger on the photographs. Maybe I wasn't meant to save either of them, but I can save his little girl. My gaze drifts to the photo of his daughter and back to Saylor—one is a smiling ray of sunshine who taught me to love again, and the other is the woman who taught me how much love can hurt.

Trent's expression turns murderous when he notes me looking at the photos. Any time he comes into my office, he flips over the one of Saylor with a snarky remark about her being an idiot, but today, it's the photo of his daughter that turns his eyes into black, unfeeling lumps of coal.

"You have to sell," he seethes, and the vein in his neck bulges like a bodybuilder on steroids. "You're going to sell because it's a damn good offer. It's plenty of money, Dante. It's time to sell." The sweat of desperation trickles down his forehead, and spittle collects in the corner of his lips.

"Ascendancy Inc. is not for sale. I've built this company from the ground up. It's a legacy to leave our family."

After losing Saylor, I was ecstatic to find out I have four half-siblings around the country—the family I've always craved but only ever had with her.

Shaking my head, I vanquish all thoughts of her. Those memories cause a longing I can't deal with today. Right now, I need to focus on my brother.

Trent makes a disapproving sound in the back of his throat.

"Family," he snorts. "You're so desperate to find one, you put blinders on to everything and everyone else. Poor Dante," he says in a mocking tone.

It takes all my effort to keep a neutral expression on my face. This isn't him. This is the drugs talking.

"Poor little Dante." Taunting me is one of his favorite pastimes. "Left home alone at five years old, so now you try to make everyone love you—to be so good that no one will ever leave you."

I crack the knuckles on my right hand, and he pauses with a snarl on his face.

I was left home alone a lot, but I'm guessing five is just when I became aware of it.

"How's that working out for you, Dante?" He says my name like a curse. "Did that piece of shit in Connecticut love you? Oh, that's right. She sent you packing as soon as—"

"That's enough," I say through gritted teeth. I place my hands in my lap but keep my fists balled tightly under my desk. I won't give him the satisfaction of a visual reaction. "Dad may have been stuck with me after my mother died, but make no mistake, he didn't want me any more than he wanted the rest of you. Why do you think we moved every two years? He's never been someone any of us could count on."

I'm still not sure why he didn't put me up for adoption, but Trent doesn't need to know that. I've already told him too many secrets, and now, I fear that was a mistake.

"I'll never regret putting family first." I sigh and glance at Saylor's picture for a split second before focusing on Trent again. "All of my family. Saylor showed me what family should look like, and for that, she'll always be a part of mine."

His sneer is full of contempt. "You'll never regret putting family first? That's stupidly idealistic." His features take on a hard edge, but his expression is vacant—my brother is no longer in control of himself. "Regret is a funny thing, *brother*. Never say never."

It's a warning, but I can't begin to fathom for what.

"Listen." I rub my forehead with my thumb and pointer finger. I can't seem to apply enough pressure to make the rising headache disappear, though. "I've worked too hard to hand this company over to some sleazy trust fund kids for a fraction of what it will be worth in five years."

His knuckles turn white on his thigh. "A trust fund kid like me?"

How did I miss this? I haven't seen Trent spiral like this since my first week in California.

After I got him out of that mess, he promised he'd stay clean. Will this always be the cycle for him?

"You're not a trust fund kid. You started working on TV shows when you were still in diapers."

"And not a day since. Is that what you mean?" He may be older than I am, but emotionally, he's stunted at eleven years old.

"Damn it, Trent. Stop putting words in my mouth."

"Sell the fucking company." Sweat gathers on his forehead, plastering his stringy hair to his skin. The vehemence of his tone is what unsettles me most. It makes warning bells chime loudly in my mind. He's grasping at straws, and he knows it.

His nostrils flare, and his face reddens, but this is about money. He hasn't had a paying gig in three years, and if he's using again, the only money he has left is probably tied up in the shares of Ascendancy Inc. that I stupidly gifted him.

I lift my hand to loosen the knot in my tie and lean back in my chair. "I'm not selling." I release a heavy sigh. "How much do you need?"

"It's not about the money." His eye twitches, calling attention to the lie.

I yell, "Don't lie to me, Trent. Not to me." I take a calming breath before my employees start asking questions. "I'll buy your shares." My shoulders are as tight as my words. It's the last thing I want to do. These shares are supposed to be his retirement plan. That's why I've worked so hard.

How long do you have to take drugs for them to cause that vacant look and sallow skin? I'm not entirely sure how he's able to function like this. It pisses me off and makes me incredibly sad. I've worked my ass off to rehab his image and his career. It's a slap in the face after everything I've accomplished and a wrecking ball in his family's life.

But he's your family. You would help him if you cared. And you owe him this. It's not his fault he had no real family who loved him, and Mike Thompson has never put anyone over himself—especially you. My inner voice is an honest asshole.

"Playmore is willing to pay double what they're worth." His tone fluctuates between pissed off and a whiny teenager. I hate witnessing this level of desperation, but it's the proof I've been waiting for—he's in way over his head. *How much could he possibly owe?*

If I'd been around when we were kids, maybe I could have…

It's not even worth going down that path. Trent is one of

two half-siblings who live in California, and where Trent is a match about to catch fire, Hunter is a self-made asshole, but at least he has his shit together. *Would he help with Trent if I called him?*

Not likely. Trent burned that bridge well before I knew I had brothers.

I doubt even having our father around would have kept him clean. Not with what I now understand about our childhoods.

We've always been on our own.

His knee bounces erratically, and his fingers tap a relentless rhythm on the arm of the chair.

"Double what they're worth *now*," I say, unable to keep the exasperation out of my voice.

A flash of bubblegum pink catches my attention through the glass wall. I glance quickly over Trent's shoulder to where Lena and Poppy stand speaking with someone in the hallway. When Lena turns toward my office, I shake my head and hold up one finger. Trent's too out of his mind to care, but she catches the gesture immediately, tightens her ponytail, then steps back.

She scans from me to the back of Trent's head in a fraction of a second, before distracting Poppy and leading her away by the hand.

Only then do I return my focus to my brother. "The value of this company grows year after year. You're looking at an instant payout instead of the long game."

He stands so quickly that he knocks over the guest chair and glares at me like it's my fault, then he kicks it to the side and paces behind it. He's agitated and angry, his moods shifting faster than a tornado.

"Sell," he hisses. It sounds like a threat, and I'm even more thankful I caught Lena before she entered my office.

I don't think he's heartless enough to endanger his

daughter, but drugs change a person. I'm beginning to learn that the hard way. Would he do something to jeopardize her future?

"Is there anything else you need today?" There's no point arguing with him. He can only hear what he wants to hear right now.

"You're going to regret it." His gaze jumps to the photos on my desk. When he stares at the one of Saylor, it's all I can do not to clutch it protectively to my chest.

My blood simmers below the surface like an underground river rushing toward an exit. "Are you threatening me, *brother?*"

He shrugs, and all hope that the man I've gotten to know over the last six years is strong enough to fight his demons is gone. Trent's losing this internal battle.

"I wouldn't threaten my own brother," he says condescendingly while glaring at my photos. "You didn't grow up in Hollywood. You may be the golden boy now, but everyone falls. Everyone. Sell. The. Company." Each word is a blow to my heart.

I regret every secret I've shared with him.

"Go home, Trent." I pull at the tension in my neck and squeeze while he holds my gaze for a beat too long. I'm not even sure if rehab will work this time. The only emotion he can access is anger. How long has the life been seeping out of him? How long have I ignored the signs? I should have kept a closer eye on him.

"Fuck you," he spits before storming out. He's like a toddler having a tantrum, knocking over piles of paper and office supplies as he goes. I force a tight smile for the few heads brave enough to turn my way. This is what I get for having glass walls.

When our audience goes back to their tasks, I drop my head against the chair's headrest with a dull thud and focus on my breathing. I only have minutes, maybe seconds, before my office is filled with sunshine and rainbows.

One. Two. Three and four. I repeat the mantra in my head until I hear the pitter-patter of little feet running down my hallway.

"Unca!"

A grin takes over my entire face before I even open my eyes. And when I do, I'm hit by a love so profound it rattles my bones.

"Lollipop," I say, then open my arms so a four-year-old ball of energy dressed in pink tulle can run straight into them. She smells like strawberry shampoo and sweetness. She's the warmth I thought I'd never feel again.

Her mom walks in behind her. Lena is the big sister I never had and has spent countless hours listening to my broken heart, but she enters today wearing a careful mask, and I sit up straighter.

She and Trent started dating a year after I moved to California, and if it weren't for Poppy, I would regret ever introducing her to Trent. Lena deserves better, and I know her Prince Charming is out there somewhere. She'll find him as soon as she allows herself to move on, but regardless of what happens in their relationship, I'm thankful for her because, in some strange way, she reminds me of the only place that's ever felt like home—Hope Hollow.

A town I haven't set foot in in over six years. Maybe it's because she saw me at my lowest and helped me up. Or because she listened without judgment and told me to get my head out of my ass when I needed it. She embodies everything I grew to love about that quirky small town in Connecticut.

"So, it's true?" she asks carefully.

I should have listened months ago when she told me she thought Trent was using again.

I nod while Poppy traces every line on my face. I hope she holds on to this level of curiosity for a while longer.

"Well, crap." Lena rights the chair Trent knocked over. "Then today's probably not the day to drop another bomb on you."

I lift one brow in her direction, but Poppy instantly pokes at it, trying to push it back into place.

"You're hairy, Unca."

This kid can pull a chuckle from me even while dread sits around my neck like a noose. "Yeah, Lollipop. It's been a long day." She curls into my side and rubs her face along the silk of my tie. Once she's settled, I give Lena my full attention. "Lay it on me."

Chewing on her lip, she tightens her high ponytail for the fourth time.

It's not often that Lena gets nervous. Not when she found out she was pregnant and Trent flipped out. Not after Poppy was born and he took off for Ibiza the same day. Not even the time Poppy dislocated her elbow. But she wrings her wrist now, and it sets off every internal alarm I possess.

"Lena, this day can't get much worse. Just spit it out," I say as Poppy draws circles on my dress shirt with her little finger.

It's true what the baby books say. I read them all while Lena was pregnant, and kids really do feed off the energy that surrounds them. I take a deep breath but still struggle to relax my shoulders.

Lena nods, then reaches into the bag she uses for the unbelievable amount of shit this child needs every time they leave the house. Who knew something so small would require enough supplies to care for a small army?

Poppy places both hands on my cheeks and plants a big, wet kiss on my lips. I love this little girl so damn much, and

I'm in serious trouble because she already has me wrapped around her little finger.

A thunk draws my attention, and my throat burns like I'm trying to breathe through a room full of smoke. Bacon in a frying pan couldn't sizzle more than the air trapped in my lungs. My world narrows to nothing but the book Lena dropped on my desk, and a low buzz fills my ears.

Seconds, or maybe decades, pass before Lena rounds the desk and removes Poppy from my lap.

My voice is hoarse when I finally find my words. "What the hell, Lena?"

"Hell, hell, hell," Poppy sings. Apparently, her ability to pronounce sounds changes depending on the word.

"You have to read it." Lena's voice is pitched higher than usual, and the hairs on my arms stand at attention even as I shake my head no because I've lost the ability to speak.

April Rain by Sassy Thompson—known to me as Saylor Greer. The only woman I've ever loved, and the only woman who asked me to leave and never return.

Seeing her use my surname for her penname in person like this is a punch to the gut. Would she feel the same if she knew I'd chosen hers as well?

"Read it, Dante. And do not leave this office until you do." Her tone is sharp and unyielding.

Lena has heard every detail of my relationship with Saylor. Every. Fucking. One. I don't know how many hours she sat with me while I tried to process the messed-up situation that ended with me fleeing to California six years ago.

I was a train wreck when I arrived here. Heartbroken, disoriented—a shell of my former self. She was the friend I needed, the one to help pull me from the despair suffocating me, and the heartbreak still remains.

Saylor's a pain that will never heal.

"Don't you think living through the loneliness is enough,

Lena?" I fight the urge to open social media and stalk Saylor's online life. "Why in God's name would I want to pick at a scab that won't heal? I know how my story ended."

She shakes her head sadly. "You know how the story ended for you." Can she hear how loud the blood rushing in my ears is? My breaths become shallow, and I can't seem to fill my lungs. She taps the book covered with raindrops and a silhouette of a woman who somehow emanates sadness. "But you don't know how it ended for her."

My mouth goes dry. I can't look away from the book. "What are you saying?" My voice doesn't sound like my own —it reflects a love lost well before its time.

"Read it. You might find that your story doesn't have to have the tragic ending you've been living all these years."

Heartbreak turns me to stone. Our love story was a tragedy. Am I really strong enough to find out how it broke Saylor too?

CHAPTER 2

SAYLOR

One month later

"What is this?" Kate screeches through our video call, and her voice echoes off the walls in my tiny office. She's a great agent, but her delivery sucks. "It doesn't even have a happily ever after. I can't shop this to a new publisher." Her lips purse into a thin line when she leans closer to the screen. "What's happening here? You've sent me three half-finished manuscripts just like this. What am I supposed to do with this shit? It's garbage, Sass."

It's times like these I regret publishing under my nickname, because when she's pissed, all those Ss hiss at me.

I forget to blink as she lays into me, but maybe I deserve her harsh words. If only she could understand that some stories don't get a happily ever after.

"You took a risk leaving Malimar Media," Kate says in her signature abrasive tone, and I'm glad I stayed in Connecticut for this meeting. "I understand why you did, but enforcing the rescission of your contract makes the other big

16

publishing houses extremely nervous. They need a new book that's impossible to turn down, and they need it now."

"Malimar wanted me to write from a script, Kate. A script with borderline abusive heroes and heroines with no backbone. It wasn't my voice, and it has to be *my* voice I listen to. And, if the whispers of his eh, business practices are true, I want nothing to do with him."

A recent scandal with Will Malimar and an actress was the catalyst to get my butt in gear.

Kate's teeth must be worn to nubs with all the grinding she's doing. "I agree, Sassy. But Malimar Media is still considering legal action against you."

Opening my mouth to release a curse-laden tirade, she cuts me off before I can get going.

"They don't have a case—Grady made sure of that. They have no leg to stand on after the hack job they did to your last stand-alone book."

I snort. Calling it my book is an exaggeration. Over fifty percent of that story came from someone else, and they published their revised version without my knowledge or consent under my name.

"But that doesn't mean they won't threaten anyone trying to take you on. Give me something so good Holiday House Publishing can't refuse it."

"Kate." I groan and press my fingers to my forehead. Talking with her is the equivalent of little knives stabbing my eyeballs. "I can't give them what I don't have. I'm burnt out, and I need a break. I told you that three months ago that twenty-two books in five years has drained me. You're supposed to be protecting me from vultures like them."

"This is me protecting you. How long do you think new publishers will wait before they find the next big thing that comes with a hell of a lot less baggage? You have a small window of time to show up with something truly stellar because if you can't deliver, they will decide you're not worth the risk."

While she stews, I sit in the silence of dead air and fantasize about ways my life could have been different.

Her sigh is heavy and comes far too quickly. "You have to do the interview tomorrow," she says.

"No way, Kate. Rebecca Henshaw is Malimar's daughter! She'll probably do something shitty."

"We know she will. Malimar has the world's worst God complex, and no one has ever successfully broken a contract with him. He will attempt to make an example out of you, but if you play nice, and keep your attitude in check, they'll have nothing to use against you. This is an opportunity to show the publishing world and Malimar that you're not afraid of him. It's the last piece of the contract you're obligated to fulfill, then we can terminate it with limited repercussions. Her broadcasts receive millions of views every week. The interview stays."

"Fine. I'll play nice at the interview. But only because it gives me a chance to pimp First Pages. She will let me talk about my literacy program, right?"

"There's no format for her segment. It runs live and is more of a round table discussion, so you should be able to promote your little literacy initiative too."

Little. Yeah, making sure children have access to currently relevant reading material is little.

"Ten a.m. You can do this, Sass. And you're doing it from home. You don't even have to come into the city. You'll be fine," Kate says right before she hangs up without a goodbye.

I'll be fine? How long has she freaking known me? There's a reason I don't do interviews. There's a reason I don't do public events in general.

I'm a liability to myself.

"I know," I mutter. And I do—sort of.

~

"Miss Thompson?" Rebecca asks, interrupting me again. She says my pen name like we share a secret, and I clench the edges of my latest book.

That tone makes me want to duck for cover. Or maybe it's because I haven't been able to get three words in about my literacy program, and the snark I've been trying so hard to keep in check is bubbling to the surface.

I bite the inside of my cheek. *Be professional. Get through this interview, and then you're free. Keep the sass in check.* That last one is the hardest to control, though.

Her lips thin into a cruel smile, and I straighten my spine as a chill works through my body.

"Would you say you pull from your own life experiences for your stories?" Her voice is too silky, too sickly sweet. She's trying to give me a false sense of security.

I shift in my chair, crossing then recrossing my legs as words of warning play on a loop in my mind. "I think there's a level of storytelling that allows an author to incorporate real-life events or emotions, and it wouldn't be realistic to say that my life doesn't filter into the stories occasionally."

"That's so interesting," Rebecca coos. She leans forward in her seat as the camera zooms in on her face. "In *April Rain*, your heroine was an orphan."

It's not a question, so I don't answer, but I do swallow hard. There's no way she knows about my history. Right?

Thank you, stupidly expensive lawyers.

When her eyes glint with malicious intent, it hits me with sudden clarity. Her father doesn't give a shit if this book bombs on the charts. Malimar couldn't keep me under his thumb, so he's starting a war.

When I remain silent, she digs in. "Did you base their lives on your own family?"

Her lips curl into a nasty snarl. She thinks she can break me but doesn't know I'm already damaged beyond repair.

My nails dig into my right palm while my left hand cradles it from view. *Focus on the pain, Sass. If you cause it, no one else can.*

"You receive criticism for the heat level in your books." She changes the topic without giving me more than a second to reply. "You write words that could easily describe a pornography scene, yet you openly promote children's literacy and programming as your charity of choice. There must be mom groups all over the world angry at you for dragging children into such sexually explicit material."

"No, I don't. That's not what—"

"And it is explicit, Miss Thompson. Graphic even. Where do you get the inspiration for that?"

Heat coats my spine, and I'm pretty sure my camera-ready smile is only a baring of my teeth at this point.

"What kind of research did it take for those *steamy* scenes in your last novel, *Come September?*"

What the hell kind of question is that? I open my mouth, but she wastes no time finishing her attack.

"Are the rumors true, and it's autobiographical? Do you regret pushing away your *one true love*, Dante Greer? I'm sure the world is curious about that relationship and how it relates to the characters in your book, Sara and Danny."

Rage has my hands trembling. My stories are not porn. But Dante? How the hell does she have that information? I've spent years refusing to acknowledge why we chose each other's surnames as pseudonyms, but her words make images of him flood my mind. They swirl like a whirlpool, and curse words sit on the tip of my tongue.

"Is it true that the love child is his? Is that why you're no longer together?"

Love child? What child? My stomach heaves, and I take a fortifying breath to keep my breakfast down.

Children's literacy. Focus on children's literacy.

That's what I'm here to freaking talk about. My nails break skin, and moisture beads in my palm. I let my body focus on that while I build my retort.

"Why are you asking this?" My voice is deceptively calm—a miracle in itself. "Did you ask Steve Bigby if he murdered fourteen people before writing *On The Fifteenth Night*? Did you ask Marla Montrey if she rode dragons to the seventh ring? I find your line of questioning offensive, ignorant, and lazy."

My words don't deter her, and she keeps talking, but the darkness is creeping in and all I hear is static.

She shuffles some papers in front of her and reality comes crashing back in violent waves. "It confuses me that you write such explicit material but are so vocal about championing children's causes. It's almost like you believe those two worlds should be connected somehow. Do the parents of these kids know what you write?"

"I don't write pornography, and I don't write for children. All my novels are very clearly written for adults and marketed to adult readers. I'm here to discuss how people can help children access current and culturally relevant reading material. What I write is—"

She laughs, and it's cold, almost maniacal. "I apologize. Most people aren't ashamed of what they write."

What the fuck?

"We'll go back to your family and why you go to such lengths to hide your identity from your readers."

Her sneer is evil—all fake softness and camaraderie have vanished.

Air whooshes in my ears as I fight back a panic attack.

"You've utilized extensive measures to keep your history

and your sister's untimely death from the public. Or perhaps it's what happened after the accident that you're hiding? It was a terrible tragedy, but it seems like someone also went to great lengths, expensive lengths, to keep the story out of the mainstream news."

She has no qualms about blasting my private life to the world. It's written all over her face.

She's not interested in an honest interview. This attack was premeditated, and her father is my executioner. I've heard the rumors. How he blackmails and strong-arms his talent, and no one is safe from his particular brand of encouragement.

But I thought I'd found the loophole.

I was wrong.

"How does the rest of your family feel about the smut you write?"

My balled-up fists ache, and the blood pooling in my palm burns like acid. I've hit my wall, and this bitch is going down.

"I'm no more ashamed of what I write than you are to admit you got this job because of Daddy. Must be nice having the backing of Will Malimar. I'm sure he opened many doors for you. But to answer your question, because you're a desperate woman willing to sabotage another to accomplish your own selfish goals, Miss Henshaw, I'll tell you this."

I lean in like I'm about to give her some juicy gossip, then stare straight into the camera and say, "Go grab a ten-inch dildo, the kind with suction cups on the balls, and then stick it to Daddy's desk. That's the only kind of fucking over either of you are getting from me. This interview is over."

∼

"You told the daughter of Will Malimar, owner of Malimar Media, to sit on a ten-inch dildo, live, while promoting children's literacy. Now they've spliced the video so it looks like you're talking about children with dildos. This is exactly what they wanted. They will bury you, Sassy. What the hell were you thinking?"

What was *I* thinking? I told her this was a bad idea. I scan my small bookstore that always calms my chaos, or at least wrestles it into submission enough that I can focus.

Ainsley squints her eyes into slits next to me as she watches her computer screen. My big sister, by a whole two minutes, is as gentle as they come, except when it comes to me. She's always been a worrier, but losing our entire family by the time we were twenty-two has made her obsessive about my safety.

When we were younger, I swear I could hear her unspoken words in my head, but not anymore. It's a side effect of shutting down and spending my days actively trying to avoid emotions. But sometimes, like now, I miss that connection.

I catch a glimpse of the views over Ainsley's shoulder. They're pouring in on Rebecca's interview. One thousand. Ten thousand. A million.

And rising.

How much is Malimar spending on advertising this shit?

Ainsley's pale face is a sickly gray color.

"You've gone viral, Sassy—viral for the wrong reasons," Kate says with slightly less bitterness. "We knew Malimar wanted to make an example of you for daring to leave his company, and you handed it to him on a silver platter. Now he's…"

We've all heard how he punishes those who go against him, and Kate was right. He's waging a war against me to set an example for anyone else who dares to even think about leaving him. He's taking it as a personal affront and has the means to make this spiral until I won't be able to show my face anywhere.

Thank God for Grady Reid Esq. and his uncanny ability to tear apart a contract everyone thought was ironclad. Hopefully, all his hard work won't be for nothing, but it's not helping to secure my future.

"I'm heading to your godforsaken town in the morning," she grumbles. "Do not talk to anyone until I get there. Do not make any public statements. And for once in your life, put a fucking lid on the sass and do as you're fucking told."

"No. You don't have to—"

"Sassy, so help me God. Close the store and sit tight. You're in desperate need of an image rehab, and there's only one person with enough magic in his arsenal to fix this shit. Just, please." Her tone is softer than I've ever heard from her. "I'll be there soon."

My scalp tingles like a bad omen—I'm in over my head here.

"Maybe this won't be so bad," Ainsley says, wrapping her arms around my shoulders. I instantly go stiff. Hugging gives the sensation of spiders crawling under my skin, not because I don't like to be touched, but because it's a prelude to feelings, and I can't allow those emotions to penetrate my armor. I spend every moment of every day trying to lock those suckers away—it's the only way to keep myself safe. And if I don't outwardly share what's happening in my heart and mind, it'll hurt less when I fail.

Ainsley and I couldn't be more different. She has the patience and grace I've never been able to hold on to. She's soft to my hard, loving to my cold heart, empathetic to a fault, and I—well, it's better for everyone if I keep all my feelings to myself. I love her dearly, but we are not the same.

Maybe she should have done the interview in my place.

"Won't be so bad?" I choke out before I can grab the anger that's become my security blanket. Anger is safe. Anger keeps people at bay, allowing safe harbor in my home and bookstore. "How can you say that? Malimar is turning the world against me, so even if I can write something, and Holiday House buys it, no reader will touch it."

The cold hands of fear embrace me like the grim reaper.

"Without readers..." A gulp jerks my chin to my chest. "Holiday won't take a chance on me. If this snowballs, I could lose my bookstore, Ains."

My throat closes as I scan the little store that's always been my dream. It's the one thing that gives me hope. "This is my entire life—the only place I fit in. If I lose it..."

"Sass." She turns the screen my way. Shoulder to shoulder, we watch as the comments roll in under Rebecca's post.

Ainsley clicks another button, and TMZ pops up with interview clips. Another browser, another site. The combination of my overnight success five years ago, my reclusive nature, and the ridiculous popularity of Rebecca's show has catapulted me into the spotlight. It also doesn't help that Malimar's vendetta means filtering it out through all his media outlets on a loop.

"Kate's right. You're already going viral, and it's not good. People are calling for you to be canceled, and those are the nice ones."

"But I—I..."

This empty store is my place to hide. A place to belong. A place that reminds me of those I've lost without suffocating in the sadness of it.

Owning a bookstore was always my dream. I drag the pendant around my neck along its chain as other dreams, broken long ago, try to enter my headspace.

Writing allows me to have the one dream that wasn't shattered.

"I know you're struggling, Sass, but you can only live on your savings for so long. Maybe it's time to consider renting your room upstairs. That should help offset at least some of your expenses until the words flow again or you finally receive your frozen royalties." She speaks to me like she'd speak to one of her patients about to get a death sentence.

Because opening my space to a stranger is exactly that—a death sentence.

I can taste blood at the back of my throat. My body reacts to stress viscerally, and today it acts like I just ran thirty miles without my inhaler and my lungs are collapsing.

The royalties from the books still on the *New York Times* list should be coming in every six months, but Malimar is using my broken contract to seize them. It's not legal, but it's also not stopping him.

Ainsley's right. Even existing on ramen, I can't survive on my savings forever.

"Sassy. This is killing me because I still believe Kate's a bulldozer, but I think you should trust her with this. And renting out your extra room will give you a financial buffer. It won't be that bad."

"That bad? Are you out of your mind? It would be horrible. It's not even a bedroom. It's half a room I use as an office. Plus I'd end up renting it to some stalker or ax murderer, because that is the kind of luck I have, admit it."

"That's true." She chuckles. "But you forget that I'm your mirror. I know what you need and what you can handle, just like you know me when you allow yourself to feel it. I'll help you get it rented. Let Kate handle the mob, and who knows, maybe having a roommate will help get you out of the writing funk you've been in. Maybe it's your next great love story waiting to be written."

My "funk" is a choice—it's being intentionally lonely

while creating happily ever afters I don't believe in anymore. But I'll never admit that to anyone—not even my twin.

"But it means I'd have to wear a bra in the morning and remember to brush my teeth before anything else. What if they mess with my coffee or play loud music?"

"You have noise-canceling headphones for a reason." Ainsley turns the sign on the door to 'closed,' and my heart spasms with the motion.

What if it never opens again? The thought sours my stomach.

"If I get murdered in my sleep, will you make sure they play ocean sounds at my funeral? It's peaceful, and shouldn't a funeral be peaceful? I mean, there won't be a ton of mourners, but you and Grady will be there. Maybe we should cancel the funeral altogether, and the two of you could go on a cruise or something. I don't want—"

"Now, Sass," she says. "I thought you saved the drama for your stories?"

Ainsley is the levelheaded one. I'm not sure when I started noticing our differences more than our similarities, but they're all I see now.

She hooks her arm through mine and rests her temple on my shoulder as we walk toward the back stairs. I fight the urge to flick her cheek off me. Skin-to-skin contact makes it harder to keep my walls up.

"Shan would have been proud of you. You know that, right?" she says.

My stomach hollows out. The pain of missing someone who was your whole world never gets easier. We don't talk about our sister very often because she's one of two people who threaten my ability to control my emotions.

It's not fair that her life ended when she'd never really lived. She spent her life taking care of us.

"Do you ever wonder if she thought we were a burden?" I ask.

Ainsley stops at the back stairs that lead to my apartment. "You mean because she took over mothering after Mom died?"

I shrug. "She was only thirteen. Grumpy took us in, but she raised us. And when he died, she was only twenty. She never even got to have a normal college experience."

Our father took off when he found out we were twins, and our mother passed away when we were seven. As far as I'm concerned, we buried him with our mother. But our sister was our last connection to our history—and now she's gone too.

"She loved us, Sass. It was hard for her, yes, but I don't think she ever regretted it. And now, we owe it to her to make the most of the lives she sacrificed for."

I nod because the lump in my throat is the sadness that still fights to take my whole world away from me. If only I'd been able to get to her. If only I'd been able to open her door. If I hadn't been with Dante...

Survivors' guilt is one that lasts a lifetime.

CHAPTER 3

DANTE

"*I*t's been a long day, and I have no idea how this will go."

I'm out of sorts. I may be known as Hollywood's it-boy when it comes to solving public relations crises, but I'm not sure even I can salvage my reputation with the story they're spinning.

Somehow, rubbing elbows with celebrities made me a celebrity in my own right, and now I'm experiencing the dark side of fame in a whole other light. It wasn't ever supposed to be like this. I had no interest in the spotlight, but the spotlight found me just the same, and I was too young to fully flesh out the possible repercussions down the road.

When I was lonely and hurting, it was a boost to my ego to have people interested in me, even if it was originally via Trent. Now I wish I'd never shown my face.

"Why?" Lena asks.

"Because," I say like a petulant child. My damn nerves are shot. I spare a quick glance at my driver in front of me, but thankfully, he stays focused on the road and not on my quickly spiraling life.

After reading Saylor's book a few weeks ago, I started making plans. Schemes. A way to force my way back into *her* life because it'll be a battle of wills. I wasn't prepared to be called in as her knight in shining armor right when my world was imploding.

I've needed her since I was fifteen years old. I blew it once —I won't do it again.

"Because why?" Lena prods, bringing the screen closer to her face. This is what I get for being best friends with a hair-stylist. She has a sixth sense and has spent countless hours reading people. She could pry gold from a pirate's hand if given enough time.

"Because she has no filter or self-preservation, for one. For two, she won't be happy to see me. And three, because Trent and my client, if I can still call Olivia a client now, are spewing their stupidly concocted story all over the tabloids about my character and insinuating Poppy isn't safe around me. And…" I don't want to admit this, but it's the only truth that makes sense. "It had to have been Trent who tipped off that reporter about Saylor and me. I was stupid to hold out hope there was enough kindness left in him not to drag Poppy or Saylor into this."

He knows I have exactly two weaknesses. His daughter is one, and Saylor is the other. He all but made that threat in my office a month ago, didn't he?

My own brother is trying to ruin me. We're a fucking reality show.

I've spent the last six years keeping my nose clean and helping clients dig their way out of their shit. I should have known that one little threat against a lying, cheating, narcis-sistic brother could undo all my years of hard work.

"Connecticut isn't so bad," she says, and I lean my head against the car window.

"I don't know, Lena. I'm back in the middle of bum-fuck

country, and I have to trust Kate Gerard, of all people." Thankfully we're on the same team, because if Kate is half as ruthless as she was when she worked in public relations, she's not someone I'd want as an enemy.

Me and Saylor. Two problems, one solution.

That's why I dropped everything and agreed to come. I'll do whatever it takes to save us both this time.

Nostalgia hits hard when I lean forward to peer out the windshield. "Poppy would love it here. It's quiet, and kids are running all over town."

Lena smiles into the screen. "I'm sure she would, but because of Trent, she's stuck in the house for a while."

I can't hide the flinch. We've worked so hard to keep Poppy out of the spotlight. Even when Trent is plastered all over the news, we've made it our mission to protect our little girl.

Because yeah, sometimes I feel more like a father than an uncle. She means too much to me to allow Trent to deprive her of that kind of love, so I decided a long time ago that if he wouldn't provide for her in every way, I would.

I swallow through the guilt as sights that still haunt my dreams come into view.

If Trent had been in his right mind, he never would have made up lies about his daughter like that. Until recently, the media had only speculated.

Is she Trent's, or is she Dante's love child?

Could she be their niece?

Are they raising her together?

Because we never confirmed anything, the public quickly lost interest in her. Acknowledging that she was Trent's daughter would only have put her in harm's way, so we remained silent.

It shows how deep his addiction has gone. He knew it

31

would filter down to affect his four-year-old, and he didn't give a shit about the damage he was causing. Who does that?

How did I let this happen?

"We both knew there was some level of risk involved in this world," Lena says gently. "You guys work with celebrities and lies. You run in those circles. Poppy couldn't stay a mystery forever, and we'll fight back. You're not the monster they're making you out to be. Poppy will be fine, so fix your narrative before he destroys everything you've worked for."

"I want to protect her."

"I do too, Dante. But the reality is, we live in Los Angeles. Her friends' parents see you both on red carpets. They hear whispers and ask questions, so we should be realistic. You're both a part of that world, and by proxy, so are we."

She must read the tension in my face—for once, I can't wear a mask—because she continues more gently. "We'll get through the Poppy drama. The truth always comes to light eventually. And I get that Trent took choices away from you, but he's painting you as some violent, abusive predator. Brother or not, you can't fix everyone, but you can solve this. You can counter the lies he's spewing."

I don't have a good track record of fixing anyone I love.

Pulling at the muscle bunched at the base of my neck, I say my biggest fear out loud. "I don't want Poppy seeing this. I don't want her to question the kind of man I am or the legacy I'm trying to create for our family."

The weight of her sadness hits me hard through Face-Time. "You're worrying about the wrong things. Poppy is four. It'll be a nonissue by the time she's old enough to understand what's going on."

Lena sits quietly while my mind spins possibilities. But there's only one logical explanation. "He's either being paid to do this by a competitor, or he's more desperate for me to sell than I realized, and both scenarios boil down to money."

"He's not the Trent we grew to love," she says gently, and it's a reminder for both of us. "It's important to remember that so we can undo this mess."

She's not saying anything I haven't already thought of, but it doesn't make it any easier.

"The world knows you as a curated form of Dante, a persona, not the Dante who runs out at four in the morning because his niece is sick and needs medicine. There's a difference, and the world needs to know that. Make them see the truth."

I rub my forehead as I think, and she presses on.

"Public Dante can be an asshole, but you aren't. Both sides of you collided last week to protect your niece, your name, and all that you've built. I get that, and the world will too, if you make them see you for who you really are. And you do that by mending the piece of your heart that should have never been left broken. It starts with Saylor. You've loved that girl for half your life. You'll be stronger with her by your side."

My gaze drifts to the lake as the car slows to a stop in front of a house I never wanted to leave.

Like I had a choice.

Rubbing my forehead does nothing to rid me of the headache that's taken root between my eyes. "I don't know how to spin this, or even if I can."

I shift in my seat as acid turns my stomach.

"The world doesn't know that Trent is sleeping with that woman," Lena says. She keeps her tone even, but a tendril of hurt snakes through her words. "And they don't know that he's using again."

"And I'm the asshole who truly believed Trent was on my side—that we were a team. Now I have no idea what their endgame is, and it's my word against theirs."

For the first time since I opened Ascendancy Inc., I can't

see the ending of this story.

"Dante." She sighs. "Their speech was staged—the entire thing was choreographed, so how long have they been working on that plan? What other attacks will he launch against you and your company?"

When I started Ascendancy, Trent had connections but no motivation. I had the motivation but no connections. I wanted it to be ours, even if I did all the work.

Trent has never spent a full day in the office, but how the hell do I prove this company is successful solely because of me when I've done everything I can to present us as a team for years?

"Poppy and I will be there for you every step of the way. But if this is just another storyline to them, one they're creating to keep Olivia's name trending and get him out of whatever mess he's in, where will you land when the lies finally come to the surface? What will be left of your company? That's what you need to be worrying about and planning for."

Dread drops like a brick into the pit of my stomach.

What if I allowed myself to go with the motions, with what was easy in favor of reaching my goals, and didn't recognize the chess pieces being laid at my feet?

The driver stares at me expectantly, and I slowly open the car door, then drag my small suitcase across the seat. Nostalgia niggles dangerously in my heart when the familiar scent of home slaps me in the face. It's summers spent at the lake and camping in the woods. It's dirt roads and fresh-cut grass. It's as familiar as Saylor and as sad as our heartbreak. It's a happy memory before my world burned to the ground. The last time I was here was a lifetime ago, and now I'm back, about to shake up her life.

I swivel my head from left to right. The old home in front

of me, with a sign that reads Pleasure Bound Bookshop, knocks the wind out of me.

She did it. I knew she had. Social media makes it too easy to keep hold of your past. But seeing it in person is something else entirely.

To the left is a storefront with boarded-up windows, and to my right is the old tackle shop. It's like this little town built itself around her grandparents' home on the lake.

Almost nothing else has changed in all these years.

Heart Lake sparkles between the buildings like strikes of lightning warning me away.

"Want me to have Poppy call you when she's done with dance class?" Lena asks. Jesus. I'd forgotten she was on the phone. *Get your shit together, man.*

"Yeah. I want to hear how she—"

The snap of an old screen door, followed by shattering glass, has me turning in place and my heart trying to drop-kick my lungs. The world tunnels, time stops, and everything goes blurry except the woman standing before me like she's seen a ghost.

And in her story, she has.

CHAPTER 4

DANTE

"Hell no. No, she wouldn't do this to me." Her words bring everything speeding into motion. It's the first time I've heard Saylor's voice in person in over six years, and it's enough to shock my heart into beating again.

I incline my head toward the voice my soul will always recognize.

"You have got to be kidding me." Her hands are frozen in midair, where she'd obviously been carrying something.

"Lena? Let me call you back. I found my Sa...my client."

I hang up before she can reply and smile at my mouthy little she-devil.

"Client? Your client?" Her voice gets shriller with each passing syllable.

The sun is so bright behind the house that it casts the porch in shadows, and it takes a few moments for me to adjust to the light.

Not a day has passed that I haven't felt her presence in my heart.

Guilt caused by shared trauma and mistakes sits heavily on my shoulders.

"No. No way," she whispers, but it carries across the distance like an arrow to my heart. Her right foot taps against the old wooden planks that have probably not been replaced since her grandparents owned the place, and when she catches me staring, she crosses her arms over her chest.

"You are not my image doctor. No way. Kate said—but—it can't be you." The column of her throat ripples when she swallows, and she makes a face like it pained her. "This new Dante," she says, pointing at my chest, "is an asshole."

Her lashes fly high when it slips from her lips, but she's wrong about me. Dante Greer is who I became to mask my pain, and I'm assuming she uses my last name professionally for the same reason. What better way to shield yourself from the world than to wrap yourself in what's already hurt you?

Her chest heaves like she's struggling for breath, but I'm entranced by her face. The wide, bottomless eyes I spent years lost in. Her thick brown hair, still too wild to be tamed, spills out of the messy bun she's made on the top of her head.

She's wearing short denim shorts and a T-shirt with a blue grumpy-looking teddy bear on it. It makes the organ in my chest skip several beats. Saylor's the same and so different that it's disorienting.

How much of a role did I play in putting those shadows beneath her eyes?

She mutters something that sounds like asshole again, and I finally find my voice.

"You know that's my public persona, and I know Sassy *Thompson* is yours," I say mildly. But it does nothing to calm her. Instead, she seems to get angrier.

How many times did I watch her doodle Sassy Thompson in her notebooks? Hundreds? Thousands? In another world, she would have been Saylor "Sassy" Thompson for real.

"Oh, I do," she mutters, tightening her features. Her face morphs into a full-on glare, but all I see is the pain she's masking as anger. "I can't go to the grocery store without seeing your face everywhere." She stomps her foot like Poppy does when she's angry, and if I weren't so disconcerted, I'd smile.

When she doesn't continue, I close the distance between us to stand at the bottom of her steps and fight the urge to scratch at the pain in my chest.

Eyes the clearest shade of blue with a ring of navy glower in my direction without really focusing on anything in particular, and it sends me spiraling through a lifetime of memories.

"Well?" she demands, drawing my attention back to the tapping of one tiny foot.

"You need me, Sass. You know you do." The nickname her grandfather, Grumpy, gave her as a child roughens my voice. It's scratchy and lower than normal, so I clear my throat.

"No," she snaps, but her chin quivers, and the ache in my chest intensifies. "I don't need you. I don't need anyone. Not anymore."

"Saylor." Her name comes out harsher than I intended. The adrenaline of seeing her for the first time in six years is threatening my control.

Does anyone call her Saylor anymore? When she was mine, everyone had made the switch to calling her Sassy years before, so Saylor was a name she reserved only for me. The idea that maybe someone else has earned that right makes me flex my fingers, but it does nothing to work out the tension locking me in place.

She marches down the steps, her shoes crunching in broken glass, and places her palm against my chest like she's thinking about shoving me. It startles us both, but the pads of her fingers press into my pec, testing the touch.

Each finger sends a jolt of electricity through me like sparks from a welder's torch, and I fight not to take an involuntary step back.

"You don't belong here anymore, Dante." Her little body shakes as her hand falls away, but I draw closer when her eyes dim for a fleeting second.

She's scared, so I keep my voice pitched low and allow her to hear the honesty in my plea. "Let me help you, Sayl. Please."

That was the wrong thing to say. Her face turns a painful shade of red at the nickname I've whispered in her ear a million times.

When did memories turn into weapons between us?

"I needed your help once, and it didn't end well. I can't do it again. You should go home," she says, putting some distance between us.

So Lena was right. Saylor wrote her truth.

Shit. She isn't going to make this easy, and I don't deserve easy, but Jesus. I was twenty-three years old. I didn't know. I thought I was doing the right thing.

I fight a smile at seeing the physical representation of why everyone in her life calls her Sassy, and she growls.

"We need each other, Saylor."

She scoffs. It's a jarring sound against the relaxing backdrop of the lake lapping at the shore behind her home. "I have work to do. Please. Leave." But her confident stance is belied when her voice quivers.

"Why won't you hear me out?"

"Because."

Damn her for making that a complete sentence. She always had, though, and I probably learned it from her, so I shouldn't be surprised. She's the most stubborn person I've ever met.

"Because why?" I wouldn't have guessed that Saylor could

39

be any more stubborn than she was as a teenager, but she is. Those heels are digging in, literally and figuratively, right before my eyes.

"Because if your pompous ass can't remember why we're no longer friends, it's not my job to remind you. Now leave."

Pompous ass?

"Friends?" The word vibrates in my chest. "We were more than friends, *Sassy*," I say in a derisive tone. I can't remember a time in our lives when I've ever called her Sassy, and now, I've done it twice.

It feels wrong on every level.

"We were never *just* friends, and you know it. That counts for something."

She glares at me. For a pint-sized thing, she can be intimidating, and it brings me right back to my sophomore year of high school. Will she lash out like she did when we first met? Will she run? I won her over once—can I do it again? My body pulses with my desire to still be someone she trusts.

I pocket my cell phone and drop my suitcase to the ground. "Fine," I concede with a condescending smirk that will irritate her. Irritated Saylor, I can work with. "Tell Kate I'm here. She hired me, not you. I'll leave when she tells me to."

This makes her pause. "Kate," she mutters under her breath. Her face puckers with the action, and my smirk spreads into a grin. "I can't believe she'd do this to me."

"Yeah, well, it seems we both have some shit to work through." Crossing my arms over my chest, I widen my stance and rock back on my heels. Her face scrunches up even more.

Game on, sweetheart. I'm not going anywhere. Not this time. I walked away from her once. Doing it again would destroy what's left of my heart, so I will find a way to repair this for all of us.

Even as the idea plays in my mind, it's already sinking into my soul as the truth, because I was always meant to be hers.

Her body shakes with pent-up energy. Anger is her default, always has been. It's as much a defense mechanism as her sarcasm.

Why do you need a defense against me, Saylor? You pushed me away, remember?

But it's not in her nature to make anything easy. I can almost see her processing information as she stands like a warrior princess who is all of five foot two. Her gaze darts back and forth like she's reading, then every muscle in her face draws tight when she's made a decision.

"What did you do?" she asks, and I'm happy to find that her curiosity overrides her emotions just like it used to.

The hitch in her voice is enough to tell me that some-where, buried deep under all that rage, there's a sliver of her that still cares for me. That knowledge electrifies the energy in my bones needed to fight, and the tension tightening my shoulders slowly unfurls. Seeing her standing here, and not in my dreams, makes breathing more difficult than it should be.

A truth I've refused to admit, even to myself, crashes into me as I stare at her. There's never been a time when I've not been in love with this girl.

All this shit with Trent has been screwing with my head. When Kate called, I'd already been contemplating selling my business. I thought it was the only way to protect my family. I built an empire once—I could do it again. But this? With Saylor? This changes everything.

I couldn't give up Ascendancy Inc. and still come for her. That's my excuse for being here, anyway. Without Ascen-dancy, Kate would have no use for me. And while Kate

41

thinks this is a job, it's more for me. So much more. This is my do-over, and I won't fuck this one up.

Lifting my arms in the air, I surrender to what will be a painful reunion. Chances are, she's already seen me on TV yelling at Trent and Olivia, and that hurts.

Does she believe that's who I am now?

Holding my palms toward the sky, I say, "Who the hell knows, Sayls? Can we call a truce in whatever war you have brewing in your head? Because I know there's one in there. I have a lot of shit to get done in the next few days. I can't do that while worrying my scary little *friend* will slice my eyeballs out with her claws."

Sadness bleeds into my words, and every muscle in her body pulls taut from her calves to her forehead, like she's physically reinforcing her walls. Emotions and Saylor have never quite gotten along. But she's always been able to drag wild ones from me, and for the first time in years, I feel like myself—the boy who would have sold his soul for this woman and the man who still will.

I became Dante Greer when I left this town. A hardened, asshole version of myself was the only way to survive. It was the one and only time Trent ever helped me.

I was practically carrying him out of the club when reporters shot out from the darkness, surrounding us like an angry mob. They wanted to use Trent's inebriated state for clickbait but instantly became determined to find out who I was instead.

"What's your name?"

"How do you know Trent?"

"Don't give them your real name," Trent slurs against my shoulder. *"Nothing in Hollywood is real. Don't give them that piece of you. You'll never get it back."* Panic clears my mind, and it takes all my strength to hold him up.

"Who are you?"

"Um, I'm Dante. Er, Dante...Greer. Trent's brother."

It was the second time in less than a month that my life changed forever.

The day I left Saylor is the day I stopped believing that there was good in this world—until Poppy.

The day I saved Trent's ass, and every day since, has shaped me into who I am today—a man fighting through life, longing for a love he thought was lost forever.

Saylor's features soften as we stare at each other. Her sharp intake of air has me blinking out of the past, but her fists are clenched so tightly at her sides that her hands shake. She's always had a war raging inside of her. It's a sucker punch to my soul that she's still fighting her demons.

"Saylor, please," I whisper, but in my head, it sounds like *I love you.*

I might be here to save her and my company, but staring at her now, I understand that my heart will never beat for anyone else.

Whatever she finds in my expression has her reacting less like a she-wolf, and she shakes her arms while flexing her fingers. It's a small victory when she holds out her palm to shake hands.

"Truce," she grumbles. "Just stay out of my way." With our hands touching, she couldn't quite keep the bite in her tone.

Always fighting. She's even more disagreeable now than when I first met her. And it makes me smile like a cocky teenager.

Lowering my head a few inches, I stare into her eyes. "That's not part of the plan, sweetheart."

Frost fills her features as she retreats.

"We don't have to be friends, *sweettits.*" God, how I've missed that mouth. "You do you, and I'll do me. Okay?"

My scalp prickles at her tone. I worked incredibly hard

once upon a time to be someone she trusted. And that all-consuming need to be in her sphere calls to me now.

I nod because I can't form words, and her anger singes the space between us. It speaks of so many stupid mistakes made in youth—hers and mine.

She's muttering curse words under her breath when the squeaky screen door opens and Kate walks out.

"What the hell are you doing, Kate?" Saylor's angry tone is clipped, but the subtext is clear—how could you go behind my back like this?

"You two obviously have...something. Whatever history is causing you to be a vibrating ball of rage right now, you need to let it go. You've both gone and fucked up your careers. The way I see it, the only way forward is together."

Pinching the bridge of my nose, I almost laugh. Kate did my job for me.

I'm an idiot. I should have seen this all along. Trent outing our relationship and connecting it to Saylor's books might be what saves my reputation and her career.

Everyone loves a comeback story. And a second-chance love story is enough to dull the shine of my brother's lies if played correctly.

"He's not moving in with me." Saylor sounds unhinged, and I can't say that I blame her. She already made me leave her once, and I was the blindsided jerk who listened.

Does she care that it nearly killed me?

I wish I could say I never looked back, but every action since I left proves otherwise. The photos, the tattoos, the lonely nights filled with memories that try to drown me.

She broke my heart, so I searched for meaning and a place to belong. I went as far away from Connecticut as I could get because I thought it was the only way to move on from her.

But now her pain slices through me with every lash of her

tongue. I've never been more wrong about anything in my whole life.

She paces three steps to the right, spins, then takes three steps back. Her hands are fluttering through the air as she tries to organize her thoughts.

But Saylor is at a disadvantage right now. She isn't seeing our plan yet, and it gives me a perverse sense of…*something*. This woman creates a reaction in me that's causing a riot, and yet the thought of annoying her until she breaks down and accepts this path forward calls to me on a visceral level.

After all, it's my tenacity that let me into her world once, and this time I have everything to lose.

"We're about to become America's sweethearts," I say, flashing her a wink.

A painful choking sound sizzles somewhere inside Saylor. Her eyes are far too wide, and her skin turns nearly purple. Is she holding her breath? She flaps her hands at her side like she's trying to pull words from thin air, and when nothing comes, she shuts out the world like she used to by skirting the glass, stomping inside, and slamming the screen door. A few seconds later, Jimmy Eat World's "A Praise Chorus" blasts from a speaker somewhere inside.

The world moved on around us, but some things never change.

The music hits me like an anvil. Her sister used to blast this album when she was overwhelmed by raising her younger sisters. It was her sign to the world, and us, that she needed a break.

Are you still living in this pain, Saylor?

I'm staring after her when Kate pokes me hard in the chest.

"I don't know all the details," she hisses, drawing my attention away from Saylor's front door. "But since you're here, I'm going to assume you know you fucked up. Make it right, and don't do it again."

This woman should be in the mob. Her threats could make a grown man shit his pants.

"I was a kid, Kate. A kid who didn't know how to handle her grief and took her word at face value without realizing how much pain she was in."

I watch as understanding hits. *April Rain* wasn't any story. It's our story. "So you walked away and left her alone?" Her voice is a harsh whisper of disbelief.

I swallow my shame because I did. She had Ainsley. She had Hope Hollow. But she didn't have me.

CHAPTER 5

SAYLOR

"*C*ome here, fishy-fishy."

Tossing another piece of bread over the railing, I lift onto my tiptoes and rest my belly against the wood to get a better vantage point.

I'm not a swimmer. Well, more accurately, I don't know how to swim. And the thought of having my face in the water with all these squiggly, slimy-looking things terrifies me. But I can't deny the beauty of their bright colors and the graceful way they glide through the water. They seem so peaceful.

What would it be like to live with that kind of peace?

My sisters tried to teach me to swim throughout the years, but nearly drowning when I was six and not being able to save my sister as an adult makes the endeavor impossible now.

And I'm okay with it.

Mostly.

But the lake was my sister's favorite place on earth. This is where I can feel her, and when I'm desperate, talk to her, so it calms me instead of scaring me now.

I lean over a little more and toss another piece of bread

into the water in case they've swum under the dock. I thought I saw a red one earlier, and I need him to come back —he's my favorite.

"What are you doing?" the deep, masculine voice of my heartache asks.

Before I can utter a single word, I fall headfirst into my sea of fish and bread.

"Swim," he barks as my head sinks below the water.

My body freezes in panic as I stare up through crystal clear water at the man who left me behind.

The razor's edge of panic muddles my brain, and my head sways when the lightheadedness hits. I close my eyes when the urge to inhale is too strong to fight, but then a disturbance in the water shakes me around. Oh God! Is that a shark? I'm going to be eaten by a shark.

I open my mouth to scream, but water silences me. It fills my mouth and throat until everything burns. I kick and thrash and jab the monster with my elbow, but the white light is drawing near, and my end has come. When the warmth reaches me, everything goes black.

"How long was she under?"

A warm mouth lands on mine as strong hands land on my breasts. Oh, God. His lips coax mine apart. This is, without a doubt, the best kiss I've had in years. Then he pulls away. No!

"Not long. I watched her go under but thought she was messing with me. I thought she was pissed that I'd startled her and was waiting for me to walk away. But then she went eerily still, and I knew…"

He kisses me again, and I lift my arm to wrap around his neck.

I blink slowly and then lock on a pale version of Dante, and everything comes rushing back.

I try to push him off me and sit up, but when I do, I vomit lake water everywhere.

Dante kneels over me with a leg on each side. "Calm down," he says gently while brushing my hair off my face. "Don't move."

I turn away from him as another wave of nausea hits and find Kate watching me with the same worried expression.

Closing my eyes, I focus on breathing and Dante moves to my side, so I roll over and place my cheek on the cool grass.

I'm an idiot.

"Are you okay?" he asks.

Sitting up, I replay the last few minutes. "Oh my god. You scared me and pushed me over the railing with your words." My head is foggy. "Wait, how did you get me away from the shark? And why were you kissing an unconscious woman? That's disgusting and nowhere near consensual."

I'm trying to brush my hair from my forehead again when he lifts his hands and rises to his feet.

"You're fucking out of your mind, woman," he says. "I asked you what you were doing, and you went overboard. Why the hell were you that close to the water if you still can't swim? And what are you talking about? What shark? This is a goddamn lake, Saylor."

He reaches forward like he wants to check for injuries but quickly pulls his hand back. "Did you hit your head on the way down? And lastly, I was not, I repeat, not kissing you. Kate watched as I fished you out of your watery grave and stood there as I performed CPR. A thank you would be customary. Not an accusation of assault, you twit."

Stunned, I lean back on my hands. Twit. I haven't heard that in years, and I almost laugh. Wait. "You didn't kiss me?"

"Trust me. I'm not into comatose, and this," he says, waving his hands around angrily, "is not my scene."

Outrage and humiliation fight for dominance in my heart, and I stand up, clinging to outrage with both hands. "Right. Oh, I know I'm not your *scene*, Dante. I've seen your *scene* all over the internet." The words are hoarse, but my tone is as sharp as his infraction and cuts just as quickly when he flinches.

I'm the worst human. I deserved every ounce of pain he inflicted back then, but I had no choice. I either hurt him for a few months or hurt him for a lifetime. I chose the lesser of two evils six years ago, even though it broke me too.

And regardless of how it kills me now, I have to hang on to the anger. Anger is easier than sadness. Hate is easier than loving someone you'll only ever hurt. And selfishly, I won't survive the pain of losing him again. No matter what else happens, I will stay angry with him.

His face softens, losing a little of the anger as he studies me long and hard, but I still see the vacancy in his eyes. He has no idea how much I needed him.

"Thanks for saving me. I'm sorry for—for what I said. This isn't going to work, Kate. I'll give up Sassy Thom—" I trip over my pseudonym. Even if he did the same thing, saying it in front of him is mortifying. "I'll give up my career before I willingly break my heart again," I say instead.

I stagger to my feet, and neither of them moves while I head for my house, dripping a pool of lake water with each step.

~

AN HOUR LATER, I poke my head out of the bathroom door and look both ways like a thief before exiting. No one in their right mind would stick around after this afternoon's display, but Kate and Dante live on another planet. The glitz and glamour of Hollywood holds no shine for me, but they're drawn to it like mosquitos to electric buzzers.

I understand why this setup makes sense to them, but I don't know or care what's in it for Dante.

Liar! You care so much that it hurts.

Jesus, Sassy. Do not let him invade your thoughts. I lost Dante years ago, right along with the rest of my life. Let him stay dead. Thinking of him as Dante Greer makes it hurt a little less. That Dante is an asshole. He's a playboy, according to the gossip blogs. Hating him as his alter-ego is easier than feeling the pain of missing him as mine.

Something tells me I haven't won this battle yet, and I take tentative steps down the hallway. He's invading the air, my space, my soul, and it hurts so much that a shudder rolls through my body.

The open living space is empty. How the hell do I face him now? It's like I'm fourteen all over again. When he first stormed into my life, I spent weeks hiding from him, but my apartment is way too small to do that now.

Guilt washes over me, and I clutch my pendant in my palm. Sometimes I wish I were strong enough to handle the emotions trying to suffocate me. I wish I could be more like Ainsley and let people in. I wish I wasn't the way I am, but life happened, and now I deal with the repercussions. But why did I have to go and accuse him of assault? My freaking mouth always shoots off before my brain catches up. That got me into this mess, and I still haven't learned my lesson.

I shouldn't have said anything until I had my feet planted firmly in reality. These are the times I wish I could know peace—even for a few days. I should make it a goal to think before I speak. This is why it's so much safer to live in my mind than to live in the mess that's my life.

But seriously, was it necessary for his lips to brand themselves on mine? Dear Universe, why do you hate me so much? It's an extra shameful kick to the teeth because I've kissed exactly two men in my life. One felt like kissing a brother, and the other still makes me forget all my fears.

At least Grady and I stayed friends.

It serves me right that the only person besides Ainsley who cares about my double life is someone who feels more like a brother.

When Grady stumbled into the New York City bookstore hosting the one and only signing I've ever done, I'm sure that the cranky girl from his hometown was not who he was expecting. Not when his own life had imploded the year before, leaving him with an ex-fiancée and enough rage to light up an entire city.

We bonded over trauma we were both too young to have experienced while walking through Central Park.

The next week, he accidentally found me at The Landing, where my sister died, and unlike other Hope Hollowans, he has always respected my boundaries. It helps that we both kind of hate people.

It makes Grady a perfect friend.

We're there for each other when it counts, and over the years, we've become each other's secret keepers. He's the only one I confided in about Dante, but I didn't even tell him the entire truth. Thankfully he's never judged me—not too much, anyway.

Staying friends with Dante would have been impossible. We've always been too combustible. And he would have spent a lifetime trying to fix me. It would have ruined him because the darkness that nipped at my soul through childhood claimed me wholly the day my sister died.

The towel wrapped around my head slips onto my face, so I unwind it and roughly dry my tangled web of hair.

I left my computer in the office somewhere. I should have

been writing instead of fish-watching, but the words wouldn't come. They never come these days. And then, I swam with the fish and almost died.

I'm an idiot. It would have killed Ainsley if I died. I can't do that to her. I'm all she has left.

"You're alive," Dante says gently, but it still scares the living crap out of me, and I trip into the office. This time, he's there to catch me, and I hate how the heat of his naked torso covers me like a weighted blanket and eases the anxiety that has me in a chokehold.

He tenses with me in his arms, and my heart crumbles a little more. It figures he would have a completely different reaction to me. *That's what happens when you hurt someone.* I hurry to steady myself and pull from his grasp.

"Why do you keep doing that?"

"Why do you scare so easily?" he retorts. His lips twitch at the corner like he's fighting a smile, and I avert my gaze to anything but his face and the new tattoos I refuse to memorize.

"Why are you in my space? Again?"

"Why do you answer every question with a question?" There's a smirk in his tone, but he's the one asking questions instead of answering them, and suddenly I'm fourteen years old again when he made it his mission to befriend me.

God, he can be so freaking annoying.

I release a long, aggravated breath through my nose, remove the towel draped over my shoulders, and toss it carelessly onto my comfy chair. Then I spin in place, trying to find him through the nest of hair that won't stay out of my face.

I'm a real-life Jane of the Jungle. I certainly look the part most days.

But me as a disaster isn't anything he hasn't seen before. Ainsley and I may be identical, but she got all the happy-shiny genes. I got whatever was left over, and once upon a time, all the messy, cranky sides of me were what he loved most.

Fucking weirdo.

I place my hands on my hips, glaring at him, because glaring is safer than apologizing. "Well?" I ask. My toe starts tapping against the aging floorboards again, which irritates the hell out of me. Having him so close causes energy to surge through my body, searching for an exit, and I can't control it.

"Ah, Saylor." Instantly his expression changes. His eyes darken and grow wide while the tendon in his neck convulses when he swallows.

"What?"

He stares pointedly at my chest, so I follow his line of sight and gasp.

The robe I got at some holiday swap party is meant for a football player and is gaping at the top. I'm exposed from my neck to my belly button, so I grab the lapels and force them shut.

Embarrassment steals all my sass, but I can't ignore the heat that lingers in his gaze. *Don't give in to the pull that ties us together. Do not do it.* It's harder to shut out my feelings with him this close.

Well, at least until he taps the top of my MacBook. "So, Sassy got in trouble, and now Saylor doesn't know how to fix it?" he asks with a hitch of his brow and a gentle smile that makes my heart weep.

Every muscle in my face pinches together like I've been sucking on lemons all day. "I don't know. Did *Dante* get Dante in trouble, and now you're here to—to, gah!" I throw my hands into the air. "Why are you even in here?"

My eyes narrow as his face transforms into an expression

I used to love. You know, before I had to refer to him as the arrogant asshole known as Dante Greer.

I want to hate him a little for using my last name, but I'm a lot of things, and a hypocrite isn't one of them, so I bite my tongue until I taste blood instead.

"I've followed your career, Saylor," he says. His body language says he's relaxed, but there's tension in his bunched-up shoulders. What does he think of me now? Did he read our story? "You're a natural storyteller, you always have been, but you can't keep the fucking sass in check." His words should sound like a scolding, but instead, they bleed with something close to pride.

"Why did you choose Thompson as your pen name?" His question catches me off guard.

My chin wobbles, and I turn away from him. I hate how he drags emotions from me. I've spent six years bottling this shit up. It's not fair that he can set them free in a matter of hours.

After a long silence, I set my expression to stony indifference and face him again. "Why did you choose Greer?"

I'm expecting him to laugh or avoid or deflect. I'm not expecting honesty.

"Because it kept me tethered to you." His voice is so raw and full of love, I taste tears at the back of my throat. It doesn't surprise me that my eyes stay bone-dry, but any hint of emotion is enough to make me double down on sucking them back into my bottle. "Why did you choose Thompson, Saylor?"

Stay strong. Telling him the truth won't mend anything. I can't give him false hope that the darkness will fade, or that I'll ever be able to live without all the sadness that chases me.

Squaring my shoulders and lifting my chin, I force a lie out of my mouth. "Because it's the only name I could write in cursive." The words scratch at my throat like they're being run through a cheese grater. He'll believe it, though, because he spent hours watching me doodle his name.

My stomach plummets with his shoulders. "At least now I know you're still willing to lie straight to my face." His words —laced with disappointment—hit like a wrecking ball, but all I can do is shake my head.

He stares at me like he's unearthing all my secrets one by one. I can't hold myself together much longer, and he seems to understand that when he nods.

"Your sass is threatening to take everything away from you. Your interview was messed up, and I can help make it right. But I won't tolerate any more lies. Not even ones you think are for my own good." That look says he knows what I'm doing.

He's been moving closer as he talks, and it makes the air too thick to breathe.

"It's what I do," he says like a promise. "I overhaul images and public perceptions. All you have to do is say yes." He stares down at me, and all those messy emotions bubble to the surface before I can lock them down.

I drop my face into my hands so he can't read me. He was always too good at that, but I can't let him. Not now. So, I dig deep and reach for the anger I need. Anger is safer than admitting that I don't fit into the real world anymore, and I couldn't even if I tried. If he stays, he'll try to fix me, and it will break him when he can't. Doesn't he understand that? There is no instant remedy for what ails me.

Even with years of therapy behind me, it's a lifelong process.

Oh, God. I'm really messed up. I'm going to be one of those cranky old ladies. A spinster? A cat lady? I can picture it now. Me in my bookstore with cats roaming free and yelling at customers not to break the spines on my books.

"You okay?" he asks, and I push my palms into my eye sockets until stars explode with every color of the rainbow.

I've always been the girl who got lost in thoughts and daydreams, but it's gotten worse over the years. It's a byproduct of hiding away from people, and now it's become an excuse not to socialize unless I'm forced to.

People always have something to say about me. I'm flighty. I'm rude. I'm too distractable. I'm unfriendly.

And the thing is, it's all true.

Shaking my head, I try to remember what he was saying. What was it? Oh, right. He's here to save me.

Sigh. That's all I've ever wanted and knew I could never have.

Rubbing my temples, I angle my face toward the floor.

"I'm sure you're very good at what you do. But this is my life. One I've fought hard to build." *I can't handle pushing you away again.*

When he remains silent, I open one eye and squint at him. "Why are you staring at me like that?"

He stands shirtless, and with my panic slowly receding, I study him and finally register the tattoos I've been trying to avoid—nautical tattoos—specifically, a sailboat across his heart. My brain immediately shuts down. Dante Thompson with tattoos is worse than the strongest drug. It's addicting, and I cannot take a hit of him.

"Like what?" he asks, and it sounds like he's laughing at me, so I drag my gaze back to his, and sure enough, he's showcasing that dimple that makes my breath catch. His blue eyes sparkle like the sun hitting the ocean at dawn, and his hair has dried in effortlessly windblown perfection that he probably did nothing to encourage. It's light brown, and my fingertips remember exactly how soft the strands are. Every memory leads to another, my mind traveling a dangerous path.

My fingers twitch like they're still grasping for him in the middle of the night. It's not fair that he's so pretty, and I hate how he can make me feel seen when I'm obviously trying to hide in plain sight.

Placing a hand on my hip, I pretend to relax into the position but angrily trace my finger in the air, pointing to his ink. "You hate tattoos."

"I hated them for you," he says with a slow shake of his head. "Your skin is a work of art. It would be a shame to have it defaced." He's laughing at me again.

My shoulders tense, and I consciously make them relax by stretching my neck from side to side and swinging my arms. *When did I turn into a prized fighter?*

"Why are you doing this?" My tone could freeze lava. "Why now? Wasn't leaving once painful enough?"

Eesh. Super-bitch called, she wants her voice back. That was unfair. I didn't give him a choice.

"The last thing I ever wanted to do was hurt you. I'm sorry that I did. I was young and stupid. I didn't know how to handle the grief you were carrying." He leans down into my space. "But neither did you."

And he left.

Because I told him to.

I was in such a dark place then. I don't even remember what I said to him. But I did hurt him. His pained expression from that day still haunts my dreams.

"But I have to tell you, Saylor. I never expected the sassy side of you to completely bury the pieces I've always loved." He scans my body slowly, his gaze coasting up my skin like a lover's caress that I refuse to enjoy.

The pieces he's always loved. Not only in the past. The fragments of my broken heart collide against each other like pieces of a puzzle that don't quite fit.

I do not still have feelings for him. I can't. Yes, I told him to leave, but he didn't fight for us either. In my darkest days, I lost the only light I had left.

Liar. My conscience can take a flying leap off the nearest flagpole.

My head pounds. Embarrassment and insecurity weigh more than I'm able to carry.

Crossing the one room that's always been intentionally Dante-free, until now, I pick up my discarded towel and stare out at the lake. This time, I keep a healthy distance between us. Plastic wheels roll over the hardwood floor when he drops into my desk chair, breaking the silence that hangs between us like a steel door.

Please don't get too comfortable. It won't end well when you see who I've become.

"Go home, Dante."

"You know I can't. Walking away from you again will kill me."

Holy hell.

CHAPTER 6

DANTE

"*W*alking away from you again will kill me."

Her face goes ashen, and I've once again said the wrong thing. She turns on her heel, grabs her laptop, and runs from me.

After Saylor storms out of the room, I stand to stare out over the lake. How do I get past her walls? A few seconds later, she's walking down her goddamn dock again. Why the fuck does she keep getting so close to the water?

I'm out of her office and chasing her down the back stairs before she reaches the end of the dock, where there are no railings.

She doesn't know that I've never let her go, that my tattoos are so I could always have a piece of her with me, or how desperately I still need her. I want her to know me now, the real me, not the Dante she obviously thinks I've become. And I need there to be a way back to us, the way we were before our lives fell apart.

I've been broken without her, and it's an ache I don't want to carry anymore.

I've tried.

Staying away from her was a daily exercise in self-torture. The call from Kate was a reprieve from the pain, but I'd known for weeks that I would come for her.

Trent just had to go and throw a live grenade into my life.

"Walking away from you again will kill me?" she says with a sad-sounding scoff. "It certainly wasn't killing him when he was partying with that model in LA less than a month ago. What does he think will happen now?"

She mutters her secrets to the lake like an old friend and holds her arms around her middle in a protective shield. "We're not the same people, Shan, but the outcome will always stay the same." Her voice trembles, and a visceral pang lances my heart.

She talks to her sister out here.

I'd give anything to be the person she confides in again, or for her to understand how my life has really been for the last six years. Once upon a time, our trust was unbreakable, but it hits me now that we ruined it in the most foolish way.

Even after all this time, she's still under my skin, and frustration blooms high, so my retort comes out with the sting of her sass. "It won't be the same, Saylor, because now I know what I'm working with." She startles, and I reach forward, but she doesn't fall, thank God. I need to get control of myself.

"I didn't have all the pieces before," I say more calmly. "You didn't tell me the whole story. But I know now." I flash her a smirk.

She scowls, but I don't miss the split-second of pain that crosses her face. Jesus. It sinks into my skin like a branding iron.

Her shoulders droop in defeat as sadness muddies her eyes and plays out across her features. "Listen, Dante." Her tone causes a tiny shiver of dread to course through my body, but I bite my lip to keep from saying anything and wait for her to finish.

When she finally looks at me, she's wearing a mask I hate. That's not my girl. All-consuming regret gnaws at my chest. Now, knowing her side of the story, I'm even angrier that I didn't fight harder for us. But there's still something inside this woman that my heart recognizes. It's there in every scowl, every touch, every word.

If there's a way back to us, I will find it.

"I know the interview was a shit show," she says, staring down at her clenched fist. "I'm an easy target because I speak without thinking. I'm not a bitch, but people accuse me of it based on my reactions. Honestly, I'm still trying to survive in a world where I don't fit. And I'm tired, Dante. So very tired."

My stomach hollows painfully with her words. But I don't move. I barely breathe. And when she lifts her haunted gaze to mine, it's all I can do not to gasp for air. I'm choking on the pain she wears like a duty, and my eyes burn as I watch her.

How can she possibly still feel like a voyeur in her own life?

"I'm trying to write something," she says, dropping her gaze to her toes that wiggle against the wood planks of the dock. "I need to write anything at this point to give to Kate before she starts selling my teeth to make ends meet, and my mind is blank. I don't think I have any stories left to tell. So, excuse me if having you back in my life sends me into a further tailspin. I'm not the same girl you knew back then, and I promise you, it's best if I remain a memory."

She turns away from me, and my fear burns in my lungs. She's too close to the water.

"I don't want to fight with you," she whispers. "I don't have time to play games. Stay in your lane, and I'll stay in mine. When this is over, I promise you won't hear a word from me again. And…"

She slides into the small Adirondack chair sitting at the end of the dock and opens her laptop. "Thank you for saving me," she says over her shoulder without making eye contact. Her voice cracks. It seeps into my chest and squeezes my heart with each passing syllable. "I don't know why you came running when Kate called, but I'll do whatever I can to make sure you can get out of here as soon as possible. Sometimes the past needs to stay in the past."

"He came because he didn't have a choice," Kate drawls as she sashays down the dock. "He needs you as much as you need him."

"Kate," I say in warning. It's not her place to tell my story. "And, Saylor, so you're aware, I'm not searching for a quick getaway. Not this time."

Kate taps her chin, but Saylor stares straight ahead, even when Kate speaks. "Fine. We'll meet tomorrow over Zoom. I'm heading back to the city, but Sassy?"

Saylor's head falls back against the weathered wooden chair. "Yes, master?"

I suppress a chuckle because neither woman would appreciate it, but my heart warms knowing she hasn't lost all the spark that made her someone I desperately wanted to love, even as a teenager.

"Congratulations," Kate says, patting my shoulder. "You make a very handsome couple."

I frown, and Saylor mutters. Even her grumbled words wrap around my heart and ease the uncomfortable agitation taking over my mind.

"Figure it out. Have fun, kids. Dante, a word?" Kate says while walking away.

"Kate! There's no way people will buy that he's—he's with

me." Saylor's hand gestures wildly in the air. I'm curious if it's because of me, but her words are my first priority.

Kate turns back with a grin I don't like. "I'm sure you two will figure it out."

Grinding my teeth, I hold up a finger to tell Kate I'll be there in a minute, then wait until she reaches the end of the dock and is out of earshot. When I'm sure we have a moment of privacy, I slide into the chair next to my child-hood best friend, my only love, the missing piece of me. My stomach leaps into my chest because I was not expecting it to be such a long drop down. Why the hell are her chairs child-sized?

"I always did like your sassy mouth, Saylor, but having me as a boyfriend won't be all that bad. I was pretty good at it once upon a time."

She's so little, but her presence at my side is enough to calm a giant. The fear she thinks she's hiding shows in the wild way her gaze jumps from one object to another. And sadness washes over me because her words and actions make it obvious that she's still trying to fight whatever demons hold her mind hostage.

I stare out over the water rippling with the breeze and take comfort in her arm pressed against mine. Maybe kid-sized chairs aren't so bad after all. "Why did you say that?"

She turns to her computer with a shrug that warms my entire arm. Where's the spitfire who was ready to torch me not two minutes ago?

"Why, Saylor? Why can you tell me to piss off and put yourself down in the same breath?"

"It doesn't matter," she mumbles.

But it does.

I turn my full attention to her now. The sun is going down on the other side of the lake, and it casts her face in an orange glow that softens her and somehow shows her

64

strength. She's grown into a goddess, and it hits me with a violent force how much I've missed her.

"Why?" I demand. When she doesn't answer, I lean over so my face is mere inches from hers. "Why, Sayl?"

She flops back in her chair to give herself some space. "I don't know, Dante." She hisses, but I love my name on her lips. I always have. "Maybe because I've seen you with your gaggle of girls."

"It's not a gaggle," I correct with an incredulous chuckle. She sounds jealous, and it makes my body buzz with hope. If she's jealous, that means she still cares. "And you can't believe everything you read. That world is created with smoke and mirrors."

"Whatever. You traded up in life. Some things never change, and I'm still me. I shattered once, I can't let it happen again. Go back to your models and actresses. Whatever you think you need from me, from this place, doesn't exist anymore. It's not your job to fix me."

What I hear is that I broke her.

She places her palm on my face, pushes me away, then rests her fingers on her keyboard.

"You're a terrible liar, sweetheart. This connection between us is clearly tugging at you in the same way it does me. If it still exists after all these years, it's not ever going away. Ever. I fucked up once, but so did you. The difference between us is that I don't intend to make the same mistake twice."

Standing tall, I roll my shoulders to deal with Kate, who waits impatiently for me at the end of the dock, while Saylor turns an ashen face toward the lake.

It's not easy to leave that woman at a loss for words, but there's no joy in it this time.

"Olivia's outburst was a shock," Kate says loud enough for Saylor to hear when I reach her. "I didn't see that coming, and I certainly wasn't expecting her to follow up with more allegations or a takeover with your business partner."

"He's not a partner, he's…never mind."

"Well, whoever they are, they're trying to bury you, and that interview this morning is creating a landslide of shit. What did you do to piss them off?"

I wouldn't give up the career I've poured my blood, sweat, and tears into or the girls who are my entire world. Trent wanted more from me than I could give, and somehow, he got Olivia on board with all his lies. Damn it. I haven't seen the new interview, but my mind whirls with possibilities.

"That's their angle," I say instead of answering her. The words vibrate with the anger I'm trying to keep in check as their plans take form in my mind. "He wants to make me the most hated man in Hollywood so he can take over my company, and she comes off as the wounded victim ready for her next close-up. I never touched that woman. She was a client. I haven't ever fucked around with clients."

I peer over my shoulder to make sure Saylor isn't watching us, then I lean in and whisper, "That's why Saylor won't be a client either. I'm here for her, our careers, and to correct the mistakes of our past. That's worth more than any kind of payment."

Kate smirks, watching me closely, and I'm reasonably certain she could be a human lie detector. "They're bringing a little girl into it now."

My eye twitches, but otherwise, I keep my icy expression. On the outside, anyway. On the inside, I'm a lit fuse racing toward the explosion.

Tinny voices break the tension. Single words echo in the silence—Dante, daughter, predator. Saylor googled me.

"Oh no," she gasps, but I refuse to look at her.

My world tunnels, and I wrap my hands around the railing to keep from trying to break something. I've never been a violent person, but my life is spiraling, and I need control back.

I should be hurt that my own brother is eagerly attacking everything and everyone I love, but the only thing filling me with rage is myself. I've always known this world was a game, and I've allowed myself to be played.

I swallow hard. "Saylor." My voice is rough, but she stands and shockingly comes to my side without her usual sass. She may hate me. She may not understand my world, but she's always understood me. She hears my silent plea.

She always has.

Kate's plan has legs, but if I'm going to survive this, our timeline needs to speed up. Ideally, we would have waited until we filled Saylor in on all the details tomorrow, but now I'm ready to beg if that's what it comes to.

"What?" Her voice is neutral, but she's twisting the bobble of her necklace along the chain. My attention catches on the platinum metal she drags back and forth. The friction against her skin causes an angry red welt to rise on the delicate column of her neck.

I hate anything that hurts her, so I lift my hand and place it over hers until she stops the offending motion. I remove my hand when she stills, but she keeps hers clasped tightly around the pendant.

Dropping my head and my voice, I hope it's enough to cut Kate out of this conversation. I need it to be me and Saylor— the way it was always meant to be. Kate may have gotten the ball rolling, but she has no place between the two of us.

"Do you see what I'm dealing with now?"

Her silence tells me it's worse than I imagined.

"Do you understand how the media and paparazzi work?" She nods but still doesn't make eye contact. "I can't allow them to feed these lies to the press unchecked. It's not only me they'll ruin. I love my niece with everything that I am. She's been the one bright spot in my life since I lost you."

Saylor gasps, and it lances my chest like a knife, but I continue.

"Her mother and I are friends—it's all we've ever been." That distinction is important because it's the truth. "Lena and Trent decided, together, to keep their daughter out of Hollywood, and I've done everything in my power to make that happen."

She's biting her lip but listening to me.

"I have to fight back, and so do you. I'll do whatever you ask of me. Please go along with this even though I've done nothing to earn this favor yet. But I need you, Sayls. I've always needed you."

She nods, and her body shivers when I place my hands on her biceps.

"What do you want me to do?" she snaps, then claps a hand over her mouth. Her snark always goes into overdrive when she's overwhelmed, so I take a step back and try to soothe her with words.

"We need to give them something else to talk about. Something that will overshadow their lies, even if only for a day." My mind races to all the ways they could spin this story. But there's no refuting that if we get ahead of it—if we create a new narrative—we can control the outcome.

The storm inside her picks up speed, and I hope that means she'll agree to what I'm asking—what we need. She's the only person I've ever met who tells entire stories with only their eyes.

For years, I've tried to force away the memory of her—or suffocate it with work. Standing before her now, I realize how fucking dumb I am. I'll always miss her because a heart doesn't regenerate, and mine stayed with her.

"L-Like what?"

"Let him kiss you." Kate's gloating, since this was likely always her plan. Her time spent in public relations before becoming a literary agent makes her a master at this game, but my shoulders still tense as she speaks. "A racy kiss will always get people talking, and it will confirm that *April Rain* and *Come September* are at least loosely based on your relationship—that will send the media and the public into a tailspin. The information is already circulating. You might as well make it work for you. People love a good second chance, Sass."

Saylor and I will never be a game, no matter how she reacts to this scheme. We're more than that. We're inevitable. She just doesn't know it yet.

Her entire face dims before she shrugs. "It's not like it'll be the first time we've lied to ourselves. But if we do this, promise me that you'll leave as soon as it's all over. And I mean it—I can never see you again after this. Got it?"

The next breath I take hurts like inhaling shards of glass. I don't want to be someone she regrets. My left hand balls into a fist in my pocket before I cross my fingers like a ten-year-old because, at this moment, I have no choice but to lie and agree to her terms.

"Done," I say before I whirl on her, pulling her in close. She fits like she was made to always be at my side.

"I'm going to kiss you," I whisper.

"Yeah, I caught that part."

"It'll help us both."

She rolls her eyes, so I wait for her to focus on me again.

"If you don't want this, say so now."

I scan her eyes, her face, her neck for any signs of distress, but all I find is her rapid pulse point on the soft skin of her neck. She licks her lips, and I mimic the move like I can already taste her. Then she tilts her head to look at me and I get lost in her eyes. The ones that beg me to be careful, not to break her, to abide by her rules.

They're the same eyes that darken as they zero in on my lips, and when her breaths become sharp inhales of air, she can no longer pretend she's immune to our connection no matter how hard she tries.

Like the stars that can't shine without the moon, we aren't complete without each other.

"Is there another option?" she asks through clenched teeth.

"Not one that will work as fast as this," Kate says, and I hate how close she is to our conversation—to us.

"The sooner we solve our problems, the sooner you can go home." Her voice trembles, but she squares her shoulders and looks me straight in the eye. "Let's do this."

I should give her a second to change her mind, but years of pent-up love rush through me and I lift her body to mine. Her laptop presses between us, but this kiss is a need, like air and water, that's raging inside me until my mouth covers hers. The second our lips touch, I relax into her warm body. This is the kind of kiss that can bring a man back from the dead.

And it does.

This kiss is years of longing and pain. It's heartbreak and love. It's coming home after a lifetime away, and I sink everything I am, everything I've ever felt for her into it. My body jolts as the electricity of life zings through my veins.

This is happiness.

In my periphery, Kate walks toward us with a phone pointed in our direction, as I knew she would. She not only plays the game, she wrote the damn rules.

Saylor's lips are timid and unmoving against mine like she's frozen, but I slowly lick a line across her seam, and she opens wide with a trembling breath. She shivers in my arms, and it shakes the ground below me. But when she hops up and locks her legs around my hips, I deepen the kiss with a groan that has my dick pulsing and my skin ablaze.

The rest of the world fades away, because here, we're not broken. There's no fear in this kiss. No, this kiss is the purest example of the love I knew existed but was too scared to fight for. With her lips on mine, a switch is flipped inside me, and everything changes.

Our kiss turns frantic, like we're both afraid that the other will vanish if we stop. Teeth and tongues clash—mine with desperation, hers with what feels like anger and pain and lust. It's evident in how her body trembles under my touch, but she uses her hands on my chest like she can't decide if she wants to push me away or pull me closer. It's a sure sign that her heart and mind are in a battle of wills.

But we both take something we're missing from this kiss, and I savor every inch of her mouth. She tastes like citrus and mint. She tastes like sunshine and life. She tastes real.

It's what I've been missing in my life—the real.

"Saylor," I groan. Her head falls back, and I kiss a line down her neck, nipping and sucking wherever I can reach like a man possessed. And I am. She's had a hold on me since the moment I saw her, and I'm an idiot for ever trying to live without her.

"Holy shit." Kate laughs. She breaks our spell, and I could wring her neck.

Saylor gasps and pulls her torso away from me while unlocking her legs, forcing me to ease her to the ground.

Her wide eyes and flushed cheeks cause an image of her naked to flutter across my vision, and another groan escapes. She lets out a strange little "eep" sound.

"It's not. We can't. You promised," she whispers, clutching her laptop to her chest like a shield before turning and sprinting to the house.

My heart can't quite decide on a rhythm that works, and it's not only because my brother's trying to ruin me. It's also because I just kissed a girl I thought I'd never hold again. And now I want to do it again.

And again.

Kate's laugh grates on my last nerve.

"Fuck off, Gerard," I snap.

Her cackle pitches higher.

"Maybe this time you'll understand what she sacrificed when you left." Her words leave bile sitting in the back of my throat. Kate Gerard is not someone you spill your most intimate secrets to. If Saylor told Kate anything about our past, maybe we both caused more damage than I realized.

I push past her without another word. Saylor is my priority.

I FIND her leaning over the vanity in the bathroom, splashing water on her face. But her shaking hands cause a lump the size of Texas to lodge in my throat.

"I'm sorry." I keep my tone gentle, but like a frightened little bird, she jumps and whacks her knee on the open cabinet door.

"Damn it, Dante. You promised." Her voice has lost its edge. She sounds almost fragile, and worse, she sounds hurt.

"I know I did. I'm sorry. I'm sorry I'm here, I'm sorry I left, and I'm sorry I asked you to help me. Using people is not something I make a habit of, regardless of what you think of me."

She stares at the floor, but I can feel her ragged breaths from across the room. "What are you doing in here?"

With a sigh, I welcome the ache in my heart because, despite what I said, we do need to use each other. "I won't let the media, my half-brother, or his minions ruin everything I've built. My niece and her mom count on me—they've been the only real family I've had." *Since you*, but she's already trying to flee, so I keep that part to myself. "I can't let them get away with trying to ruin everything I've built for Poppy."

Or for trying to ruin you. Does she know it's Trent who tipped off Malimar's reporter?

Her head snaps up, and her irises are filling with questions.

"They named her Poppy?" She sounds like I broke her spirit with that question.

"They did."

"Who? Who chose it?" Saylor's voice cracks, but her spine stays rigid—a little warrior planning her next attack.

"I did."

I think she might stop breathing, but when she drops her gaze, her confusion becomes palpable. I'm sure hearing that I named my niece in her honor is the last thing she was expecting.

"My favorite flower?"

"Yes."

"Why?"

"Jesus, Saylor. Because, okay?" I let out a frustrated breath and tug on the hair at the nape of my neck. "They couldn't come up with a name. And regardless of what you saw on gossip sites, until the day Poppy was born, you were still the only person in my life who could make me come alive. I needed you to be part of me—of my life that I was living without you."

Her eyes are wide and searching.

"However I could have you." My voice is barely audible.

She takes a small step back.

"Poppies are the flower of remembrance and hope—you

73

taught me that. I wanted a reminder of you every day to keep the hope alive that it wasn't our end."

Saylor shakes her head, but the movement is so slight and sad that I force myself to give her space.

"Her—her mother?"

"I've told Lena all about you. She was my first friend when I got to California."

I drop my forehead into one hand, the other resting low on my hips. This is not how I envisioned telling Saylor about how my life spiraled when I found out my father had spawned four other children, but nothing ever goes to plan with her, so I shouldn't be so surprised.

"Poppy's four, Saylor, and she's amazing—anything and everything good I've ever tried to be is reflected in that little girl. I can't let her believe, even for a second, that she's not a priority in anyone's life because while it's true she wasn't planned, she is loved, even if my brother can't be bothered. I remember what it was like growing up like that, with a father who was indifferent, and I vowed to never let her feel that way if I could help it."

She nods but won't look at me.

"And you have a brother?"

I pinch the back of my neck, then stretch it side to side. There's a lifetime of information and no easy way to explain it. "Three of them, actually. And a sister, but I haven't met her yet. Apparently, my father got around each time we moved."

She drags her necklace back and forth on its chain.

"I found out from those genealogy tests we did." This causes her to step back and tilt her long lashes up at me. "When I left here, I needed something or someone to fill the Saylor-sized hole in my life, so I went in search of Trent, since he was closest in age to me. He was a childhood actor who was struggling with drugs and booze. I stayed with him for a while, got him clean, and helped him get a few jobs. Life snowballed from there."

"I'm glad you had someone." Her voice is so low that I strain to hear her.

"What did you see online?" Right now, Saylor and I feel like a team. It's not lost on me that the one person I'm placing all my trust in is the one whose trust I may have broken beyond repair. "Scandals and drama like this don't simply happen in Hollywood. They're carefully, meticulously orchestrated. Which means they've been planning my demise for a while."

"I—I…you should google it yourself."

I run a hand through my hair, tugging roughly on the ends. "It's that bad?"

She nods.

"Please look at me, Saylor."

I hear her gulp, and even though my world is turning inside out, it pulls a small smile from me. Finally, she lifts her gaze but keeps her head bowed.

"Please tell me?"

"Please google it," she murmurs.

My stomach drops out. If anyone has the motivation to cause me pain right now, it's Saylor. And she refuses to do it.

"I can't. My phone was in my pocket when I pulled you from the lake. It's currently in a bag of rice, drying out."

"Shoot." She picks at her bottom lip, and my gaze lingers longer than is polite. "Come on," she says. "Meet me at the sofa." She eases past me in the doorway, careful not to touch me, and runs to her office while I stand beside her coffee table. She's in front of me a second later with her laptop, motioning me to sit, so I do, and she places the laptop on the coffee table, then presses play.

She stands opposite me, rocking from foot to foot, as the scope of my nightmare plays out in front of me.

CHAPTER 7

SAYLOR

"What we had wasn't love, and it wasn't professional." This is where a horrid woman named Olivia flashes the camera a sickeningly sad grimace. The mind-numbing image burned my retinas when I watched it earlier. "Men like him don't know how to love. I realize that now. It's a power trip for them. He's a predator, and I'm not the only one to fall into his web of abuse."

Dante flinches, and his skin turns a sickly shade of green. "He doesn't love anyone but himself. Not even his own brother. What he did with Trent's girlfriend is unacceptable. He even named the baby—his niece. That's beyond twisted. He's been masterminding people's careers for so long that he forgot we're actually people when the cameras turn off."

This god-awful actress lowers her gaze and wipes away a nonexistent tear. "How can that child's mother allow that little girl to spend any time with him? He's dangerous and violent. If he lashed out in front of cameras, imagine what he's like in private."

Olivia fake sobs, and I clench my hands into fists to keep

myself from sticking my finger in my mouth like a dramatic teenager.

"I didn't know what else to do." She shakes her shoulders like I want to shake her. It should terrify me that I still have so many protective reactions for Dante, but it doesn't. What I am scared of is how those feelings wrap around my body like a long-awaited embrace.

"I thought I had to do what he said, but I've never been so terrified." The nasal voice of the worst actress in America snaps me back to the moment, to Dante's face, and I wish I could erase the pain I find there. "Can you imagine how scary that life must be for a little girl? Trent has tried to keep him away from Poppy, but he's still inappropriately close to her mother."

Oh God. Oh. God. I might be sick. None of that is true, I know that in my bones, but what kind of monster would try to tear a little girl away from people who love her like that? Because that is the only thing they can possibly gain from this narrative. Child services will have to intervene, right? What will happen if he can't see his niece?

I'm definitely going to be sick. As much as I need to keep up my walls, it's becoming harder by the minute because I have never been able to forget Dante's greatest wish—to have a family.

His body vibrates, sweat rolls down his temple, and a new vein throbs like a snare drum in the center of his forehead. But it's his tears that tell me the truth.

The grating sound of Olivia's voice plays in the background as a man steps up beside her. Him. Trent. I recognize him from shows I loved as a child, and the magazines in the grocery store.

He has the same strong jawline and elegantly slanted nose as Dante, and like their father, their high cheekbones and chiseled features always make them look like they're smiling.

But it's the piercing blue eyes that give them away. There's no mistaking the family resemblance. But where Dante's mother was Italian and gave him his sun-kissed complexion, Trent has strawberry blond hair and fair skin.

"Dante?" His gaze is unfocused, so I gently close the laptop.

I'm not sure what to do, and it causes me to fidget. I can't do feelings in real life. I was never very good at them, and since my sister died, I've become a master at shuttering them all behind a protective wall. They're messy and uncomfortable and never work out how they should. Real-life feels are Ainsley's department, not mine. I'm good for a quick comeback and a fuck off.

And isn't it just a kick to the taint that the only person who can drag compassion from the dark, dank dungeon of my soul is Dante flipping Thompson?

The floor creaks beneath my feet, and I attempt to still my swaying limbs.

I didn't think it possible, but his body continues to coil tighter until I'm sure he'll explode.

"Dante," I whisper, slowly moving closer, like I'm sneaking up on a cat with a travel carrier. I'm not even sure he's able to hear me right now. This kind of rage has a way of blocking our reality—I should know, I've been fighting it for years. "Dante," I try again. "What can I do?"

What am I even saying? I'm not the consoler. I'm the one who intentionally blocks emotions, and I certainly can't care about his. Not anymore. Right?

Startled, he blinks rapidly, causing more moisture to fall from his sky-blue depths. He doesn't open his mouth when he speaks, his jaw locked so tightly that I'd need a crowbar to open it.

"That's not true," he says, pointing to the computer. His words are filled with so much venom that the sting hits from six feet away. "I can't believe they used Poppy like that. I—I can't believe he betrayed me. Trent is my brother. I let him into my life. He knows..." His gaze pierces mine until I blink away the intensity of the moment.

"Trent knew about you." He sighs and drops his head into his hands as it hits me. He's the reason Malimar knew about my sister. Dante told Trent everything.

"I'm an adult who entered that world willingly," he says, and I try to focus on his words through the blood pumping in my ears. "You guys didn't. With Poppy, they didn't want her growing up like the assholes we work with. Trent was adamant that she have a better childhood than he had. With you, I thought he understood. I thought..."

He leans forward, placing his forearms on his thighs. Then he begins to shake, and something I've avoided for years burns through my body like wildfire—empathy.

Losing the ability to sympathize was the first step for me shutting down all those years ago. But the pain inside me now is too real, too visceral to be anything else.

And it scares the shit out of me.

I scan my home like an answer will magically appear, but when it doesn't, I desperately wish I had forced Ainsley to come over.

It takes three tries to dislodge the knot in my throat. It hurts going down and leaves the bitter taste of regret on my tongue. Then I sit next to the asshole—who isn't feeling like an asshole at all.

"Er, Dante. Do you want to talk? Or," I half whisper, half screech, "even better, can I call someone for you?"

His gaze is wild when it finds mine, holding me hostage in his pain. I don't even dare breathe.

"I have to call Lena," he says with broken words that make my palms sweat.

Remembering he doesn't have a phone because of me, I hand him mine. He takes it but then stares at it, unblinking.

"I don't remember her number." His voice is monotonous, flat, and so dang defeated.

I clutch my necklace with one hand while my other curls around my thigh. The pain of my nails digging into my flesh grounds me, allows me to think.

"Did you have an iPhone?"

His lips twitch on one side like that was a dumb question, and he's trying not to smile.

"What? Not everyone is Apple obsessed." My tone is haughty, but at least it puts a little life back into his eyes. I don't even know why I say it other than to disagree with him. I am an Apple girl.

"Says the girl with a MacBook Pro."

Is he reading my damn mind now? "Not me," I say with a careless shrug. "Sassy Thompson has a MacBook Pro because she's testing out formatting software."

I pointedly ignore how his face lights up when I say my pen name.

Then I get an idea.

"Wait. What if you sign into your iTunes account on my MacBook? Then you can call or FaceTime, right?"

He nods, so I sign out and hand him the computer.

Dante's large hand encompasses mine in the exchange, and he doesn't let go. "Do not ever allow anyone to make you feel as though you're less than or like you don't deserve the world. Not ever again. Not even me. Do you understand?"

His command leaves me breathless, and my mind spirals as a story unfolds. Images and scenes fly across my vision like a movie reel—so quickly that I can't keep up.

"Yeah, yes," I say to get him to release me.

Then, while he navigates to FaceTime, I run across the room for my notebook. Holding it to my chest, I blink away tears and am so taken aback by the action that I almost crash into the side table.

I haven't cried since Shannon died.

My legs are weak and shaky as I blindly return to the sofa and settle on the far end. The familiar FaceTime ring sounds, but I tune it out, because words are coming and the scenes make sense. I have to get them out before I lose them.

I scrawl notes across the page at an alarming rate as one idea after another pours out of me. From the corner of my eye, I know that Dante glances toward me every once in a while, but I can't break my concentration. If my hand stops, my ideas may vanish.

That's how it works. My brain is a bitch sometimes, and she loves to play games with me. One second, I'll have the most fabulous storyline, then I blink, and it evaporates like it never existed.

I'm not sure how long I plot, but when I finally come up for air, Dante still has his face directed at my laptop.

But it's not an adult on the other side. It's a beautiful little girl with eyes so similar to her uncle's that I do a double-take. Her hair is lighter, and her lips fuller, but there's no mistaking the relation.

It hurts to breathe watching them, but I can't tear myself away.

"I'm sorry you have to miss the end-of-school party, Poppy."

My gaze lands on Dante, and the pain I felt earlier squeezes the air from my lungs.

"It's okay, Unca. I'm goin' fishin' with Grandpa, and I got my pwetty dress on for the pictures, and tomorrow I'm going to wear a party dress and wave to them—"

"Lollipop," he interrupts, and my ovaries damn near explode.

"Yeah, Unca?" Geez, she's sweet.

"Who is taking your picture?"

"My fans," she says, showing off perfect little baby teeth. "I'm a pwincess."

"What?" Dante growls. He rubs his hand roughly through his hair, and I get the sense he's trying not to rip it right out of his head. "Yeah, sweetpea. About them, ah, I need to talk to your mom again."

"Okay. I is making cookies with Granny now."

"Love you, sweet girl."

She leans forward and places a big, wet kiss on the screen. He lifts two fingers to it and holds them there.

I watch silently as she jumps up like the world doesn't suck, and a woman who could get away with never wearing a drop of makeup fills the screen while wiping the little girl's kisses away.

"Do you hang out with anyone who isn't ready for a magazine cover?"

Dante's unexpected laugh has me snapping my lips shut. Crap. I said that out loud.

Awesome. At least it's true. This woman is effortlessly beautiful.

"It's not a big deal," the woman says as she finishes cleaning the screen.

"Lena! It is a big deal. This is disrupting her entire childhood and your lives. Can you even work?"

"Dante." Something about this woman's tone is so soothing that even the flutter in my chest is calmer. "We got them to back off the property, and Dad's got the gates closed again. We'll lay low until this all blows over."

She masterfully avoids the question about work.

"What if it doesn't?" His concern stunts his words.

"Then you'll come up with another plan, like you do for everything else, or I'll find a new normal."

My mind swirls with words again. Plans. Plot twists that

connect my story with Dante's life. No matter how hard I try to separate them, they keep swirling into one connected story.

"What if I can't fix this?" His voice is hollow, and there's no arrogance left—only fear and blinding love.

This is Dante Thompson, and he couldn't be more different from the Dante splayed across the tabloids for the last few years.

He's going to make this so freaking hard simply by being himself.

"You will," Lena says gently. "And if you don't, we'll still figure it out like we always do. But…"

"I know. I should have listened when you said something was off with Trent. For fuck's sake, Lena. You've been my best friend since the day I arrived in California. I should have listened to you." That bit of information is a slap across the face. Did he replace me that quickly? "I'm sorry, Lena."

"Stop apologizing for things you couldn't control. The bigger issue you need to address is that Trent got at least some of your clients to turn on you, so how will you find out what employees he's turned too?"

Suddenly his problems seem so much bigger than mine. I was the only one to feel the repercussions when I lashed out. Dante has people depending on him.

Loneliness wraps its cold fingers around me, and I shiver like I'll never be warm again.

His heavy sigh eats up the silence. "It could be the entire team. I don't know who to trust, Lena. But I'm countering his move before he can do more damage."

"Um," I interrupt because even when I'm trying not to get attached, I'm still a nosy asshole. "How do you know your team was involved?"

"Dante?" Lena asks, and he swirls the camera toward me.

"Lena, this is Saylor. Oh shit." He smacks a hand to his forehead. "I mean Sassy. This is Sassy Thompson, *the* author."

I'm not sure what possesses me to try and comfort the name-dropping ass, but I do. My hand lands on his forearm, but it's not gentle like when Ainsley does it, and it hits like a slap, so I immediately take it away.

"Somehow, I don't think your, um, friend gives a shit about who I am." Internally I cringe as I turn toward the camera.

Lena smiles warmly, and it lights up her face. I don't explore why I instantly want to trust her. "You couldn't be more wrong," she says with a gentleness I've never had. "I've waited a long time to meet you, Saylor Greer, and I'm super happy your favorite flower wasn't a geranium or something. Poppy could have had a very difficult childhood." She pops a dimple, so I continue before she asks the questions dancing in her inquisitive eyes.

"Um, so, anyway. How do you know?"

Dante sighs, and it blows his hair around his forehead. "Because the reporters didn't simply happen upon us the night I threatened them. That restaurant isn't a normal hotspot. That type of ambush in Hollywood was carefully created by puppet masters who understand what kinds of stories the world wants, and only a select few people on my staff would have known where I was that night."

"Puppet masters. You mean you. You're the mastermind."

"Yeah." He sighs. "Usually, anyway. I pull the strings and choreograph break-ups, make-ups, and everything in between. Drama in Hollywood is almost always scripted."

His confession doesn't sit well with me. Would I be doing the same thing if I had been strong enough to go with him? My stomach flips over at the thought. Creating drama in people's lives feels dirty and wrong, but who am I to judge? I write words people can get lost in, so is it really that different?

"It's shitty because I should be able to trust my team. They're all on my payroll, and I hand-selected them all," he says, staring straight at me. "But my brother will sell my soul, and apparently, everyone I care about, to get what he wants."

I still don't understand, and my confusion must show on my face.

"Saylor." It should piss me off that he uses that name. No one in my life calls me Saylor, not anymore. But my body responds like I've saved that piece of myself for him. "You understand what I do, right? Why Kate called me to help you?"

No. My mind is still working through the mental gymnastics of having Dante suddenly back in my life.

My fists clench, and the knuckles on my right hand crack.

"I own the most sought-after public relations firm in California, Saylor. I'm who all those celebrities call when their lives are falling apart. We say they're in some sort of rehab, but truthfully, they're usually on the beach somewhere while I find a new way to spin their bullshit to get them out of trouble. Or I create buzz around a new 'relationship' when there's a movie to promote or an album to sell."

"You're a professional liar," I say, twisting my lips into a frown.

His smile is sad. "That's one way to spin it. This is the first time I've needed the spinning, though."

"Same," I grumble.

"Think of it as a mini time-out," Lena says. I scrunch my nose and scratch my neck when I realize she's talking to me.

"Um, I may have told the daughter of a very important person to stick a dildo to a hard surface and spin. Or, you know, something like that, during a live interview that was meant to promote childhood literacy programs. The way they've spliced the video makes me look…" I tear my gaze away from the screen. "I'll need a little more than a time-out."

Her face softens with her words. "I'll admit. I saw it live before they edited it to the mess it is now. It wasn't your fault, though. She was obviously digging for something, and she's the one who came off as unprofessional, not you. It really sucks that they can manipulate that stuff like they did," she says with a kindness my heart says is real.

Yeah, they edited the hell out of the replay. My cheeks heat. "You're one of the millions and counting, then?"

She nods. "Afraid so, but I'm also a big fan."

"I hate her," I mutter.

Lena's laugh is throaty and carefree.

"Oh, not you. I mean, I don't know you. I…"

"I'm not a fan of Rebecca's," she says like you'd tell someone they were being silly. "I'm a fan of yours. I'm the one who pushed Dante into reading your books. They got me through a pretty dark period of my life, and when I read *April Rain*, well, I knew."

My skin prickles as I turn my wary heart toward Dante. "You read my books?"

He nods.

"A—All of them?"

Another nod. "I told you I'd always be your biggest fan, but admittedly, I didn't read any of them until about a month ago. It was—too hard."

My chest collapses, and my breathing comes in short bursts. No one notices that I'm spiraling, though. Lena turns her attention back to Dante while my entire world is being put through a shredder.

He knows.

He knows my fears and my regrets.

He knows how I pathetically held out hope.

And he still came back.

Is that what I'd hoped for all along?

"So, you do have a plan, right?" Lena asks.

Dante says he does, but I've never seen him so crestfallen. In my mind, he's always been Superman—above the pain we mere mortals feel daily.

"Kate Gerard is Saylor's agent." I don't miss Lena's flinch. I knew Kate was a hardass, but I didn't know her reputation was this widespread. "She got the ball rolling tonight. We'll hash out the details tomorrow."

"What better way to silence all their claims than flooding the world with a real-life tragedy turned happily ever after? People are going to eat that up." Lena sounds like she's swooning, but my head is seriously about to explode.

"But we're not," I mumble. "We were friends. We. We're…"

"More than I valued," Dante says, with so much meaning packed into those four little words that I fight the urge to flee.

"Can you pull off a love affair for the ages? 'Cause I've got to be honest, Saylor is a little green and maybe a lot pissed off. I'm pretty sure she still hates you, and you already know I'm on her side there."

My left eye twitches. In the book, I did place most of the blame on the hero. It wasn't fair, but it's what sells. Did he tell Lena the truth? How he left me here? And why? But she's wrong about the hate part. I hate that I've loved him all these years. I hate that I couldn't move on. I hate that nothing has changed, and my reasons for pushing him away are still valid. But I've never hated him.

Dante pierces me with his gaze—those eyes that have haunted my nights for years—and my stomach tries to flip. This is the connection I've never had with anyone else, and it's the one that tells me he could still get me to drop my panties with a single command.

No. My panties stay on. On, Saylor! All the way on. I sink my fingernail into my earlobe when he stares at me. I'm so screwed. That's all there is to it. He's in my head, and if I don't hold onto my self-control with both hands, he'll be in my pants. Once that happens, my heart doesn't stand a chance. But then he'll witness the darkness when it finds me, because it always does, and we'll both be fucked.

There's no happy ending in this story for me.

"I know we can," he says without shifting his focus from me.

"You do?" I ask.

He gives me a soft smile. "You've never put up with anyone's shit. There's no reason to start now." He slowly scans me head to toe, prompting goosebumps to sweep over me. "We made some mistakes that cost us years we'll never get back."

I shake my head—it wasn't a mistake. It was the right thing to do.

But he continues, "So, we might as well let the world fall in love with us while you learn to tolerate me again."

His damn smirk hits me right in my core.

"Well, I like her already," Lena says like we're destined to be best friends. Her approval wraps around my body like poison ivy, and an unbearable itch flares over my skin. I can't do friends. They lead to feelings and all the unpleasantness that comes from trying to deal with them.

Dante holds out his hand with his thumb and forefinger spread wide, and my throat goes dryer than the desert. When I don't move, he leans down and fits the V they form between my thumb and forefinger, then he gently taps the delicate skin there with his thumb.

It used to be his reminder to put my claws away.

He tamed my sass, and I encouraged him to live loudly.

"Trust me? Just one more time?" he says under his breath without letting go of my hand.

I hate that my body reacts to the hope in his voice. I hate that I'm flooded with emotions trying to claw their way to the surface. I hate feeling so out of control but not swirling with the darkness that can keep me in bed for days. But mostly, I hate myself for knowing so intrinsically that this man will always own a piece of my soul.

Why am I doing this? Aliens. That's what it is. Aliens have taken over my body. It's the only explanation for even considering going along with these idiotic plans that will surely send me spiraling into the abyss of depression when he leaves.

I hope the aliens aren't slimy, and they let me say goodbye to Ainsley. My poor sister would be devastated otherwise.

"Saylor?"

I drag my gaze to him, but my mind is spiraling with stories and what-ifs. I stare at him without blinking, and he squeezes my hand again.

Crap.

"Are you okay? I know this is a lot, but…"

"So, um." I pull my hand from his and tug on my earlobe. It's suddenly itchy, so I run my nail along the fleshy part of the lobe, allowing it to sink in far enough to become uncomfortable.

I haven't been paying attention, and I do this a lot. I guess that's something a second-chance romance partner should know.

"Well, here's the thing." I try again. "The stories? The ones that I used to tell you out loud?" I sneak a peek in Lena's direction. I'm pretty sure she'll be keeping her daughter away from the unhinged lady after this. "Well, now my imagination rivals a fantasy author's, but it's all in my head."

89

Because I try not to leave the house unless someone drags me out, and even then, not long enough to talk to anyone.

They stare at me like I have two heads. Don't they know what kind of crap fantasy authors make up? Everything. Literally everything.

"Stories start and stop in here all day long," I say, pointing to my head. My eyes are so dry it hurts to close them. Crap, when did I stop blinking? "Well, not recently—but today—I don't know. Sometimes I get lost in my mind multiple times a day. If I'm ignoring you, it could be on purpose. It's probably on purpose," I amend. "Or it could be because my characters won't shut the hell up. I'm weird. And strange. And it's probably why I don't have a lot of friends."

Well, that and I push everyone away, but I don't tell him that.

It's become so unbearably hot that I can't resist fanning my armpits.

Real classy, Sassy. But at least he's seeing me for what I am. A mess just trying to survive.

But the freaking guy stares at me like I harnessed the sun. Maybe he needs to speak to my therapist. The way his gaze sears my skin is not normal, and words bubble up in my chest.

"Er…" My brows pinch together, almost painfully, when he smiles at me. "Ah, I do much better in my bookstore, sometimes. So yes, you will have to say my name multiple times. Yes, I embarrass a lot of people because of the way I am. I'm not the right person to make America fall back in love with you. If anything, I'll only turn you into a meme too."

"Oh, she's perfect." Lena laughs.

"What?" The perfect meme maybe, but nowhere near perfect.

How the hell did that not scare her off?

Dante is still staring at me. Without moving my head, I shift my gaze left, then right. Being under his scrutiny is worse than telling my sister I crashed our only car into the Weathersfield's barn when I was supposed to be grounded.

My legs itch like a million red ants are marching up them. And now "The Ants Go Marching" plays in my mind. I casually run my hand down my shins, but the sensation won't go away.

When I can't take the creepy-crawlies or the way he's watching me anymore, I leap to my feet, searching for an escape, but this is my stinking home, and I end up spinning in a circle.

Think, Saylor. Where should I go? My room? Maybe Ainsley's house. I'm still spiraling when he grabs my arm and tugs me down to the sofa—right next to him.

"I think so too," Dante says.

What? He thinks what too? Oh, right. Lena isn't put off by my special brand of dippy thoughts and ideas. Maybe she should visit my therapist. Oh, maybe I can get a group discount for us all!

Dante leans into my line of sight, and I blink to bring him into focus. My throat gurgles, and I'm not sure if I was going for a laugh or a scoff, but a messed-up version of both escapes.

He shakes his head with a kind smile and, without looking away from me, says, "Lena, I'll have security to your parent's house within an hour. Maybe now would be a good time to take a vacation."

Jesus, Dante. Stop staring at me.

My gaze ping-pongs between the two of them. They would make a beautiful couple. Oh, lord. What if they were stranded on an island? During a storm. And there was only one bed. They could fall in love.

Ah...what? My stomach revolts against the direction of my thoughts.

Lena says goodbye from somewhere in the background. Shit. Somehow, I missed the end of their conversation, and now embarrassment makes me look like an even bigger dork because she's grinning and waving at me.

"Oh, crap. Sorry. Bye?"

She nods, then blows Dante a kiss before the screen goes dark.

He holds me tight against his side. Could he sense that I was about to flee? His fingertips flex against the exposed skin between my shorts and T-shirt, and it pains me to admit I never even flinched at the contact.

"We'll figure this out, Sayl. Together this time."

This time.

What the hell did I fall into?

CHAPTER 8

DANTE

"*H*oney, I'm home," I sing as I enter Saylor's office. A sick satisfaction blooms in my chest because with that kind of greeting, she won't be able to hold back the sass.

Stirring a reaction out of her is my new favorite pastime —I can't get enough of it. Any response from her is better than the years of silence we've enforced on each other.

"You don't want to call me honey," she says with a wag of her finger. "Trust me, I'm no bumblebee. I'm the mean one with a painful stinger."

I'm not even sure what that means. None of her words have made any sense since our meeting this morning when Kate announced that Saylor and I are in a fake relationship, though I have no intention of keeping it fake. The meeting lasted over an hour, and Saylor was not happy that Kate called me her muse—but even Saylor can't deny that she's suddenly writing again with me in the house.

It makes me fucking giddy, but honestly, I'm surprised she hasn't called Ainsley in for reinforcement yet.

Saylor stands in the corner, with her arms hanging and

fists balled at her sides. The anxiety is still there, but it's clouded with something close to fear too, and it makes my stomach clench reflexively.

She's even more beautiful now than the day I met her. Her wild mass of hair that may never be tamed makes me itch to touch it, and she has a few more freckles covering her nose. But her dimples are the same, even if I've only seen a glimpse of them since I've been home.

Though not tall, she's all leg, and the cutoff denim that seems to be her wardrobe of choice these days showcases the toned and tanned skin of a runner. It makes me chuckle because Saylor has never run a day in her life.

Unless—has that changed too?

My heart constricts in my chest the longer I watch her. I used to be able to get her to laugh and relax without even trying. Who does that for her now?

"Listen, Sayl. I appreciate you going along with this arrangement, even though it isn't what you were expecting. So if there's anything I can do to make your writing—easier, let me know." I flash her a grin full of innuendo. The way her grumpy face heats in reaction to me is enough to make my cock weep for all the time we've been apart.

I love how her hooded gaze falls down my body before snapping back to my face. There's more emotion in that one look than I've experienced over a lifetime without her.

And Jesus, I'm a jerk for wanting to push her on it. A thought crosses my mind, and my lips curl into a lascivious smile. Ripping my T-shirt over my head, I stalk her slowly. We have so much baggage to talk about, but I remember how her beautiful mind works. We won't have any of those conversations until I can get her to let down her walls and show me the fears that lie beneath.

"Would it help if I walked around shirtless?" I ask, tossing my shirt to the side. "Lena was right. In the past month, I've read every book you've written. Even the one they made into that terrible movie."

She scoffs, trying to appear offended, but she must agree they butchered the thing because she carefully skirts away from me without arguing.

"You've got quite a dirty imagination," I say, unable to contain a groan. "I was shocked they cut the Jacob's ladder from the film, though. Seems like something women would want to see." I shimmy my hips with my palms pointed to the sky, and she quickly shields her eyes with both hands.

"No," she blurts. When she peeks through the cracks in her fingers, I laugh so freely that I don't even recognize the sound. "Wait. What are you saying? Are you—are you pierced? Down there?"

I laugh again, and this time I clutch my stomach. People think it's her attitude that always got her in trouble, but truthfully, it's her inquisitive nature. She can't help herself.

Rubbing my chin, I walk toward her with an exaggerated swagger. When I'm close enough to touch, I lean in to her personal space, and the scent of mint and wildflowers fills my nostrils. It evokes a million memories and throws me off-balance for a second, but when I hear her teeth snap together, I pull back to study her face.

"I guess you'll have to find out," I say with a husky drawl. It wasn't my intention, but in an effort to seduce my way into her trust, I've only succeeded in riling myself up.

"No way. Nope. The pictures I saw doing research were more than enough. If that thing is pierced, keep it the hell away from me."

My cheeks already hurt from smiling. "Does that mean if it's not pierced, you're willing to say hello?"

Her right hand grasps her necklace and drags the pendant along the chain, but she's not about to snap, either. Even the vein in her temple is relaxed.

"No." She drops her pendant and places her palms on my chest to shove me away, but we both freeze.

The hairs on my arms stand on end, and my goddamn dick twitches like it's waving hello.

We remain frozen in this position, and she uses her index finger to trace the outline of my sailboat tattoo, my own Saylor forever branded over my heart.

Can she feel the energy between us? Alarm flashes across her features, and when she snatches her hand away, I almost fall into her. Her hands breathed life into me and sucked it all away when she lifted them.

It's not normal. Reactions like this don't happen to everyone. They happen to those of us tied forever to another soul.

Her touch only reinforces one thing—she is mine, and I'll do whatever it takes to show her that.

Saylor's mouth hangs open, and the color rises high on her perfectly sculpted cheekbones, so I assume she at least felt—something. She blinks slowly, gracefully, like a butterfly hovering over a flower. She's perfect. She's still got that wide-eyed innocence about her, even when she's lashing out with her barbed tongue.

"How the hell did I survive missing you all these years?" I make no attempt to mask the longing in my tone.

Gone is the butterfly, and in its place is a hummingbird with rapid-fire blinking that breaks her trance, and she slides along the wall to get away from me.

"You're just out of sorts," she says with a slight tremor that gives her away. "Don't even pretend that was—anything. I'm not someone you'd give a second thought to if we weren't stuck together in this nightmare."

That hurts, and I deserve every biting word. Or the image of me that I've portrayed deserves it, anyway.

She's right that I'm out of sorts, but it's not entirely from this situation. The lack of her touch left me bereft, and I need her essence to fill me again, so I move slowly toward her.

"I understand why you might think that, but don't you dare pretend that was nothing. You and I both know better than that. If you're scared, say you're scared, but don't ever diminish us to *nothing*."

I take a deep breath to calm my temper, count to ten, then continue. "Who I am on TV and in magazines is not me, Saylor. It's a role I play when I leave my safe spaces. Dante Greer protects me and my family. When I'm him, nothing and no one else matters. I learned a long time ago to put blinders on. Had I not done that?"

I take my time perusing her, from her pretty blue toenails up to guileless eyes of the same color.

"Get real," she says scornfully before I can finish my thought. "I knew the first time I saw you in a magazine that you had the ability to be an asshole, but I've never known you to be intentionally cruel. I don't exist in your hemisphere, whether you're Dante Greer or Dante Thompson. This," she says, running her hands up her torso like Vanna White, "is not what you want on your arm, and I refuse to be a time filler for you."

Frustration roars in my chest. "Why do you do that?" I ask through clenched teeth.

"Do what?" She's not quite yelling, but her voice has risen a few octaves.

"Talk about yourself like that?"

"I'm a realist. Plus. I've unfortunately seen the girls you date, and I've seen Lena." She pauses, and her face twists like she's contemplating something terrible. "Ugh, fine, Lena is lovely, but I've seen her now too. We are not the same."

My body releases a month's worth of tension at her words. Doling out compliments is not easy for her, and Lena deserves all the love and friendship the world can give her.

"Who said I want the same? Who said I want the plastic, vapid, money-grabbing faces from those magazines? There's a reason I'm still single after six fucking years, Saylor, and she's standing right in front of me." I'm so close to her now that the navy outlining her irises like a wall protecting its fragile center becomes more pronounced until all that's left is a guarded darkness.

Her chin quivers, but stubborn to a fault, she juts it out and holds her ground. "I'm well-versed in the scale of beauty, Dante." Every time she says my name, it sounds like a curse. Is she doing that on purpose? "I write about beautiful people and the love everyone on the planet is searching for, but I make it a habit to never lie to myself, either."

I set my jaw with a snap, and the muscles in my neck twitch in agitation. She is truly the only person who could ever piss me off like this.

"I'm pretty, but I'm weird," she says as she flits about the room, away from me. Her movements are jerky and agitated. "They cancel each other out for people like you. I was a placeholder in your life, but I don't get the fairy tale. I write about it so people like me can have the fantasy of it. You left Hope Hollow behind and never looked back. That's real. That's the truth. So don't come in here and blow smoke up my ass. Just…just…" The first glimmer of real emotion passes over her face. "Please, Dante."

She tries to flee again, but I gently wrap my fingers around her wrist before she can escape. Her fist releases almost immediately, and that's when I notice the nail marks in her palm.

"What the hell, Saylor? Doesn't this hurt?"

"Not as badly as feelings can." She tries to pull free, but I hold her to me.

"I left because of what you said to me. What you told me to do."

She drops her head, and her long lashes fan out over her cheekbones.

"Why are your feelings hurt if you got exactly what you asked for?"

I read her book—her answer was right there, waiting for me in black and white. It's too coincidental for it not to have been, at least in part, autobiographical.

She tugs her hand free and heads to the bedroom.

We have so much to talk about. So many mistakes to sort through. So many lies to undo.

But I'm literally speechless, and my heart is behaving like it was set on fire.

How do I reach you now, my sweet, sassy Saylor girl?

CHAPTER 9

SAYLOR

"I don't understand," Ainsley says gently.

I'm pacing back and forth in front of my bed. The one queen-sized bed because that would be my luck. I've written that trope enough to know what people think happens, but in real life, the hero got the sofa, and the heroine locked herself away in the bedroom.

Crap. We are not the hero and heroine anymore. Why won't my brain get that message? I'm freaking annoying as hell sometimes.

It doesn't help that our meeting with Kate was an epic shit show. Somehow we came out of it with a plan for a fake relationship and Dante believing he's my muse. My freaking muse.

"Sass, can you stop moving for one minute? You're giving me motion sickness."

I drop dramatically onto my bed. Propping my phone up on the pillow, I lay on my belly with my chin in my hands.

"I'm writing."

"Okay. That's good," she says juggling the phone while she ties her shoes. I shouldn't be bothering her right before another twelve-hour shift. She's probably exhausted, but she's the only anchor I have left.

"No! No, it's not, don't you see?"

"Ah, no. You'll have to be more specific." Ainsley sits on a bench in the hospital locker room, props her phone up in a locker, and clips her badge to her shirt.

Ainsley was meant to do great things, and I prefer the land of make-believe.

"Dante's here. Somehow, I got roped into a kiss that turned into a fake relationship, which turned into him moving into my apartment—with me."

"Dante who?" She's obviously not paying attention as she adjusts her ponytail.

"Dante," I hiss. "Dante Thompson."

The silence makes my heart thump erratically against my chest. Ainsley moves so slowly that I'm worried her connection is failing.

"Dante? Your Dante is living with you? And he's your muse?"

"No. Why does everyone keep saying that?" I ask as Dante yells through the wall, "Yes, I am. Happy to help. Missed you, Ains."

"What the heck?" I leave my phone on the bed and stomp over to the door. How dare he be all charming and sweet. He hasn't been part of our family for years. Wrenching the door open, I poke my head out, expecting him to have his ear pressed to the wall but find him lounging on the sofa. "Do you have superhuman hearing or what?"

"No, sweetheart. You happen to be a little shrill at the moment, and since we do need to sell this relationship, and your bookstore is technically open downstairs, it's probably best if you blabbed our secret a little more quietly."

"Hey," I say, pointing my finger at him. When the heck did

I turn into an angry old lady? "I'm talking to my sister. That's allowed. Kate said so."

He stands quickly and is in front of me a second later. How in the world does he move so gracefully when I fumble around the world like a drunk girl hearing P!nk's "Raise Your Glass" at two in the morning?

Life isn't fair.

"She did say that, didn't she?" His words are buttery smooth. Why, oh why, do I have to react to him? Him! Of all people, he has to be the one to break my feelings ban. This is why he was never supposed to come back. "She also said to act like we're actually in a relationship. That means we should be out doing something."

"Out?" I gulp. "Out where?"

He stares at me, and I shift my weight from foot to foot. Geez, Dante. I'm not a Rubik's cube you can't solve. "I don't know, Sayl. The beach? A park? A fucking walk? Anything outside of these four walls."

"I—I don't go out." I say it like he suggested we get dinner on Mars, because for me, they're the same. "And we already established I don't swim when you hauled me from the lake. You and me outside is a freaking mess."

"Granted, we're unconventional, but we're not a mess." His hypnotic voice matches the shimmer in his eyes.

"What? Of course, we are."

His face practically glows. He's wearing the same expression that could always get me to freefall straight out of my comfort zone. I take a giant step back. And then another.

"I'll finally teach you to swim."

I stumble back another step and shake my head. "I—I don't swim."

"I remember. I'll teach you. I'll keep you safe, promise." He flashes a dimpled grin that reminds me of book fairs and football games. He would keep my body safe, there's no question in my mind about that, but the answer is still no.

I can barely swallow, let alone make my words work. They come out frog-like and painful. "I don't swim," I repeat.

"Maybe it's time," my traitorous twin says from my bed. I forgot she was listening.

Dante pokes his head over my shoulder, and rainbows shoot from his eye holes as he pushes past me and belly flops onto my bed like he's seventeen again.

"Why, hello, beautiful sister."

How the hell can he be so happy-go-lucky when the sky is literally falling all around us?

"That has never worked on me, Dante," she says shyly even as she turns an embarrassing shade of red.

"Obviously," I snort.

"Don't hurt her, or I will cut you into little pieces. I learned how to do it in med school." She's too soft-spoken for the threat to be menacing, but I love her for trying.

"I'm not going to hurt her." He turns his head, and his gaze devours me. Electricity shoots between us, making the entire room feel charged. "Give me the *CliffsNotes*, Ains. How do I get Saylor out of her shell? What should our second chance first date be?"

"Ah…" Poor girl. I can picture her discomfort without ever looking at the screen. "I don't suppose you want to hang out dusting her books?"

"If that's a euphemism for something dirty," he says with a cluck of his tongue that has me grinding my teeth, "you need to take some vocab lessons from your sister."

"Ugh. No, D."

I suck in a breath. My sister falls right back into easy banter with him while I'm a hot mess of half-cocked stories.

And he's laughing like he hasn't been missing from our lives for the last six years. *Easy on the sass, Sassy. It's your fault he's been away.* A shiver runs down my spine like a kiss from a ghost.

"Tell me where to take her," he says, dangling his feet off the edge of my bed.

"Well. How brave are you?" she asks. I don't recognize that tone. My sister never stirs the pot or participates in gossip of any kind, yet that tone from her mouth puts me on high alert.

"I've always been brave. And I've had to grow a pretty thick skin in California."

I don't dare speak, but I slide my pendant along the chain from one ear to the other while I listen.

"Well then, take her to Three Brothers Brewing. Grady keeps her favorite wine behind the counter, and he'll be able to help."

"Ainsley!"

"Gotta go," she yips right as my phone beeps with another call.

Dante drops his head with a groan. "It's the lady viper."

My lips twitch because it can only be one person. "Ains, we'll call you back. Okay?"

"Yeah, *we'll* call you back," he says with a disarming grin.

I dart my gaze toward him, and heat creeps up my neck.

"Not we. I mean me. I'll call you back." I'm reaching for the phone when he wiggles his fingers at my sister, then clicks the green accept button, and the screen fills with Kate's face.

Dante's body deflates at the sight of her. Hmm. I guess Kate Gerard has that effect on everyone.

"Dante," she snips. "Is Sassy there?"

"Why am I *Dante*, but she's *Sassy?*" This time his tone is teasing.

Oh my god. He's like a whiny little toddler. Yup. Keep

thinking that—anything to counter the other thoughts stirring in my body.

"Because they're both masks of people whose asses I'm trying to save. Is she there or not?"

He turns the screen toward me, and his smile melts into a frown, so I reluctantly come closer. Rolling his shoulders, he sits on the edge of the bed, and I'm forced to sit next to him so we're both visible on my iPhone camera.

"I sent the extended video to *Page Six*. It'll go live any minute. It'll take a while for them to track you down in Hope Hollow, but make no mistake, they will. Spend this time getting Hope Hollow on board with this new relationship. Make the people who know you best believe in the fairy tale, or it'll never work."

"But…"

"Sassy, it'll be fine. When I went searching for you, no one in that town would give me the time of day. If they think you've forgiven him, they will protect him too, at least long enough for our plan to work."

It's so annoying when she's right.

"We're heading to the brewery," Dante announces.

It's a testament to how much that surprises Kate when it actually shows in her expression. "You are?"

"Sure." He shrugs.

"Well, if you can sell this to Grady, you can sell it to the public."

Why did I ever introduce her to Grady? If I'd known she'd throw it in my face like this, I would have kept his friendship to myself. This is what having two glasses of wine does to me. It makes my mouth all loosey-goosey.

"But why?" I demand. "Why do we have to sell this here?"

"Because, Sassy, you've managed to piss off Malimar, and now the court of public opinion is the only one that matters.

Social media makes and breaks people every day. We need it to make you. So if either of you wants to work again, you will make this look like the most romantic story ever created, or they'll cut you off at the knees. Trent and Olivia have turned Dante into enemy number one, and you? You've turned Will Malimar's princess into a dildo meme. He won't let that go unnoticed, and he's a vindictive son of a bitch. Get your shit together, put on your happy faces, and fall back in fucking love."

Dante opens his mouth, but Kate isn't finished.

"Sex sells stories. Make Hope Hollow believe you're having the hottest sex in Connecticut, so when the soul suckers invade, we have the seeds of a love story the world is already interested in planting roots."

"You want us to have sex?" My voice quivers like I'm one hundred years old, and my knee bounces wildly against Dante's thigh. My brain starts spinning with the tempo of Jimmy Eat World's "The Middle." It's chaotic and makes my heart race, but somewhere in the angry beat are words I cling to.

"I don't care if you fake it, Sassy. But do whatever you have to do to make it appear real."

"You want me to lie." I stare up at Dante. "To everyone who has stuck by me my entire life."

"Anything else?" he whispers. There's tension in his voice as he stares at the phone.

"No. Sell it," Kate demands, and he turns to me with an apologetic shrug. "I have to go. Remember, sex sells. So sell the shit out of this tonight." She hangs up, but Dante continues to hold the phone out in his palm while he watches me.

"How are your acting skills?" Even wearing a wary lopsided grin, he still looks like a rockstar who graces the bedroom walls of teenage girls everywhere.

"About as good as your writing skills," I mumble. "Probably. Maybe worse. Probably worse."

He bumps my shoulder with his. "Then maybe we need to make this real."

Sparks shoot down my spine. "What?"

"Before I got you to fall in love with me, we were the best of friends. Let's start there. Think of it as me trying to woo my way back into friendship like old times." He stands, then turns to face me. "Saylor Greer, let today be the first day of me winning back your trust. But…" He seems unsure for the first time since he walked back into my life, and stares at me with an unreadable expression. "Are you and Grady a—thing?"

I almost choke on the name. "Grady? Grady Reid?"

A low rumble erupts from somewhere within him as I stare at him in utter disbelief.

"May I remind you that you're the one who came crashing back into my life with your string of women plastered all over the tabloids?" *Zip. Zip. Zip.* I drag my pendant across the chain like an angry bee.

It's harder to calm myself with him so close. It's why I use my bookstore to hide. It's my sanctuary where I can fall apart, be pissed off, and eventually calm myself down. It's safe, and Dante Thompson is more dangerous than a nuclear explosion.

"None of that was real, Saylor. It's all about appearances and nothing more. But if you are in a relationship, it kind of fucks up our plans here, don't you think?" The grit in his tone is new. I've never heard him sound like this before. Did he show up here assuming I'd always waited for him—that I'd been alone all this time?

He'd be right, but what hurts more is knowing that he didn't wait for me, even if he did exactly what I told him I wanted. I take it back—I am a hypocrite.

Your book told him you waited for him. The voices in my head need their mouths duct-taped shut.

Pain sears my eyes, and they grow hot with the moisture I'm no longer accustomed to, so once again, I grab ahold of anger, regardless of how irrational it is. "It's only now occurring to you that I might be with someone? That someone could love me? That they would stay?"

Low blow.

"Jesus, Saylor. No. That's not what I'm saying."

I can't listen to him anymore. Everything hurts. After years and years of protecting myself, my insides shake in fear. Fear that feelings I've attempted to bury aren't as deep or as broken as I need them to be.

"Go to hell, Dante. Go straight to hell."

CHAPTER 10

DANTE

"*I* hate to admit it, but it worked," I say when Saylor finally lifts her head from her laptop with glassy eyes.

"What?" she asks while blinking and glancing around the room like she expected to be alone.

How did I ever forget all her quirks? Every one brings forth a new memory that makes me desperate to learn more.

It's almost midnight, and she hasn't moved from the table since six hours ago, when she'd tucked her feet underneath her and started working, so I joined her. I should have been focusing on my work, but I spent most of the time watching her.

She's freaking distracting in the best, most painful of ways, but it gave me time to take in her home. It's not messy, per se, but there are piles of clutter in places that make me smile. What shocks me is there are no photos of anyone anywhere. Saylor used to carry a Polaroid camera with her everywhere, so why is her home lacking the love she used to showcase so proudly?

I take in the mismatched pillows and throw blankets from

the sofa that were tossed haphazardly after making my bed last night, and I bite the inside of my cheek to hold in a chuckle. We couldn't be more opposite. At my house, every available surface is covered with pictures of those I love, and there's not a pillow out of place, but it's never felt like a home, either.

Saylor feels like home.

Her relationship with Grady set her off tonight. More accurately, my interest in it set her off, but I saw the heartache play out in her eyes. Then she was too pissed at me to go to the brewery, so I attempted to make dinner. It was edible, but only barely.

Why didn't I fight for her—for us—back when it would have made a difference? Saylor leans forward in her chair, curled in on herself, swinging her necklace around her neck in a daze, and her lips turn down in sadness. Everything about the position screams broken.

If I did this to her, I'd never forgive myself, but there's something else she's fighting, and I will figure it out.

"You okay over there?" I ask. She turns her head and finally focuses her attention on me.

"Oh." She clenches her fist in front of her heart as she brings herself out of her made-up world and rejoins me here, in her home above the little bookstore she always wanted.

"Do you always lose yourself so completely in your work?" I sound tired, and I am. But it's the kind of tired that comes from running away from problems instead of fixing them, and I'm not doing that anymore.

She glances at her keyboard, and I watch as she saves her work. It's something she's done repeatedly over the last few hours. She does it like she's used to losing things. "Um." Her focus shifts as she watches the rainbow-colored wheel spin. Once it's saved, she turns her attention back to me. "I mean, don't you?"

"I do, but I guess it seems different because I'm always in it with actors. The stuff I make up is entertainment, sure, but it doesn't grab people and wrap them in a hug like your words do."

"Yeah, well, I don't play well with others." She clasps her hands over her head and leans side to side, exposing a small sliver of skin at her waist. That tiny bit of her causes an ache deep in my core.

"Are you hungry?" I ask. I haven't felt this unsure of myself since the day I walked into Tri-High. I hated that school. Well, until I met Saylor, anyway. She made everything more tolerable.

It was Sassy who helped me that day, but it was Saylor I fell in love with.

And now I'm met with a scowl.

"What?" I ask, shrugging my shoulders like an insecure teen. "You barely ate anything at dinner."

"I can't help it," she snips, then takes a deep breath. "I wasn't expecting to be sitting next to a jealous asshole who only sees what he wants to see when he wants to see it." She says it calmly, but the words still cut.

I fight hard to relax my features as I study her. She has her guard up, surrounded by a ten-foot wall and a moat full of piranhas. But all I see are challenges to be won. "I apologized for that. I needed to know if we had an obstacle I wasn't aware of."

"No, Dante." Her shoulders hang heavy, like she's tired of holding herself together, and I would give anything to be the one to support her. When she lifts her head, all the emotions she's trying to hold in check crash into me. "I'm not in any kind of relationship. Totally and completely alone, is that what you want to hear? Grady is the friend I found when I needed someone most."

Her eyes glaze over, caught in a memory, maybe, but she

blinks them clear, void of emotion. "We tried to hook up once. When we were both hurting so much, we just wanted to feel—something—anything but the nothingness we lived in. But we realized pretty quickly it was like kissing a sibling." She wrinkles her nose, and it eases some of the uncertainty that had settled in my gut.

"Saylor." I can barely hear my own words, but she does. She always did. Sometimes it felt like I didn't even have to speak them. She had a way of understanding me that I've never experienced with anyone else.

"Please, Dante. Don't. We're six years too late." She glances away, and her statement weighs down the silence because it is a lie, and we both know it. "My sister died. Her baby died. I nearly lost everything in that watery grave, then I lost myself, and when I came up for air, you were gone too."

"But you told me…"

She shakes her head. "It's fine, Dante. I can't go back to that time in my life. Please, if you ever cared at all, let the past stay in the past. We'll get through this mess, and then we'll go through with our futures like we would have a month ago. On different paths. We don't need to mix them up again."

Her phone dings, and she lifts it to her face. It shows how deep her concentration runs, because she didn't hear those notifications once while she was writing.

We need to talk, though. If the story she wrote is true… Fuck. If it's true, I've been mourning a loss for years that never should have happened.

A light shade of pink creeps down her neck, making the buzzing in my chest more prominent. "Guess the kiss worked."

She turns her phone to face me, and the image on her screen makes my heart fill with relief. It's the only way to describe it. It causes a light inside me to flare brightly because you can't fake a kiss like that.

"You did good, Sayl." And I mean that in every way possible because that kiss still lingers on my lips, and it's imprinted on my soul for eternity. It's the kiss that told me we would be okay.

"Thanks. I think," she grumbles. Then she stands from the table and slips on her shoes.

Nervous energy crackles in my gut as I watch her. "Where are you going?" It's midnight, and she lives on a lake. She can't seriously be considering leaving right now.

"For a walk." She opens the door and jogs down the back stairs like we're not in the middle of a conversation. I'm tripping over myself to slide my feet into flip-flops and follow her.

"By yourself?" I ask when I catch up to her. Saylor Greer is a one-woman show with no need for side characters, but I don't want to be a side character. I want to be her hero. The one who earns her love. The one who holds her when she's breaking. The one she doesn't need but wants anyway.

Her slim shoulders lift, but she doesn't look my way. "It's what I do."

"What? What is what you do?" Panic is rising in my body faster than a tidal wave.

"After I write. I go for a walk to mull over my scenes and where I want my story to go."

"But it's midnight and pitch fucking black out here. You can't swim, and you don't even have a flashlight."

She stops like she's only now considering this. "It's not an issue. I've lived here my entire life. I stay away from the lake, and I walk the same path every night."

"Every night?" How can she still not possess an ounce of self-preservation? My heart hammers against my chest as a

113

real fear of losing her consumes me. "You do this every night? By yourself?"

"Why do you ask so many questions?" She sighs, and I imagine an epic eye roll in there too.

"I'm trying to get to know you," I admit. "You're everything I remember and nothing familiar. I haven't figured out how to reconcile that."

"Well, hopefully you'll be able to head home soon, and you won't have to worry about it. I'm not a puzzle to be solved, Dante."

What would she do if she found out I'd been scheming, planning, and waiting for the right time to reenter her life for over a month? Or that I've always known California wasn't my home because she wasn't there? What would she say if I told her a giant Saylor-sized hole was missing in my life?

We walk a few paces in silence, but I watch her from the corner of my eye. Being stuck with this woman doesn't feel like the prison sentence she makes it out to be.

She walks with her face pointed to the stars, and I use the opportunity to memorize every inch of her. It hits me then that her shoulders aren't squared, and her fists aren't clenched. She's not even holding onto her necklace for dear life.

"You're calm out here," I say after studying her for a beat. "Or at least, calmer than I've seen you."

"I told you. I don't do well with people anymore."

I chuckle because she's never liked people, and she shoots me a dark expression.

"It's quiet out at night," she continues. "People don't *usually* try to talk to me. And it's really hard for overwhelming anxiety to sink its claws in when you're engulfed by a sky full of stars. It reminds me that I'm a small cog in the wheel of this universe. There's a whole world of problems that exist outside of my own. But I have a hard time remembering that through the noise of life sometimes."

I reach over and take her hand in mine. She flinches, her body tensing from her forehead to her toes, but she doesn't immediately pull away, and my shoulders relax. It's funny how physical my reactions are to her even now.

"Practice," I say in explanation while lifting our joined hands. I draw the line at kissing the back of hers, even though I want to, because I'm pretty sure she'd send me home, and I'm not ready to be away from her.

She scowls in response. My entire body smiles. When she doesn't fight me, it's a small victory in the war of Sass.

"I like this version of you," I admit. "But I like all the versions of you." I always did. Her fingers twitch in my palm like she's attempting to flex them.

"It's a mask," she says. "We all wear them." She guides us back toward her house but allows our hands to stay connected.

"I get the Sassy mask," I say. "And now, I've experienced it, too. Does that mean you're showing me Saylor now?"

"You make it sound like I have multiple personalities," she grumbles.

"No, I think you're very intentional with who gets to see what sides of you. But I wonder if anyone gets the whole woman anymore."

She slips her hand from mine and tucks a stray piece of hair behind her ear. "Not everyone knows who they are. Some of us are just protecting the pieces we recognize the only way we know how."

Oh, Saylor. I'm glad it's dark out so she can't see the emotion welling in my eyes for the pain she thinks she's hiding.

I watch her profile as we walk. "Is this the path you always take?"

She hesitates, then shakes her head. "My walks are for me and me alone."

"Jesus, Saylor. Do you tell anyone where you go?"

She shakes her head again, and I file this information away, adding it to the list of things we need to talk about.

I don't realize we're home until she turns toward the dock.

My breath stalls in my lungs as we walk single file, then she sits with her feet dangling over the edge. Once she's settled, I join her to make sure she doesn't fall in.

"Why do you keep getting close to the water if you're scared of it?"

"Oh," she says, sounding genuinely surprised. "I'm not scared of the water." She lifts her gaze to mine, and her eyes sparkle when they catch in the moonlight. She's so damn pretty but sadder than I've ever seen her. I want to kiss away that pain. Hold her fears. I want to be the man I always said I'd be.

"It's actually quite soothing," she says, staring dreamily out over the water. "I just can't bring myself to swim. That's a panic I can't control."

She opens her mouth wide when she gasps, and it hits me that it was a truth she didn't mean to tell, but I let her search my face for the love and understanding she'll find there.

Her gaze drifts to my lips, and her tongue slips out to wet her own. I moved closer as she spoke, and her scent, like salt air and citrus, fills my nose and assaults my mind with memories of us together. I want to kiss her again so much it hurts, but the pain she hides behind shuttered eyes keeps me in place.

I have to go slow.

She leans back on her elbows and stares at the sky, so I do the same. We're far enough removed from her life in that house that I let my guard down a little. And it's so easy to do around this mercurial little woman with a giant broken heart because out here, we're still us.

Her chest rises and falls with a slow rhythm I'm starting to understand only happens for her with great effort. She struggled with anxiety and depression in high school, more so in college, but seeing it in action now, I know she wrote a lot of truths in that book of hers. She calls it the darkness because that's how it feels when the depression consumes her.

"What are you thinking?" she asks. It's not quite a whisper, but it matches our gentle surroundings.

"I'm fascinated by how you work and how much of yourself you give when doing it. It's admirable." It's the truth. Even as teenagers, she had more focus than I did.

"Yeah, well, Van Gogh once said he put his heart and soul into his art and lost his mind in the process. I feel that on a cosmic level sometimes."

She brushes her hand on her leg, presumably to give herself something to do, but it's her detached tone that rattles around in my mind and causes words to stick in my throat.

How the hell does she lock down her feelings so easily? I've been with her for less than a week, and mine are clawing from inside my chest to be set free—for her. She's not this unfeeling, detached person she's trying to be, but I don't know how to get past her wall.

"I bet you do," I say. "I watched your face as you wrote today. I was completely immersed in the story through your expressions. It must be exhausting living in the hearts of so many characters all the time."

She shrugs, but her mouth hints at a smile. "At least I'm feeling something I can control."

A panic she can't control. I'd bet good money that she's

117

spent years attempting to wrestle all her emotions into a tiny shatterproof safe so she can throw away the key.

She sits up and leans toward the water, nearly giving me a fucking heart attack, so I use it as an excuse to wrap an arm around her waist and hold her to me. "In case you try to tumble in again," I say. But even as I say it, we both hear the lie.

My arm fits around this woman like a second skin—like she's the piece of me I've been missing. She doesn't pull away, even though her entire body has turned to stone, and I mark it as another win. For the first time since she told me to leave Hope Hollow, to leave her behind, I fully understand what a terribly tragic decision that was—for both of us.

"Are you okay?" I ask again. Eventually she'll have to tell me the truth.

She sighs, and it's like an exorcism. The tension that controls her body releases one muscle at a time, and she relaxes into my hold. I'm so grateful I swear my heart expands in my chest.

"I'm not used to having people around. Ainsley likes crowds, all the people. She likes the noise even if she doesn't participate in it. I get lost in it and…"

"And you worry about finding your way out."

Saylor's face purses again. I forgot how much I love it when she does that. It means she's thinking. It means I'm not getting a knee-jerk reaction out of her but a thoughtful, real answer. "Yeah."

"We need to talk, Sayl. About everything."

In the distance, a door slams, and it's like a hypnotist snapping his fingers. It brings Sassy back just when I was getting to see her again as Saylor.

"We've talked more in the last two days than I've talked to any of my neighbors in months. We are talking."

It's too late for the conversation we need to have, so I pivot.

"For what it's worth, Miss Saylor Sassy Greer, I see all of you. All the pieces that create you are worth knowing and trying to keep forever. The sassy ones. The sweet ones." I lean in so my nose grazes her ear. "The scared ones. Even the insecure ones. Remember that."

I stand before she can reply. I don't want her ruining the moment, and she will if given enough time. She won't be able to help that mouth of hers. Holding out my hands, I gesture for her to come with me.

She may act sassy, but Saylor is who she's protecting, and I make it my mission to get to know her—Saylor and all her pieces.

She places her palm in mine, and I lift her easily. The scowl on her face feels right, and it makes my soul lighter than it's been in a long time. How can her scowl make my entire body zing to life with happiness?

Saylor stops in the middle of the dock, and my pulse picks up when my gaze lands on a bear of a man blocking our exit.

"So it's true?" he growls. He's too far away for me to read his features, but there's a familiarity between them that makes fire creep up my spine. This must be Grady.

"Showtime," I whisper.

"No, Grady. It's not," Saylor says with a sigh while also dropping my hand. What the hell? We have a plan to follow. "But we have to pretend like it is. I screwed up at that interview, and he's got his own..." She peers up at me, but my shadow makes it too dark to read her expression. "Stuff. It makes sense that we work together to fix everything."

I hate that she's confiding in him. Hate that he gets this unguarded piece of her I no longer have.

"America's sweethearts, Sass? Honest to fucking God."

Grady doesn't hold back. It must be why they get along so well. Saylor wants direct, honest, and brutally real. It's why she works so well with Kate.

His gruff exterior isn't what I remember from high school, but it's who Saylor trusts.

Unease coils in the pit of my stomach. *Real.* Who is the real Dante Thompson now? I've been running from him and the emotions he didn't want to face for years, but that's who I must find if I want a second chance.

"Did you eat?" he asks as she walks closer. I follow behind, but with a distance between us that feels catastrophic.

She glances over her shoulder and shrugs. "Sort of."

He holds out a paper bag with grease stains on the bottom, and I can smell the fried food from here. Even if this isn't a romantic relationship, it's clear that he cares about her. A lot. And based on her more relaxed demeanor, she cares for him too. That means he's someone I need on my side.

"Thompson, you're bringing home a metric ton of baggage that took years to undo. I hope you know what the fuck you're doing. Same goes for you, Sass."

She walks to him, and he wraps her in a hug while whispering something I'm too far away to hear. The sight makes my heart shrivel up and catch fire right inside my chest. She isn't stiff or uncomfortable in his arms. She fell into him like he was her safe space—like she trusts him—and everything in me wants to cry out because she's not even like that with Ainsley anymore.

Something happened between these two to form this kind of bond, and now it's not only distance separating us. It's misunderstandings and mistakes causing a chasm far wider than the miles separating Connecticut from California.

Yeah, Grady. I'm beginning to understand exactly how much baggage we're wading through.

Sometimes in life, you have to free fall and hope that someone will catch you on the other end. For Saylor, I'm willing to take the leap and trust and pray that she'll be with me when we land, because it's time we buried our ghosts.

CHAPTER 11

SAYLOR

"A Hollywood golden boy walks into a bookstore and falls..."

If I could shoot my sister with eyeball lasers right now, I would. At least the intensity of my glare makes her stop talking.

"This isn't funny, Ainsley. And it's not a joke. It's only been four days, and I'm already climbing the walls."

"I mean, it's kinda funny. Who would have guessed your sass would land you in a relationship with America's favorite celebrity sidekick? With *your* Dante, of all people."

"It's not a relationship. It's a situationship. It's..."

"It's about to get real," a deep male voice says. How the hell does his tone wrap all the way around my body like that?

I keep trying to figure out how I got here, but it's all a blur. I mean, how did I go from a live-streamed network interview to a situationship with the only man to ever break my heart, to living with him in my tiny hometown that's about to be overrun with paparazzi?

"This isn't normal. None of this is normal," I mutter. I jab my pointer fingers into my temples and rub small, hard circles there.

Can anyone else feel my anxiety? I swear it's shooting off me like fireworks.

I lift my head right when Dante takes the sunglasses off his face, and my stomach hollows out because he removes the Hollywood mask right along with them. It's the first time I've seen it happen. But it's distinct. It's how he carries himself and the sexy-but-guarded expression he keeps plastered to his face. When he sheds all that, I'm left with the boy who taught me to drive. The man who stayed up late with me in college so I could study for finals.

I'm left with Dante.

My Dante.

In here, it's so easy for him to be the Dante I loved all those years ago, but out there? Out in the world? He's Dante, the man who rubs elbows with famous people, smiles for the cameras, and never has a worry or fear.

"How do you do that?" My shoulders are so tense around my ears that when I roll them back, my spine crackles.

He shrugs. I don't have to explain what I'm asking. He's always been able to speak Saylor. "It's a part. Out there, I'm Dante Greer." A sexy smirk tips the corner of his lips. "It's self-preservation, just like your sass."

Ugh. Eyeroll.

"But how do you turn it off so quickly?" My voice sounds constipated, but I can't change it. I'm out of my comfort zone, away from all that I can control, and it makes my guard spike to mountain-like heights.

His smile is soft and genuine. It gives the impression that it's only for me, but it's a reminder of how much pain he can cause—how much pain I can cause too.

"Because now I know who I am and who I want to be."

Each of his words flows through my skin, a needle stitching up the tears.

"Show off," I grumble.

"So, how is this going to work exactly?" Ainsley asks with far too much glee in her tone for my liking. I swear to God, if she claps her hands like an excitable cheerleader, I will push her right out the front door.

She always liked Dante, even after he left. It's the only time in our lives she wasn't on my side.

Then the bookstore door opens with a snap of wood hitting wood, and men with boxes waltz through to my back stairs, followed by two more men with even more boxes, all wearing Jolly Joggers Moving company T-shirts.

"Up the stairs," Dante directs.

"Ah, what the hell are you doing?" I hiss through my teeth.

He flashes the room a playboy smile that doesn't move when he speaks. "We're moving me in, Sassy. And we're making a production of it."

My head throbs. "But I thought...I thought..." What? What exactly did I think? "We've been here for all of like ten minutes." More men walk through my store. "How much stuff do you have? There's no way that's all going to fit in my apartment."

Shit! Are they going to touch all my stuff? My heart runs wild in my chest. I really don't want them messing with my belongings.

A small crowd forms outside the door, but thankfully I recognize most of the faces. The comforts of a small town come with the discomfort of everyone all up in your business 24/7. There's not a lot of privacy unless you're an outsider. Then they'll close ranks faster than a group of moms at a Black Friday sale.

"Half of them are empty," Dante whispers in my ear. He lingers long enough to give the impression of a private moment. I ignore the goosebumps that sweep over my arms and down my neck, but when he inhales, a chill works through my body, and I shiver.

His hand slides to my lower back, and he ushers me to my favorite stool behind the counter, hands me my glasses, opens my laptop, and presses a chaste kiss to my forehead.

"This won't take long, and then we have some things to discuss." His gaze burns into my soul while I search for the closest exit. "You're not running, Saylor. And I'm not leaving. Not this time."

My mouth is so dry that my tongue sticks to the roof of it. I need to start drinking more water. It's not normal to become so dehydrated from simple words. Ainsley sits in the corner of the bookstore, looking like I feel. When she leans forward like she's going to stand, Dante turns his attention to her.

"I'd like you to stay. I hope we won't need a mediator, but considering how our friendship started the first time, I don't want to take any chances." He flashes a lopsided grin, and my chest aches with memories of all my firsts. First kisses. First dances. First and only love.

Wait. How we started? Heat spreads across my exposed skin. We were forced teammates in our speech and debate class when he first made it his mission to win me over, and I did not go down easily.

My sister's expression shouts a thousand messages at me that I can no longer receive. They bounce off me like I'm standing behind a plexiglass wall. We used to know everything about each other, and then I taught myself to reject any outside emotion.

I taught myself to compartmentalize and block feelings because it's the only way to stay safe, but now, here Dante is, six years later, force-feeding them to me by the spoonful.

"Please," he adds so softly that I turn to make sure his lips are moving.

I face Ainsley, silently pleading, but I can't tell what either of them needs because I don't have that connection, Not anymore. Not with anyone.

Not ever again. If there's no love, there can be no pain.

I should have told him that back then. Maybe then he would understand.

His gaze sears my skin, and I fight against the memories floating in his electric blue depths.

No. No.

His mere presence can suck me into his vortex. He doesn't even need to try, and that's why I couldn't let him love me. He was always happiness and sunshine with a side of mischief, and all I had to offer was gray, bleak sadness. Now, I can't even offer him that. I'm just…empty.

"Saylor." His lips move, but the words sound distorted. They hit me like the roar of a thunderstorm, but without the rain to soothe me. Blinking rapidly, I try to focus on his lips as he speaks. "So many mistakes," he says. A chill grabs me and seeps all the way to my bones. "So many misunder-standings…"

My body shivers, and my teeth clatter. The rapid click, click, click drowns out the rest of what he's saying. Memories pass through my mind like postcards, each one more painful than the last. And in my head, I hear Dante begging me not to do this. Not to end us. Not to be so cruel. Not to lie.

Ainsley wraps a blanket around my shoulders and guides me to the back room through the fog settling over my exis-tence. She leads me to our grandmother's old armchair. It's bigger than a chair but not as big as a loveseat, and I curl into it just like I did as a child.

Just like I did *then*.

Dante crouches down so we're eye to eye, and all the fears I've tried to avoid are swimming in his. This is what I didn't want for him. More memories try to break my solitude, but I fight and push them down as far as they'll go.

This. This is why I can't keep him. When the sadness comes, I'll only drag him into the dark, and he deserves all the happiness the world has to offer him. He won't get that with me. He can't, because I'm not strong enough to do it for myself yet, and I refuse to be the one to snuff out his sunshine.

His heavy hand brushes the sweaty hair away from my face, and I breathe in through my nose to keep from hyperventilating.

"Give her a minute," Ainsley says from somewhere within the room. I can't tell where she is because everything is spinning and unfocused.

He angles his face toward my sister's voice, but his gaze never leaves mine, I feel it. He covers me with his warmth, and I fight hard to focus on their words.

"Why did I listen to her?" Dante's voice is a choked sob, and guilt takes purchase when too many emotions claw their way to the surface of my mind. I'm not strong enough to fight them off all at once.

"She didn't give you a choice. We didn't know what to do," she says. There's a commotion in the store, followed by the soft click of a door closing, but I'm paralyzed in memories I've tried so hard to forget. "You did what she asked, Dante."

"I shouldn't have listened." Leaning forward, he gently places his lips on my forehead, and a single tear rolls down my cheek. "I should have come back. But I'm here now, Sayl. I'm sorry it took me so long."

He continues to stroke my hair as I count, breathe, and

count again. Into my throat for one—to my chest for two—to my belly for three, and release.

"Why did you come back, Dante?" Ainsley asks.

I'm still fighting through my anxiety attack, but my ears narrow in on that question.

He's not back for good. He can't be. Silence descends as we stare at each other, and when the seconds drag into long minutes, I push myself to sit and call on all my strength. I don't fall apart anymore. Not anymore—I can't.

I see his answer before he says it—he knows I lied.

"I read *April Rain* and *Come September*," he says quietly. "Lena read them first and then threw them at me. She told me not to leave my office until I'd finished." He cups my cheeks and stares so intently that I'm sure he's reading every secret I've ever kept from him in my irises. "You wanted me to come back."

It's not a question. It's my truth. I shrug because doing anything else feels too monumental right now. When he didn't come back, I convinced myself it was for the best. It's what was right, and I was doing it for him. Somewhere along the line, it became my truth.

"You made me leave because you *thought* it was best for me." His words are harsh but full of conviction. "But you never fucking asked me, Saylor. You made all the choices and broke me in the process. You told me you couldn't love me anymore because I'd always be a reminder that your sister's death was our fault. *Our fault.* It wasn't even close to being our fault, but I've lived with the guilt and heartache of knowing you believed that shit for six long years while you've been here doing—what? Living half a life?"

Ainsley gasps, and nausea rolls through me in waves. I don't remember saying any of that to him. I only remember the scathing letter he sent me a week later telling me he would always love me, but he'd never be able to forgive me. It was a goodbye letter filled with the pain and anger of someone who lost the love of their life and needed them to hurt too.

And I understood why he wrote it, even if I didn't remember the words I used to push him away.

I deserved it. And I carry his words with me every single day.

"Hello?" someone calls from the front of the old house.

"I—I'll go," Ainsley says. "It's probably the movers."

Dante nods, but I don't have the energy to even move. Every muscle in my body aches with the tension that's been holding me together all these years. When a tremor shakes my body, I will myself to fight harder, to not break, but it's a battle I can't win.

"The only person to blame for Shannon's death is Benjamin. He intentionally ran her off the road that night. He is the only one at fault, and he will pay for his stupidity for the rest of his life."

Benjamin—Shannon's almost father-in-law. My body shudders, and the taste of bile fills my mouth.

"Talk to me, Saylor." He cups my cheek with the softest of touches.

I close my eyes and sink into his warmth even though I should pull away from him. Nothing's changed, but his caress is a comfort I can't give myself. And if I tell him the truth or about the darkness that controls me, he'll stay out of a sense of duty, and then he'll resent me.

It's taken six years, but with intensive therapy and constant work, I've come to terms with it—that the shadows I live with will always be hiding in the dark corners of my mind, just waiting for their time to return.

He wears his heart on his sleeve so full of timeless love and hope that it breaks me. If he pushes, I won't be strong enough to lie to him again.

"It won't change anything," I whisper.

His warm lips land on my cheek, and his deep exhale ghosts across my skin. When he drops his forehead to mine, his words are my undoing.

"You're wrong, sweetheart. It'll change everything."

My stomach clenches, and I dry heave, but he still doesn't pull away. If anything, he holds me tighter. He protects me. He loves me even though I don't deserve it.

I try to shake my head, but he holds my cheeks gently, lovingly, in his palms. "But it can't change everything. It can't. I can't. I won't." The words break on a sob that is sure to open the floodgates of my pain.

"Tell me, Saylor. At the very least, I deserve your honesty, don't you think?" Each word he speaks sounds more pained than the last.

My chin trembles.

"Tell me." He pleads against my skin as his heartbeat drums dramatically in his throat. "Talk to me, baby. Please."

I should have known he'd penetrate my armor. I shouldn't have agreed to this. But it's his final words that rip me open and leave me bare.

"I need to know that we were real." His voice cracks and my eyes snap open. "I need to know that you loved me as much as I love you. That's what's tearing me up inside, Saylor. Our love was real, I felt it. But…" His face crumples, and every ounce of pain I've caused this man breaks through my chest like a bullet. He's blowing the plexiglass wall I've built around my heart wide open.

It is real, I want to scream. But the fact that he thinks my love is past tense crushes my vocal cords. In my head, we're still real. In my head is where we'll always be real, but it can only ever be a dream. I won't ruin him because I'm too selfish to let him go.

God, please help me. Please. Please don't let me hurt him again.

Please make this pain in my chest go away or take me away from here now. This is a pain I'm not strong enough to survive without ruining everyone I love. I know I'm not. I never have been, and that's why we're both hurting now, but he doesn't deserve to carry my broken soul.

He watches me with a determination that bleeds his feelings through his tears, begging me to say something—begging me to be honest. But it's the torment in those tears that forces me to talk.

"I broke, Dante." My words are no more than a whisper, but his fingers flex on my cheeks, and after a breath, he slowly pulls back enough to study my face. "I shattered into a million tiny pieces, and the only thing my mind would focus on was that if I hadn't been with you, I would have been in the car with her. Maybe I could have done something."

"Or, more likely, you wouldn't be here either," Ainsley says gently.

When did she return?

There's so much liquid pooling in the back of my throat that I might drown in all the tears I haven't shed. Each swallow brings more mucus for me to choke on. "But…"

"You sent me away because you said it was too painful to be with me. You blamed me, Saylor. I couldn't stand that I was causing you more pain."

I shake my head. "I know, okay? I know. But I didn't blame you. I blamed myself." My voice breaks, and Ainsley rushes to my side. Dante shifts his weight so he's fully seated on the floor between my legs.

"But why didn't you ever call, Saylor? You knew I would never go against your wishes. If you loved me, why didn't you contact me when you realized…" He doesn't finish his thought, but he means when I remembered I'd always need him. It's what I wrote in my book, and his question is one that I've asked myself a million times but never had an answer for.

Today I do.

"You built a life so quickly out there. You—You started showing up in magazines a month after you left. I was never going to fit in that world. The more I saw, the less I liked. It was easier to blame you and hate you than admit that I ruined us. To admit that my mind betrayed me and broke me —turned me into a person I didn't recognize because I couldn't handle what life was throwing at me."

I stare at the ceiling when the connection between us is too much to bear, but I'm all in now. I have to tell him everything.

"The whole time I was in the mental health clinic, I had this daydream that you were out there waiting for me. Or that you'd come back for me. I only remember fragments of what I said to you that day. So, when I left the hospital, I continued to allow myself the dream that you'd come back for me, even after seeing the life you were building. That was always the plan, right? The hope kept me going, even though rationally, I knew. I knew I could never keep you without breaking your spirit too."

I lift one shoulder and force a crooked smile that threatens tears. "Your life kept playing out on social media, and I...I stopped living. Ains begged me to call you, to talk to you and try to explain how broken I felt, but how could I ask you to come back to this when your life looked so...complete?"

"You ask, Saylor. You say you made a mistake." He's angry. I don't blame him, but he doesn't shout, even though the vein in his neck tells me it's taking great effort not to lose his shit. "You should have told me," he says more calmly. "You're you. I would always have come back for you, sweetheart. How could you not know that? But I thought, I truly thought I would hurt you more by forcing you to see me."

"Our lives didn't connect anymore," I say. It's a wet, raspy whisper. Ainsley places her head on my shoulder, and I don't shrug her off. Her tears soak my arm, and somehow it strengthens our connection, the one I thought I'd severed irreparably.

"I tried to get her to reach out," she says. "But the more I pushed, the more she retreated. I was in med school, and even I couldn't help. I wasn't exactly sure what had happened, so I stayed silent too."

Dante sighs and smiles kindly at my sister—the only family I have left.

"Shannon was always our safe space, especially after Grumpy died," Ainsley says quietly. "We were technically adults when the accident happened, but twenty-two-year-olds still need their security blankets. We still needed her so desperately, and we were drowning in our loss."

I nod and choke out more explanations that mean nothing now. "We were so young and freefalling through emotions we had no idea how to handle. And then for her to die so suddenly and violently in that car was…none of us handled it well."

"I'm sorry I didn't do more to help you both through this," Ainsley whispers.

This isn't another burden for her to carry. She was grieving in her own way. Neither of us was there for each other like we should have been. For the first time in as long as I can remember, I tilt my cheek to press it against my sister's head. She shudders beneath me and cries silently. She always has.

Time passes, but the three of us stay immobile and connected like a strange little triangle until Dante clears his throat.

"You—You're still not doing well, are you?" There's no accusation in his tone, only sadness and something too close to love for me to acknowledge.

I tilt one of my shoulders up in a shrug. I've only told my therapist everything, but maybe hearing how messed up I feel will show him why he can't stay with me. "I have night-mares sometimes. My anxieties are more nuanced and fickler than most. My fears, irrational as they are, control my day-to-day life. My weirdness is more intense."

"You're not weird, Sassy." Ainsley uses a tone I imagine her using with her stubborn patients. She stares at me for a long moment, scanning back and forth like she's decoding a secret message, and for the first time since we lost Shannon, I hear her voice in my head. *Take this chance and let him in. You are lovable and worthy of good things. Let him love you.*

"Thank you for asking me to be here for this," she says to Dante without releasing my gaze from hers. "Thank you for remembering how easily I feel her pain, but I'm going to head home and let you two take it from here."

She stands, and I grasp for her hand. It surprises me as much as it does her. "Are you going to be okay?"

Ainsley doesn't hide her emotions from me. Watery eyes sparkle through pain and happiness, reaching me like rain-drops on a cloudless summer night, warming my chilled body.

Maybe, just maybe, I'm not as broken as I believed.

"I am now," she says. With a nod to Dante, she scurries from the room, and moments later, I hear her close and lock the front door of my bookstore.

Dante stands and slides into her spot next to me. "Tell me." It's not a demand. It's a plea to let him in, and I'm too tired to find any snark.

"I—I don't handle being close to people very well. According to my therapist, knowing I could lose them hurts too much, so I keep everyone at arm's length. Not everyone allows it, though." Arching my right brow, I point out the nonexistent space between us, and he chuckles.

"I'm not moving unless you tell me you need physical space. Emotional space is no longer an option for us."

My brain says, *hell no. Step back. No touching.* But my heart bleeds for him, and I'm too stubborn to tell him so. Instead, I shrug and let my body sag back into his. "My therapist said I've been trying to shut off my emoters." I laugh, but nothing about this is funny. "I lock things away and keep them inside to shelter others from my pain—and so I can't be hurt by theirs either. I haven't had an attack like this in years because I work hard to exist in the emptiness. It's easier to avoid emotions because they shred me to pieces when I let them in."

"Saylor." He drags out my name as if it pains him. "But you do. You feel things in the stories you create. If you didn't, your readers wouldn't connect to them like they do. You're still experiencing the painful things, the happy things, the things that let you know you're alive. But you're living them through the safety of your mind."

Silence fills the room, but my thoughts are playing over a loudspeaker in my head.

"Do you think I'm crazy?" My biggest fear is spoken in the darkening room, and there's no taking it back, because the truth is, most days, I'm not sure myself.

"No, Sayls. I think you're hurting. I think you're unmoored and lost your last safe place to land—you lost me."

Until tonight, he's mostly followed my social cues and rarely pushed past the walls I wear like a last line of defense. Now, squished together into a double chair, he takes control. He wraps an arm around me and hauls me up while he leans back so my body is draped over his, my head on his chest, and that's when the dam breaks.

His comfort doesn't send me spiraling down. It lifts me gently into the emotions I've kept embargoed in my mind.

Years and years of unshed tears find their way into the button-down shirt of the one man I thought would never hold me again.

"Fall, baby. I've got you," he says against the top of my head. And I do. I free fall into the pain I've spent a lifetime hiding from, secure in the knowledge that he'll catch me when I'm done.

It is a trust fall, and I'm not sure I'll ever be able to land.

CHAPTER 12

DANTE

"You're still here."

I'm sitting on the steps of Saylor's back porch with my head in my hands. It's late, though I have no idea what time it is or how long I've been out here trying to make sense of a nonsensical situation.

Lifting my head so my elbows are on my thighs and my chin rests in my palm, I blow out a harsh breath through pursed lips, then look down at Grady at the bottom of the stairs.

"Yeah, I'm still here."

He stands like an angry linebacker with one hand on his hip, the other hanging stiffly at his side, and his chest puffed out like a rooster. On second thought, the guy might just be so big that he doesn't have to preen. He's huge.

I don't remember him being so pissed off all the time, though. But both times I've seen him now, he's been wearing a scowl so entrenched on his face that he looks more like the leader of a biker gang than the lawyer he is—or was, maybe. I've never met an attorney quite like him.

I'm not sure what happened to him, but even I can tell he's not the same man he used to be.

"Where's Sass?" he says roughly.

Tilting my head, I study him. He's two seconds away from ripping my head off.

"She's sleeping." Thankfully, once she had cried herself to sleep in my arms, she didn't awaken when I carried her to bed.

Even if he's been good to her, he doesn't get access to that piece of us. I hate that he has any part of her at all, and I don't care if it makes me sound like a petulant child or a jealous asshole.

"Ainsley said she had a rough night." He lifts his hand to the back of his head and rubs his neck, relaxing his face a little. He's not wearing a scowl now. No, that expression is full of concern.

Why the hell did Ainsley call him?

My jaw works back and forth, trying to keep the question in.

"Listen," he growls, at the same time I say, "Did you need something?"

We glare at each other, neither of us willing to back down. I knew Grady a little in high school. I was closer in age to his younger brother, Harrison, but these towns are so small that everyone knows when you take a shit, when you check your mail, and when you run away. Unlike LA, there's no hiding here.

He's a good guy, but if he's trying to stand in my way after everything Saylor and I've been through, I will ruin him.

"Goddamn drama," he mutters under his breath before clomping up the stairs and dropping a bag to the floor before sitting next to me. I glance over my shoulder to make sure he didn't wake up Saylor.

Eventually I face him, and he's holding out a beer.

"Ains said you could probably use one, and after seeing your brother's face all over the news, I assumed she was right."

Fucking Trent just won't give up. He and Malimar seem to be duking it out for the biggest twat award. I take the beer, but discomfort makes my shoulders tense.

"Trying to poison the competition?" I chuckle like an asshole because I'm not sure how to respond to his seemingly sincere gesture.

Is it a rule that everyone over twenty-five has to act like a dick to live in this town?

He snorts, and the sound is full of disdain. "You're no competition. Trust me."

That raises my hackles.

"What's your plan?" he asks, surprising me.

"What do you mean?"

He takes a long pull of his beer, and the label catches my attention when he lowers it. "Are you drinking root beer?"

I immediately hold up the bottle in my hand. It says Red Reid-er, pale ale.

"I don't drink much these days." He's staring out at the lake as he says it, so I'm able to study his profile. He's still the same Grady I knew, but different somehow. Sad, maybe.

We sit in silence for a while, long enough to make me uncomfortable. "You come by a lot?" I tried to sound casual, but the jealous nature of the question is undeniable.

He turns to me with his bottle hovering over his lips like he's frozen in time as he studies me. After a brief pause, he takes a sip. He never takes his gaze off me until he wipes his mouth with the back of his hand.

"Sassy and I have an understanding that's none of your business."

My hand tightens around the beer bottle, and I'm afraid it will shatter.

"Listen, Grady. Our history is—complicated."

He surprises me when he turns suddenly to face me. He leans against the pillar, and I push back against the one opposite him. At least six feet separate us, but it's still not enough space.

"Is your future going to be too?"

"Our..." My mouth hangs open while I figure out what I want to say. "Honestly, I don't know." I run my hand through my hair. "I have no fucking idea."

He's quiet and thoughtful as he watches me.

"Would you have come back if you'd known?" he asks quietly, almost hesitantly.

"Did you know?" I accuse. Grady and I weren't friends, and granted, I cut off everyone from Hope Hollow when I left, but if he knew? If everyone knew? Why didn't they do something to intervene?

Unless, maybe, she wasn't hurting over us as much as I was. But that's not what she said in her book. That's not the impression I got when she cried herself to sleep in my arms.

Endless possibilities run rampant in my mind. My thoughts are so loud that I almost miss Grady's next words.

"Not until her last couple of books," he admits. "We probably should have known—*you* probably should have known."

Fuck you, Grady Reid.

"Well, I know now." My frustration is at an all-time high, so the words are harsh and angry.

"Now you know," he agrees amicably. "But what are you going to do about it?"

I stand abruptly, and he shakes his head, then takes his time to rise with me.

"That's not really any of your business," I say.

"Sassy is my business, Thompson. She has been since the night I found her at The Landing."

The Landing?

Those words hit like a throat-punching, stopping my breath.

The Landing is where Shannon's car went over the cliff.

"She's struggled and fought for herself for years. Don't fuck that up. You can't 'test the waters' with her..."

"I don't need you lecturing me on Saylor."

He lurches forward until we're toe to toe.

"This isn't a game, dipshit." The muscles in his forearms flex at his sides, and he deliberately takes a step back. "She's stronger than she gives herself credit for, but losing a love like yours once already almost crushed her. I don't want to see what happens if she suffers another loss like that."

"You sound like you're talking from experience." I try to keep the sarcasm out of my voice, but my emotions are messy and I'm all over the place. Frustrated, I look him in the eye and infuse my words with as much compassion as I can. "Sorry. I mean..."

"Betrayal and loss often feel the same," he says cryptically before turning away from me and jogging down the stairs.

"Do you love her?" I blurt before he hits the bottom.

I'm losing my damn mind.

He pauses and tilts his head to the sky. "Like I said, Sassy and I are not your concern. But because it sounds like she doesn't need another fucking interrogation, I'll tell you this. I will always have love for her. But I'll never be in love again."

What the hell does that mean? Does he mean he'll never love her again? Someone else?

"The wheels are turning so fast you have smoke coming from your ears. Stop worrying about what I'm doing, and figure out what you want. Either way, it's going to be a bumpy road."

He jogs down the last step and tosses his bottle in the recycling bin at the corner of the house. It irks me that he struts straight to it. How often is he here? I'm the one here now, though, and I need to remember that. I'm the one she loves.

That's a fact that's embedded in my soul like my next breath, because he's right. But it wasn't only Saylor who was almost crushed by the weight of our loss. I don't want to live through losing our kind of love again, and I'm willing to do whatever it takes to make sure I don't have to.

$\sim$

"HI," Saylor grunts as she walks past me toward the kitchen.

I chuckle despite my exhaustion. I couldn't shut off my mind last night and haven't gotten any sleep.

Saylor was never a morning person, and after seeing her the last few mornings, she might be even worse now. The anxiety that sits like a trapped cat in my stomach eases a bit. At least I still know some things about her.

She moves through her home with her left eye closed and her head tilted like she's trying to avoid all the sunlight.

My little vampire.

"Good morning, sunshine." I flash her a wink then sip my coffee.

"Oh, God," she whines. "Why are you so happy?"

I choke, and coffee comes out of my nose. She sounds exactly like Oscar the Grouch.

Her face pinches even more as I mop up the muddy liquid and laugh.

"I forgot how much you hate mornings," I say after she has a mug in her hands.

"Ugh." Now she sounds more annoyed than angry, but there's a healthy dose of irritation there too. "You're already dressed?" she asks after she finally opens both eyes.

"Went for a run too."

"Why? Was someone chasing you?" She places the coffee

cup on the table, then leans forward until her cheek is pressed to the cool wood.

"Was someone chasing me?" I chuckle. Trading my chair for the one beside her, I reach over to place a hand on her back but pause midair when I realize she's serious. "No one was chasing me, Sayl. I couldn't sleep, so I was burning off some energy. It helps me think."

"That's not normal," she groans. Then she lifts her head only high enough to take a sip of coffee. After inhaling deeply, she sits up, cradling the mug between both hands and staring at it like it holds all the world's secrets. "Was it because of me?"

I don't answer at first, and she adds, "Not sleeping? Was that because of me?"

An internal debate wars in my head. How honest does she want me to be? But between remembering how she felt in my arms last night and seeing her hesitation and uncertainty this morning, there's no going back—I'm all in. So, I tell her the truth.

"It's everything combined. You. Me. Poppy. Trent and Malimar putting out new press releases every other day. Our past." She keeps her gaze focused on the steam rising from her mug, but it gets sucked into her mouth when she holds her breath. That's the moment I know. We'll never fix the past, but I sure as hell can fight for the future we should already have.

Leaning forward, I tuck a piece of hair behind her ear, and she releases a shaky breath. Then I slip my index finger under her chin and turn her to face me.

"And also, our future."

Her hands shake, and coffee spills over the side of the mug she's holding, so I remove it from her grasp. Her fingers immediately ball into fists, and I remember the nail marks I'd seen earlier.

"Don't hold in your emotions, Saylor. I can handle them. I promise."

She's shaking her head no with her mouth open, but no words come out.

"I had a lot of time to think last night," I tell her.

Her gaze falls to mine once more, but her breaths are shallow. Her chest heaves like she's the one who went for a run.

"Let's go over the facts. Okay?"

Her lashes flutter, but I'm pretty sure she tilts her head in agreement.

"Good. Fact—I didn't want to leave."

"Dante—"

"Fact, you didn't want me to leave."

"But—"

"Fact, if I had known what was going on, I never would have left you in the first place."

"That's my point—"

"Fact, and this is a pretty fucking big one—I've been miserable since the day I stepped on that bus. You've haunted my dreams and stolen my days. No one has been able to compare to you. No one has made me happy except for Poppy."

"Poppy," she says. With trembling hands, she reaches for her coffee again and lifts it to her lips. She's hiding behind the mug, and I let her. For now.

"Yeah. That will be an adjustment." I envision Poppy's chubby little hands moving Saylor's face around so she can kiss her wherever she needs a kiss, and my smile grows.

"So, the way I see it, this is our second chance."

The coffee slips from her hands and crashes to the table, sending light brown liquid everywhere.

She jumps up, knocking my mug over in the process, instantly transforming into that rapid-fire state of hummingbird. I stand calmly, place my hands on her hips, and move her out of the way before grabbing the paper towels while she buzzes around the room.

Right. I need to remember that her reactions are big. And sometimes messy. But always her.

"Second chance. Second chance?"

When I turn, she's holding a towel to her T-shirt, but her gaze is on me as I cross the room with deliberate steps and stop right in front of her.

"Perhaps not a second chance. How do you feel about a do-over?" She opens her mouth, but I'm only a breath away, and I move in slowly. Painfully slowly, so she's aware of my intentions. When she makes no attempt to stop me, I seal my lips over hers.

A groan rumbles in my chest and settles deep in my throat. Yes, here's to do-overs and new beginnings.

CHAPTER 13

SAYLOR

*D*ante moves slowly with his eyes wide and searching mine, like he's asking for permission. Permission to kiss me. Permission to love me. Permission to keep me.

It's the last one that has my lips parting on an inhale, even though everything in my body screams that this is a bad idea. But I bled myself dry last night, and now I'm not strong enough to push him away. And what scares me more is that after years of hurting for this man, I don't want to push him away. Having him for a short time is better than never having him again. Isn't it?

Am I a terrible person for wanting the comfort only his touch can bring when all I've done is cause him pain?

Will I survive the inevitable fall?

His tongue slips out and runs along his bottom lip, leaving a trail of moisture in its wake. Our noses press together, and then his mouth is on mine, stealing all my complaints before I'm able to voice them.

And it's because he's watching me so closely that I sink into a kiss that tastes like home and feels like safety.

Old fears of dragging him into my darkness and new fears of Poppy, Trent, and our careers fade into the background when his hands cup my face and angle it the way he likes.

He always did like control of our kisses, and it's the one place I was more than happy to give him that power.

His teeth graze my bottom lip, and my entire body sings with life that's been missing. He makes no effort to deepen the kiss or rush it. No, Dante Thompson is happily, thoroughly reacquainting himself with my body through this lazy brush of lips and tongues.

The longer he owns my mouth, the more my body lights up. That nervous energy that lives inside me gathers itself and darts through me like a colony of bees protecting their queen before settling deep in my core—a constant buzz of need and desire.

I might come from a kiss. A freaking kiss.

When my body is about to snap, he pulls away. My mouth follows him before I catch myself, and I blink rapidly to clear my vision.

He may have just kissed me stupid.

"Hi," he whispers, still holding my face in place.

It's like waking up from the most pleasant dream after a lifetime of nightmares.

"Hi."

"I'm going to be real honest with you here, Sayls."

My mind is a swirling tornado of activity.

"I've missed you so damn much," he says.

I nod when my throat is too itchy to speak.

I can't bring myself to say the words. Not when there's so much left unsaid. Not when he'll realize there can't really be a do-over for us.

"Tell me what you're thinking," he says. His hands release

my face and land on both of mine with a gentle squeeze, forcing me to stay in the moment.

"This is going to be hard."

"What is?"

Slipping a hand free, I wave it between the two of us. "It's going to be hard not to get attached."

He takes a step back and leans against the counter, wrapping his fingers around the edge of the granite. "Why shouldn't we get attached, Saylor?" There's that tone again. The one that tells me he's doing his best to stay calm, but now my body sparks to life with a completely different energy—anxiety.

"For all the reasons I told you last night." Despite the quiver in my voice, I stand tall and gather the strength not stolen by his kiss. "The reasons I never reached out to you once my anxiety and depression were better managed. My life is here." My hands gesture around my home again. When I notice how aggressively I'm waving, I tuck them under my armpits to avoid reaching for him.

He tilts his head, waiting for me to continue.

"And your life is there." I nod a little too animatedly with my head toward the door. "In California, I mean. You have a family and clients and a life that's not conducive to a reclusive author who only likes going out when everyone else is asleep. I have days…"

I pause to press my fingers into my temples like it will make this easier. "Not as many as I used to, but there are still times when my mind tricks my body into feeling pain so excruciating, I can't even get out of bed. There are days when I wake up in the middle of a panic attack so awful, I black out."

His face crumples, but I'm on a roll and keep going.

"You're happy, and I'm—not. You like running, and I can't even do a silent meditation. You're confident and successful, regardless of what's happening with your company right now, and *this*"—I point aggressively at myself—"does not work in that lifestyle."

He swallows slowly, and my focus locks on the bob of his Adam's apple. "Are you done?" he asks when I just stare back.

Am I done? Ugh, how dare he? My mouth hangs open in exasperation, but what am I going to do? I am done—I think.

"For now, I guess." My shoulders roll forward, and I hop up onto the island. Even this conversation is exhausting. What the hell is going on with me? If this is what feelings do to you, no wonder I've tried to embargo them in a tiny bottle.

"First of all," he says, holding up a finger. "You're not a this. You're you, and you're even more beautiful and amazing than you were when we first met. Second." Up goes another finger. "Yes, I do have a niece to think about. She will never be an afterthought. Third." He holds three fingers out in front of himself. "California was my exile, and I'm ready to come home. Fourth." He stalks closer with his fingers raised. "It crushes my heart to know how bad your attacks are and that you struggle alone sometimes."

He stops an inch away from my knees, and my legs separate automatically, like they've been waiting for him. Dante's hands land on my thighs as he slides between them, and his thumbs gently pass over my skin in a soothing rhythm.

"And I really hate that I haven't been here for all your dark days, but the threat of ones in the future will not scare me away."

"You don't even know me anymore," I say.

"I'm going to, though."

"Ugh." I exhale a harsh breath that pushes my hair off my forehead. "I need you to listen to me. You don't know what you're asking. You don't know what—"

"Then tell me. Talk to me. Teach me."

My palms land on his chest, and I take a second to soak in

the comfort that simple touch brings, then sadly push him away. He moves back, and I slip off the island. Walking around it, I put some distance between us.

"I don't like people…"

"You never did."

"I have manic moments, usually when I'm writing, when I can't focus on anything, and other times when I'm so focused, I don't see anything else."

He doesn't say anything, and my heart spasms in my chest. People say they understand and can be compassionate for invisible pains, but I've experienced it firsthand—it rarely works out that way.

"You saw my panic attack. What you didn't see are my bad days. The days when I don't get out of bed until Ainsley or Grady come roll me out and force me to shower or get fresh air."

The muscle in his jaw bunches at the mention of Grady, but he wants the truth. This is my truth.

"I don't want to be like that, Dante. I don't. But there are days when I'm powerless to it. People call it lazy or entitled. But it's not a choice."

The emotion that clouds his eyes steals all the air in my lungs.

"Do you have those a lot?" he asks with so much concern that tears burn the back of my throat.

How the heck do I have any tears left?

A rush of irritation shoots up my spine like a roller-coaster, and I have no idea where it comes from, but I'm shocked when it sits at my shoulders instead of finding release with sharp words or a bitter tone.

What's more, I'm aware of the change. Usually, my snark has a mind of its own.

The base of my neck itches, and I contort my face into a frown. "Not anymore," I say in a rush that sounds like a confession. "But I do, sometimes."

"So, sometimes we'll deal with it."

Shaking my head, I turn away from him and grab a new mug. I take my time pouring a cup of coffee, and when I face him again, I'm ready to tell him what he's been avoiding.

"So, what are you going to do? Change your entire life and move back here? See if we work out? You're not being practical, Dante."

"That's exactly what I'll do. Or I'll go back and forth until we figure it out. No matter what you say, you won't scare me off again."

Challenge. Accepted.

Placing my mug back on the counter, I inhale deeply and deliver the final blow.

"Is someone who's cranky, unfeeling, has no control over her mouth, and is known to have horrible, debilitating anxiety with bouts of serious depression someone you want to have an influence on your niece?"

His face falls, and I don't have to continue. We're done. It's what I wanted, right? So why does my heart choose this moment to jackhammer against my ribs?

Dante's neck muscles flex, but his face is doing something else. Is he…? Are his eyes laughing at me?

My fists press into the flesh around my hips as I watch him. The crinkles at the corner of his eyes become more pronounced, and they damn near sparkle, or maybe twinkle. Whatever it is, they freaking shine like a disco ball.

"Did you hear what I said?"

"I did," he says calmly—too calmly. It makes me decidedly un-calm.

I stretch my eyelids wide and give him my best "and?" expression while my chest vibrates uncomfortably. That makes the corners of his lips twitch.

And he still doesn't say anything.

"Well?" My voice is two octaves too high and a lot of decibels too loud.

"Here's the thing. No matter what I say, you're going to have a comeback. That's your thing. You're sassy when you're uncomfortable. You retreat if it makes you feel safe. So, instead of responding to all your..." He scans the room like he's searching for a word.

"Issues?" I offer.

"Points," he counters. "Instead of addressing each point, I'll say this—you are more than the sum of your parts. You have anxiety, but you also have strength. You have depression, but you also have love."

"But Poppy. And—And Trent..."

"All points that need to be addressed. But the one I'm starting with is us."

My grip tightens around my necklace until the cool metal bites into my hand, and then he's there, opening my fist and gently caressing the skin of my palm with his thumbs.

I forgot how touchy-feely he is. And like when I was fifteen, I don't hate it.

"I believe in Kate's plan, with one minor adjustment I haven't told you about yet."

He starts tracing slow circles around the sensitive skin on my wrist, and it's hard to focus on anything else.

"Hmm," I say when he seems like he's waiting for me to say something.

"We'll go along with Kate's plan. We'll show the world who we are. And while we're doing that, I'll get you to fall back in love with me—for real."

He smirks. Of course, he smirks. He doesn't doubt that I love him. What he's really saying is that he's going to wear me down until we're so entwined with each other that we don't know where one ends and the other begins—again.

Falling back in love with him isn't the issue here. It's that this time when I fall, and he realizes the damage I carry is too much, there won't be anything left of me to catch.

"Trust me, sweetheart. From this day forward, always trust me."

CHAPTER 14

DANTE

Saylor stumbles out of her room. It's become quite the morning ritual. But today, she stalls in the doorway, so I hurry to close the laptop with Trent's new media stunt and Malimar's latest smear campaign. I've just closed out of the last webpage when a loud noise echoes in the room.

"Did…was that…?" I ask as my mouth hangs open.

She covers her mouth with both hands and shakes her head wildly. But she's also shaking like she's holding in laughter.

Her face turns so red I fear she's not breathing. Finally, a laugh escapes as she breaks wind, and then it's a symphony of laughs and farts.

Tears wet her cheeks, but she doesn't stop laughing. "Why?" she says, doubling over and gripping her stomach. "Why do I have the humor of a ten-year-old boy? Why do farts have to be so funny?"

With no idea what to say, I shrug and laugh too. It takes her a full minute to get herself together, but when she does, her morning grouchiness falls back into place.

Maybe mornings are like hangovers to her. That's how it looks, anyway.

She angles her face toward the floor and shakes her head. "Don't. Say. Anything," she grumbles. "I forgot you were here."

And just like that, grumpy Saylor is back. I step closer, and she must hear me because one eye opens in panic. "Do not come closer." She shimmies a little, and I almost laugh as she tries to inconspicuously fan her rear end.

"We need a new sleeping arrangement," I say instead of bringing up her rather epic gas attack.

It's been three days since my declaration that I would fit into her life, which means it's been way too many nights of me sleeping on a couch made for toddlers.

She holds up a hand and stumbles over her feet. No matter what time she wakes up, it's always the same. Her brown hair is in some sort of tangled knot that falls every which way, her face is scrunched up, trying to block out the sun, and she has an inability to form complete sentences.

Grunts are her preferred form of communication until at least eleven, and it's currently nine forty-five. But I do store away the fact that farts can make her laugh before her grumpy side takes over.

When she stops in the middle of the kitchen and sucks in a deep breath through her nose, a low chuckle rumbles in my chest and I move around her to reach for a coffee mug. I keep an eye on her, which is more for my benefit because she chose to sleep in a tiny tank top and shorts that ride dangerously low on her hips, and make her a cup of coffee.

When I'm done, she doesn't look at me, but her chest rises and falls slowly. She's controlling her breathing. Yesterday I thought she fell asleep standing up, but now I know she's trying to pull herself together so she doesn't snap at me. That seems like progress.

I quietly step in front of her and hold the mug under her nose, allowing her to breathe in the aroma of the dark roast, but not close enough that if she has a sassy-sized reaction, she'll knock it out of my hands.

The frown lines around her lips relax when she holds out her hands. I offer it to her but don't relinquish it until she lifts her gaze to mine.

"Good morning, Oscar the Grouch."

I wait, hoping she'll growl at me like she did the last time I called her that, and I'm only mildly disappointed when she doesn't.

"Ugh. Fine. Good morning." She squints one fiery blue orb at me, and I release the mug. "We are to never, ever talk about this morning, ever."

If I smile any harder, my face will split in two. "Deal."

Her cheeks are tinted a lovely shade of pink as she lifts the coffee to her lips.

The last couple of days have been hectic. I've been putting out fires almost as quickly as Trent starts them, but I can sense his desperation escalating, and it scares the shit out of me because the moves he's making are unpredictable.

Saylor, on the other hand, has been writing, which is great, except she hasn't left the house. Without leaving the house, we have nothing to show the world.

That's why she's up so early, for her, on a Saturday.

"I can't believe the Lemon Festival is still a thing," I say with a grin.

"Why?" she barks, and I swallow a chuckle. She's feisty this morning. "It's Hope Hollow. Turning lemons into lemonade is practically the town motto."

She sips her coffee, and I can literally see her physical reaction. The second it hits her lips her body uncoils like a spring.

"You're like a yo-yo," I say without thinking.

She turns her glare on me. "Are you saying I've gained weight?"

"What? No." Whatever else is in my expression, there has to be a healthy dose of confused and taken aback, because what the hell, Saylor?

"A yo-yo? Like a yo-yo diet?" She tugs at the hem of her tank and tries to cover herself with her coffee cup.

She's not wearing a bra, and my gaze zeroes in on her tits like a sex-starved teenager. I've never felt desperation or longing so acutely. Being near her and not making her mine is slowly chipping away at my self-control.

I blink and shake my head before flashing her a sheepish grin. "It has nothing to do with your weight. You're beautiful. I said you're like a yo-yo because I've been watching you. Your body goes from wound and ready to snap to relaxed and peaceful four hundred times a day." I bend my knees so we're eye to eye. "Like a yo-yo."

She carelessly lifts one shoulder. "Welcome to anxiety, Dante. Good times had by none."

I snort, trying to hold in a laugh.

"You think my anxieties are funny?" She lashes out, her words like a whip in a silent room.

"No." My smile makes my cheeks hurt, but I'm not sure anything could wipe it from my face.

"Then why are you laughing?" This time she does growl.

"Because, Oscar. I'm trying to figure out when you went from dealing with the bad days to letting them own you. You're close to becoming a full-on curmudgeon, and you're stronger than that."

Her nose scrunches up, and her mouth hangs open with a loud scoff.

"It's okay. I'm here now. Just like old times. I'll teach you to have fun again."

"I have fun," she mutters.

157

"Do you?"

"Yes," she says with an indignant nod of her head.

I step forward, invading her space until her breath almost touches my bare chest. "When's the last time you had fun? Really had fun. Not a laugh or two. When was the last time you had so much fun that you lost track of time and the world around you?"

She tilts her head up to look at me.

I can't keep my gaze from tracing her lips as I speak, and my words dip low with desire. "When was the last time you were so fully immersed in *fun* that you forgot to worry, or plan, or overthink?"

She swallows, and I watch the column of her neck work. Her creamy skin pulls taut as she stretches to meet my gaze. The wild pulse of her heart at her throat is entrancing, and I want to run my tongue over it. I want to…

"We—should—probably… Oh shit." She bounces on her toes, smashes her coffee into my chest, and then runs to the table in the corner.

By the time I set down her mug and turn to her, she's holding two different pens in her right hand. Is she writing with them both?

Moving closer, I sink into the chair opposite her and watch as she scribbles across the paper. With a flick of her thumb, she switches between the different colors without ever having to put a pen down.

It's pretty impressive, actually. I lean forward, trying to peek at what she's writing, when I notice what she's writing in. It's a notebook I remember, or a duplicate, anyway. To her right is a giant stack of them, all carbon copies of the one I gave her all those years ago covered in poppies.

She did keep a piece of me with her after all.

"It's a resort," she mutters to herself. "On an island. His

entire company is supposed to be there for a court-mandated team-building weekend because he's an ass. But…"

I lean closer to see what she's writing. It's words like tension and lustful. She flicks the pen again, and this time she writes *pulsing*, and my cock decides it likes that word.

Jesus. I'm even turned on by stupid fucking words now.

Another flick, and she writes *longing glances*, *desperate*, *needy*, and *wanton*.

"Saylor." She doesn't stop until I place a hand over her paper.

"What…"

"If I can give you this much inspiration with a simple conversation, imagine the inspiration you'll get"—I lean in to whisper in her ear—"when we're out having fun."

The hairs at the base of her neck rise to attention as goosebumps cover her flesh. My heart throws up a fist bump in victory, and I inhale her scent, thankful it's one of the things that hasn't changed.

Salt air and citrus. My little summer raincloud.

She shivers, and I lean back. I can appreciate her flushed cheeks and blistering gaze with some distance between us. How would she describe them in one of her books?

"You're so sexy. So. Damn. Sexy."

She looks from me to her paper and back again.

With her attention trained on me, I infuse my voice with a rasp and deepen the tone. "Come have *fun* with me, Sayls."

She's nodding and pointing one delicate finger toward me when she gets to her feet. "I have fun." Her tone is slightly less grouchy. If I hadn't seen her body react to me, I'd worry we might be a lost cause.

But Saylor is feeling everything I am. She just has to give herself permission to explore it.

Luckily for us both, I'm nothing if not persuasive when I

want something, and I can't remember wanting anything more than I want this woman.

"Get dressed, sweetheart. We make our debut at eleven." I'm so freaking giddy at the prospect that my cheeks hurt from the perma-grin I've been wearing for the last hour.

As expected, Saylor scowls, but it's too late. I already saw it in her eyes. Hope.

CHAPTER 15

SAYLOR

"Are you all set for a couple of hours?" I ask Lilly.

"Oh, yeah. Totally," she says with stars in her eyes. She already has a stack of books in front of her. She's worked odd hours for me for about six months, but I knew the day Grady walked his little sister in my door it had nothing to do with the paycheck.

Lilly Reid is as obsessed with books as I am. She's a romantic, though, and still thinks love is all you need. I guess that's easy to believe when you're sixteen.

"You didn't want to go to the Lemon Festival?" Dante asks from the doorway. He wasn't exactly thrilled to see Grady drop her off this morning, but he played nice.

"Oh, no. Kai has to work…" Her face turns a brilliant shade of pink at the mention of her boyfriend. I don't know much about him, but I've met his mom and stepdad a couple of times. It makes me laugh because it must infuriate Grady. As her legal guardian, he takes protective to a whole other level. "But he might stop by later," she says quietly.

Alarm shows on Dante's face, but I shrug. Lilly is a smart, responsible kid, and I trust her.

"Okay, well, there are more lemon pops in the storage room if you run out." As a business owner, I'm obligated to have something lemon-themed for anyone who comes in today. I bought the sourest, tartest ones I could find. The passive-aggressive act makes me feel better about my required participation.

My gaze jumps to Dante briefly. Remembering his declaration to make me have fun has my cheeks heating uncomfortably.

Lilly nods when I return my attention to her. She's waiting for us to leave so she can read, so I walk toward Dante and usher him out the door.

"Is Grady okay with her boyfriend dropping by? It's not like there are a ton of customers to keep her busy," Dante asks as soon as the door closes behind us.

"Probably not, but don't worry about her. She'll be busy. The kids always come to the bookstore. It's become like a rite of passage for them. Every year I get the sourest lemon treat I can find. They all flock to the store to see who can handle the sour."

Yeah, I'm a little proud of that.

He lifts his brow and graces me with that dimple I love.

"Two people threw up last year."

"You sound very proud of that achievement too. I'm sure the parents loved you for it," he says mockingly.

Indignation rises in my gut as I tug the pendant around my neck. "I'll have you know, one of them was a dad. It's not only kids who take my challenge."

"Interesting. And is there a reason you took that particular angle on Lemon Fest?" He removes my hand from my necklace and lifts the chain himself.

He studies it, and an uncomfortable heat coats my skin.

"Your—face is laughing at me." I try to sound annoyed, so he won't stare too closely at my pendant, but it's not working. "Yes, actually, there is a reason. No one likes too much sweet. There has to be something to balance it all out."

"Like you and me," he says, dropping my necklace while his swirling pools of emotion stare at me like he can decode all my secrets.

"Huh?"

He leans over and takes my hand. "Your circle, it has dates in Roman numerals."

Shit. Shit. Shit.

If he notices my sweaty palm, at least he's gentlemanly enough not to say anything. And I definitely don't want to admit that my heart syncs to his the second we touch.

"The day your sister died, and the day I left Hope Hollow." He lifts the hem of his shirt and points to the pole in the center of his boat tattoo. There, hidden in the details, are the two dates I wear around my neck like a noose. "We've always been connected, Sayls."

My eyes burn, and I can't seem to swallow. Shaking my head, I take tentative steps forward with him griping my hand like I'll disappear. We walk a while in silence, and I think he's letting me work through the atomic bomb that keeps trying to light its fuse inside my mind.

He breaks the silence first, bringing this conversation full circle. "I balance out your sour attitude. Sweet and sour. You and me."

That drags me from my thoughts real quick.

"Are you saying you're the sweet one?"

He stops and slides a salacious gaze my way. "It depends on what we're talking about, I suppose." The heat creeping over my skin continues to spread lower. Why does my body insist on reacting this way? His focus never wavers from mine as he cups my cheek and leans in to whisper in my ear. "From what I remember, you certainly tasted the sweetest."

Air hisses through my teeth. The sharp inhale expands

my lungs while my heart thrashes in my chest. Is this what we're doing now? He said he'd get me to fall in love for real, and this feels so real that my core spasms at his words.

I'm not going to survive him.

"But if we're talking about disposition," he continues, like he didn't just start a riot in my world, "there's no contest, Oscar. If we were a trope, you'd be the grump to my sunshine."

Dante ghosts his nose over the shell of my ear and along my jaw before planting a deceptively gentle kiss against my lips. When he pulls back, I'm panting and struggling to remember what we were talking about.

Yup. I'm screwed. Seven ways to Sunday, screwed.

And he knows it. It shows on every inch of his face—from the crinkles around his cerulean depths to the lazy uptick of his lips.

"But I did like how you reversed that in *April Rain*. It's fun seeing you as a sunshiny heroine."

Right. Grumpy-sunshine.

"You are not the sunshiny one," I grumble when my mouth remembers how to form words.

Surprise lights his face. "No? Are you saying you are?"

"I…well." The scowl that forms on my face says no, not sunshiny. But am I truly the grumpy one in this relationship? Crap. I *am* the grumpy one to all his stupid sunshiny early morning happiness.

"Sassy? Oh, thank God you're here."

Peering around Dante's large frame, I realize we've hit The Common.

Hope Hollow is one of three towns that surround Heart Lake, but we have the largest town center, affectionately known as The Common. Standing there with her hands on her hips is Cassie Holly.

Cassie would describe herself as my best friend, but that's

only because she refuses to take no for an answer. She grew up down the road in Chance Lake, but all three towns are so small and close together that they might as well be one community.

"I'm going to kill Mrs. Shelly." Cassie glares at the tent she came from, and I bite my lip to keep from laughing. Her high school and college sweetheart, who broke her heart when he entered the NFL, is grinning like a fool from inside. "She signed James up to run the Tag 'em and Bag 'em booth with me. With. Me. I cannot take another second of his puppy dog eyes and sickly sweet words. You have to come over to balance it out."

"Because she's grumpy?" Dante asks with an impish smirk.

"Well, yeah," Cassie says with an inflection that actually means *duh*.

"I'm not grumpy," I growl.

Two heads swivel in my direction.

"Okay, fine. Maybe I'm grumpy right now, but it's early. And he's making me be social." I jab my thumb in Dante's direction.

"That must be it, Oscar. Come on, game time." Dante drags me closer to Cassie's booth but keeps us on the periphery, likely knowing the gathering crowd will send me running home. Does he remember that, or is it something he's learned?

"Is this too close?" he whispers.

"Yeah." My voice cracks at the single word.

Warmth spreads through my body at the tenderness of the moment, but honestly, the crowd isn't what's setting off my fight-or-flight reaction. It's my hyper-focus on the man next to me.

He is too close. Too close to me. Too close to my emotions. Too close to making me break.

That's how it always was, though. *It could be again if you give him a chance.* I dig my nails into my palm and focus on what's happening around me.

"The rules are the same every year," James shouts. "Each clothespin is numbered, and each target has a point value. You have two hours to tag 'em, and whoever has the most pinned at the end wins."

Tag 'em and Bag 'em has been a highlight of the Lemon Festival since I was a kid. Unsuspecting targets are chosen randomly, and you have one hour to stick your clothespin to them without them removing it.

"I can't believe this is still a thing," Dante laughs. The carefree sound wraps around my anxiety like it can keep my fears at bay. Freaking Dante.

"Oh, it's intense. You have no idea. Last year Harrison Reid almost got arrested for removing someone else's pin."

Dante's gaze slides to me, assessing. He's trying to figure out if I'm telling the truth, but he'll find out soon enough.

"You may work in teams. However, you'll only receive one set of numbers," James says. "And now, the moment you're all waiting for." He glances at the crowd to make sure this year's targets aren't in attendance.

James reads off the first four names, but everyone is waiting for the whale—the top target. Anticipation fills the air, but the anxiety of so many people around me clogs my throat.

"And, finally," James says, dragging it out. "This year's Moby Dick is—Grady Reid."

No one moves for a full five seconds. Once it sinks in, gasps and outcries fill the silence.

"No one can get close to Grady."

"That's impossible."

"This is supposed to be hard, not a death sentence."

Dante leans in conspiratorially. "So, if we bag Grady, we'll be the talk of the entire festival, right?"

Shit. He's really enjoying this. I ball my hands into fists so I don't claw at my neck where I'm sure I'm breaking out in hives.

I shrug and roll my shoulders. "Probably. But Grady has been Moby Dick for three years in a row. No one's gotten him, not even his brother."

To my left, Grady's brothers, Harrison and Adam, stand with their heads together, probably plotting against the eldest Reid, and everyone else must have had the same idea because they're all branching off into partners.

"Game on, Oscar. How about a little side bet." There's mischief in his gaze, but damn him because I like it.

"What did you have in mind?" I aim for bored, but the words come out breathless, and my fist slowly unclenches.

"If we bag Grady, you agree to a date—a real one. With me," he adds, like he needs to clarify.

"Dante."

He stands in front of me and places his hands on my hips. "Fun, remember?"

Yeah, I remember just fine.

"Go," James shouts, and people scatter around us.

Colors fly by, but my focus stays on Dante.

"No one has even come close to Grady. You know that, right?" Dang. Even I heard the sarcasm in that sentence.

"I'm not everyone, sweetheart." At my scowl, he chuckles and says, "Maybe sweet-tart is a better nickname."

"Ha. Ha. Ha," I say dryly. "Just because I like what I like and hate everything else does not mean I'm grumpy."

The lines of his face fade when he suppresses a laugh. "Okay, Oscar. Whatever you say. Do we have a deal?"

"Fine," I mutter. "It's not like you'll get Grady. He's as

likely to shoot you as he is to toss your ass to the ground, so I have nothing to worry about."

He steps forward until our bodies are almost touching, standing so close that the heat radiating off him warms my skin, and his spicy scent fills my nose. The anxiety that normally shimmers through me is pushed down to my toes.

"Oh, Sayls. You've seriously misjudged how much I want this date. And you have no idea of the lengths I'm willing to go to get it either."

"Fine. I hope a date is worth your life," I say with an eye roll I don't mean.

"Not any date. A date with you. That's worth so much more than my life because my life has been on pause without you in it. A date with you is what will give me life for the first time in six years. That is worth any risk I have to take."

The blood rushing in my ears makes me lightheaded. I'm supposed to be the romance author, but he keeps coming up with proclamations that make me sound like Dr. Seuss.

He pulls back with an expression that says he knows what he's doing to me, and this is only the beginning. He walks backward, never breaking our connection until he reaches James, who gives him a small pouch with his numbered pins inside.

"Oh, Sassy," Cassie coos. She always freaking hovers. "You're done for. That boy might be even more in love with you than when he left."

"He doesn't even know me anymore. And you're one to talk. James is tracking your every move."

"James and I are a different story for another time. But you and Dante? Time may have passed, Sass, but really think about if you've changed or not."

"What's that supposed to mean?" This is why I don't socialize. Everyone has an opinion, and it's fucking exhausting. And Cassie is the worst. She has boundary issues and no problem inserting herself into anything she deems a worthy cause.

"It means you've been going through the motions of life, but you haven't been living. Experiences are what change us, shape us, help us grow. You've intentionally avoided experiences because they make you feel. So, you say he doesn't know you, but have you grown all that much since he left?"

Vicious words sit on the tip of my tongue, but she holds up a hand to ward them off.

"Sorry, babe. That's a lot of tough love right there, but if no one else will tell you the truth as we all see it, then I will. You deserve happiness. You need love. But you have to decide if you're worth the risk, because that man there? He's all in. It's up to you to trust yourself enough to believe it."

"Maybe people should put blinders on and mind their own stinking business." My skin is on fire. I need to get out of here before I turn into one giant hive.

"No can do, babe. This is what friends do for each other."

"And exactly why I don't like having friends." It's not the truth, but it's the nicest thing I can force out of my mouth right now.

"Oh, you love me. Even if you don't say it, I know you do."

She's out of her mind. She also sees everything through rose-colored glasses.

"Cass?" James stands behind her, and I watch the ice freeze over her expression.

"No," she growls. "See ya, Sass. Good luck today. I'm off to run Cherry Pie."

Okay, so rose-colored glasses for everyone except the man who broke her heart.

"Shit," James curses, following her into the crowd.

"That's a lot of history to unpack right there," Dante says, making me jump. How long has he been standing there like a creeper? Freaking Cassie and her stupid thoughts on love and happiness.

"Yeah." I don't elaborate, scratching at my neck with my knuckles so I don't leave marks.

He holds up his bag. "We've got some time before I make my move, so Frozen T's or Cherry Pie next?"

I close my eyes and inhale a long, pitiful breath. Today is going to test every level of patience I have.

"There's no way I'm putting on a frozen T-shirt."

"Cherry Pie it is," he says. "Just like old times."

Memories assault my vision, and I stomp my feet, pretending to kick off dirt to hide my shaking, but Dante snags my elbow and pulls me into his side. And just like that, the tremors ease.

Our first time together.

Our first Lemon Fest.

Our final moments.

It all comes crashing back with wave after wave of sensations until my body trembles, and I can't move.

"I remember every detail of every conversation and every moment we've ever spent together. And I look forward to all that we'll do in the future. Together."

"Together," I repeat.

How do you feel about a do-over, Saylor?

A different kind of nerves flutter in my chest as an emotion I can't quite reach dances on the periphery of my existence.

It feels dangerously like hope.

CHAPTER 16

DANTE

*E*veryone gives us space as we walk deeper into The Common in silence. My false bravado that I could actually tag Grady felt like the right move at the time, but now my mind whirls with different scenarios as I try to devise a plan of attack.

I wasn't lying when I said failure wasn't an option, but I also might be Grady's least favorite person right now.

"I'm not doing that." Saylor's voice drags me from my thoughts.

I follow to where she's pointing, and a deep, unexpected laugh escapes my mouth and lightens my worries.

People sit at picnic tables with pies in front of them. Well, shallow tins made to look like pies. They're actually filled with whipped cream and cherries.

"The rules are simple," Cassie says with wicked intentions written all over her face. "The objective is to fish out five cherries. However." She pauses for dramatic effect. "Your hands must remain behind your back, and if any whipped cream lands on the table, you're disqualified."

"Oh, come on, Oscar. This is an easy one."

"Easy?" Her voice vibrates with annoyance. "You can't use your hands. You can't spill the cream. Trust me, it's anything but easy."

Cassie spots us in the crowd. I haven't spoken to her since my senior year in college, but I recognize that look. The question is, will she use her powers for good or evil? In my case, will she use them to help or hurt my chances with Saylor?

Honestly, with her, it could go either way.

"And," she says, "the first round is done in pairs. Each cherry plucked must be transferred to your partner, who will spit the pit into the appropriate bowl. But remember, no hands." She waggles her brows, and some people standing in line shift positions, not wanting to partake in the innuendo-laced game.

So, helping it is. I nod in thanks and flash her a wink. I can use all the help I can get.

Saylor backs away, but I hook my arm with hers and coax her forward. "It'll be a good show for everyone," I say under my breath, nodding at our surroundings and reminding her we're here for publicity.

There are already a few phones pointed our way, and she stiffens next to me. My face has been in the tabloids even more than normal, thanks to my dear old brother. For the first time since I returned to Hope Hollow, true irritation overrides my happiness at being with Saylor. Even though publicity is our end goal, my jaw twitches as I fight to control my protective instincts.

She frowns. "They don't live here. They're only here for the festival. No one who lives here would invade our privacy like that."

"True, but that's also what we want. So, let's give them something Instagram-worthy."

"I haven't played games in…" She snaps her mouth closed,

and I step in front of her, then bend my knees so we're nose to nose. It's my favorite way to talk with her because my lips are only inches away from hers.

"Since when, Sayls?"

She drops her gaze and shakes her head.

"Are you telling me you haven't participated in Lemon Fest since I left?"

The hard line of her lips tells me I'm right.

"Oh, Sayls." Sadness infiltrates those two words like a painful harmony.

My mind flashes back to our last Lemon Fest together. We'd won the Cherry Pie competition. We'd dominated most of the games that year because we were so in sync.

Acid rolls around in my gut as her words from the other night take shot after shot at my heart. *Your life kept playing out on social media, and I...I stopped living.*

Clasping her hand in mine, I walk us to the table with the fewest number of people and take a seat. She eventually slides in next to me.

A piece of hair keeps falling into her face, so I tuck it behind her ear. My heart gallops every time my skin touches hers. "It's time to start living again, and that starts today," I say like I'm sharing a secret. "Plus, I want you to remember how good I am with my tongue."

Her skin flushes crimson, and not from the hives.

Yeah, she's remembering all right.

Cassie drops a plate in front of me with a wide smirk.

"Traitor," Saylor hisses, but it only makes Cassie's eyes dance with mirth.

"Tough love, babe. That's what I'm here for."

Saylor crosses her arms over her chest and pouts as we wait for everyone to get a plate.

"Ready?" Cassie calls after a beat. "Go."

With heat in my veins and dirty thoughts in my mind, I

get to work. I hover above the cream and part it with my tongue, searching for a cherry.

"Disqualified," Cassie calls out. I lift my chin to confirm it's not me, then plunge my tongue deeper.

When it hits fruit, I stretch my tongue as far as it will go, trying to scoop the cherry from underneath. As soon as I trap it, I sink my teeth in to lift it and turn a lust-filled gaze to Saylor.

Her flushed cheeks tell of memories not fit for public, and my cock reacts. I watch the flush work its way down the column of her neck, then lean in. Our lips touch, and I transfer the fruit using more tongue than necessary. Her body melts into mine.

We're so close that the light freckles kissing the bridge of her nose stand out, and when I pull back, she sits frozen and wide-eyed with whipped cream on her lips and chin.

"I've missed you, Sayls. So, damn much." Her nostrils flare. "Eat the cherry, sweetheart. Then spit the pit. People are watching."

She snaps out of a trance I hope is sexual in nature because there's nothing I want more than to show her how well I remember her body.

Her jaw works as she eats the fruit, and I go back to searching.

The second one takes me longer, but three more people are disqualified by the time I catch it.

With the cherry between my teeth, I say, "Come here, Sayls. I need your lips." My voice is rough with need, and I love how her pulse surges in her neck as she leans in.

Her lips brush mine, and a low rumble vibrates in my chest. I wasn't thinking about how my body would react to this game when I dragged her over here.

Saylor pulls away more quickly this time, but her face is scarlet, and I chuckle before heading back in.

The third and fourth go quickly, but the fifth one keeps slipping away.

"Hurry up, Dewey. Mom, that guy only has one left," a child says in front of me with a slightly panicked voice.

"I'm trying, kid." I glance over to find my competition. I've never seen him before, but based on his small cheering squad, I'm assuming he lives here.

Determination sets in when Saylor's thigh presses against mine. I'm not losing this game. For some reason, it's symbolic, and a loss is not an option.

Finally, I snatch up the last cherry, and Saylor is so wound up that she crashes into me. She may have tried to hide it, but her competitive streak would make any professional athlete proud.

She drops the pit into the bowl and jumps up with a loud, "Whoop! We did it!"

I stand, wiping the whipped cream from my face, smiling as I watch her feet tap into the ground in a victory dance. She lifts her head, and I stalk toward her slowly. When I reach her, I wrap my arms around her and pull her to me so her feet dangle in the air, and I fucking consume her.

It's a kiss meant for the bedroom. It's a kiss that feels like home. And when we finally break apart, she's gasping for air, but I don't set her down. Not yet. Holding her fills a Saylor-sized space in my soul, and I want to keep her forever.

"Ah, hell," she mutters, dropping her forehead to my shoulder. "I guess that was good for the amateur paparazzi over there, huh?"

"That's a bonus." She lifts her head, but her face furrows into a frown, so I lick a dollop of whipped cream from the corner of her mouth and say, "That kiss was for me."

Her shoulders tremble, but she says nothing, so I slowly lower her to the ground.

"Dante and Sassy are the winners," Cassie announces,

then hands us our certificate for free fried dough. "You'd better get moving. Grady is growling at anyone who comes near him. He's removed three tags and is pissed that he's the target again this year." She laughs, and I'd bet good money that she had a hand in choosing him. "But come on, he makes it so much fun."

She shrugs and returns to her Cherry Pie duties, but dread sits in my gut. How the hell am I going to tag a grumpy Grady Reid?

Saylor watches my face like she can read all my thoughts.

"Fine," she says with an eye roll. "The secret to tagging Grady…" Apparently psychic after all, she leans forward and crooks her index finger my way. "Is Lilly," she whispers. "She's his weakness because he's responsible for her. And I guarantee she'll be on board to help."

Her face shines brighter than the sun, and the slight lift of her lips is an arrow to my heart. She's still grumpy. She still doesn't care for crowds. But for the first time since I've been home, she's the Saylor she used to be, and I'll take any progress I can get.

"Why, Saylor Greer. If I didn't know better, I'd think you wanted us to win."

"Whatever. I just don't want to listen to you whine if you fail." The muscles tighten around her mouth, but the hard edge that usually accompanies her words is nowhere to be found.

"Fair enough. Let's go win this thing, huh?"

My phone sounds with a series of pings, and I fish it out of my pocket before she can respond. I set a notification for anything with my name or Saylor's attached to it, and sure enough, social media updates flood my screen.

Sassy Thompson offends prominent mother's group.

Trent Bailey is worried for the future of Ascendancy Inc.

The king of spin is getting cozy with Sassy Thompson. Is it possible that her international bestsellers are based on their real-life love story?

It's the last one that has sweat beading at the base of my neck. That was almost too fast.

Sassy leans over my arm to read the headline, and her body tenses against mine, but I can't tear my gaze away from the photo accompanying the short article about us.

It's a still from the video that Kate took. But the expression Saylor's wearing as I leaned in to kiss her gives me pause —hope, and heat, and fear. I swallow, but messy emotions are stuck in my throat. Hope and heat I can work with. It's the fear that scares the hell out of me.

"We'd better head back to the bookstore and talk to Lilly," Saylor says quietly.

"Yeah, okay." I lead her away from the crowd with a hand at the small of her back, but the fear in that picture brands itself in my mind as a reminder of how much pain she's been living in.

~

"So, WANNA HELP?" Saylor asks Lilly after explaining the situation.

"Oh, heck yeah, I do. Grady will hate it! I know exactly how to get him here too." Her face beams with excitement. She seems like a good kid, but I imagine the chance to prank an older brother like Grady doesn't come along often.

"He's seriously going to hate me now," I mutter.

"Grady hates everyone," Lilly says with a shrug. "Well, except me and Sassy. So blame us."

She lifts her phone and taps away. I'm almost nervous to find out what she'll say that will send Grady running. When she's finished, she flashes us a smile that makes me nervous.

"Quick," she says, jumping down from her stool. "We need to make it look like books fell off the shelf."

"What did you tell him?" Saylor asks but hurries to the far side of the store with Lilly.

"That I was putting away books, and a shelf broke. I said I'm fine, and Kai is coming to check on me." She glances over her shoulder with a shit-eating grin. "It's not that he dislikes Kai, but there's not a chance he'll let him check on me without chaperoning."

She and Saylor pull down a row of books. "When he gets here, I'll sit on the floor. You'll have to be quick to get the clothespin on him. But he'll be a little ragey thinking I might have gotten hurt, so he won't be as vigilant about his surroundings."

"That's…"

"It's not nice, but neither was he when he chaperoned homecoming and kept pulling Kai back by the collar when he got too close while dancing with me. A little payback never hurt anyone," she says.

"He's definitely going to kill me," I groan. "So much for getting him on my side."

The overhead bell chimes when the door crashes open. "Harrison, I swear to God, I will end you if you come near me with that pin," Grady roars.

I peer around the bookshelf as Lilly drops to the floor. Grady scans the store before landing on me. The muscles in his shoulders eat up the space between his chin and chest as he stalks closer. Behind him, Harrison and Adam smirk.

I glance at my watch. I can't make a move until the final minutes, but guilt hits my chest when Grady pushes past me.

"What happened? Where's Kai?" The words fly from

Grady's mouth as Harrison and Adam flank me on either side.

"Genius," Adam whispers.

"Getting Lilly to rope him in was both impressive and fucking du-umb. He's going to kill you," Harrison says.

Harrison was one of the few people I considered a friend when I lived here. Even when I came home from college for the summer, he was the only one besides Saylor I did anything with.

He's someone else I owe an apology to for cutting him out of my life. But it'll have to wait for another day.

"Yeah, he's going to be pissed," I admit, even as I inch forward.

There are less than five minutes left in the competition, so I make my move. Placing a hand on Grady's shoulder, I lean over him, pretending to check on Lilly. His low growl has me lifting one hand even as I clip the pin to the material of his shirt with the other.

"What happened?" Grady demands.

"I said I'm fine. Nothing even hit me. Admit it, you came running because I said Kai was coming," Lilly says with more than a little sass. Maybe letting her hang out with Saylor wasn't the best idea he's ever had.

"Then why are you on the floor?" His face is pinched with concern, and I don't think Grady can say anything without growling.

"Ugh, Grady." She gives the kind of annoyed shrug that would make Saylor proud. "I'm organizing the books so we can reshelve them."

Saylor snorts when she's unable to hold in a laugh, and it makes Grady suspicious. He stands quickly and glowers at the room, assessing the situation with his back to a bookshelf.

Two more minutes.

"Lilly, what the hell is going on?" he asks, glaring at me.

Somehow, he's figured out this is my doing, and I'm thankful for all the hours I've spent in the gym. There's no way I could take Grady, but I'm almost confident he couldn't actually kill me, either.

One minute.

Lilly stands, and the flash of her purple sundress must grab his attention because he finally stops glaring at me.

"Epic," Harrison laughs.

"Admit it, Grady. You came running because you thought I'd be alone with my boyfriend," Lilly taunts.

"You're sixteen," he says through clenched teeth.

"Time," Adam announces while pushing his glasses up his nose with his pointer finger.

"What?" Grady glares at every person in the room while Saylor doubles over laughing. It's a sight that stops everyone in their tracks for a full thirty seconds, and a pride I've never experienced fills my heart.

Harrison steps forward, breaking us all from our shock, and lifts my arm like a heavyweight fighter who just won his match.

"Dante, one. Grady, zero." Harrison steps to the right, partially blocking me. Is he also worried that Grady might charge me like a raging bull? While I appreciate the effort, Grady would bowl over the both of us without breaking a sweat.

Instead, Grady reaches for his back as far as his muscular arms will allow. But it's Adam who plucks my pin from his shirt.

Grady's eyes do something strange. They aren't quite sparkling, but there's humor in them that he's trying to suppress.

"Fucking stupid games," he grumbles, then stalks toward the door. I'm not the only one who noticed his voice was missing some of its usual bite, and we all stare at him with dumbfounded expressions on our faces. Before he reaches the door, he calls over his shoulder. "Be at the brewery tonight at seven, Thompson. We have stuff to…discuss."

When I don't respond, he turns with a smug expression. "Unless you're a chicken," he taunts. "Sassy, you too. Don't want you missing book club again."

"Ah, shit, Grady," she grumbles. "That's not fair."

"Payback's a bitch, my friend. See you both tonight."

"What happens at the brewery tonight?" I ask. Harrison and Adam are still standing on either side of me.

"The ladies of Heart Lake meet for Sexy Sips and Scenes. The guys? Well, it's supposed to be poker. But really, it's a bunch of smack talk," Adam says.

"Better wear your thick skin tonight, man. Grady will be in a mood for sure." Harrison laughs. "And I'll let you make up ghosting me by giving me front-row seats to the shit show."

Guilt swamps me. "I'm…"

"Nah," he says, smacking my chest with the back of his hand. "I read the books. I get it."

Saylor's head snaps up. "What do you mean, you read the books?"

"Come on, Sassy," Harrison says with a flush to his cheeks. "You must know everyone's been worried about you, right? So, when whispers of your story spread faster than cheap vodka at a bonfire party, we all read it."

Her face pales.

"We're all just glad you're giving life another shot," Adam says shyly.

Her mouth drops open.

She always did feel like an outsider in her own life. Maybe now she'll start seeing how much people have always cared.

CHAPTER 17

SAYLOR

"This is the worst idea in the history of ideas," I say as Dante steps out of the bathroom in nothing but a towel. "Why are you naked?"

He stares down at himself, then back at me. "It's hot as balls in there, Oscar. Why doesn't the fan work?"

"I never got around to having anyone fix it. I normally shower with the door open to let the steam out."

Naughtiness seeps from his every pore. "Don't stop on my account," he says with a sexy lilt.

My throat is too dry to respond, so I roll my eyes instead. It feels safer.

"Are you ready to go?" he asks as he crosses the room then digs into the suitcase he keeps propped against the wall.

My shoulders tense. Am I feeling guilty over a suitcase? Ugh. I probably am. I should have at least given him a drawer or something. Stupid, messy emotions. I liked it better when no one bothered me enough to force them out of me.

You know that's not true. Geez! What the hell is wrong with my conscience these days?

He slides a pair of boxer briefs up his legs and under the

towel, but because I can't stop ogling him, I catch a sliver of his muscular ass cheek as he covers it.

How the heck do you get muscles like that in your ass?

Dante drops the towel and waits for me to meet his gaze. "I really love how you're looking at me right now, but we won't make it to Grady's if you don't stop."

I puff out my cheeks and hold my breath before spinning on one foot and staring at the wall.

I don't have to hear him to know he's closing in. The heat of his body is the force field that has always drawn me to him.

He runs one long finger up the outside of my arm, and I watch goosebumps rise in his wake. Every inch of me wants to curl into his touch like a cat. Even his fingers are sexy. There's something fundamentally unfair about that.

"I liked the game we played today." His voice is whisper-soft, but it causes a riot of sensations across my skin.

"Okay." I breathe the word like a prayer.

"Every time your lips touched mine, it was an exercise in self-control not to say 'fuck the game' and drag you home."

He inhales deeply, and I shiver. I'm not cold. Not even close. But he makes me want. He makes me need. My body is a traitorous sun-drenched landscape, and his touch is the first drop of rain.

"Do you know that I've ached for you? Ached, Saylor, for years."

My breathing becomes shallow as I hang on to his every word. It makes me wobble on my feet, and I reach out to steady myself against the wall.

"Every day, when I'd sit at my desk, I'd get lost in your picture. Lost in memories and fantasies and dreams. It was so much easier to stare at your face and imagine what life could be like than suffering in the loss life was."

My head spins, and I'm swimming with questions when I

turn to face him. He's so close that I can smell my shampoo on him, honeysuckle and juniper. My scent mixed with his natural one is a mind-numbing aphrodisiac.

I lick my sticky, parched lips, and his gaze sharpens as he follows the movement. Why is it so stinking hot in here? I can't breathe, and my skin is kindling, ready to catch fire from his flame.

"You have a picture of me at work?" It's the only question my mind can grasp because I know where all my pictures went. They were too painful to see, so they're all in a box at the back of my closet now. I can't believe he was still holding on to one of them after all this time.

Sadness falls over his expression. "Saylor, I have pictures of you everywhere. I couldn't let you go. There's one from graduation on my desk. One of us together at a concert on my mantel. A collage of our life together in the hallway. You've always been here." He points to his heart. "And you were never far from here," he says and taps his temple. "You and Ainsley were my family. I couldn't just let that go."

"Didn't your dates find that..." A sharp edge of jealousy slices my heart into tiny pieces.

Strong fingers grasp my chin and tilt my head toward the ceiling. "You cannot believe everything you read online or in magazines. Have I dated? Yes. Has anyone even come close to easing the ache of missing you? Not a chance. I've been living in a hell of my own making for years, Saylor. Years. You're the balm to that ache. You're the only one who can pull me from purgatory. It's only ever been you, sweetheart. Don't you see that?"

The sound of my heartbeat whooshes in my ears, and salty emotion settles in the back of my throat.

"What about you, Saylor? Has anyone been able to erase me from your heart?" His voice trembles as if he's in pain.

I could lie and tell him that he doesn't still live rent-free in every part of me. It would probably convince him to walk away after this is all said and done. But the pain in his expression stops me. He may not understand what he's in store for, being with me, but even a bit of him now is better than seeing him and not having him as mine.

So, I shatter my walls and give myself to him, knowing there will be nothing left of me the next time he leaves. But his presence weakens me. Too weak to have him here and not long for who I used to be—too weak not to have him.

I only hope the time we have together, this temporary reprieve, will be worth the eventual fall.

Words stick to the roof of my mouth, so I do the only thing I can think of. I show him. Surprise flashes across his face as I throw myself at him, but he catches me without hesitation.

He's always caught me.

His words, his honesty, and his devotion have snapped the tether holding me back, and I can't get close enough. My hands claw at his bare chest, trying to reach his mouth, and when he slowly, painfully slowly, lowers his mouth to mine, my heart explodes as wildly as our kiss.

It's a teeth-smashing, lip-crushing, soul-rendering kiss that leaves me breathless. One of his hands wraps around my neck and holds me tightly while his other hand grips my ass possessively, lifting me to him, waking up every dormant cell until my entire body is alive and throbbing.

My hands slide down his chest, memorizing every curve and dent of muscle, but I still can't get close enough to him. I want him with a need so powerful I might combust if he doesn't ease the desire building between my legs.

I've gone from keeping him at arm's length to *give me that entire length* in the blink of an eye. Eventually I'll regret it, but right now I don't care. How can I when I'm alive for the first time in years?

Have I really been dead inside for six freaking years?

When the what-ifs and what-nexts invade my mind, I dig a hole in my chest and bury them, however temporary, with Dante's love.

Courage spikes when his hardened shaft presses to my center, and I allow my hand to drift to the band of his boxer briefs. But he pulls his hips back, slows our kiss, lowers me to the floor, and new panic ices my veins.

Why is he stopping me?

"I'm not going anywhere," he says with his lips hovering over mine. "That means I have to find my place in your life —in all aspects of your life. With Ainsley and even…" He turns his face away from mine. "Even with Grady," he grumbles.

Heaving breaths burn in my lungs as I process what he's saying.

"You—You still want to go to Three Brothers Brewing? Now?" My voice is squeaky and a bit annoyed. "Now? When I'm—When I want to…"

"You have no idea how much it's killing me to pull away right now."

I glower at him, and he chuckles, then reaches for my hand. Before I can find a retort, he places it over the thick ridge of his erection.

"Killing me, Saylor. But I'm not going to fuck up this time. I will make an effort with everyone who matters in your life."

"But what about me?" I cannot believe I whined like that. What the hell is happening to me?

He takes a step forward and crowds me against the wall. "Oh, baby. Trust me. I'm not forgetting about you. While you're at that sexy little book club, I want you to remember what it felt like to have my head between your legs and my thumb stroking your clit like my favorite guitar. I want you to remember how I pulse inside you and how your walls choke my cock when you come."

"That's not fair," I say with a shaky sigh.

"But think about how ready you'll be for me when we get home. Because I am coming home tonight, sweetheart. In your bed. In your body. In your heart."

He retreats to pull on more clothing, leaving me dumbfounded.

Holy mother of shit in heaven. I don't move. I don't even dare to breathe for fear my denim shorts will press against my clit and I'll come on the spot. I should have worn leggings.

"Breathe, Sayls. You only have to make it through a few more hours." It's a dark promise of what's to come.

I finally exhale a long breath and fight the urge to double over with my hands on my knees.

My entire body vibrates, and I'm afraid that if I move an inch, sparks will fly from my limbs. It's been years since I've had this kind of energy flowing through my blood, and it's all because of the man I pushed away. In only a few days, he's brought me back to life in ways I hadn't even acknowledged I was missing.

What will he do to me in a week? Two?

He turns a crooked smile my way and finds me staring at him in the darkening room. "You ready?"

The lump in my throat decides it's not budging, so I hum my agreement. "Mm-hmm." I also don't dare open my mouth because I have no idea what might fly out with my mind a whirling firestorm of emotions I've repressed since he left.

Dante wraps an arm around my waist and walks us to the door. I'm halfway down the stairs when he says, "There's not a day that's passed that I haven't been in love with you."

I freeze. The sounds of him locking the door hit my ears like a steel drum, and then the thump, thump, thump of his footsteps brings him so close his body heat infiltrates my own through our clothes.

"I'll take your dark days, and I'll take your sass, your insecurities, and Oscar-ish ways. I'll be here to catch you, but please, promise that you'll let me in because I won't survive losing our love twice."

Everything goes fuzzy when my heart rate triples, and I'm forced to focus on the handrail so I don't fall. This is a different kind of panic. This is the kind of panic that speaks of truths because I won't survive it either.

"Come on. Grady is probably waiting to kick my ass."

He takes hold of my hand and leads me down the remaining stairs. If he notices the war happening in my heart, he doesn't say so. He simply takes care of me as we head toward the covered bridge leading to Three Brothers Brewing.

I won't survive losing our love twice.

His words play on a loop in my mind.

Will I survive the inevitable end when he realizes I'm more work than I'm worth? Because he will, won't he?

A blast of icy-cold air cuts through me when the wind rustles the trees, and I spin my head left to right. But my mind is playing tricks on me because I could have sworn I heard my oldest sister's voice swaying with that breeze.

Crap. Maybe I am losing my mind.

THE WALK to the brewery normally takes fifteen minutes, but Dante allows me to drag my feet, and we arrive twenty-five minutes later. He droned on about life and what he's been up to. I should have been listening. I wanted to listen, but the devil on one shoulder was antagonizing the angel on the other.

They fought over Dante the entire walk and blocked out most of his words. By the time we arrived, neither had been a clear winner.

"Did you work it out?" he asks when we reach the parking lot.

"Huh? Work what out?"

"The storm that's brewing in your head. I'm guessing it's your wants fighting against what you thought you needed." There's no condescension in his tone, just understanding that comes from a soul-deep connection with someone.

"No, it's still kicking up dust."

He tugs on my hand, and we stop at the front door. "So let it. But don't lie to yourself either. We've both been telling ourselves what we thought we had to in order to survive. But now we know the truth. Now we can fight for what should have been ours all along."

"What's that?" I ask when he reaches for the door.

"Love."

He doesn't say anything else. He doesn't have to. Love is what you fight for, and somewhere along the line, I convinced myself I couldn't have it.

But what if I can? What if he's right? What if I've been wrong this entire time?

My questions are forgotten the second we enter the bar. Ainsley spots us first and darts straight for me, followed by old Mrs. Walker, the organizer of Sexy Scenes and Sips.

"You made it," Ainsley sing-songs before wrapping me in an awkward hug, then she turns and does the same to Dante. I only bristle a little at how natural affection is for them.

"Well, Sassy. Good to see you, dear," Mrs. Walker says, holding a copy of *Come September*. "It so happens this was our read this month."

"Wonderful," I grunt. Just what I freaking need. Why in

the world would they read my book? There are millions of romance novels out there. Why choose mine?

"Come on now, Oscar. It won't be that bad," Dante murmurs into my hair before he kisses the side of my head.

"We've got words for you too, Dante Thompson." Mrs. Walker scolds. "But I'll save those for the bookstore. Now, Ainsley—"

She's interrupted when Mr. Walker joins us. "Dr. Greer," he says, cutting in front of his wife. "I need to see you immediately."

Ainsley's face instantly turns professional. "What's wrong, Mr. Walker?"

"I've got ah, a problem. Again. I think Millie's book gave me an," he leans in to whisper, "STD." But Mr. Walker is in his seventies and refuses to use his hearing aid, so it sounds like someone trying to talk over a football game.

Ainsley stands stoically, but Dante and I lose our composure.

"Mr. Walker, I assure you, you cannot get an STD from a book," Ainsley says in her most professional voice, but I heard the quiver. She's trying not to laugh too. "STD is a sexually transmitted disease. I believe your rash is from walking in the woods and not killing all the poison ivy that lines your property."

"No," he says with a wave of his hand. "It's not only the book. It's what she's doing with—"

"And that's our cue to move along," Dante says with a hand pressed to the small of my back.

"Good luck," I mouth to my sister. When I turn back around, we're stopped by a human wall of Reids.

Awesome. This night cannot end fast enough.

"Grady, what are you doing?" I ask.

"Book club's waiting for you, Sass," he says in a much gentler tone than he uses for anyone else. I guess when you see someone at their worst, you tend to treat them with kid gloves forever.

Placing my fists on my hips, I wait until he stops glaring at Dante. "Are you going to be an ass?"

"Nah, Sass. We're going to come to an understanding, is all." Grady's stern expression doesn't give much away, but the ticking of his jaw means he's grinding his teeth.

"Ease up, Grady. I'm a big girl."

His face softens for a fraction of a second. "Yes, you are."

"Fine. I'm going to be right in there. Don't start anything." I glance between the three Reid brothers and Dante. "Any of you."

Each man gives a different version of okay, and I begrudgingly walk away. Instantly, I miss the heat and security of Dante's hand.

How quickly things change.

"Poker table. Now," I hear Grady demand. I turn and find Dante's gaze roaming my body. A lazy smile hooks the corner of his mouth upward. He's not worried.

But maybe he should be.

CHAPTER 18

DANTE

"*I* thought we were playing poker," I say. Grady's assembled a crew at a long, rectangular table instead of the customary round one. With three chairs on one side and one on the other, it looks more like a trial.

"We are," Harrison says. "Eventually." He stands behind Grady with a lazy uptick of his lips but he's the only one smiling.

Grady sits left of center at the table. To his left is Matty Miller, who was always the most-liked kid in town, and to his right is James, but his attention is singularly focused on Cassie—who appears to be the center of attention in the tasting room where book club is taking place.

Guess I'm not the only one aiming for a do-over.

Behind them, Harrison and Adam stand like security guards.

With the exception of Haphazard Harrison, I was never very close with any of them. I only moved here during my sophomore year of high school, and Saylor consumed my entire world from the moment I saw her. But I can't deny the twinge of jealousy that they've all been able to remain friends after all these years.

Would I be part of the group if I hadn't cut them all off?

In college, I came home and stayed with Saylor during the summers. My father had already moved on. Two years in the same place was a record for him to begin with, but Saylor's family felt like home, so I stopped chasing him all over the country.

"It's about time you came back to fix your shit," Grady grumbles as I slide into a chair opposite him.

Harrison's chuckle makes Grady growl, and I sit back in my chair with a smirk.

"Since you're here, let's air it out. You took off and cut everyone out of your life. Now you're back, and you have amends to make." Grady cuts a pointed glare in my direction. "So, make them."

"No offense, Grady, but who died and made you sheriff?"

"You did," he says through clenched teeth. "The day you vanished and hurt people I care about, you brought this on yourself."

Everyone remains silent and staring while they wait for me to respond.

"Listen, Grady," I say with a sigh. "I get that you're protective of Saylor. But this is between me and her."

"You're in town." Grady's voice is deadly calm, but the firm set of his jaw and the way his left eye twitches belay that composure. "You're participating and acting like you'll be here a while. But we all know what happened the last time you left. What's going to happen to Sassy when you leave again?"

Irritation gives way to white-hot anger at his gall. I didn't have all the information when I left last time—now I do.

"When I left, I thought I was doing the right thing, but I have never stopped loving her." My blood boils, making my words come out in a thick staccato. "Saylor has never been far from my life, even when we were on opposite sides of the country. But now I have the truth, and nothing, not even you, will get in my way of getting her back." At some point in my speech, I'd leaned forward, my hands gripping the edge of the table and the muscles in my arms straining with tension.

Everyone is eerily quiet, and no one moves. The air is as thick as smog in LA, but Grady and I continue glaring at each other, waiting for someone to break.

Finally, he nods. "That's what we needed to know. Now tell us how we can help."

Confusion must show in my expression because he pinches the bridge of his nose, takes a deep breath, then explains. "Someone is coming after you and Sassy. She hates being plastered all over the fucking world, but she's doing it, presumably for you and her career. So, tell us how we can help fix the fucking problem."

Stunned, I sit back and stare at him. This guy curses more than the rapper, DaBaby. Poppy and her fairy foul mouth jar would have a field day with him.

I lost a good chunk of money to that jar last year, but I've gotten better at catching the curses now.

He glowers in return, and somewhere in the back of my mind, a memory tries to surface but can't quite break through. And then it hits me. The night Shannon died, this town showed up for Saylor and Ainsley just like they are now.

Another memory, this one of Mr. Reid arriving at Saylor's grandparents' house and offering me a job the first summer I moved in with the Greers.

A smile tugs at the corner of my lips. I've missed this.

Harrison laughs, but when I look at him, his expression morphs into concern. "We're not your enemy here, Dante. But Saylor's been through so much, we need to make sure you're in it for the long haul." He places a hand on Grady's shoulder. "Sass and Ainsley are like…" He drops his gaze to the floor, and I'd swear his cheeks flame. "They're like sisters to us."

Grady grunts and nods. "Let us help. It'll make all these assholes feel better."

"Us?" Miller laughs. "As if you're not sneaking around town in the middle of the night fixing shit no one asked you to and then denying it."

My jaw hits the floor. Is he visiting more than Saylor late at night?

"We're talking about Dante," Grady growls. "What can we do?" His words are rough and disjointed, like his threshold for peopling is running thin. He's the male version of Saylor. It makes me understand him better and possibly have a little more compassion toward him too.

"I appreciate the offer," I say, making eye contact with each man in turn. "But I've got it handled. My brother—" The term sticks in my throat. Betrayal will do that, I guess. Trent might be blood, but he would never step in like these guys have.

Scratching behind my ear, I avert my gaze and drag in a breath. I forgot how small towns get all up in your business if they believe it's for the greater good. It's how I imagine a ridiculously large extended family to behave.

A prickle of awareness crawls up my neck—Saylor's watching me. She tugs on her necklace, and the worry shows in the furrow of her brow.

I'll do anything for this girl, and if that means airing my shit, that's what I'll do.

Flashing her an easy smile, I turn back to Grady and lay it all out. "After I left Hope Hollow, I discovered I have four half-siblings throughout the country. Trent is one of them, and he's in a bad place. I'm his scapegoat, but I'm handling it.

If you want to help, you'll make sure no one gets to her when the paparazzi show up here trying to dig up shit—because they will come. The last thing she needs is to feel like she's not safe in her own town. And the way Trent runs his mouth, they will show up in hordes."

Each man studies me as I speak. Different emotions play across their features, but they all have the same goal. Keeping someone they care about safe.

Grady nods, but it's Harrison who speaks. "And your brother?"

I choose my words carefully but finally decide to go with my heart. "He was the family I always wanted, but he's put Saylor and my niece in danger physically and emotionally. I can't force him to stay clean, and I won't stand by and allow him to hurt the two people I love most in this world. If it comes down to him or them, I'll choose them every time."

Grady's body relaxes infinitesimally, and he finally nods like he's made a decision. "We'll call a town meeting to discuss the rats," he rumbles.

My lips twitch. Town meetings around here used to be more entertainment than business. Saylor and I would come just to watch the show. Are they still the same?

He sees my smirk and leans forward into my space. "But I swear to God, Thompson, if you hurt her again, I'll tie you up and pick you apart piece by piece, and they'll never find your body."

I also lean in to show him that he will not intimidate me. "If I hurt her again, I'll dig the hole myself."

Silence.

Brutal, unrelenting stares.

Then this bear of a man does the last thing I expect. He laughs. Loudly. "Good enough," he says and a smile slides across my face like a proud parent.

This is the side of small towns I was never part of before,

and witnessing it now is fascinating. But as much as I want to follow the other drama they're now discussing, something about a yoga studio owner and Miller, their voices become muted when my gaze catches on Saylor, sitting alone at the bar.

She's as far away from the crowd as she can get, but she's turned sideways, so the tiny dip of her lip is more pronounced. When the magnetism we wear like a tether calls her to me, she glances over her shoulder, and there's no mistaking her sadness.

She shifts her focus from me to Cassie standing in front of the crowd, and the chasm between Saylor and life has never had a more heartbreaking visual.

"Well, this was one hell of a welcoming committee." Harrison chuckles.

Pinning Saylor with my gaze, I say, "Welcoming committee? It felt more like an interrogation."

I hear a rumble that means Grady is holding in a growl. When I turn to him, his neatly cropped beard enhances the twitch of his jaw. "This is the kind of welcome you get when those who care about you are sick of you fucking up your life for a stupid-ass reason."

"And," Harrison says with a playful shrug, "all the ladies are in the book club. We're bored. Plus, you deserve a little heckling after the shit you've pulled. Consider it your initiation back into town."

These guys are something else.

"What they're saying," Adam says while pushing his glasses up his nose, "however ineloquently, is people around here missed you. Keep that in mind before you run off again."

"Since when did you all become therapists?" I ask, but there's a hint of wry amusement in my tone too.

"When everyone forgot what matters in life." Grady stares

straight ahead as he speaks, but the ghosts he keeps hidden shadow his expression.

He's not only talking about me—he's talking about himself. Then he blinks, and all emotion is erased from his gaze. "Deal the cards, Harrison, and don't fucking cheat. I'll be back with beers."

He stands abruptly, and I watch him walk away. What the hell was that about?

Grady hides behind his gruff exterior, but one thing is clear—he cares about everyone, even when he doesn't want to.

"You heard the man. Spread out and put your money where I can see it. The girls took the round high-tops to the tasting room, so we're stuck with the jury table." Harrison chuckles then waggles his brows at me. "Now, tell us how you plan to get the girl."

I groan. "When the hell did you turn into a teenage girl?"

James shifts uncomfortably in his chair and says, "If you love her, fight. You'll never forgive yourself if you don't."

He has no idea that I've already learned that lesson the hard way.

CHAPTER 19

SAYLOR

"Were you nervous about writing this story or secretly hoping he'd read it and come home?" Mrs. Winters asks.

"No, Mrs. Winters." Even moving across the room hasn't stopped her incessant questions.

No one told me until tonight that over sixty percent of this book club are also members of Senior-Cycle. Something must happen when you hit seventy that activates your *no fucks left to give* button, because everyone my age gives me a wide berth.

Well, everyone except Cassie, but she has the people-pleasing gene like Dante.

I don't suffer the same affliction.

"But the sexy times in the gazebo during a rainstorm. Someone must know if that actually happened," Mrs. Walker says, fanning herself.

Mr. Walker sits beside her, pretending not to be interested, but he reads these books faster than anyone, and I can see his detested hearing aids from here. Plus, he's my best customer.

"What did Dante think when he read them?" someone else asks, and sweat trickles down my spine.

Great. I'm going to walk out of here with swamp-ass. I avert my gaze, choosing to stare at the gleaming bar in front of me and silently praying they'll all leave me the hell alone.

"You'll have to ask him," I grumble, not caring if they can hear me or not.

"When will you give them their happily ever after? Are you waiting to see how you and Dante get yours before you write it?"

My head hits the cool bar top with a thud. Maybe if I get a concussion, they'll leave me alone.

I'm not even sure where that question comes from. Why does this room have to be so small? Grady seriously needs to check the fire codes because we are definitely over capacity in here.

"What about when the hero took her standing up at the county fair behind the food trucks? Is that even possible? Did you ever get caught?" Mrs. Walker has no shame, but my entire body tries to shrivel up from embarrassment.

"Okay, people, tone it down," Cassie says after standing on a chair to get everyone's attention. "This is supposed to be book club where we discuss the dynamics of the hero and heroine, plot, you know, all things story. We're not here to put Sassy on blast. She didn't sign up for a Q&A session."

I take back everything I've ever said about having friends. Right now, I could kiss Cassie Holly.

Low grumbles of dissatisfaction filter through the semi-private tasting room we're set up in, but eventually, they die down, and Mrs. Walker leads the discussion on character motivation. I tune them out. I wrote the damn thing—I don't need to dissect it now too.

A glass of white wine appears in front of me, and I follow the arm holding it. Grady. "Hey," I mumble, taking the glass.

He doesn't sell wine in the brewery, but he always has a pinot grigio for me and mysteriously has various kinds for other people who show up occasionally.

The guy is a big teddy bear with the heart of a giant and the attitude of a porcupine. But he's a good friend to those of us who need him and probably to those who don't yet know that they need him.

"Hey," he grumbles in return. "We put Thompson through the paces over there."

I turn my head toward him so fast, my hair swings and blocks my vision. "Why would you do that?" I hate how my chest flutters with nerves. Dante's a big boy, he can take care of himself.

Grady throws me an *are you serious* expression with one raised brow and turned-down lips, then shakes his head.

"Because we all want you to be happy, and no one wants to see you…" He doesn't finish that sentence, but we both know where he was going with it—no one wants to find me on The Landing again—where Shannon took her last breath.

Grady and I are close because he found me sitting on the rocks there when I didn't know where else to go. It was the lowest point in my life. I'd pretended to hold it together for nearly a month, but that night I couldn't do it anymore. I couldn't deny that I needed help after that, so I pushed Dante away, then checked myself into the hospital.

Since then, we've met each other there anytime one of us was struggling. Grady's depression is different from mine, but we understand each other in a way that's hard to describe.

"I've never given an opinion before," he says. His voice is pitched low so only I can hear him, making me swivel on my stool toward him. "But I think you were wrong to push him away." He holds up a hand to stop me when I open my mouth, ready to fire a snarky defense.

"I know why you did it. But now that I've read *Come September*, as your friend, I'm obligated to tell you that you fucked up." His brows furrow as he stares at me. "I don't want you to get hurt again, Sass. But I do believe that man loves the hell out of you even now."

My throat tightens. Since when does he have retractable walls in the brewery? I need them to stop closing in on me.

"Did everyone and their freaking mother read it?" I grumble.

"Why wouldn't they, Sass?" He sounds almost angry, and Grady rarely gets angry with me. "Everyone in this damn bar loves the hell out of you, but we didn't know how to help." He shakes his head, and his features relax when he rakes his fingers through his hair. "Trying to push our way in only made you retreat more, but don't think for one second that this entire fucking town hasn't been rooting for you because we have."

My throat is too tight to breathe properly.

Raucous laughter comes from the poker table, and we both incline our heads that way. The men are picking up cards with mischief radiating from their bones. "He never stopped loving you. That's something you don't just walk away from 'cause it's hard. That's something you fight for because it's worth the risk."

"That's, yeah." I rub my now-sweaty palms on the denim covering my thighs. "I." Damn it, why is my voice so pitchy? Clearing my throat in a way that sounds like a fisher cat, I continue. "I think you're right. But what if love isn't enough? What if he can't handle—me?" For the first time in a long time, I wear no mask. I don't hide my fears. I've torn down my walls and asked for help in rising from the ashes of my broken life.

"If you love him, trust him enough to try. He deserves that chance."

I lift my tenuous gaze to his. "I thought you didn't like him?"

He flashes me a rare grin. "I don't like anyone. But I can respect a man who goes after what he needs, and that man needs you. Almost as much as you need him. I will always be here for you—you're one of the only people I can tolerate at length—but you deserve a love only he can give you."

I bump his shoulder with mine. "When did you start playing matchmaker?"

"When some asshole started spreading lies about my best friend and forced her hand at fixing the biggest mistake she ever made." His words set off explosions in my chest.

Why are my emotions on steroids now? Once the floodgates opened, they obliterated the dam that held them in check.

"I think I liked it better when you were an asshole," I say.

"Oh, Sass. I'm still an asshole." He chuckles, then hardens his tone when someone clears their throat. "But I'll always be a better friend."

"Am I interrupting?" Dante's voice covers me like an electric blanket. I'm suddenly too warm, too overloaded with sensations, too—alive.

"Always," Grady growls, but there's a sliver of humor on his face when he winks. I laugh and turn toward Dante.

"No, you're not interrupting. Grady is just being a good friend. But I've hit my limit with peopling tonight. I'm going to head out."

Dante's expression falls blank. "I'm only here for you, Oscar. If you're leaving, then so am I."

Grady chuckles. "Only he could get away with calling you Oscar and keep his balls intact. Remember what I said, Sass." He turns his head and lowers his voice so only I can hear him. "Let him try."

Rolling my eyes so hard they ache, I peer around Dante to

the poker table and find all the men watching us. When they catch me glaring at them, they immediately turn their heads every way but mine. And they say women are the ones who gossip the most. I snort. Apparently, they've never met the men of Hope Hollow.

"What about poker?" I ask.

Dante aims his scowl in Grady's direction. "It's not poker. It's more of a therapy session, and my time ran out."

Grady shrugs. "It is poker, but you had to pass inspection first."

"Did I pass?" Dante's cute when he's nervous. He pushes his hands deep into the pockets of his shorts and rocks on his heels. He wants to be here—it shows in his open expression that reads like a book. He wants to belong, just like he did at fifteen.

Grady assesses him with cool indifference. "Remains to be seen." He tilts his head in my direction. The unsaid words speak volumes. *It depends on how we proceed.*

Dante nods his head but takes my hand in his. "Ready to go home?"

Home.

The contact of skin on skin sends an electric current running through my body. It sizzles and crackles the air between us, and for better or worse, I couldn't turn back now, even if I wanted to. I hope my therapist is ready for me because this path I'm choosing is covered with thorns and buried in memories I've spent years trying to forget.

CRICKETS CHIRPING over the waves licking the shore are the soundtrack to the multitude of fears spiraling in my mind on the walk home.

Dante also seems lost in his head, and I can't stop myself

from checking on him out of the corner of my eye. What the hell did the guys do to him?

We arrive at the back door of my house, which has a private staircase leading to the apartment upstairs so we don't have to go through the bookstore.

I remove the keys from my purse, but Dante takes them from my hand and unlocks the door. Anxiety creeps up my spine and lodges itself in my throat when he still doesn't say anything. Is he rethinking our...situationship? Did the guys warn him away from me and my...issues? That's what I'd do, isn't it?

There are fourteen steps to the top, I've counted them every day since I was a kid. Tonight, each one makes my muscles burn and my heart hammer inside my chest, but it's not from the physical exertion—it's the mental one. What happens now? What happens tomorrow? When will he leave me and go back to California? Will he come back?

He holds the door open, and I enter the apartment first. Then the door swishes closed with a near-silent click, but I don't hear Dante's footsteps. *Did he leave?* Tiny dots litter my vision, and sweat gathers on my upper lip.

It's terrifying how much I want him to be here and how quickly he's secured himself in my life. I turn slowly with dread weighing down my limbs, only to find him leaning against the door with a boyish smile that makes his dimples pop and his eyes glow in the moonlight.

"I've missed you," he says.

I release a breath so deep I'm sure it reaches him across the room. "We were only apart for an hour."

I grab the pendant around my neck, the one I made from my sister's engagement ring, and twist it back and forth on the chain. I had her diamond cut into smaller ones and the jeweler created two beautiful stars out of it. One for me and one for Ainsley. I had them set mine so it appears to float in a thick ring of platinum. Ainsley kept hers small, and she wears the delicate star like I wear mine—as a connection to a life once filled with love.

Dante was right about the dates, though. They're etched into the precious metal circle that gives me something to hold on to when I feel like I'm drowning.

He shakes his head. "I would dream about you." His slow, measured steps do nothing to ease the erratic thump of my pulse. "And then I'd wake up with a hard-on so painful I had to count to ten before I could walk." His voice grows raspy. "But that was nothing compared to the pain of realizing I didn't have you. It was like losing you over and over again."

The pendant around my neck makes a zip, zip, zip sound as I drag it back and forth—it's a comfort to me. It's so loud in my head that it blocks the rapid thoughts swarming rampant in my mind, and I can't stop myself from doing it tonight.

"Did you dream of me?" he asks. More steps. My heart sprints like it's in the running for a gold medal. "Does your body remember what your mind tried to forget?"

Holy hell.

"Tell me, Saylor. Did you miss riling me up and trying to set me off by simply breathing?"

He presses his body into mine, and the hard ridge of his erection sets my already simmering pulse on fire.

Dante places his palms on my hips, but I barely register them moving because his words glide over me like melting wax, stealing my concentration. "I want all your sounds, Sayls. The moans, the cries, your groans and screams."

He slides his hand into my hair, and I fight a whimper, but the second he tugs on my ponytail with enough force to shock a gasp from my lungs, the mewling sound he was chasing slips free.

"Yes, Saylor." His answering groan vibrates through my skull and has a direct line to my clit. "Tell me you remember."

"I remember." For the love of all things holy, I remember. Even when I tried to forget, he infiltrated my dreams and chased away my nightmares.

His teeth gently nip at the tender skin of my neck, and I groan, but it's his words that resonate through my soul. "Are you ready to make new memories with me?"

I shiver as his warm, wet tongue licks a line down the tendon stretched taut in my neck. He continues to walk me toward the wall until I fall into the frame, rattling the window.

Standing on my tiptoes, I try to reach for his lips, but he pulls back a fraction of an inch. My brain is hazy, and I don't want words. I want to feel—us. My harsh, panting breaths echo in my mind and sound like an explosion in the darkness of night.

"Are you going to let me touch you?" His throaty voice scratches against my skin. "Make you come?"

The only light in the room filters in from the moon that's high in the sky, but I miss nothing. I nod eagerly, and his blue eyes, framed in white, turn dark as night.

"I need you to think about this, Saylor." He sounds tortured. "Because if you let me touch you, I won't ever be able to let you go. Do you understand me?"

Logically, yes. At this moment? I couldn't even spell my own name.

"I mean it." His voice has a rough edge, but if it's anger or desire, I couldn't say.

I lift my face to his. The determination is there in the steely set of his jaw. His hands flex like he's fighting for control, but still, words elude me.

"If you let me touch you again, Saylor, that means you are mine. And I'm yours. I won't share. I won't debate. And I sure as fuck won't walk away ever again. So, before you let me touch you, think about what that means, and what I'm saying. Are you ready for forever?" His words dip low, and if he were anyone else, I'd be frightened by the sheer magnitude of what he's saying. But with him, all I hear is a promise. "I'll never let you go."

The intensity of his stare makes moisture pool between my legs. My heart is trying to escape my chest, but it's not panic or fear causing it to take flight. No, my body is reacting to the sincerity of his words—to the honesty of his statement—the knowledge that after all this time, I'm still the one. And even though my response is as visceral as a panic attack, this is something much more dangerous.

This is love, and despite my traitorous mind screaming at me, telling me that I'll only hurt him again, my body caves and ignores all the warnings.

"Touch me."

He pauses for the briefest of moments while searching my face for the deeper meaning. *Take me. Hold me. Love me. Never let me go.*

He reads it all in the blink of an eye, and then I'm airborne, resting in his arms, as he carries me to my bedroom.

Sounds fade into nothing until all I hear are our hearts beating in tandem as we fall back into us.

CHAPTER 20

DANTE

"*T*ouch me," she says.

My heart does a painful jump stop in the center of my chest as I set her down on her bed.

I study her face for signs that she heard what I said because I meant it all. I won't be able to walk away again. Doing so would not only break me, it would *ruin* me. It would be the equivalent of setting myself on fire and putting it out, only to do it again.

And I'm not a masochist.

Swirls of blue color her eyes until I see nothing but the truth, and my body hums with electric awareness. The room is so charged that I expect lights to flicker off our skin.

"Be sure about this." The warning bears repeating because she needs to understand how deadly serious I am. "If this happens, there's no going back. This is it, Sayls. I'll fight until my final breath to make sure you're mine. If we fall into bed right now, it might as well be falling into forever, because that's what it'll be. Our forever." My words break on the last few syllables, and it intensifies the painful weight trying to crush my lungs.

If she pushes me away, I'm not sure I'll survive it. She's staring at me like a wounded puppy, but I want her words almost as much as I need her love. It's an acknowledgment that we'll be a team and navigate this shitstorm together—no matter what life throws at us.

"Mio amato." She says it on a whisper of a breath, and a single tear slips down her face.

I press my fist against my breastbone hard enough to bruise, but it does nothing to calm the riot inside me that's fighting every pore for release.

Mio amato. My love. She took Italian in college so one day we could visit the village where my mother was born. She refused to say it the day she sent me away. Instead, she called me Dante with a cold, detached tone, and it sliced me open. The way she said it hurt almost as much as the words themselves.

"Say it again," I command through clenched teeth. It's the only way to keep my body from vibrating right off the bed. I'm a hair's breadth away from hitting the limits of what I can handle, and a grateful, choked sound gurgles in my throat when she opens her mouth.

"Mio amato." Saylor's lashes flutter slowly, and her expression flips back and forth between terrified and content faster than I can blink.

I keep my focus on her as I step off the bed and remove my shirt, then toss it to the floor. My shorts and boxer briefs drop to my feet. The sound of my belt hitting wood cracks through the silence of the moment. And then I'm standing before her, bare, wanting, and so full of love I fear I might actually implode.

"My love," I whisper huskily, then crawl up her body. She's lying on her back with her torso propped up on her elbows, watching me, memorizing me, fucking loving me.

She swallows noisily, and it lightens the moment. She's so

beautiful, and funny, and caring, even if she hides it behind a prickly exterior. And she's mine. After six long years, Saylor Greer is mine once more.

I place my hands on her hips and slip them beneath her T-shirt. Her skin is soft against my rough fingers as I lift the fabric. She falls back onto the bed when I remove it completely, and I sit on my knees, staring at her creamy skin with a dusting of freckles crossing her chest and shoulders.

"Dante." She shifts and tries to press her thighs together, but she can't get the friction she seeks because I'm straddling one leg.

It makes me deliriously happy. She's on the verge of combusting too, and I can't look away from her visible discomfort.

"I know what you need, Sayls. But I'm going at my speed. It's been too long since I've seen this body, and there's not a chance in hell I'm going to rush this."

"Dante," she growls and rises onto her forearms again with a scowl so fierce a lesser man would cave.

But not me.

Moving slowly, I advance on her like a panther circling his prey. When my hands are close enough to touch, she releases a shaky breath, but I hover them above her skin.

She whines in protest and thrusts her chest forward, pressing her tits into my waiting palms, and I finally come undone.

I work my fingers into the cups of her bra and yank it down so her breasts spill out over the top of it.

"Holy shit," I say reverently.

Her nipples pebble under my scrutiny, and the view makes my cock jerk against my leg as precome leaks from my slit. Saylor reaches between us, her silky hand wrapping around my shaft, and I allow it for a long moment while I revel in her touch before nudging her away.

Her furrowed brows drop into a scowl, and confusion clouds her eyes.

"You're going to come for me, sweetheart. Multiple times before I sink my cock into your needy little hole. You're going to come on my lips, my fingers, and then I'll do it all over again. I want you to make a fucking mess of this bed so when I do enter you, your arousal is all that fills the air."

Her chest heaves harder with each word that leaves my mouth.

"Can you do that for me? Can you come all over my face? Because if you do, I'm going to drink from you like a man dying of thirst."

"Holy shit. And you say I have a dirty mind."

Those muttered words pull a chuckle from me that releases all of the worry that's been holding me captive, and I hold the tab of her zipper between my thumb and forefinger before slowly sliding it down. When it reaches its end, just above her clit, I press down hard enough that her body jerks toward it, wanting it, needing the pressure. A quarter of an inch more and she'd get exactly what she wants.

Her stomach quivers, and I press down again before hooking my hands into the waistband of her shorts. I tug them down over her hips, pausing to kiss and nip her skin whenever the need arises.

"You do have a dirty mind, Sayls. But I put your words into practice."

I carelessly toss her clothes, and she gasps. Her noises have always made me feel more animal than man, and tonight I'm holding onto control by a quickly unraveling thread.

"You weren't wearing panties."

The devil that lives inside my girl shows himself in her rosy cheeks. "They were bothering me."

I run a lazy finger from her ankle to the juncture of her

thighs, connecting each freckle as I go. I allow my hands to roam her skin, but my gaze zeros in hungrily on her pussy.

Leaning forward, I tug roughly on the neatly cropped landing strip of hair. It's new, and I'm not sure if I like it. It causes a murderous bout of jealousy I've never experienced before.

She writhes on the bed and thrusts her wanting mound into my hand.

"Who is this for?"

She gasps, and her back arches off the bed, so I do it again, and her hands lift to caress my face.

"Who is this for, Saylor?" I'm a growling boar right now, but fuck me if I can control it.

"Me. You. Ah…" Each word leaves her mouth on a pant. "Research." She moans, and the muscles in my jaw relax.

"Research?" I ask as I lower myself to the bed. She opens her legs wide, making room for me, and pleasure ripples through my body when she grinds against me.

"For a character. Spice. Geez," she whimpers, then I slide a finger through her damp skin, and it evolves into a loud moan.

"You're already wet for me, sweetheart. But it's not enough. When I'm done with you, you'll have no idea where you begin and where I end."

"That's what I'm afraid of," she mumbles, even as she rides my hand and lifts hers to pluck at one nipple.

"No need to be afraid." I trace my finger around her clit, teasing, winding her pleasure higher. "We're a team, and I've always got you."

I don't give her time to respond. I'm too out of my mind and ravenous for a taste of her, so I stiffen my tongue and run it through her folds until I find that sweet bundle of nerves that I've missed. Taking it between my teeth, I strum against it with my tongue until her skin glistens with perspiration.

I bite down harder, and she screams my name, but I ease up right before she comes.

"Asshole," she moans. Then I press two thick fingers into her and grab my cock with my other hand. I squeeze myself just this side of painful to keep from coming before I've even felt her wrapped around me.

Saylor's pussy clamps down on my fingers, and I attack her clit with vigor.

Forget what I said. She'll come once and then again when I'm inside of her. I can't wait any longer than that to slip into her wet heat.

One flick.

One moan.

One twist of my fingers.

And she comes apart below me in the most sensual symphony of moans and screams and my motherfucking name.

I lap at her entrance until she stops shaking, and I silently curse myself for going without her for so damn long.

My muscles are wound so tightly I could crack into a million pieces, but I hold my thickening length in my hand and guide it through her wetness. Once I'm coated in her, I pump against her clit until panic flashes in her expression.

"You can take it, baby." I move my hips faster and apply more pressure to my cock as it rides that over-sensitized bundle of nerves.

"I've missed you, Saylor."

She nods. Does she understand, or is she too blissed out to hear reason?

"I never stopped loving you," I admit, and it's still the most liberating confession I've ever made. Her body is glistening and primed for another orgasm already. "I still love you. That will never change."

My words are her undoing. I halt my movements and take in every inch of her body. Her eyes pinch closed, and her mouth falls open, emitting the most delicious sounds I want to swallow. The flush of her skin sparks more flames of desire.

"How much of your body will blush for me?" I ask, staring at her thighs that convulse around my body.

Leaning down, I press my lips to hers in a gentle kiss. When I pull back, my words ghost over her lips. "I love you, my sweet and sassy Saylor girl." Her heart shows in her expression because tonight she's not guarded, and it takes my breath away.

Her body pulses with the aftershocks of her orgasm, but I'm not ready for this moment to end, so I press her knees to her shoulders and enter her with one long, torturously slow thrust.

"You're so"—a grunt escapes as her warmth wraps around me—"tight," I say through clenched teeth. Her inner walls flex and squeeze, trying to keep me out, and I'm forced to make smaller, more shallow thrusts. "Let me in, Sayls. Please, for the love of God, let me in."

Let me into your body, your life, your heart.

My words send a rush of warmth to her opening. Thank fuck. Her natural lubrication covers my cock as I seek entrance to the most private piece of her. Then, finally, her walls quake around me before finally relaxing enough for me to get the last inch inside of her.

When I'm seated fully in her warmth, my pelvis rubs against her clit, and I give her a second to acclimate to my size, but I never release her gaze from mine.

Together, like this, as one, I feel whole for the first time since our lives spiraled so far out of our control.

"God," she says, arching her back as much as she can with me pressing her knees into her chest. Her neck strains, and her rapid heartbeat fluttering against delicate flesh calls to me. I'm completely entranced. "I—I forgot how long and, fuck," she groans again, "how thick you are."

Irritation and pride fight for dominance in my mind. I am truly a possessive Neanderthal when it comes to her.

I push forward with one rough, shallow upward thrust, and she narrows her eyes at me.

"I never forgot how tight *you* are, Saylor. Or how you choked my cock when I went as deep as possible. Or how you'd mewl when I'd grind against you and push a little deeper."

I reach around her and squeeze her ass until I reach her slit, then run a finger over her, spreading her arousal back to the puckered skin I was searching for.

"And I never forgot how you scream and writhe when I slip past this ring of muscle." I pause, searching her face for approval, and I get it when she presses back against my finger. When it slips inside her ass, I adjust my hips and pummel into her with years of pent-up frustration and love that had no outlet. She's the only one who could ever tame the beast within, but now we've set it free.

"Dante." Her head thrashes wildly on the pillows and her fingers land on my chest with a slap. One hand marks my skin with her nails while the other twists and pinches my right nipple.

She does remember.

My thrusts are uneven and primal. I piston into her like I'm trying to get deep enough that she'll never be able to leave me again.

"You. Are. Mine," I say, slamming home with each word. "Say it."

216

Glassy, lust-filled eyes the color of a summer sky give a slow blink.

"Say it, Saylor. Goddamn it. Say it." I sound out of control, but she does that to me. She can break me, she can ruin my control, and she can make me whole.

"Yes," she cries out loud enough to shake the roof. "I'm yours. I'm yours. I'm yours." She sobs as violent tremors course through her body. It's a confession of her own that will terrify her as much as it will set her free. But I'm too lost in the moment to soothe her fears—that'll come later. The rhythmic pulsing of her pussy milks my dick until I explode.

I collapse, my body sheltering hers, and we slowly come down from the sex-induced high. Our breathing evens out and syncs.

It's the calm in the middle of a storm headed straight for us. We may not be as strong as we once were yet, but our connection, the way we fit together, is that once-in-a-lifetime love she writes about. We will weather whatever comes our way. Of that, I'm sure.

Eventually, as the perspiration dries to our skin and a chill creeps in, I ease out of her. Despite my dick being hard again, her head lulls drowsily, and my body is fighting a decade-long exhaustion.

"Stay here," I murmur. "I'll get a cloth to clean—oh, shit. Saylor…"

"I felt it. It's okay, it's not your fault. I didn't think about a condom either."

"That's not your job." Panic falls through my body like dominoes. What the hell is wrong with me?

She scowls and presses on my chest. "What century are you living in, Dante?" My body tenses at my name. I guess mio amato will take some time to become a habit again. "Women are as responsible for safe sex as men. I'm on the pill, and I have condoms, I…"

"For who? Are you sleeping with someone else?" My heart doesn't beat for a full thirty seconds as she stares at me. A jealous beast roars in my ears, and he sounds ferocious in my words.

What the fuck is going on with me? I've never had a jealous bone in my body, but it's found a light within me when it comes to Saylor. First with Grady, who I probably owe an apology to, and now here, in our bed.

I'm an asshole.

She slides up the mattress and crosses her arms. "For your information, they've never been opened, but they're a precaution, just in case." Her eyes, like burning embers, glare at me. "How many people have *you* slept with since you left?"

The calm of a moment ago begins to rattle and shake.

"Three," I say, watching her reaction closely.

The muscles in her face tighten, and she swallows multiple times but doesn't say anything. Guilt consumes me. It always did. It's why I didn't keep relationships.

"What about you?" I ask gently while trying to keep the rage from consuming my tone. I don't mean to be a hypocrite, but for fuck's sake. Imagining her with anyone else is screwing me up. *What do you think it's doing to her, asshole?* I try to swallow past a boulder of guilt in my throat, but it doesn't budge.

Her chin shifts like she's grinding her teeth, then her gaze drops to her lap, and her hand tugs her pendant along the chain.

She doesn't say anything, but she slowly shakes her head.

None. She slept with no one. More proof that she stopped living. And the worst part is, I can see more clearly why she thought I'd moved on.

"I'm sorry. I'm so sorry." The words are so quiet I'm not even sure she hears them, but it's an acknowledgment of my mistakes, of hers, of ours, and it's a promise to fix our entire fucking world.

Exhaustion consumes me as the enormity of the last few days wash over me. It's evident on Saylor's face too, with the dark circles trying to peek through delicate skin. Every inch of my body screams for rest, but I walk on dead legs and grab a wet cloth from the bathroom.

Her head is still bowed when I return, but she allows me to clean her legs. It's so much more intimate than anything else we did tonight. And I love it so much more. This is a trust she's giving me. To care for her body. To protect it from harm. Now I'll have to convince her to give me her heart too.

When I've cleaned her the best I can, I sit back on my heels and stare at her until the weight of the silence makes her look up.

It always did. She loves the silence, but not when it's deafening.

I toss the towel to the floor and slide under the covers while her gaze stays on mine. Once we're settled, I pull her body to me, and she rests her head above my heart as I recline against the headboard.

My mind races. I need to say something—acknowledge what I've done and she didn't do. I can't allow regret to derail us though, so once again, I tell her the truth.

"I never moved on, sweetheart. There's no replacing you, even when I desperately wanted the pain to stop—it's always been you. It's time to start living again, and I want to do that by your side."

I allow my chin to droop and kiss the top of her head.

Saylor's breathing evens out almost immediately, and her body sags into mine as sleep overtakes her.

It takes some maneuvering, but I lay us both flat, with her still on my chest, and I run my fingers through her hair while thoughts of our future play out like a black-and-white movie.

But I'm ready to enter our lives in living, vibrant colors, and I'll blow up the world to keep Saylor at my side because failure is not an option. Not this time.

With that promise running through my mind like an oath, I drift off to a peaceful, sated sleep.

CHAPTER 21

SAYLOR

*W*hy am I so freaking hot? Taking stock of my body, I can't quite register what's happening. There's a heavy forearm draped against my bare skin near my ribs with a hand splayed open on my collarbone like a human necklace. I rub my legs together. Hmm, no pants on either.

Geez, Sassy. Get your shit together. I close my heavy lids again, willing my brain to wake up for a change. It must be super early if I can't think. Am I hungover? Maybe I'm hungover. That would at least explain things.

But my head doesn't hurt, it's—blissfully empty.

Then why, for the love of the goddamn sun, am I sweating into my pillow? I hate being hot, and I roll over with a groan. Please don't let the AC be out again.

Well, I try to roll over. I only make it two inches onto my side when I hit a human wall.

"Argh. What the. How the. What?" After my initial scream, each word pitches higher until I sound like a shrill stadium announcer.

"Good morning, Oscar. Glad to see you wake up angry and it's not only me who makes you that way."

Finally, I suck air into my lungs like it'll be my last, and I push up onto my knees, which causes the sheet to pool at my sides. My snarled hair blocks my vision again, so I pull it from my face with both hands. I'm still crushing my hair to my skull when my vision clears, and a too-charming smile nearly blinds me.

"Dante," I hiss.

"Don't do it," he demands. His voice is husky with sleep and wraps around my core like the most powerful vibrator.

Like lifting a zipper, every muscle in my body tenses in a slow incline from my toes to my ears, even as a flush races across my skin. Memories invade every sense. Images of him above me and in me. His smell. His touch. His words. Our taste.

"Do what?" Jesus. I am bitchy in the morning. That's easy to forget when you wake up alone every day for years.

"Don't pull away." He lifts onto one elbow and does a lazy perusal of my body. The heat in his gaze licks across my skin like flames. I'd be convinced his hands were on me if I wasn't presently glaring at him.

"I'm. Not." My teeth clench until my jaw aches, and I'm not sure if it's my normal morning attitude or fear of what comes next.

"Are you sure?" Is he mocking me?

Am I sure? He told me his rules. He said if we did this, he wouldn't be able to leave again. He said...

"Saylor?"

Jesus. When did I close my stinking eyes again? Am I dreaming? As inconspicuously as possible, I pinch my thigh. "Ouch." Dang it. Not sleeping.

Dante's rich silvery laughter makes my nipples pebble to painful points. My body has always had a physical reaction to the sound of him. It's annoying and pretty inconvenient at the moment.

"You're not dreaming, Oscar. And you're not going back on your word. I'm here with you, and that's not changing."

With one harsh tug from his muscular arms, I fall forward into his kiss, and my body uncoils into a pool of mush. Soft lips and rough whiskers kiss me and ghost over my jaw, down my neck, and back again. The scrape of his stubble abrading my skin is the most delicious kind of pain.

"Sassy?" Grady's voice slices through the air like a bullhorn.

"What's he doing here?" Dante grumbles.

"What? What time is it?"

I crawl over him and reach for my phone. Noon? How the hell is it noon? "Shit. We overslept. He's dropping Lilly off for her shift." I roll again and misjudge the edge of the mattress, and I land on my ass with a loud thud.

"Sass?" Grady's boots clomp loudly up the stairs, the sound pounding in my skull as I scramble to do—something. This is what I get for giving him a key.

"Ah, I'm coming. Hold on," I yell.

Dante laughs and moves languidly through the room. But he still manages to get dressed before I've even stood up.

"I've got it," he says, offering me a hand.

I'm enslaved by his needy gaze that never leaves my naked body as I uncurl from the floor.

"Fuck." He sighs before turning and going to intercept Grady.

"Tell him I'll be down in five," I call to his back.

Fuck doesn't begin to cover it. Something tells me my life is about to get really freaking messy.

But at least you're living. I spin in place, and a chill wraps around my body as sweat dots my skin. The words that ghosted through my mind sounded exactly like my sister, and they were gone as quickly as they came. It's enough to stall the air in my lungs.

God, Shan. I miss you. I'm not someone who prays often, but I do occasionally speak to my sister, and the urge to ask her for a sign bubbles in my throat. *Am I going to be okay?*

～

THE AIR IS thick with tension when I make it downstairs, but I can't read Dante's or Grady's expressions.

"What's up?" I ask, and both men turn to me with varying shades of unease, but neither says anything.

"They're seeing who has the bigger schlong," Lilly says from her perch at the register where she's reading. I fight and fail to hide a smirk. After her parents died, Lilly retreated from everything she normally loved. And it seemed to get worse when Grady became her guardian. They had growing pains figuring out their new dynamic. But in the last year, she's started to show signs of life again.

"Lilly." Grady's voice cuts through the tension.

Lilly shrugs. "They're both giving each other warnings when the truth is, Dante is in love with you, and Grady loves you…" Grady's face turns purple. "Because you're his best friend and he struggles with boundaries, he's here making sure Dante doesn't mess up, and Dante is telling Grady that he's got it covered. There, was that so hard?"

Throughout her entire spiel, she never once took her eyes off her book. I would have laughed if the testosterone in the room weren't cloyingly dense.

Dante does.

"Yeah," he chuckles. "That about covers it."

Grady's face shifts from purple to a slightly less angry shade of red.

We're making progress.

"Are you—"

A FaceTime call cuts off my question. The telltale ring has us all reaching for our phones.

Dante lifts his. "It's Lena." He accepts with a wide grin, no doubt excited to see Poppy. His expression is sad whenever he talks about her. Being away from her is getting to him.

Will he resent missing out on her everyday life if he stays here?

"What's wrong?" Dante's voice changes in a heartbeat.

"He— I — She was at dance. I." Lena is dragging in painful, sobbing breaths in between each word, and I reach for my pendant on reflex.

Zip. Zip. Zip. The sound of the chain reflects the harshness of my breath as I cross the room to stand beside Dante.

Lena's beautiful face is streaked with tears and mascara. The air shifts as Grady moves forward too. If Dante has a Mr. Fix-It complex, Grady has a savior one.

"Take a deep breath," Dante says. His voice strains and his pain hits as hard as my own.

"He. I brought P-Poppy to dance. I only left to get a coffee down the street." We can understand her words, but it's filtered through fear and pain that lances my heart. "When I was walking back, I saw him taking her from dance. Her arm. His grip. She was crying, and I ran. He, he was trying to take her, Dante. And he was on something else this time, he had to be. There was no emotion when he grabbed her hard enough to bruise."

Dante's body begins to vibrate next to me.

"He didn't let go when I grabbed her around the waist. He didn't let go when I begged him and she cried out in pain." She chokes on a sob so broken it causes a sensation that rivals my worst panic attacks. "He pushed me and pulled her, but I didn't let go. I…"

"Lena." Dante's voice is tortured. "Do you have Poppy now?"

She nods, and tears spill out over her cheekbones.

"Where. Is. Trent?" There's a deadly calm to his tone that I'm sure is for Lena's benefit. He hides how his body shakes and his knuckles turn white, but I'm witness to it all.

I place a hand in the center of his back, and his breathing slows, but nothing will bottle up the fear vibrating through him.

Grady stands on Dante's other side, so close you couldn't slip a piece of paper between them, and for Lena's sake, I'm glad only Dante is visible on the screen. Together, they're a wall of barely contained rage hidden behind layers of muscle.

"I don't know. One of the dads from dance saw what was happening and stepped in. I'm not sure what to do," Lena cries. "He went to my parents' house this morning, but we were already gone."

Dante doesn't say anything as he processes this information. I can tell he's trying to fix this. Find the solution. Create the game plan, but it's Grady who shocks me by speaking.

"Bring them here." His lips barely move as he speaks.

Dante turns his head in question.

"Bring. Them. Here," he repeats.

"I know what it's like when someone loses themselves so completely into addiction."

His confession knocks the wind out of me. Up until now, I thought I was the only one who knew his story.

"It will escalate," Grady continues. "He will keep coming for everyone you love. Bring them here where they can be safe while you figure out how to contain him."

Grady doesn't say anything else as he retreats and leans against the wall. Am I the only one who can see how unnaturally his chest rises and falls?

I stand in silence as Dante talks to Lena.

"You take the summers off anyway, Lena. He's right. It might be best if you came here. We'll cover your expenses with Trent's payouts from Ascendancy Inc."

"Is that even legal?" she asks.

Dante shrugs. "I'll worry about that later. The most important thing now is to get you here, so I have everyone I care about safe. Then I'll figure out what the hell to do about my brother."

I don't hear Lena's response. My mind is doing its thing at the most inopportune time. I try to focus, but a story about a protector and a single mom unfurls as they speak.

By the time Dante faces me, I'm deep into the plot. But when he stands in front of me and places his hands on my biceps, I blink to bring him into focus.

"I should have asked you, Sayls. I'm sorry. I…"

"What?" I shake my head to clear the story webs from my mind. "What are you talking about?"

Dante shoots Grady a nervous expression.

"About Lena and Poppy coming here. I reacted, but I promise you, Lena and I have only ever been friends."

If the situation weren't so dire, I'd laugh. Not once did I question his loyalty.

My mouth drops open with short puffs of air, and perspiration dots my upper lip.

Not once did I question his loyalty.

Grumpy's voice rings in my head. *"Loyalty and love are what will keep you sane, Sassy. Loyalty and love. Don't ever take it for granted."*

"Saylor?"

I shake my head so hard that I get dizzy. "No. Sorry. Of course. It's fine."

Dante and Grady share another expression that annoys me. Ugh. The last thing I need is them ganging up on me.

"I'm serious. Sorry, I just…got lost in my head for a

minute." My fist flies to my hip, and I let the sass explode. "I told you that would happen, and it does. I'm fine."

I can tell he doesn't believe me, but he doesn't say anything else.

"Where are we going to put them?" I tilt my head to the ceiling. "Can we even get a bed in my office?" My office is technically another bedroom, but the problem with these old homes is that the room is the size of a modern-day walk-in closet.

"They'll stay with me," Grady says with an eerie calm that freezes everyone in place.

"Ah, what was that big guy?" I'm sure I heard him wrong.

"The apartment above my garage is the safest place in Hope Hollow, and it's as close to you as you'll find around here. They'll be at least forty minutes away if they stay in a hotel. There's an apartment next door, but that building has been boarded up for years. It'd take six months to renovate. It's the only option." He finishes on a growl, daring us to question him.

"But why?" I ask. This is the most un-Grady-like thing I've ever seen him do. He doesn't like people in his space. Even when his brother lived there, he was an unbearable asshole. My gaze snags on Lilly, who is watching this unfold. Her expression is soft, with a smile playing across her face.

I'm seriously starting to rethink my whole abducted-by-aliens theory, but Grady's next words send a shard of ice straight into my veins.

"Because no one should live through the fear of losing a child like that. No one should be terrified that the boogeyman is lurking in the shadows. And if his brother"— he hooks his thumb toward Dante—"is as far gone as the blogs say, that's all that family will ever know until he's stopped—or dead."

Silence hangs like the threat of rain.

Lilly and I gape at Grady. Dante vibrates with fury. And we all just stand there, in stunned silence.

Grady's nod breaks the trance. "Get them here. I'll make sure the apartment is clean and has everything they'll need." He's already halfway to the door.

"Grady," Dante calls.

He pauses with his hand on the doorknob.

"Thank you."

Grady responds with one curt nod, then leaves my bookstore, with the rest of us wondering what the hell happened.

CHAPTER 22

DANTE

*S*aylor stands beside me at baggage claim in JFK Airport, but she's shifting her weight from one foot to the other, and her neck has an angry red line from tugging on her necklace.

I reach over and take her hand in both of mine. "I'm glad you came with me."

"I'm not much help. You're supposed to be worrying about them, not if I'm going to have a nervous breakdown and embarrass you in front of all the cameras." Her nose scrunches as soon as the words are out of her mouth, and my jaw ticks as I remember the twenty or so men looming behind the glass wall with cameras pointed in our direction.

The pointer finger of her other hand traces a pattern on her thigh, and I'm momentarily struck by the movement. It triggers something familiar—a memory, perhaps. She splays her fingers wide on her thigh when she catches me staring, and I'm dragged back to the present.

"I will always worry about you, Saylor, but not because I think you'll embarrass me. So, get that shit out of your head right now," I say, shaking my head. At what point did she lose all her confidence? And how the hell do I help her get it back?

"Unca!" My body relaxes when I hear Poppy's shoes smacking against the tile floor. I squeeze Saylor's hand, then release it as Poppy launches herself at me. Lena is right behind her, carrying multiple bags.

"Unca. Unca. Unca. I missted you the mostest."

"You missed me the mostest, huh?"

The little girl in my arms nods in earnest.

"Yes. I did. Wight, Mommy?" Lena jumps at her name, and she worries her hands.

"Sure thing, sweet pea," she says.

Poppy's hands land on my cheeks, and she peppers my face with sloppy kisses, but I speak through it. "You're safe here, Lena. And we'll keep it that way even if—*he* shows up in town."

Pudgy fingers poke and stretch my face every which way. "I missed you a ton, Lollipop. Not sure if you can beat that."

She frowns at me, but somehow it still reminds me of sunshine. "Oh, I did. Unca. I so beat you."

Saylor laughs to my right, and we all track her in slow-motion. She freezes instantly with her hand holding her necklace in a death grip.

Lena moves forward to introduce herself, but Poppy pushes off me with her legs to propel herself at Saylor.

Luckily, Saylor moves quickly and catches my wild little niece before she face-plants on the floor, but she holds Poppy under her armpits and away from her body. What does she think Poppy will do, bite?

I fight back a chuckle.

Poppy and her lack of need for personal space don't allow it for long, though. She reaches out with her legs and draws herself to Saylor like a spider monkey.

Saylor's face has turned a scary shade of gray as she wraps

her arms around Poppy. Not that Poppy gave her any choice as she tries to lock her legs around Saylor. I'll take it as a win that she didn't immediately drop the little girl.

But even grouchy Saylor is no match for Poppy and her lack of boundaries. I watch in amusement as Poppy leans in and plants kisses all over Saylor's scrunched-up face.

"Poppy, give Saylor some space," Lena says, but it falls on deaf ears. Poppy is in her full-on look-at-me phase.

"You is more pwetty than your pictures," Poppy gushes, and Saylor holds my niece's gaze.

Disbelief forms in the wrinkle between Saylor's brows—always the skeptic. I told her she's always been a part of my life.

"You've seen pictures of me?"

Poppy shifts, blocking Saylor's face from view. Lena stands at my shoulder, and we watch the two most important girls in my life meet for the first time.

"Yup." Poppy pops her P with a flourish. "Unca's gots them eveywheres. Ev—ery—wheres. His desk and his bed and his walls and his money holder and…"

"Okay, there, motormouth," I say, pulling Poppy away from Saylor and resting her on my hip. "We should get going." I nod toward the paparazzi, and Lena flinches.

"I only checked one bag. It should be…oh, there it is." She runs forward and hauls the large suitcase off the carousel, and she's back a second later with open arms and pulling Saylor in for a hug.

Yeah, this will be an adjustment for Saylor, and that thought makes my teeth ache from the sweetness of it all.

"It's so nice to finally meet you, Saylor."

"Ah, okay," Saylor replies with a pale face. "You too?"

Lena breezes right over her discomfort as Saylor takes bags from her hands.

"Dante has talked about you nonstop for years, so I feel

like I already know you. I'm sorry we're crashing into your lives like this. And for that phone call a few days ago." Lena is uncharacteristically jumpy and stares down at her feet. "I wasn't at my best. I can usually hold myself together better than that."

Saylor shocks me when she places a firm hand on Lena's forearm, halting her forward motion. Saylor's body tenses like she's shocked herself too. "It was a terribly traumatic experience," she says in a solid, kind tone. "Dante would have been worried if you didn't react like that."

Then she pulls back just as quickly as she'd reached out. Her finger dances across her thigh again, and a little more color drains from her face. She said I would have been worried, but her expression says she would have been too.

Lena's eyes fill with moisture, and she takes a step back. "Thank you. For that. And for all of this. We'll try to stay out of your way so you can write. Poppy doesn't exactly make a peaceful environment."

"Actually," I start, then shift Poppy to my back so I can take Lena's suitcase in one hand while holding Saylor's in my other. Poppy clutches my neck and restricts my breathing. I didn't quite think this through.

"You fool. I've got this," Lena says, taking the suitcase back so I can prop Poppy up with one arm.

"Sorry." I shrug.

She chuckles and pats my bicep. "Lead the way," she says, pointing in front of her.

"But what I was going to say is"—I glance to my right to gauge her reaction as we walk toward the exit—"you're going to stay with Saylor's best friend, Grady. Well, not in his house, exactly. He has an apartment above his garage. It's secluded and secure and only a few miles from us. It's the best we can do, Lena. The closest hotel is forty minutes away, and Saylor's guest room isn't big enough for the both of you."

"Whatever you think is best. I trust you." She has always taken things in stride, but there's a fragility to her tone today, presumably because Trent has thrown her off-balance.

Saylor surprises me by squeezing my hand, so I return the gesture before releasing it and pulling her close. I drape my arm over her shoulders while I remove Poppy from my back and tuck her into my side, shielding her from the photogs.

The four of us huddle together as we exit the safety of the terminal and push through the throng of photographers. Thankfully, JFK is used to this, and security arrives within seconds to escort us to my rental car.

They stand guard while I buckle Poppy into her car seat, then we all slip into the SUV and drive home. There's a war brewing, but I also can't shake the sense that this is exactly where we're all meant to be.

Together.

～

I TURN right onto Grady's dirt drive and take it slow over potholes and turns I'm not used to navigating yet. When we finally pull into a clearing, Grady is sitting in front of his house in one of four Adirondack chairs that were not there yesterday.

That's not all that looks different. There are also potted plants hanging from the guest house balcony, a swing set that's only partly constructed in the corner, what looks like a kiddie pool, and pink plastic toys littering the yard.

"What the fu—unicycle is all this?" Saylor asks. She chances a quick peek to the back seat with a guilty expression. It's cute, but I'm more impressed she caught herself. It's taken me years to get my curses under control around little ears.

"It seems Grady might be more excited about having guests than he let on," I say, barely suppressing a laugh.

Lena leans forward between the two front seats and gawks at the sight before us. "Did he...did he do all of this for—us?"

My heart pinches. Lena hasn't had the easiest life, and she never takes charity. It's all I can do to get her to take money from me that I promised is coming out of Trent's company shares. It's not, but he's not paying child support, so I had to do something.

"It's not his usual modus operandi, that's for sure," Saylor says, a little wonder sprinkling her tone. She shrugs. "First time for everything, I guess."

Poppy fell asleep halfway home, so the three of us sit there and stare at Grady through the windshield.

After a few moments, he stands briskly, obviously annoyed at our slack-jawed ogling.

"Are you just going to sit there and stare at me?" He doesn't raise his voice. Not really. But we all hear him clear as day anyway. He points an angry finger at me. "Do not make this weird, Thompson."

Shaking my head, I open my door, which wakes Poppy. This kid is the polar opposite of Saylor because she wakes up singing. The song of the day today is "Bibbidi-Bobbidi-Boo."

Grady's going to love it.

Opening my door spurs the girls into action, and they exit the car while I grab Poppy. As soon as she's unbuckled, she squirms until I set her on her feet, and then she takes off running straight to Grady.

Well, huh. That's new. Poppy normally shies away from new men, but Saylor and Lena are almost to him, too, so I hurry to catch up, and I'm just in time to hear Poppy say, "You're big."

"Yes," Grady says. At least his tone is gentler than anything he's used with me.

Poppy waves her hand, motioning for Grady to come closer, but he frowns at us because she's already nearly touching him. Then she uses two hands to gesture, and he slides gracefully to one knee.

She places both hands on his shoulders and pats him like she's about to pronounce him king. "Do you have friends?"

Grady flashes a panicked expression my way, silently pleading for help, and I laugh.

"Kids," I offer. "Poppy calls all kids friends."

He shakes his head in response and scans every inch of the little girl.

I squeeze Lena's shoulder affectionately, but all the color has drained from her face like she's seen a ghost as she watches Grady with Poppy. I have no idea why. Maybe it's because she hasn't been around a lot of good men in her life? Grady may piss me off, but he is a good man. I'll need to remember to tell her that.

"Nah," Grady croaks, then clears his throat and tries again. "I don't have any kids." Poppy moves forward and climbs onto his bent knee, hugging him tightly around the neck so she doesn't fall off.

"So why ya have so many toys?" She's fascinated by him, and my shoulders shake with silent laughter at his obvious discomfort.

Saylor smacks my chest, but her eyes are smiling too.

Grady tugs at the back of his neck. "I guess I thought you'd need some stuff while you were here."

Poppy reacts like an old-school cartoon with big expressions and even bigger gestures. "You gots this stuff for me?"

"To use," Lena says, stepping forward. Her voice quivers, and her hands shake. Trent has scared the shit out of her.

236

"We're borrowing them. You have to give everything back when we go home."

Grady's face pinches together, and his cheeks turn red. "No, you don't," he tells Poppy.

"Yes, she does," Lena says, standing her ground. "We work hard for our—toys."

Poor Grady. He means well, but he needs to learn not to step on momma bear's toes.

"And sometimes, it's okay to take a gift," he grumbles while standing and taking Poppy with him. He rests her on his hip like it's the most natural thing in the world.

Saylor makes a choked sound next to me, and it expresses everything happening inside my head. Damn it, Grady. Back down! Mayday, mayday, mayday. I try to signal him, but he's already zeroed in on Lena.

Well, now. That's—interesting. I haven't seen Grady pay this much attention to anyone since I've been home, and that includes my girl. I quickly look to my left and find the same bewilderment on Saylor's face.

"I appreciate that," Lena says through clenched teeth.

Oh, shit. It's my turn to interrupt.

"Ah, Grady, this is Lena. She greatly appreciates your kindness. Lena, this is Grady. Compromises are hard-fought with him, but you'll work it out." I don't hide the mirth in my tone as they stare at each other.

If looks had a temperature, theirs would be nuclear.

Something haunts Grady's expression as he studies Poppy's features.

"My butt wiggle giggles when I faht. Does your butt wiggle giggle when you faht?" she asks.

His nose wrinkles, and Poppy's entire body shakes with laughter.

Saylor snorts but holds in a laugh. "Why are farts so funny?" she asks, clutching her stomach like it hurts.

Lena's face is a horrifying shade of red, but it's my niece who saves us all from having to say anything.

"Gwody? I gots to pee."

Grady splutters and practically sprints up the stairs to the apartment, with the rest of us scrambling after him.

He opens the apartment door, sets her on her feet, and points across the room to the bathroom. She takes off running, and Lena pushes through, saying, "Excuse me," and follows Poppy to the restroom.

It's only been two days since I was here dropping off new linens, so I immediately notice the changes he's made in here too. Grady finds me taking it all in but cuts me off before I can say anything. "Do not say a word. I needed to update the place anyway. This merely sped up my timeline. Plus," he says grumpily, "she doesn't have to do everything herself."

"No," I say gently. "But it's all she's ever known, so take it easy with the pushy neighbor bit, okay?"

Poppy runs full speed out of the bathroom and attaches herself to Grady's leg. Lena returns a moment later.

"False alarm. Poppy has a strange fascination with restrooms. I'm still hoping it's a phase," Lena says while attempting to detach her little girl, but it only makes Poppy cling harder.

"It's okay," Grady says in a low, controlled voice. "I'll, ah, show you the place." He reaches into his pocket and produces a key that he quickly shoves into her hand. She pulls back from his touch like a rocket, and Saylor's smirk practically shines from across the room.

"Yeah, okay. Thank you. Grady."

He studies her face for a fraction of a second before he goes real estate agent on us and shows them both around the apartment. At this point, I'm not even surprised to find Poppy's room decorated with ponies and flowers. But again, Grady glares at me, the warning clear: don't say a word.

Lena is still trying to pry Poppy off Grady, so she misses the entire interaction happening above her head.

I mime zipping my lips shut, but humor must spark in my eyes because he growls. And because Poppy is sitting on his foot and clinging to his leg as he walks through the apartment, she hears it and growls back.

He stops short and looks down at my niece. "Did you growl at me?"

"You's started it, Gwody." She shines her magic on him, and the miracle of all miracles happens. Grady Reid smiles.

"I did, didn't I?" I can't read his expression, but there's an unexpected kindness in his tone.

Poppy shrugs, releases his leg, and runs into her room to touch everything, so I stand beside Grady. Lena's and Saylor's voices are a low murmur as they walk back into the living room. Appreciation hits me hard as I glance around the apartment. It's above and beyond anything I ever expected. But that doesn't mean I won't rib him a little.

"If I knew that all it takes to get you to smile is to call you Grody, I would have done it a long time ago, but if you tell me your butt wiggle giggles, I'm officially calling us friends."

"She didn't say Grody. She said Gwody. It's different."

"Sure it is, pal. Sure it is." I clap him on the back, and he turns, trying to shrug me off. "Thank you, Grady, for all of this. Whatever ghosts forced your hand, I appreciate that you made the effort more than you could know. I owe you one."

He brushes past me in the hallway. "Don't hurt Sassy, and we'll call it even."

It's not, but I'll file his favor away for another time. Something tells me he'll need it at some point.

He pauses in the hall but doesn't turn back to me, and I can tell he's trying not to laugh when his shoulders shake. "Everyone's butt wiggle giggles. I've just never heard it put quite that way."

My unexpected bark of laughter fills the space between us. "My new goal in life is to get you to say your butt wiggle giggles as often as I can."

A growl vibrates in his chest, then he stalks off, but I'm happier than I've been in a very long time. This is family.

With one last kiss to the top of Poppy's head, I join the adults in the family room.

Grady is explaining how the alarm system works, and I drop my hands to my hips because that's definitely been upgraded since I stopped by the other day.

What are you hiding, Grady Reid?

By the time he leaves, Lena's exhausted, so I quickly check the fridge to make a list for the store, but it and the cabinets are already fully stocked. Fucking Grady.

"Are you okay?" I ask. Lena's a little shell-shocked, and even Saylor is showing concern on her face.

"Yeah, thank you, both. I didn't mean to sound ungrateful. It's just. And I…"

"Shh, it's okay," I say gently, pulling her in for a hug.

"I'm so tired, Dante. Bone-crushingly tired."

Guilt gnaws at my throat. "You've been through a lot, Lena. But you've got us. Let us help, okay?"

She nods, then pulls away.

"We'll let you get to bed," Saylor says. "But I saw Grady left his number by the toaster, so I wrote mine down, too."

"If you need anything, call us," I say. "We'll come by in the morning to get whatever else you'll need."

"And, um, Lena?" Saylor shifts her weight from foot to foot, and her voice wobbles a little. "Grady might be gruff and pushy, but he's one of the best men I've ever known. You will be safe here."

Lena nods thoughtfully. "I'm not used to being in someone else's care."

Saylor's gaze cuts to me. "Neither am I, Lena, but I'm

—trying."

Lena charges Saylor and wraps her in a hug, but she stands like a statue, and when she can't take the affection anymore, she pulls away and shakes a shiver from her body.

I hug Lena too, and then we wait outside to hear the lock engage. When it does, I follow Saylor down the stairs. "How come she got sweet Saylor, and I get Oscar?"

My girl stops at the bottom of the stairs wearing a haughty grin. "You said you wanted to get to know me again. All the pieces of me, right?"

"I did say that, didn't I?" I ask, stepping into her space.

"You did, so you get all of me, Dante." Her smile falters. "If you can't handle that, tell me now."

I sweep her into my arms and carry her to the car. "Oh, I can handle it, Oscar. And I will. Over…" My lips touch the shell of her ear. "And over and over again."

"You can make anything sound dirty, can't you?"

I wiggle my brows. "Jealous?"

She shakes her head, wearing a scornful expression. "No. I'm…" She stares off into space like she doesn't have an answer.

Placing her in the passenger seat, I follow her and gently kiss her lips. "Me too, Sayls. Me too."

Me too, I love you so damn much. Me too, I'm never leaving you again. Me too, I'm finally whole.

I shut her door and round the hood. A flash of light catches my eye, and I find Grady sitting on his front porch with a lantern of all things, watching the front door of Lena's apartment. I lift an arm to him and wave. He acknowledges me with a quick nod, so I slide into the driver's seat, even more sure that coming home was the right decision.

I start the SUV and put it in drive. "Let's go home."

She nods and then rests her head against her seat. It's a quiet drive, and I've never been more at peace.

CHAPTER 23

DANTE

Saylor curls into my chest, and I finally set my phone aside. She's still dead to the world, but I've been up for hours.

The social media alarm I set for our names started going off around two this morning. The photos from the airport went into circulation almost immediately, and Trent, drunk or high, I can't tell from the pictures, lost his ever-fucking mind.

I haven't slept since, and I do need to get moving. But I want nothing more than to stay tucked away in this bed with her. Messy, snarled hair covers her face and tickles my chest, so I tuck it behind her ear with one finger.

It springs back the second I move my hand, and I stifle a laugh.

"Oscar," I say, checking the clock. If anything will make her grumpy, it's being woken up at nine. "Saylor."

She groans and rolls away from me, but I cage her in before she can get far. "I need to check on Lena and Poppy. They'll need a car, and she'll want to make a plan for her time here."

"Mm-hmm."

"Trent is denying parentage." Animosity and disgust make my words ragged and harsh.

That has her flopping onto her back and squinting at me with one eye.

"Explain," she barks.

She throws her elbow over her face to block out the sun, and I take the opportunity to study the rest of her. She has more freckles than she used to, but her lips are still full and permanently stained a beautiful shade of pink that people pay good money for.

She lifts her arm a couple of inches to prod me along, and I smile at her. It's a lazy, satisfied smile because I will wake up to this grouch every morning for the rest of my life.

"Dante," she growls.

Happiness slips away with my sigh, and my entire body deflates like a sad balloon animal. "Trent reposted a picture of Lena and me hugging at JFK while you were holding Poppy."

Saylor removes her arm and sits up. That sexy little V forms between her brows as she pulls her knees up to her chest and rests her chin on them. "What did he say?"

I rub my temples with enough pressure to leave indents. "Nothing. Until this morning."

She doesn't move, but her expression is suddenly alert.

"And…" she prompts.

"And he posted a video an hour ago saying he's not Poppy's father and that I got Lena pregnant when she was engaged to him. It's not true, but the public will question it now because we never confirmed or denied who her father was before. No one is even listed on the birth certificate out of an abundance of caution."

It was easy to do because Trent refused to visit the hospital.

Her jaw drops open, and pain flashes across her features.

"They were never engaged, Saylor. Lena and I never dated. We've never been anything but friends."

She nods while staring at a spot on the wall in front of us.

"I believe you. Through everything, I've never once questioned your loyalty. Not once," she says, but her tone is unreadable. "What else?"

"Nothing good, and everything that will eventually hurt Poppy. Trent was one of the most sought-after child stars of his time, and people still love the memories he evokes, so they eat up whatever he does, even if it's to his own detriment. He's been chasing fame for so long that now he figures any press is good press."

Saylor rocks in place but doesn't say anything.

"He goes out of his way to make sure it's his name that's trending, and sometimes, that exposes Poppy. Thankfully, the press eventually gets bored with our silence about her, and they'll find another story, but this is a direct hit. This is a landmine of gossip."

I watch her carefully as I continue. "I wish I'd known more about how Hollywood works when I first got to California. If I had only done a little research, I would have tried harder not to become a celebrity by entanglement because now when he needs that hit of fame, I'm an extra layer he can pepper in to get the attention he craves."

My sigh feels like an exorcism. "He gave this whole speech about why there's never pictures of him with her. He said it's too painful to see his niece and that she was a daily reminder of the deceit that happened right under his nose. In his house."

"Fucking motherfucking cocksucking dickhead," she mumbles.

"That about sums it up, yeah."

"First, he says you're a danger to his daughter." She rubs her temples with both hands. "Now he says she's not his daughter. What the hell is wrong with him? Why would anyone believe him? What are you going to do?" Her eyes snap open and pierce me with the emotion in them.

"He's becoming more unhinged by the day, which will work in our favor. We can take the high road here and not come out any worse for the wear. He'll dig his grave with his lies, and we'll show the world the truth. That all of us—you, me, Lena, and Poppy—are a happy, healthy family. He's being dramatic though, so this news will find an audience because they don't care about the truth."

Anger burns hot in my stomach, and I have to consciously make an effort to stay calm. "I'll make an official statement, then talk to my lawyer about removing him from Ascendancy, which I should have done a long time ago. After that, I'll put out fires as they come."

That impressive impersonation of a bobblehead is back, but I give her some space because she's clutching her necklace, which likely means she's working through things in her head.

"I'm running over to Grady's to pick them up. They'll need a rental car for now. Do you want to come?"

Shouting draws our attention to the closed window.

"What the hell?" I jump out of bed and pull back the curtains to find Ainsley fighting through a crowd that's trying to get the money shot and has no desire to let her pass until they do.

"Shit. Get dressed," I say. Then I pull on some jeans, grab a T-shirt, and run down the front stairs to the bookstore.

"Dante?" Saylor yells behind me, but I'm already down the stairs and running to the front porch. "Ainsley," I shout over the crowd. She must be in the middle of the growing circle, but she's being swallowed by a sea of vultures. "Ainsley," I call again. This time I draw the attention of one of the photogs.

He moves back enough for my gaze to snag on eyes wide

with fear and exactly like Saylor's. My stomach clenches. I should have prepared her for this.

I don't have any shoes on, but I run down the porch steps, hitting the bottom stair when I hear Saylor burst through the front door behind me.

"Get the fuck off my property."

I love this woman, but she's truly a PR nightmare.

"Say—Sassy. Stop. Get inside. I'll get Ains."

"Wait. There's two of them?" someone in the crowd says.

"Sassy? Which one are you?" a man asks Ainsley.

Without giving her a chance to answer, I wrap my arms around her and guide her through the shit show.

"I'm calling the sheriff," Saylor yells from the door, but at least she's retreating. "Step foot on my property again and see what happens." She shakes her fist in the air like a ninety-year-old woman.

"We're on the sidewalk. Public property," one of them says.

"Bullshit. I built that sidewalk myself. The public side-walk is on the other side of the street, asshole." Saylor charges forward like she's going to fight them, but I snag her around the waist, haul her and Ainsley inside, then slam the door.

When I set Saylor on her feet, I'm pretty sure she has steam billowing from her ears, but she rushes to Ainsley. "Are you okay? Did they hurt you? What the hell is happening out there? Don't you have to be at the hospital today? I'm going to get a gun. Why are you here?"

For a woman who doesn't like people and supposedly hates leaving her house, she charged the mob like an angry mama bear.

"Whoa, slow down there, killer." I grab Saylor's hand and pull her back with a gentle tug because Ainsley seems like she needs a minute to gather her thoughts.

"Ah, geez," Ainsley says breathlessly. "What the heck was that?" These two are polar opposites. Saylor curses like a villain, and Ainsley sounds like Snow White.

I stare at them both. Ainsley folds in on herself while Saylor winds herself up into a tiny ball of fury.

"They got here faster than I thought they would," I admit.

"If they're here…" Saylor spins on me, and my heart stutter steps. She's worried about Poppy and Lena too.

"Yeah," I say, twisting my neck to relieve the unbearable tension settling in.

"I'm going to get a gun," she says matter-of-factly.

Ainsley and I spin on her and say, "No," at the same time.

Saylor rolls her eyes—she really should teach a master class on annoyed behaviors.

"Not a real one. Geez. But I do have a BB gun upstairs."

I can read her thoughts as clear as day, and while it's funny, I also don't put anything past her. "No weapons, Oscar."

She huffs and plops down on one of the many armchairs she has throughout the store.

"You have to keep the store closed today," I say gently.

She gives me a death glare but nods.

"Wow. That's…intense," Ainsley says. She's still shell-shocked.

"Sorry about that. I thought we had a few more hours."

She shrugs but joins Saylor in the armchair. Seeing them huddled together is a time jump that instantly brings me back to high school. Ainsley leans into Saylor, and Saylor leans away from Ainsley, but they both take comfort from each other in that strange embrace.

This is what a family is supposed to look like—weird, unique, amazing, accepting.

I want to rip Trent's head off for ruining that for us.

"Let's go to Grady's and get the girls," I say, patting my pants, already knowing I don't have my keys.

"Ah, that's a negative." Saylor snorts like I said something funny.

"What?" I snap. I've only been short-tempered with her a few times, so it shows how on edge I am.

"I'm not walking into that." She points to the sidewalk. "You go get them. Ainsley and I will stay here. Well, wait. Ains, don't you have to get to the clinic?"

I finally take in Ainsley's appearance, and sure enough, she's wearing scrubs and slip-on shoes.

"I do," she says. "I was stopping in to make sure you'd seen the news."

"We saw it," Saylor grumbles. "Fine, I'm fine, Ains. Dante, you can drop Ainsley off in Chance Lake on your way to Grady's. I'll be here when you get back."

I open my mouth to argue that there's no chance in hell I'm leaving her here, but there's no mistaking the determination in her steely expression and squared shoulders. It's a battle I won't win.

"I'll be gone for less than an hour. Do not let anyone inside. Do you hear me?"

"Yes, Dad," she says with enough sarcasm to choke a teenager.

This time, it's me who's rolling their eyes. "Come on, Ains. We'll take Saylor's car. It's in the garage."

Ainsley kisses Saylor's cheek, then stands. "Don't do it, Sassy."

I turn to watch them. Ainsley appears to be scolding Saylor, and I almost laugh. "Don't do what?"

Both girls turn to me. Saylor is wearing a troubling grin, and Ainsley is scowling. If anyone else walked in right now they'd probably mix them up based on their facial expressions alone.

"Anything," Ainsley says, then heads toward the garage.

I hitch one brow in Saylor's direction, but she shrugs and walks to the window.

"Stay inside," I say again. Suddenly I'm nervous. But not for Saylor. For the photographers, because she's very visibly plotting against them.

Shit. I pick up my pace and jog to the car. The sooner I leave, the sooner I can get back.

CHAPTER 24

SAYLOR

"Sass? You okay?" Grady asks. He hates FaceTime, but he always answers.

"Oh yeah. *I'm* fine."

He pinches the bridge of his nose, and I can't stop my lips from curling up. "Sass. What the hell are you doing?"

Instead of answering, I prop my phone up against the window. It takes a few seconds for the lighting to adjust, but I hear his low curse when it does.

"How long have they been out there?" he groans.

I shrug, even though he can't see me because the camera is pointed out. I'm too busy pulling up my Home app on my iPad. "Not sure," I finally answer.

"Where's Dante?"

I chuckle. "He's on his way to your house to get Lena and Poppy."

"He left you there alone? With those assholes outside?"

Annoyed, I pick up my phone again, turn the camera to face me, and scowl at him. "I was not going back out there. And I'm not his possession to leave behind. I'm a person, Grady."

"Don't start this shit…" His face falls when he realizes what I'm up to. "Sassy Greer, do not do it."

That makes me laugh out loud. "So, counselor."

"I'm not a practicing lawyer anymore, Sass."

"You are. You do all my contracts."

"One contract a year does not make me a lawyer." Grady gets super growly when he's frustrated, and I can't control my smile when he does.

"So," I say over him, "I've already told them to get off my property. I even recorded myself doing it. I also warned them that it's almost game time and they need to stay off my property. That means I'm covered, right?"

"Goddamn it, Sassy." My stomach cramps from holding in my laughter. Grady jumps around his house, grabbing keys and shoes. "It depends on what you're doing." He looks away from the phone, then turns back to me. "Dante's here. Do not do anything until we get there."

"I can't guarantee that, big guy. As long as I've warned them…"

"Jesus. Don't shoot anyone," he demands before walking outside. "We'll be there soon."

"You might want to wear a raincoat." I chuckle and toss my phone on the bed.

Opening my bedroom window, I poke my head out. How many are down there? Five? Six? The assholes are on my grass now. Fuckers. I just seeded that shit.

Well, seeds need water, right?

I hit a button on my iPad, and the sprinklers shoot to life at full blast. Grown men shriek and trip over each other, trying to gather their equipment. Laughing, I grab the bucket full of balloons near my feet and climb through the window onto the roof of the front porch.

Finally, the Lemon Festival and all its "fun" is coming in handy. Thank you, Matty Miller, for the water balloons.

I put a penny in each to weigh them down and filled them with whatever else I could get my hands on. Whipped cream, shaving cream, ketchup. I sit against the house so I'm hidden by the overhang and turn off the sprinklers. Then I even give them three whole minutes to walk away on their own.

When they don't, I launch my second attack. Tossing a balloon into the air with my left hand, I aim and shoot it with the BB gun in my right. Mustard explodes everywhere, then shaving cream and ketchup.

One after another, the men curse and slip on the grass in their hurry to leave my property.

I keep tossing balloons into the air even after they cross the street and yell at me. Unfortunately, I can't reach them over there, but watching the colors explode in midair is oddly satisfying.

Tires screech to a halt in front of my house, and I hang my head. Freaking Grady didn't even give me ten minutes. He and Dante jump out of my car with twin expressions plastered on their faces.

"Jesus, Sass. I told you not to…"

I toss another one into the air and shoot it. Shaving cream explodes over Grady's head.

"When the hell did she learn to shoot like that?" Dante asks.

Grady wipes angrily at his face. "I taught her," he says through a clenched jaw.

Dante doubles over laughing, and I send another one flying. A mix of ketchup and relish explodes in the air, and Dante narrowly avoids it falling on him.

"I'm going to sue you," someone shouts from across the street.

I stand up on my roof and shout back. "I told you to get off my property. I warned you that it's game time. It's not my fault you didn't listen."

"What are you, ten?" another guy yells.

"I'm not the one chasing around women and children with cameras to make a buck," I shout back. Below me, Dante is ushering Poppy and Lena inside.

"Get. Inside," Grady grumbles behind me.

Startled, I jump, but he wraps a fist into my T-shirt and pulls me back. "Now, Sassy."

"Fine," I say with a smirk, then climb through my bedroom window. "Pretty good aim, huh?"

He glares at me for a long time, like he can't decide if he wants to toss me out the window or pummel me. "Enjoying yourself?" His head is tilted to the side, and his features soften with something I don't understand.

"Yeah, I guess. But they deserved it." I hand him the BB gun before he can take it from me.

He places it on the nightstand, then laughs. Grady freaking laughs. It's not inhibited, and he doesn't cut it short, he simply lets it run its course. "It's good to see you smile, Sass."

I freeze, while mentally tallying my body's reactions. My shoulders aren't touching my ears. My fists aren't clenched. I don't have a blinding headache.

What is this? I lift my fingertips to my lips and sure enough, my mouth is smiling.

"Feels good, doesn't it?" he asks.

My throat is grossly dry. "Yeah," I admit. "It does."

"Saylor, what the hell?" Dante asks, storming the bedroom.

Grady reaches back out on the porch roof and grabs my bucket. "How did you even do this that quickly? Dante couldn't have been gone more than twenty minutes."

"I was motivated."

"You're a PR nightmare." Dante laughs. "Are there more balloons in there?" he asks Grady.

He peers into the bucket. "A few. Why?"

"There's more in the kitchen." Two sets of eyes turn to me.

"What?"

"You warned them it's game time, right?" Dante asks. His eyes sparkle with mischief and my arms tingle with awareness.

"Yes," I say warily.

Grady and Dante eye each other. Are they? Are they teaming up on me?

"Then you'd better run, Sass," Grady says with a grin I've never seen before.

My jaw hangs open in disbelief for half a second before I take off as fast as I can. I run down the stairs and out the back door but hear them running after me. Geez. They sound like elephants.

Dante's strong arms grab me from behind, and he lifts me off my feet.

"Payback, Sayls." He holds me in front of him and turns me toward Grady.

"You wouldn't," I seethe.

Dante's breath tickles my neck as he walks us away from the water and into the grassy area between my house and the abandoned building next door. "Oh, I would. All's fair in love and war, right?"

"Dante. Don't you…"

My words are cut off when Grady hits my belly with a whipped cream-filled balloon.

"I'm going to lick that off you later," Dante says before nipping at my neck. He's still holding my arms at my side, and Grady launches another attack.

"Me too. Me too. Me too," Poppy cries, running for Grady.

He sets the bucket down and lets her choose one. To no

one's surprise, she carefully sifts through them until she finds a pink one.

"Look, Mommy!" She holds up her treasure, and Lena walks to her. Poppy throws it when she's close, and it explodes with bright yellow mustard all over Lena's legs.

Lena and Poppy both stare straight ahead, wearing matching dumbfounded expressions.

Time seems to stop as we take in the mess around us. And then all hell breaks loose as we dive for balloons.

Somewhere in my mind, I register that the photographers are probably having a field day, but we're all laughing too much to care.

My arm freezes midair. *I'm* having too much fun to care. Instinctively, I search for Dante, and he's already watching me. He has so much life and love emanating from him, it's hard not to gawk. But then he nods with a sexy smile, and belts me in the chest with a chocolate-syrup-filled balloon.

Grady stands in front of Lena as Poppy tosses balloons at him. I watch it bounce off his legs three times, but he stands perfectly still while she picks it up and throws it again and again until it pops.

Dante walks toward me, and everything else slows to a stop. All the colors of life fade to black and white, except for this man, covered in every sticky substance I could find. He's the shot of color that fills me with life.

He stands before me and cups my cheeks with messy hands. The world hits fast forward around us, and I commit this moment to memory, hoping that if I lose myself in the future, this is a moment in time I'll never forget.

My heartbeat whooshes in my ears as he lowers his lips to mine, and I swear I hear cheers from the peanut gallery.

When Dante pulls his lips away with a sexy grin, I laugh because I wasn't hearing things. Most of the photographers across the street are laughing and snapping picture after picture. It's truly such a strange profession.

To my left, Grady and Lena are facing each other, with Poppy dancing in the grass between them.

"What the hell is happening?" I whisper.

"Life, sweetheart. Messy, happy life."

CHAPTER 25

DANTE

"*D*on't be mad at her," Grady says.

The girls went inside to clean up. Grady and I rinsed off in the lake, and I stayed with him while we waited for his brother to bring him a change of clothes.

I tuck my right arm in closer to my side, then turn my head toward him. He's also sitting, hugging his left arm into his body, and I laugh.

"Why are Saylor's chairs all kid-sized?"

Grady gives me the side-eye, and a hint of a smile ghosts over his face. But at least his shoulders relax. We're sitting in Adirondack chairs, but they're tiny and squished together so they fit at the end of the dock. We're so big that, even if we put our arms on our own armrests, our elbows fight for space like we're sitting in the middle row of an airplane.

Why are we cramming ourselves into opposite sides to avoid touching?

We seriously have issues. Laughter releases the rest of the tension in my shoulders, and I'm pleased when Grady shakes his head and grins.

He relaxes, too, but our elbows still fight for dominance in armchair realty.

Finally, we settle, and our elbows rest somewhere in the middle.

"I mean it," he says, staring over the lake. "This probably doesn't look great for her professionally, but this was the most Sassy-like thing I've seen her do since high school when you guys filled The Common's sprinkler system with Dawn."

I open my mouth to refute it because we agreed to take that secret to the grave, but he holds up a hand to stop me. "Don't even try to deny it. Harrison charged all the soap to Dad's account at Chancey's Market."

I cringe. "Dammit, Harrison," I say, but I'm smiling. "He never was one to think things through."

Grady chuckles. "No, he's not. But Sass…"

"I get it." Dragging a hand through my hair, I release years' worth of loneliness with a long exhale. "I'm not upset with her." Not really, anyway. "But I need to spin this so it doesn't feed into the narrative that Malimar is spewing about her."

"Why not tell the truth?"

If only it were that easy. "And what truth is that, all-knowing one?"

"Don't be a smartass," he grumbles. "She already told them it was game time. So, tell them it was family game time. That's what you want to show the world, right, that you're a stable, happy family?"

"Why, Grady Reid, are you calling me family?" I lift my fist to my chest and flutter my eyelashes at him.

"You're a dick. But you know as well as I do that blood isn't the only way to make a family. Sass is family to me." He glares, daring me to contradict him. I don't because I think he's right. "That means if you're her family, then I guess you're mine too."

"I love your enthusiasm."

His head falls back against the wooden chair with a thud. "What the hell am I getting myself into?" he mutters.

My phone goes off with a series of alarms, and I lift it from the chair. The first is a text from Kate.

Kate: What the fucking fuck is this?

Kate: Picture sent.

It's a paparazzi shot from family game time.

Me: Game night.

Kate: How the hell is this helping?

Me: She's happy, Kate. Let her be happy and let me spin this in her favor.

Kate: …

Me: Trust me. I love her and I'm not going to let anything hurt her.

I watch the three dots appear and disappear six times before she replies.

Kate: Fine.

Shaking my head, I flip back to the web page I had open. "TMZ has the pictures already."

Grady leans into my space to watch as I scroll.

Someone caught a picture of us after I got Saylor with the

chocolate balloon. We're face to face, smiling, and I swear the love shines over us like a halo. But it's her eyes and the story they tell that gives me goosebumps.

"You can't fake that kind of love," Grady says. His words are thick with emotion, and he pulls back to stare at the clouds moving overhead.

"No, you can't," I reply, then scroll to the next picture. This one shows Poppy from behind, but I'm focused on the expressions Grady and Lena are wearing.

I turn to him, then back to the picture. If Saylor and I were emitting love, these two are shouting something else entirely, but it's not hate on their faces. What the hell is it?

Holding my phone up so Grady can see, I ask, "Do you know Lena?"

His eyes pinch at the corners before he focuses on me. When he sees the picture, he pauses for a fraction of a second, but it's enough for a landslide of emotions to cross his face. "No. Not any—no. I don't know *her*."

I watch him closely, but he shuts down quicker than Saylor.

"Listen, Grady. I don't want to break this truce or bro bonding..."

"We are *not* bro bonding."

"Fine, I don't want to disrupt whatever this is," I say, gesturing between us. "But Lena is my family. The only real family I've had since losing Saylor and Ainsley. If something's going on..."

"There's not. I told you. I don't know *her*."

The way he says it has my spine tingling. "If you don't know her..."

"I knew her brother. A long time ago, when I lived in California. Before I moved home."

My brows rise in surprise before the rest of me catches up. "That's a hell of a coincidence. How do you know Asher?"

Grady shakes his head, then stands. "Not that brother. The other one. Luke."

He walks away, leaving me more confused than ever. Lena doesn't have a brother named Luke.

I stand too, ready to talk to Lena, but Harrison intercepts me before I reach the porch.

"How did I miss the party? I saw the photos online. What the hell, man? My pretty face would look great on TMZ. Luckily, there's a few rando's still hanging out in the front." He kisses his fingers like a chef's kiss and I chuckle. Does anything ever bother this guy?

"It was impromptu," I say, trying to get around him. But the thing about Harrison is he has a way of getting you to do things before you realize you're doing them.

Which is how I end up on the beach with him, building a makeshift fire pit, while Grady and Lena deal with the throng of people Harrison invited over.

"You know, you're not supposed to invite people to someone else's house."

"Nah, Sassy doesn't mind. It'll be a warm-up for the Fourth of July. She hasn't been to that in years. Consider this a pre-party to help acclimate her to us again."

"That's not…" I stop talking and focus on the stones I'm stacking when I catch sight of Harrison crossing the yard, grinning at Ainsley like a lovesick puppy.

Freaking typical, Harrison. He has great ideas, all right, and he still gets other people to do his bidding.

"I'll finish this," Grady grumbles. "You go get cleaned up."

Whatever truce we had on the dock is obviously over. He's locked up tight, and his body language screams *talk and you die*, so I don't say anything. Instead, I search for Lena, but when I find her, she's standing and laughing with Cassie, so I change directions.

261

Whatever is going on between Lena and Grady will have to wait.

Halfway up the porch steps, I hear Poppy's squeal of laughter and stop in my tracks, listening, watching, embracing everything happening around me.

Someone told me once that life happens in a million tiny moments sewn together to create the tapestry of your story. If that's true, I desperately want a million moments like this, with laughter as the soundtrack, and love the glue that binds us forever.

The screen door crashes open, and Poppy comes barreling through with an ear-piercing screech followed by little girl giggles.

Lilly and a teenage boy I've never met run past me, groaning like zombies, and chasing my niece.

Grady looks up at the same time, and we acknowledge each other with a simple nod.

I can't say what he sees, but I'm staring at a man longing for normalcy and fighting it all at the same time. A moment later, his attention is snatched away when Lilly and the boy who must be her boyfriend, Kai, run through the yard with little kids in tow.

Shaking my head, I walk inside to find Saylor.

She's not in the bookstore, so I make sure the front door is locked, then head upstairs to the apartment. I find her sitting at a window in the family room, chin resting on her knees, watching the chaos unfold below us.

She appears so small and fragile like this, but she's also missing the sadness she's been wearing like armor since I arrived.

"Hey," I say gently.

Her eyes swim with emotion when she lifts her head to find me.

"What's wrong?" I cross the room in three long strides, lift her from the chair, then sit with her in my lap.

Her expression is unreadable, and she shakes her head like she doesn't want to talk, so I pull her head to my chest and hold her.

"Are you okay?"

She nods.

"So far, I don't think we'll face any lawsuits for property damage." I chuckle. Hopefully that refills her sass well.

"I warned them," she groans before pulling back to study my face. "Did I make things worse?"

"No, Sayls. Different? Yes. But not worse. So far, everyone likes what they saw. I'll put out another statement tonight to help tip the scales of public opinion in our favor."

"Okay." One of her hands sways with the pendant, and the other pinches her earlobe, but her gaze lingers on the window and the people below.

"What else?" I ask, brushing her hair off her face, then cradling her head between my hands.

When she frowns at me, I nod toward her necklace.

"What else is bothering you?" I ask again.

Her gaze drifts back to the window before focusing on me. "It's just...today was. Today was good. Right?" The insecurity in her tone deflates my heart.

"Yes, Sayls. Today was really good." I turn us so we're both facing the window. "And it's not over. The Reid brothers are here with Lilly and her boyfriend. Cassie is here."

"Ainsley too," she says.

I nod, trying to gauge her reaction. "It's a lot of people."

Saylor tries to swallow so hard she coughs, and I run a soothing hand over her back.

"I seem to remember things like this happening a lot when we were growing up. One neighbor talks to another and another until there's a full-on barbecue no one planned for."

"Mm-hmm," she says, biting her bottom lip and holding her pendant in a viselike grip. "But it's never…it's never happened at my house before."

"Saylor, those people out there? They all love you. So many people in this town love you, they've simply been waiting for an invitation back into your life. Maybe now they're done waiting, but they all want what's best for you, sweetheart."

"I—I know. I just…I've never had a party here before."

Pulling her closer, I rest my forehead against hers. "I hate that you've missed out on so much."

"You don't understand." Her voice trembles. The soul-crushing vulnerability makes my skin burn like it's being peeled away from my body.

"Then tell me, show me what I don't know," I plead.

"It didn't happen overnight. And I know that people think I'm a freak."

"Stop."

"Please, let me finish."

My gaze searches hers, one eye then the other, and I finally nod.

"People don't always understand a pain they can't see. And when I got out of the hospital, I felt too empty to put on a happy face anymore, so I stayed home. I wrote, and I read, and I did everything I could to keep myself out of bed. In my heart, I knew if I allowed myself to stay in bed like I wanted to, I'd die there."

My heart bucks like a rodeo bull, and I fight a mental battle to keep my chest from heaving when it doesn't feel like I can get enough air.

"But, sometimes, it happened anyway. I'd have a depressive episode, or I'd forget to take my meds, and then it would get worse. My entire body felt like it had been hit with a sledgehammer, but outwardly, I looked fine. I'd be like that for days or weeks at a time. Grady and Ainsley would stop by, force me to go outside, put my feet in the grass, eat, and shower. And I'd crawl back into bed as soon as they left."

The noise of her necklace on its chain fills the brief silence.

"It's not that I didn't want to shower, or eat, or—" She pinches her forehead between her thumb and fingers, but I keep her close. Is she shutting me out? Or is she strengthening her resolve?

"Those were the times when I wished—I just wished I wasn't here." My hands tighten involuntarily around her hips at the confession. The invisible stranglehold on my lungs intensifies. "I wished I wasn't such a burden on them. I wished I could feel normal."

It takes multiple attempts before I can make my mouth form words, and when I do, each one is a painful whisper. "You are normal, Saylor, and my wish is that you would have trusted me enough to tell me the truth. I wish I had been here to put your face in the sunshine, hold you, or help the neighbors understand the depths depression can drag you. Saylor…"

I wait until she lifts her head. "I've loved you since I was fifteen years old. Love isn't only about happy times. Love means you hold someone in the dark and scary times. It means you trudge through that darkness together until you both emerge into the light. Do you want to, Saylor? Do you want to take your life back?"

A tear slides down her cheek when she nods. She wipes at it angrily, like crying makes her weak. Doesn't she understand it shows more strength to be vulnerable than it does to hide?

"It's not that easy," she confesses. "I don't know how,

Dante, and my attacks are not something I can control, and without control, I'm untethered. Everything is changing so fast. I'm scared I won't be able to control any part of my life now. It's like you blew into my heart and knocked down everything that kept me safe. You tore down all my walls in a matter of days, and now emotions I've intentionally kept at bay hit me like a tsunami. I can't block my emotions with you in my life, I never could. I can't even tell you what my triggers are anymore. And I worry..."

I don't press her. She'll continue when she's ready.

She blinks. Swallows. Takes a deep breath. And then her shoulders fall. "I should be strong enough to do this on my own, Dante. What does it say about me that I need you to feel whole—to feel anything? That I need another person to be my strength?"

"Do you trust me, sweetheart?"

She's nodding before I finish the question.

"Then trust me to keep you safe. We'll deal with your triggers together as they happen. Okay? And all that matters is that you do allow yourself to feel and to live. You are so strong, Sayls. Needing another person doesn't make you weak. It means you understand that perfection is a board game, not a way of life. You're strong because you acknowledge your weaknesses, and you're brave enough to borrow strength from someone you trust until you find your own, but that never means you don't have strength of your own. You do, and I see it every day in everything you do."

She doesn't respond, but the doubt on her face speaks volumes.

I tuck a wild strand of hair behind her ear. "It's called being a team, sweetheart." I keep my tone soft but firm. "Everyone needs love, and love fits differently for each person, so get the should-be's out of your head and start worrying about what you need. Tell me what you need, and

I'll do the rest. That makes you strong, and it'll make us strong too."

"Promise you won't end up resenting me if I can never be the Saylor I used to be."

"Oh, baby." My heart splits in two, and pain sits like razor blades in my gut. "I won't resent you for that. No one is the same person they were six years ago or even two weeks ago. We're constantly evolving, but now we'll grow and learn together."

"This is all so fast," she says again. "I'm afraid you don't understand what you're getting into with me. When the sadness comes, and it will come, you might hate me, or worse, leave me for dragging you down into it with me."

"It is fast, and it's not fast enough. There's love here, Sayls. Between us, the love will always exist. The bad days will come, and I'll love you. The sad days will come, and I'll love you. The hard and happy and shocking days will come, and I'll love you. And because of that, we'll weather your storms and embrace the life we can have together. Love is about the good, the bad, and the ugly, and I'm here for it all, Sayls. I'm here for it all, and I'm not leaving."

I pepper her cheeks, forehead, and lips with kisses, then wrap two protective arms around her like a shield and hold her in silence for a few beats. I hold her until her pulse evens out and her body releases the tension that was holding her muscles hostage.

"So," I say. "This party. Remember how I said all those people love you?"

"Yeah," she mutters into my chest.

"Well, they're also more observant than I gave them credit for. They want this for you. And they want it for themselves. They've missed you."

She pulls away and studies my expression. "What does that mean?"

"It means Adam brought over a grill. Cassie brought over some food. Ainsley stopped and picked up the dessert. Grady and Harrison are building a firepit on the beach. They've missed you, sweetheart, so they brought the party to you, on your terms, in your space because they love you enough to make concessions to fit into your life any way you'll allow. And I will too."

She stands and presses her nose to the window like a wounded little girl as the activity unfolds in her backyard.

"That seems like a lot of work for one person."

Shaking my head, I stand behind her, and rest my chin on her shoulder. She has no idea how loved she is. "That's my point. They're willing to do it because that's what you do when you care about someone."

"What do I have to do?" There's a slight tremor in her voice that gives purchase to her fears, but I'm so proud of her because it means she's not backing down. She's taking control of her life, or at least controlling the pieces she can, and I've never loved her more.

I kiss her shoulder, then turn her to face me. "All you have to do today is be yourself. They'll understand if you need space, but they're here to show you that they've never left you and they never stopped caring. So try to embrace what they're offering, even if you have to do it from the periphery for a while."

"I'm nervous." Her chin quivers, and I smile, hoping I'm able to mask the sadness of the moment from her.

Of all my failures in life, leaving Saylor alone was my worst. Maybe I couldn't have fixed her, but I could have supported her. And I'll spend a lifetime correcting that mistake.

"You survived the Lemon Fest."

"You were kissing me," she huffs.

"If that's what it takes to put you at ease, I'm at your

service day and night." She shakes her head, but a snorted giggle escapes too. "I'll be by your side the entire time," I say more seriously.

She looks at me and presses her lips into a thin line. She doesn't believe me. But she will.

"I promise. I need to shower and change. You go make a big thing of lemonade for the kids, and I'll meet you in the kitchen, okay?"

"You promise?" she asks, insecurity lacing her tone.

I swallow past the emotions clogging my throat.

Bending at the knees so we're face to face, I kiss her softly. I'll never stop loving how her lips mold to mine every time.

"I promise." It's a vow that she swallows down when I deepen the kiss. By the time I pull back, she's a little dazed, and there are no visible signs of stress to be found, but now that I know they live inside her too, and I'll help her fight through it all.

I always knew love could heal, but who knew kisses could ease the soul?

I turn her toward the kitchen. "Make the lemonade. I'll be out in ten minutes."

She walks away but glances over her shoulder three times, like she's trying to convince herself that I'm real. Then she turns into the kitchen, and I take the fastest shower of my life.

CHAPTER 26

SAYLOR

By the time we make it outside, my backyard has been transformed.

Adam Reid stands at the grill with a laser thermometer pointed at whatever he's cooking. Grady and Cassie are pulling camping chairs from cars and placing them around a homemade firepit. Lilly has all the kids sitting crisscross in the grass playing duck, duck, goose.

Dante stands beside me on the porch as I take it all in. When he squeezes my hand, I realize he's been touching me —supporting me—this whole time. Ocean-blue eyes stare down at me, and his smile soothes my rising tide of panic.

I return the expression. It's not as sunshiny as his, but I'm trying, and my smile isn't as forced as it once was.

Sensing my presence, because she always does, Ainsley turns from her conversation with Harrison, and the happiness she sends my way buoys me with her strength. As she looks at me, I study Harrison, who's staring at my sister with an odd expression on his face. I can't tell if he's confused or bewitched, but it's an expression I've never once seen on him before, and I almost laugh.

"You okay with all this, Sass?"

Grady's voice startles me. I was so focused on our siblings that I didn't notice him approaching.

"Yeah, I think—"

A little tornado of a human comes running around the house, interrupting me. Matty Miller's daughter, Izzy, has always felt like a kindred spirit. If nothing else, we share the Jane-of-the-Jungle appearance.

"Do you know I thought his name was Miller all these years?" Dante says, and Grady laughs.

"I only know two people who call him Matty, so as far as I'm concerned, he is Miller," Grady says.

Miller rounds the house a second later, dragging a wagon full of coolers like it weighs a ton. He's unlike anyone I've ever known. He gets along with everyone, cares for everyone, and is always the first to offer a hand, expecting nothing in return.

I'm not surprised that he's here since he's probably one of the few people Grady considers a friend. Miller yawns behind his hand and stretches from side to side. I've always thought of him as some energizing entity that never expires. But that's not the man walking into my yard right now.

"Sorry I'm late," he calls to no one in particular. "But I've got the drinks. The green cooler is for the kids, the white one is for the adults." He pulls it to the edge of the firepit, then spins in a circle until he spots us and flashes me a smile full of kindness and hope.

Strangely, it heats my body from the inside, making me sweat. It's way too warm. I try to take inventory of my limbs and what this sensation is, but I'm coming up blank.

What is this feeling, Sass?

Dante leans down and whispers in my ear. "It feels pretty good to let love in, doesn't it?"

I blink rapidly as shock takes over. They're all staring at

me now, and it hits me like a Mack truck even as the hair on my arms stands up straight—Dante's right. My body is reacting to an overload of love, and it's not as awful as I expected.

Miller jogs up the steps and wraps me in an awkward embrace since Dante won't release my hand. I forgot he's a serial hugger, and my entire body goes rigid.

Miller chuckles and quickly pulls away. "We'll work up to hugs, then." His expression turns serious but not unkind. "This is real good, Sassy. Baby steps. We're all here for you. We've missed you."

A tree trunk of emotion clogs my throat, but Miller's expression is the epitome of kindness, and it's difficult to keep my scowl in check, but I'm trying.

"We, ah, we would have done this sooner, but we weren't sure." His cheeks redden, and he drops his gaze to his shoes. "Well, we're doing it now."

I stare at his face, trying to understand the emotion there, but I must be rusty. He's not feeling guilty, is he? Why would he feel guilty when I'm the one who shut everyone out?

Dante kisses the side of my head, then says, "They missed you, Sayls, but they weren't sure how to help."

"Help?" I'm not even sure if I say it out loud. There's nothing they could have done. Surely, they understand that. My mental health is a battle I've had to fight on my own. Isn't it?

"Ready?" he asks, gesturing toward the fire pit. "The Lemon Fest was overwhelming for you, I get that."

I shake my head and try to rid my spine of the uncomfortable tingle Miller's words caused.

"But it's because we walked right into the fray," he continues. "How about we sit at the fire pit and let things unfold naturally? You can stay put and observe until you're comfortable."

"I feel stupid, Dante," I mutter. Both he and Miller offer nothing but patience as they stand on either side of me, though. "I've known most of these people my entire life. I saw them at the stupid Lemon Festival, and at the brewery not that long ago. Having them in my space shouldn't be this traumatizing or hard, or—"

"I'm going to stop you right there," Dante says. "The first thing we're going to do is get the word *should* right out of your vocabulary. You shouldn't be able to do anything except what is right for you in the moment. Stop putting the assumed expectations of others on your shoulders, Saylor. Because you're not anyone else. You're Saylor Greer, and you're perfectly imperfect because you're human—we all are. And it's already been established that we all love who you are. Struggles and all. Okay?"

"Ditto what he said." Miller laughs. "He's right. There are no expectations from any of us. If you hang out for an hour or six, we're just happy to be with you, okay? And to add my two cents, I think this is different than the brewery or the festival because this is where you've shut yourself off. It's different because you're, with a little encouragement"—he winks—"inviting people to be part of your space. You're inviting them to be part of your life again."

I nod and take control of the knot stuck in my throat. "Fine," I bite out with more surliness than I intended. "But the two of you need to stop being so sappy. If I cry in front of everyone because of you two morons, I'll never forgive you."

Miller's laugh booms out over the open lake, and Dante chuckles while guiding me down the stairs to my favorite Adirondack chair set up at the fire pit. He sits to my right.

No sooner do we sit than Cassie fills the chair next to me, handing Dante a bottle of beer and me a glass of wine. Then she pulls a spiked seltzer from the pocket of her shorts, pops open the top, and holds it out for me to cheers.

With an exaggerated sigh, I do.

"Cheers to second chances, new beginnings, and…" She glances over her shoulder, and I follow her gaze to where James is walking into my yard. Did she sense his presence like I do Dante's? The instant he turns in our direction, she snaps her head around so fast that her braid slaps across her face. "And…" She swallows hard. "And to love that lasts a lifetime."

Dante speaks first. "Cheers."

I copy him, then we all lean back in our chairs and let the sounds of a party wash over us.

"Sassy." A deep baritone slices through the air suddenly thick with tension. "Thanks for having me."

I open my mouth to tell him that I didn't actually invite anyone, but Dante squeezes my hand and answers for me.

"Good to see you, James. Help yourself. I have no idea what there is—it's kind of a last-minute potluck."

James holds out his hand to Dante, and they shake.

"Appreciate it," James says before casting a worried expression in Cassie's direction, but she dutifully ignores him, staring off into space like she can do it forever.

James's sigh could be felt in Antarctica. "Sounds good," he says, turning back to Dante. "I picked up some salads on my way over." He holds up a shopping bag with a shrug. "I'll go set them down." He chances another peek at Cassie before bowing his head and walking away.

"How long can you keep this up?" I ask. Cassie and James were like Dante and me. Childhood sweethearts who did the unimaginable and made it through college still in love, then suddenly, it was over in the blink of an eye. It's the one thing she's never droned on about.

"He has to give up eventually." She stands and brushes off her shorts with agitated movements. "I'm going to give

Ainsley a hand in the...somewhere," she says, then walks off in the opposite direction of James.

"Something else that hasn't changed in all these years," Dante says. The warmth in his tone tells me that whatever he's thinking makes him happy.

"What's that?" I ask, but my gaze is still taking in the impromptu party happening all around me.

"Small towns are never short on drama." He chuckles, but there's no malice in his words. He says it more like it's something he's truly missed. "And the photographers out front are documenting it all. Happy, messy life."

I shrug, lift my feet into my chair so I can curl into a ball, and watch everyone having a good time. I'm surprised by the happiness attempting to escape my body, but everyone gives me a minute to breathe, which I appreciate.

"You doing okay?" Dante asks.

"Yeah," I admit. "This is a lot easier than the Lemon Fest was."

"You're in control here, Sayls. You call the shots. When you've had enough, we go inside and call it a night. You need a little more of that in your life. Instead of being controlled by circumstance, let's start trying to control your narrative. This is your story, sweetheart, and you can write it any way you want."

His words run in a loop in my mind. Even when Miller and James sit next to Dante and engage him in a lively conversation, I get lost in the idea that I can control my outcome. I can write my own story.

Ideas filter through my mind, and questions sit on the tip of my tongue, but for once, I try to store them in my mind and reenter the real world that's happening around me.

Laughter covers me like a blanket while children run in circles around me, reminding me of happy memories, like camping with my sisters and learning to bake a cake. For so long, my mind held me captive to the sad memories, the gut-wrenching truths. But somehow, the man I thought I couldn't keep is giving me everything I thought I'd lost. He's giving me a life of balance—dark and light. He's giving me a life built for love.

∼

NIGHT FALLS, and everyone settles into chairs around me, but it isn't suffocating. With Dante at my side it feels normal.

"Do you always travel with a blow-up movie screen and a film projector?" Harrison asks Miller.

He chuckles. "Only when there will be a ton of kids and not much to do after dark. I like to be prepared. Plus, I've been wanting to try it out."

The air shifts, and the chair next to me groans with new weight. "Hey," Grady says. He leans back and lifts his head to the stars. "You doing okay?"

I shake my head with a smile. He and Dante couldn't be more similar, but they would never admit it. Angling my body toward Grady, I catalog his appearance. Tightness in his jaw, check. Squared shoulders ready for a fight, check. A scowl that could scare ghosts—well, it might be there, but his head is on a swivel searching for someone, so I'm not really sure.

"Yeah," I say. "This is better than I expected. But…"

He turns his head toward me and raises one brow while he waits for me to continue.

"Are you okay? You look tired." I lean in and lower my voice. "Are you having nightmares again?"

His gaze darkens, then he shuts his eyes for a long second and effectively shuts me out too. "No," he finally says, then places a hand on my forearm. "Just been sorting through a lot of—history lately. Don't go worrying about me, Sass. I'm good. You're good. We're going to be fine."

When I don't reply, he lifts his head with a pointed stare. So why does it feel like he's lying?

He quickly changes the topic. "How's writing going?"

I purse my lips until I'm sure I can answer without demanding he tell me what's wrong, and he chuckles.

"Writing's fine," I say while staring into the fire, even though it's not. I have three different stories going, and I can't finish any of them.

On the other side of the firepit, I watch Lena fall into a chair with Poppy in her lap. When I turn back to Grady, his attention is on Lena as well.

Interesting.

"But I do have a question," I say. When his jaw clenches, I smirk. "About my contracts."

Slowly he drags his gaze away from Lena while stifling a yawn. What the hell is going on with him?

"Are you sleeping?" I demand. My tone is harsh, and I try again. Old habits die hard and all. "Well, are you?" This time my voice pitches high enough to gain the attention of everyone in our circle.

Maybe I'm not ready for parties after all.

"Yes, Sass. I'm sleeping. What's your question?" he asks. Dante squeezes my hand. It's a warning of some kind, but I can't heed it. Stupid social cues, I never did quite understand them.

"Then why are you so tired?"

"Sassy," Grady growls. "I'm. Fine. What. Is. Your. Question."

My entire face pinches as heat climbs up my skin. Pointing a finger in his space I say, "Fine. But we're not done talking about this."

He gives one curt nod, so I return one.

"Fine," I say. "Good. Then my question is, my contract says Malimar owns Sara and Danny, right? But…" I bite my lip because I'm not even sure I want to do this. There's a song that talks about stories being unwritten, and it plays loudly in my head. Maybe my story with Dante was never meant to have an ending, but I need all the information just in case.

"What if I write the ending—the third book—like a complete stand-alone novel and change the character names, location, etc.? Could I publish it then? I never gave them an outline or plot points or anything, but readers would know it was their happily ever after because of what the characters will go through."

He taps his fingers against the armrest of his chair. "I'd have to go over it again, but one thing is for sure, I would strongly encourage you to use a different name. Either your real name or a new pen name. Honestly, Sass, publishing isn't my forte, but I can probably tell you if anything would prevent you from creating a new world to end your trilogy without blatantly finishing your trilogy. Give me a few days to review it and consult with a law school acquaintance, then I'll get back to you."

"Thanks, Grady." I allow my face to twist into a full smile, which shocks us both. He bursts into a belly laugh that has everyone turning in our direction again.

"You're welcome, Sass. It's good to see you like this."

"It's nice to be like this," I whisper like a confession.

"I'm proud of you. Take things one day at a time, and you'll be fine."

His brother Adam interrupts us, and Grady stands to help him with the grill, so I turn my attention back to the lively conversations happening around me.

My mind is running in circles, but my body isn't acting like every second requires a fight-or-flight reaction. I'm… content, and that makes me happier than I've been in years.

Dante's hand squeezes my neck, then he pulls me to him for a kiss. "I love you, Saylor. And I'm so, so proud of you."

Maybe I should feel guilty that something as innocuous as a barbecue is praiseworthy, but tonight, I'm taking Dante's advice and letting the *shoulds* go. And with it, I let the unrealistic expectations I have for myself go too. Instead of feeling like I should be able to do something, I'm focusing on what I can do, on how being content can truly bring me peace.

Life isn't only about reaching for the stars—it's about reaching for what makes you complete.

Ainsley's silky laugh draws my attention, and my smile matches hers as I watch her.

I'm not naïve enough to think depression and anxiety won't sink their claws into me again, but maybe, with Dante by my side, I can be better about accepting help from those who love me.

My head lolls to the right, and I watch Dante's animated expressions as he talks and laughs with Miller. Everything in my body slows down. My heart rate is calm and steady, and my breaths come easily.

Holy shit. I'm relaxed.

It's the last thing I remember until Dante lays me in bed.

CHAPTER 27

DANTE

"Our official statement is that we've always been in love. But like many young adults, we made mistakes that took years to correct, and now that we have, we'll fight to keep our love intact and private—forever," I say. My teeth are clenched so tightly that I almost expect the enamel to crack. Kate has been busting my balls for the last two weeks.

"You're not listening to me, Dante. Since your little family photo op, people are more convinced than ever that *April Rain* and *Come September* are your love story. And that's good. It distracts from the crap your brother is saying and shows Sassy in a new light, especially when she's seen with the kid. She's always been a little reclusive, so Malimar's bullshit was believable. But because people are interested in your story, it also means they're curious about her mental health struggles."

"That's not something we're giving up for public consumption. It's a private war that she has every right to keep to herself." I intentionally lower my voice so I don't disturb Saylor in her office. "It's a battle she fights every day. It's not a gimmick or a sales pitch."

Saylor's words have been flowing, and I've set up a mobile office at the kitchen table. We've settled into a new normal without too many roadblocks, except for Trent. My fist flexes at my side every time I think of him.

"Of course it's not," Kate snips. "And that's not what I'm suggesting. I'm saying that mental health still has a stigma attached to it. Sassy writes real characters who suffer from real, everyday struggles. It's why people connect to her stories. This is an opportunity to show people that they aren't alone, and she can address what it's truly like to live with a mental illness instead of making donations every month or sharing links in the back of her books. It's something she's passionate about, meaning now is the time for her to make a difference. It'll also help show the world that she's not this monster Malimar is still making her out to be."

Saylor's mental health will never be a marketing ploy. But she's right about one thing—Malimar. He's making this attack personal. The gossip about someone of Saylor's popularity should have died down weeks ago, but he's keeping it at the forefront of everyone's minds.

That piece of shit doesn't like to lose, and Saylor is getting the blowback of his God complex with every dollar he spends smearing her name. But Kate still doesn't understand what it means to live with mental illness. If she did, she wouldn't be pushing this narrative when it's still so fragile in Saylor's mind.

"The answer is no. Not right now. We're not jeopardizing her progress to fix her image. The risk is too great, and I'm not taking that chance."

"It's not your decision to make," Kate hisses.

But my responsibility is Saylor, and my voice is lethal when I speak. "It is, though. It is my call. Thank you for getting me here, but your job is getting Saylor deals. My job as her PR rep is her public image, and my job as her boyfriend is to protect her, even if that means protecting her from someone who thinks she's helping."

Kate's face turns molten. I've never seen that shade of red on anyone.

"It's time we adjusted priorities and responsibilities."

"Are you threatening me?" she snarls.

"No, Kate. I'm not." Here comes the headache I get every time we talk. Rolling my shoulders, I tame the tightness in my tone. "We're on the same side here. And I know, even if you don't admit it, that you care for Saylor. We can work together toward the same goal, but you have to let me do my job and stop stepping on my toes."

She pinches her nose and rests against her chair. "I do care about her," she says. Her tone isn't one I've heard before. She almost sounds human. "I've always cared. It's what her sister would have wanted."

This surprises me, and I lose the edge in my voice. "You knew Shannon?"

She nods. "We were roommates in college before she went home to care for the girls. She was the only fr—she was a good friend. She did a lot for me. I owe it to her to make sure Ainsley and Sassy are okay."

Now it all makes sense. I'd wondered how they met but kept forgetting to ask.

"I get that, I do. We are on the same team here, Kate." I hope she can hear the sincerity in my tone because anyone who loved Shannon is someone Saylor needs in her life.

Her sigh is heavy, yet cutting. "Fine. I'll back off. For now," she clarifies. "But I want to be in on any major decisions. It will be helpful as I'm working with other publishers, and—" There's a long pause. "I do care about her."

"I know you do, and I can work with that."

She stares at me with her lips pursed. She wants to say something snarky but instead says, "Okay. Keep me posted."

"Will do," I say, but she's already disconnected the video call.

Opening another web browser, I scroll through the notifications and follow Trent's activity. He's making it easy since he's out all fucking night calling the tabloids and alerting them of his whereabouts.

I'll have to make some tough decisions soon. Half of my clients have already bailed because of the scandal, but for some inane reason, I'm holding out hope that the Trent I grew to love as my brother will do the right thing.

I hate that I can't fix him. I hate that my professional life is spiraling, and I have no control over it.

Constant knocking on the screen door grabs my attention and makes me smile. Poppy's here.

I hear the chair roll across the office floor right before the door opens. "Is she here?" Saylor asks, poking her head into the hallway so only her face shows in the doorframe.

"She's here," I say, walking toward the stairs, but the *zip-zip-zip* of her pendant stops me in my tracks.

"I'm not a good babysitter," she says, her words vibrating with fear.

God, I love this woman. "I'll be right here the entire time," I say, hoping it'll comfort her.

The knocking continues, but I don't move until Saylor's gaze lifts to mine.

"Okay," she finally says. "But there's a reason I don't even own a plant, Dante. I don't trust myself to care for anything or anyone else. I barely take care of myself some days."

Tilting my head, I watch as she twists her necklace. "Is that what you think?" She shifts in her seat, obscuring herself from my view. "That's not how I see it." She scoffs, but I continue. "You've spent all this time going to therapy.

Fighting the bad days by yourself—and with help when you allowed it. You have gotten yourself here, Sayls. You've been taking care of yourself. That counts for something."

"My therapist said I avoid caring for anything or anyone, so I can also avoid losing them."

Knife, meet heart.

"What do you think?" I ask as the screen door bursts open and crashes against the wall.

She shrugs. "I thought if I didn't love, I wouldn't get hurt. I told you that."

"And I told you that you do love. You love Ainsley and—Grady." Admitting that is like swallowing a cup full of glass. "And even though you won't admit it yet, you love me too."

Poppy's feet clomp up the stairs as she sings a song I don't recognize.

"I understand your fears. I do. And life is full of risks, but if we don't take a chance sometimes, we'll miss out on all the beautiful options life has to offer too."

Saylor frowns, but can't maintain it when Poppy launches herself into my arms.

"We are worth the risk, Saylor. A calculated, well-executed risk that I will navigate with you. Trust me?"

Poppy kisses my face. "Hi, Unca. I wub you."

"Love you too, Lollipop." She wiggles out of my arms and charges Saylor, who is prepared for her this time.

Uncomfortable laughter bubbles out of her as her face scrunches up tight and Poppy kisses every inch of it.

"I wub you too," Poppy says, standing only inches away from Saylor's face.

Saylor's face pinches, but I implore her with a gentle nod of my head. "Trust, Sayls."

"You're asking me to trust an awful lot of things lately," she mutters.

The corner of my mouth twitches. "Only the things that matter."

"Fine," she says under her breath, then gawks at Poppy with what I can only describe as a half smile, half grimace. With a resigned shrug of her shoulders, she says, "I love you too, squirt."

Poppy's gasp makes me laugh.

"I is not a squirt," Poppy says indignantly, planting her hands on her hips in a way that reminds me of Saylor. "I is a big girl. I pee on the toy-yet and every-ting."

"Thank goodness for that," Saylor says, standing with Poppy in her arms. She's slightly more comfortable holding her now, but it's still awkward as hell with her back arched away from the little girl and Poppy trying to claw her way closer.

Relief rolls through me when she puts her down.

"Hey," Lena says when she's halfway up the stairs. "Sorry about barging in. I think Poppy can pick locks now."

Saylor's burst of laughter has me smiling. "I knew I liked that kid."

"Well, thanks for watching her. I guess I'll need to figure out our plans sooner or later, but it's nice of Grady to introduce me to Mrs. Winters. I wish I had my cosmetology license here, but working the front desk is better than nothing."

Grady has been exceedingly—surprisingly—helpful. When I asked Lena why she'd never mentioned another brother, I wasn't impressed with her answer that he'd passed away before I landed in California so she never brought him up. But no matter how much I press them, neither will speak about it. For someone who thrives on information, it's brutal.

"Can you believe Mrs. Winters asked if I wanted to buy the salon?"

That snaps me out of my wayward thoughts so fast I have whiplash.

"She did?" Saylor and I ask at the same time.

Lena stares at the floor, so I can't read her expression.

"Is that something you want?" I ask cautiously.

When she lifts her head, it's written all over her face. She wants this.

"Are you—are you considering moving here permanently?" Nothing would make me happier, but her entire life is in California.

"Would that be weird? Following your pseudo-brother-in-law across the country?"

"No," I say, as Saylor asks, "Do you like it here?"

"I do," she says as her eyes fill with tears. "In California, I'm terrified every time Poppy goes outside to play." We all turn to the little girl dancing circles to whatever song she hears in her head. "People actually talk to each other and help each other here. I'll never get that in LA."

"I'm not a pseudo-anything, Lena. We're family. And if this is something you want, I'll do whatever I can to help."

Her smile brightens, so I turn to Saylor, trying to gauge her reaction, and I'm relieved to find her expression unguarded. She's happy and letting the world see it—she's letting us in.

Lena turns to Saylor. "Do you think it's weird?"

Saylor shakes her head. "No," she says quietly. "I think sometimes you find where you belong by accident. And if this feels like where you belong, you should be here."

"It's a big move," Lena says, glancing at her watch. "I don't have any idea how to begin the process, but right now, I have to get to the salon."

I hug her. "Go. Talk to Mrs. Winters. Ask what she has in mind, and we'll figure out the rest." My gaze falls on Saylor. "As a family." Her cheeks flush, but she doesn't disagree.

Lena watches the interaction, then kisses Poppy. "Okay," she says. And there's an instant change in her demeanor. I'm an asshole. How have I completely missed how stressed out and anxious she's been? "It's settled then," she says with her arms spread wide. "We're moving to Connecticut."

We say our goodbyes, and Saylor settles on the sofa with Poppy. The two of them sit with their heads angled toward each other but not touching, a compromise I guess, while they watch a cartoon about singing ponies.

Finally, the pieces of our story are falling into place.

CHAPTER 28

SAYLOR

"Unca, I need my googly eyes," Poppy says.

There was only so long we could keep this little tornado inside, so as soon as Lilly got here from school to watch the store, we brought Poppy out to swim.

She dances around in a bright pink swimsuit with an attached ballerina skirt, a floppy hat that has some kind of foam holding it out of her face, and an unconditional love that snags my heart like a fishhook.

"Goggles." Dante chuckles. "Did your mom pack them?"

Poppy stares at him, nodding her head. "Yes, unca."

His smile grows. Meanwhile, I'm standing over here trying not to sweat through my T-shirt and fighting the shallow breaths attacking my lungs.

I told Dante that I'm not afraid of the water, and I haven't ever been, but watching this little girl twirl around with no fear brings back memories. I was only two years older than her when Shannon fished me out of the lake.

Truthfully, I should have died. I never understood what miracle happened that day to bring me back to life.

"Saylor," Dante says. How many times did he call my

name? I hadn't seen him move, but now he's in front of me, holding my biceps and beaming like I'm his entire world. "More stories?"

Right. Because I space out when I'm writing. That's good. Let him think that. I refuse to let him believe for even a second that I'm afraid.

I'm going to be stronger than my fears.

"Yeah, something like that."

He kisses the side of my head and walks toward the house. "I'll be right back." He calls over his shoulder. "I'm going to grab her goggles."

"What? No! No, ah, I'll get them." But he's already halfway across the yard. "Dante." Panic fills my chest, but he's too far away to hear it.

He waves. "I'll be right back."

Then he's gone. I'm still watching the door when I hear a soft splash, and icy terror blurs my vision.

Screaming, I sprint for the end of the dock. "Poppy. Poppy, please?"

Lying on my belly, I search the water for her, but there's nothing pink, so I scramble on my knees to the other side.

Oh, God. Oh God, no.

She's in the water, staring up at me with a smile.

A strangled cry is ripped from the depths of my soul when I hear footsteps pounding on the dock, and Poppy's head breaks the water's surface.

I gasp for breath like I'm the one drowning, and memories intermingle with the scene before me until I can't tell what's real.

Shannon's car at the bottom of the cliff.

I try to blink away tears, but the nightmares play on.

Dante and I rounding the bend as her taillights fell from view.

Her trying and failing to get her door open.

Her hand slipping from the glass she couldn't break.

Poppy.

Staring up through the water as darkness surrounded me.

Dante's arms reach past me and pull her tiny body out of the water. Their lips are moving but I can't hear anything.

Why wasn't I holding her hand? Why did he leave her with me? Why did he trust me?

The world around me is dim, and her muted laughter yanks all the strength from my muscles. I sink to my ass when my knees can't hold me up anymore, then Lilly is taking Poppy by the hand, and I succumb to the full-body tremor.

I'm so cold.

Dante pulls me into his lap, rocking, and presses my head to his heart.

Thump. Thump. Thump.

It beats steadily against my ear. Each strong beat is a reminder that I couldn't have saved Poppy.

Why didn't I learn to swim?

My mind is a vicious vessel for horrible memories trying to suck away every ounce of happiness I have. And I hate it. I hate it so much that my mind betrays me like this. I hate myself for allowing it to happen.

"Oh, Sayls. I should have told you that she's been taking swimming lessons since she was six months old. I'm sorry. I'm so sorry."

She can swim. Babies can swim. She can swim.

My breaths are short, harsh puffs of air.

An event that lasted less than a minute has burned itself into my soul for eternity, and every fiery image brands me like a hot poker.

Failure.

She could have died, and it would have been my fault.

"Shit." Grady's grumble comes from somewhere behind us. "She already saw the article?"

Dante shifts quickly and dislodges my head from his chest, so I push against the wood and sit up. He continues to hold me tight, and the dark cloud seeping into my mind stays on the periphery, but life is still happening around me. I'm a voyeur, watching it all from outside.

"It's okay, Sass. It's been a long time, and his father is still in jail. It will all be fine after…"

Rubbing my temples, I replay Grady's words. Between Poppy and whatever Grady's talking about, nothing makes sense. My head is fuzzy, and the dizziness is already settling in.

Get your shit together, Sassy. My internal pep talks could use some work.

"Deep breaths, Sassafras. You've got this." A chill ghosts down my spine, but it doesn't make me cold—it's more like a gentle hand caressing my back and this time, I do hear Shannon's voice.

"What are you talking about?" Dante's voice is eerily calm.

Grady turns a shade of white I've never seen on him. "You haven't seen the article?"

"My phone's inside." Dante stands and hauls me up with him. His arm wraps protectively around my shoulders.

Grady looks ill, and whatever he's talking about suddenly feels terrifying.

"Be strong, Sass. Be strong."

"Shan?" It's stupid and inane, but I still search my surroundings for my dead sister.

Dante and Grady share an expression of concern and seem to come to a silent understanding that has them ushering me toward the house without a word.

"What happened?" Grady asks.

"Poppy went in the water," Dante says gruffly. "She didn't know Poppy can swim."

"Fuck."

They keep talking about me like I'm not here, but I don't want to be a passenger in my life anymore. Not anymore. I clutch my necklace, and for the first time since she died, I feel Shannon surrounding me, encouraging me, trusting and loving me.

Once we reach the porch, I refuse to go any farther. I sit on the top step and press the heel of my palms into my eyes while I fight memories, both old and new, as my lungs burn with the need for more oxygen.

Poppy is fine. I am fine. I repeat those two sentences like a prayer.

My head aches, but I don't want to go inside. Somehow, staying out here, I'm empowered, and I want to be strong, but I need the warmth of the sun and the memory of my sister to do it.

It makes no sense, but deep in my soul I know it's the truth.

Both men stand in front of me like armed guards. I sit in their presence and soak in their strength.

"Tell me," I say quietly, staring at my feet.

The air shifts, and I'd bet money they're speaking in hand gestures and facial expressions.

"Please, just tell me."

"Ah, Sass." Grady's words are pained, but he sits down on my left, followed by Dante on my right. "Trent gave an interview about the two of you."

"Motherfucker," Dante hisses.

Unable to speak, I nod, encouraging him to continue.

"He said some of what you put into the books, embellished others, but confirmed the books were about the two of you. But then—then he talked about—Shannon."

Dante stands, muttering something I don't understand, and his heavy feet pound against the old wood before I can make sense of what Grady's saying. Rage makes Dante's muttered words bleed together, but I get the gist.

He's going to kill Trent.

Then Grady's words sink in.

"What did he say?" I keep my voice surprisingly calm considering the riot exploding in my ears.

"Everything," he says quietly. So quietly, I'm compelled to look at him. Even Dante stops raging and stands eerily still at the bottom of the stairs. "He told them about Kingston Corp."

At this my mind is on high alert. Blake loved my sister, but we had no idea how powerful his family was until it was too late.

Grady opens his mouth to continue, and I fight through memories to focus on his words.

"He explained how Blake's father was involved in her accident, and how he helped you after, scrubbing any news of it from every media outlet to protect you, and then he made up a bunch of shit. It's all tangled up in half-truths and full-on lies. Then he…"

Grady scratches at the scruff of his jaw.

"What?" I ask, and I don't flinch when he takes my hand in his.

"He insinuated that the accident was your fault. That Blake's father wasn't the only one chasing her that night. And he told them you were in a psychiatric hospital after."

Nausea makes me double over and put my head between my legs. We weren't chasing my sister that night, we were following her to Buttery Cuts Steakhouse to celebrate my last semester of college.

What is wrong with this man? Why can't he just leave us the hell alone?

"Where the fuck did he get that information?" Dante

roars. "I didn't tell him about the hospital. I didn't even fucking know." His wild gaze jumps from me to Grady.

"Trent must have gotten it from the book." I knew that was a possibility, right?

"I'm going to destroy him," Dante vows. "He's so high he has no idea what he's saying or any regard for who he hurts."

He's tried to find another solution for weeks to protect Trent from himself because he thought he owed it to him. Dante pulls both hands through his hair until it's standing on end. I can sympathize with that urge. Physical pain is easier to deal with sometimes.

"He's dead to me now." His voice is lethal. His gaze burns a hole into my chest. "I will end this, Saylor. Now."

"Gwody," Poppy screeches from behind the screen door. Lilly runs up behind her, but it's too late. Poppy barrels through the door, wraps her arms around Grady's neck, and hooks her legs around him like a human backpack.

"Hey, munchkin." Thankfully Grady has a surprisingly easy way with her, because it's taking Dante some time to compose himself.

"Sorry about that," Lilly says.

"It's okay." I'm shocked at how calm I sound.

Something has shifted in me. Or maybe something broke that can never be fixed. Or maybe what was broken is trying to heal itself. Whatever it is, I am different.

I have something to fight for now—me...and them. All these people love me, and anger that someone is trying to take this away again sits like acid in my gut.

Grady stands with Poppy still attached to his back.

"Gwody makes the bestest pancakes ever," she says with a sunshiny smile. She has no idea of the bombshell she dropped, though.

"You had breakfast with them?" Dante asks. It sounds like an accusation, but it's only confusion on his face, and it gives me a reprieve from the turmoil happening in my mind.

The beauty of distraction.

"Ever-we day," Poppy says cheerily, but not loudly enough to cover up Grady's groan.

"I'm helping," he grumbles.

"Uh-huh." I nod, but even he can't keep a straight face amidst the chaos of the moment.

My stomach hollows out, nearly knocking me over. I'm smiling. I'm not panicking. I'm not falling apart. I'm just— absorbing information and—I'm living.

"Don't, Sass."

But that growly bear routine doesn't intimidate me.

"Why don't I take Poppy with me? It'll give you two a little time to prepare. Because it's Kingston, the story is spreading quickly," Grady says.

Dante's back to pacing and doesn't respond.

Kingston. One of the wealthiest families in the world. One of the most powerful too. And yet, we only ever knew Blake as the man who made our sister smile.

"I'll call Lena and tell her what's going on," Grady says when he gets no reply from either of us. "I have to stop at the brewery for a few minutes, but she can play with Harrison. She's probably better at following rules than he is. Then I'll take her home and wait for Lena to finish work."

Grady turns to me for direction when Dante still doesn't respond, but all I can offer is a shrug.

Finally, Dante stops moving and focuses on us. "Yeah, thank you, Grady. If Lena says it's okay, that would be helpful," he says, but he's distracted. His gaze jumps from one object to another, and I can tell he isn't seeing anything at all. He's planning. Scheming. Plotting revenge.

Heavy silence covers us like soaked denim in a rainstorm. It's uncomfortable and heavy.

Grady dials Lena on speakerphone, and it rings three times before she picks up.

"I'm at work. I can't talk right now."

Grady's face pinches and the tips of his ears turn red, but he doesn't let it deter him. "Check the trash papers. I'm at Sassy's house now. Is it okay if I take Poppy home with me? They have some—stuff to handle."

A light clicking sound comes through his phone, and then a sorrowful gasp. If I had to guess, Lena was googling as Grady spoke.

"Um, okay. That's okay. You—you've babysat before, right? On second thought, maybe I should tell Mrs. Winters I need to—"

"Lena," Grady says, and silence fills the line once again. "I was nineteen when Lilly was born, not nine. I've babysat before. I can handle it."

"Right. Okay. Well. I'll be done around seven. What about dinn—"

"I'll. Handle. It."

I'm pretty sure I hear Lena swallow through the phone. "Okay."

"Okay," Grady replies, then hangs up.

"Lill, can you pack up Poppy's stuff?" I'm not even sure if it's Grady or Dante who asks, but Lilly's feet sound on the wood, and then the snap of the screen door echoes across the lake.

The Reids pull everything together while Dante and I stay outside, facing each other in silence while we both work through what this news will mean.

I don't know much about the Kingstons other than Blake has tried and succeeded at keeping them away from us. And Trent is correct that Blake whitewashed the devasting news of my sister from the internet, but he's wrong about the reason. Blake was trying to protect Ainsley and me, and he's been a silent force in our lives ever since.

He paid off our student loans. He helped me turn the first floor of my grandparents' house into a bookstore. And he does it all while drowning in his own pain and with little to no contact with anyone.

The last time we spoke to him, he was still living in a rundown house on Block Island. What will this news do to him?

CHAPTER 29

DANTE

*I*t's been two days since fuckface dropped a bomb onto our fragile foundation, and I'm no calmer now than I was then.

The only thing that has kept me from jumping on a plane and draining the life from my brother with my bare hands is that Saylor has held up remarkably well. So well that even her therapist hugged her.

Will this hit her like a landslide eventually? I don't have a clue, but I've been so damn proud of her. I told her I would always catch her, and I will. But seeing her catch herself? Jesus, that stole the fear from my heart.

The sooner I can cut ties with everything in California, the sooner we can move on with our lives. I don't give a shit about my legacy anymore. All I care about is ending this and keeping my girls safe.

"What happens if I simply shut down Ascendancy Inc.?"

Grady's been sitting at our table for over an hour, pouring through contracts, bank statements, and everything else I could pull together without stepping foot in my office.

He sits back and removes his glasses. "You'll lose a ton of money, clients, and probably your reputation."

"But it can be done?"

Grady glares at me, and the muscle in his neck twitches. "I don't advise it, but it can be done."

"Is there anything in there that could stop me from starting over in New York?"

Papers crinkle when he flips over pages until he gets to the one he's searching for. "If you sell Ascendancy, yes. There's a noncompete clause to protect shareholders. But if it simply folds?" He shakes his head and annoyance flows from the action. "No, there's no contingency for that in any of the documents I've seen, but I would be cautious in how you go about informing existing clients of your new company. If Trent or any other shareholders are inclined, they could make a case against you. But, of course, that would take work on their end."

That won't be a problem. I've already bought back the minuscule shares I'd sold to outside parties.

"Can you start the paperwork for a new PR firm? Name it Sway," I say, ready to move on, my mind already jumping to the next steps.

"I'm not a practicing lawyer anymore." He pushes the papers away from himself. "Is there anyone else with shares to Ascendancy Inc.?"

Rolling my shoulders to work out the tension living there, I nod. "Lena has five percent."

Grady's expression goes from annoyed to furious faster than I can explain, and he slowly drags the papers back to his side of the table.

"She has five percent that I gifted her, and I'll buy them from her before I shut down Ascendancy Inc. I'll do the same thing when I open Sway. I'm doing everything I can to protect her too."

He pulls on his beard as he watches me. "She could put that money into her salon."

I bite my tongue because I can only handle one fucked up situation at a time, and I have no doubt the situation between Grady and Lena is seriously fucked up. "Mm-hmm."

"Fine. I'll get the ball rolling, but find another attorney. I'm not doing this anymore."

"But you will." I flutter my lashes. "For me, or are you doing it for Lena?"

"All that matters is that I'm doing it. What's your plan now?"

I lean over the table and lower my voice. "Going back to California to settle this shit is the only option. I have a house to sell. Lena has an apartment I'll pack up if she wants me to. And then I'll ruin Trent's entire life."

He studies me like I confuse him. "This is a lot to give up," he says, nodding toward the table.

"No. Saylor was a lot to give up. Ascendancy is the physical representation of heartbreak that had no other outlet. This"—I gesture to the paperwork—"is the easiest decision I've ever made. I don't need any of this. I never wanted to be famous, so walking away from LA is no hardship, trust me. I'll gladly spend the rest of my life waiting tables if it means I have Saylor back. Love is worth more than money and fame. It's worth more than my time or energy. She is worth everything. She's worth fighting for."

"She's stronger with you by her side." His voice is pitched low, so Saylor can't hear, but there's love behind his observation.

"So am I."

"She's holding up better than I expected." He doesn't have to say anything else. We can hear them outside even with the windows closed. Hope Hollow has been overrun with media

300

vans and reporters for the last day and a half, and more show up daily, if not hourly.

"But," he says, tugging on his beard, "me talking to you isn't betraying her. We made a deal a long time ago to look out for one another, and this is looking out for her." He scowls and points a finger at me.

"Ah, okay." I straighten my shoulders when unease settles across my skin.

"She's holding up, but I don't know if she's holding together."

"What do you mean?" Going to him for advice on the one person I've loved for almost half my life would grate on me if I didn't need the information so badly. The fact that he's coming to me means more than my pride, though. It means he trusts that I'm here for her.

"She has—I don't know—tics? Tells? She does things that maybe she's not even aware of when her mind is filling with more than she can handle."

Mentally I run through the last couple of days, trying to pull anything from my memory bank to corroborate what he's saying, but I come up blank.

"It took me years of helping her dig herself out of the darkness before I picked up on them. It's simply a matter of time spent in sadness and grief with her that I've learned these things. You'll learn them, too, probably much faster than I did."

Guilt is a dirty bastard. I should have been here for her.

"She digs her fingernail into her earlobe," he says, and an image of her the other day hits me hard. "That's the first one I noticed because it leaves deep grooves in the skin."

"Like her palms," I say as more memories come into focus.

"Yeah, but her palms are when she's trying to shut down something emotional. The ear and her necklace are the two that happen the most. But there are others that show she's struggling, and they become more obsessive when she's entering a true depressive episode."

My expression must be giving way to my fear because he adds, "There's not a ton of them, and it hasn't happened in a long time. But when they do, it's our job to make sure she keeps fighting, even if that means simply getting her outside for five minutes a day until she can do it on her own."

Reality crashes into me like a heavyweight fighter. Saylor isn't only dealing with things that make her sad. She's fighting demons that drain the life from her.

"I write in cursive with my pointer finger," Saylor says, entering the room.

"I…We…" I stumble over my words, but she shrugs and slides into the chair next to me.

"It's okay. Maybe Grady should have let me tell you, but I understand why he didn't." She turns to him. "We've been through a lot together, and I would have done the same thing." She angles her body to face me. "I would have told you eventually. Probably. The truth is, I'm not aware I'm doing them most of the time. And I did talk to my therapist this morning, you know." She looks from Grady back to me. "I will be fine."

"Yes, you will. I believe that with all my heart." Even as I say it, though, her skin draws taut. She's forcing a smile for my benefit. When I catch Grady's attention, I know I'm not alone in my surmise. "Grady was just confirming what I already knew."

Her gaze flickers between mine and Grady's. It's the first time her mask has fallen since the news broke. I have suspicions that she cried in the shower after Grady left with Poppy, and it pains me that she didn't let me in, but once I fix this, I'll be back and will never leave again.

"I need to go to California and deal with all this."

"I know."

The words are injected with false cheer that instantly makes me grind my teeth.

"Don't do that, Saylor. Don't hide your emotions away for my benefit. If you're sad, be sad. If you're pissed off, be pissed off. I'm a big boy, I can handle it."

Her posture deflates, then she shifts in Grady's direction, and he nods.

"It's not that," she says. "It's not that I want to hide things, but this will be hard for you, too. I don't need you worrying about me on top of everything. I said I'll be fine, and I will."

Grady clears his throat. "You know, Sass? For the first time in a long time, it sounds like you truly believe that."

She nods. "I do. I need a support system, and I'll still stumble occasionally, but I do want some agency over my life." Her nervous gaze finds mine, but there's truth in her words. She's always been a fighter, and now she's beginning to believe in herself again.

Grady stands, blinking fast when moisture suspiciously appears on the side of his face. Then he wipes his cheek on the outside of his bicep and collects the papers before I can respond. "I'll start on this stuff and keep tabs on everyone while you're gone, but make sure this"—he holds up a packet of papers—"is what you want to do." He turns his back on us, but his voice is thick with emotion.

"I won't change my mind," I tell him. "I have enough savings to hold us over until I'm back on my feet."

He nods, rounds the table to kiss Saylor's head, then pats me on the shoulder and leaves. It's the most emotive gesture he's had toward me that wasn't anger or disgust.

Progress.

"You've always thought you have to fix everything and everyone," Saylor says softly, and I find myself longing for Oscar. This muted version of her isn't my girl. This is someone fighting fear, and I hate that any part of it is my fault. And Trent is my fault. I should have never confided in him.

When Grady opens the door at the bottom of the stairs, our sanctuary is flooded with shouts from reporters and questions that all jumble into one loud, chaotic disruption.

Her finger glides across the table, and I can't look away. Is she writing my name? Has she always?

"This isn't only your mess to clean up. I have to find happiness within myself, Dante." Her gaze burns a hole in the side of my face, but I follow the movements of her finger.

"Do you always write 'Dante'?"

Her finger halts, and her cheeks flush, then she lifts that finger to tap at her necklace. "It's because we were talking about it."

"There's nothing to be embarrassed about, Sayls. But a cursive D is distinguishable. Is it always my name?"

"Probably." She shrugs, but my heart is tripping over itself at this information, and it's hard to focus when she keeps speaking. "I will figure out my career and my mental health. Me." She taps her fist against her chest twice, drawing my attention back to her. "I appreciate your support, but don't for one minute believe you have to save me. I told you there would be highs and lows being with me, but the lows are not something you can find a solution for, okay?"

No, it's not okay. I'll always have the urge to make everything right for her. But telling her that would start a battle neither of us has energy for, so instead, I tug her to the sofa and pull her down into my lap.

"I'll try," I say when she's settled against me. "But fixing things and people and situations is a part of me. It's who I am. I will respect boundaries, but it doesn't mean I have to like it."

"No," she laughs. "It doesn't."

"How's Ainsley doing?" I ask, sobering us to the moment.

She stiffens against me. "She's okay. She spoke to the clinic in Chance Lake, where she's doing the rest of her residency, and they agreed it's safer for her to work in the Connecticut Medical Center until the media circus clears. It sucks that she's so far away, but it's for the best."

Shit. That's one less person for Saylor to lean on.

"Stop," she orders. "I'm not going to spiral while you're away. You're thinking the worst because you haven't seen me at my worst, or at my best in a long time, but you're asking me to trust you, so you need to trust me too. Grady will help if I start to struggle. It's okay that you don't understand our relationship, because we understand each other and know when to push the other out of their minds and into life. He *is* that *friend* for me, like I'll be for him when he needs me."

She presses on my chest until she's sitting high enough to be eye to eye. "Plus, I have something to fight for. I want to be someone strong enough to fight for herself. When I pushed you away, I thought I had to live the way I have been. I thought it was all I could handle, but then you burst back into my life and made me admit that I was wrong. I can fight for me while also fighting for us. I won't always win, though, Dante. You should prepare yourself for that. I don't like those episodes. I also can't control them, but I can promise to fight through them. And I will. But I can only do it if you're doing what needs to be done for you and Poppy."

"I know." And I do. She's the strongest person I've ever met. She just forgot that for a while. But we're still fragile, and I hate that I have to leave her so soon.

"And Grady is checking on some stuff for me," she says, pulling me from my fears. "If it all works out the way I want, I'll be able to take control of my career too."

This drags a chuckle from my chest. "For someone who isn't a lawyer anymore, he's doing an awful lot of lawyering."

She laughs and it settles deep into my chest. "He is. He

loved being a lawyer once." She lifts her shoulder. "But things change."

"Did you know that Grady and Lena have met before?"

"What? When?" Surprise radiates off her like static cling.

I shrug. "I'm not sure. Neither of them will talk, but somehow, they're connected through her brother, Luke."

Saylor tenses in my arms and is quiet for a long time. "Just because someone has a story doesn't mean we're entitled to it. They'll tell us when they're ready."

I'm not happy about it, but she's right, so I let it go. "I'm going to fly out tomorrow."

She nods. "Okay."

"I'm not sure how long it'll take. I'd like to figure everything out so I never have to set foot in California again, but there's a lot to do. I'm going to shut down Ascendancy." This isn't news. We lay in bed last night, discussing every possible scenario until sunrise.

This is the fastest and cleanest way to be rid of Trent. He has nothing left to hurt us with, so there's no reason to hang on to something that doesn't exist anymore.

"I emailed a realtor this morning about putting my house on the market, but we've never talked about a permanent living situation."

Her breathing turns shallow against my chest, and her clammy palms dampen my T-shirt.

"Sayls, I'll do whatever you want. If you want me to find my own place, I'll find one as close to you as I can possibly get." I cup her chin, drawing her face toward mine. "If you want me to stay with you, I'll do that too. There's no pressure, and there's no wrong answer. The ball is completely in your court, and I support you either way. I'm not going anywhere."

"I mean…" She tries to pull away, but I hold tighter to her chin. "If you want to stay here, I won't kick you out."

Warmth settles over my heart. There's my sweet, sassy girl.

"Is that right?" I inch closer to her face.

"I guess. You'll probably be a big baby about it if you have to find a place of your own. There's not much turnover in Hope Hollow."

"So, you're saying you're doing me a favor."

"Yes."

Laughter lightens the load weighing heavily on my shoulders. "Well, I guess I should thank you for your very magnanimous favor then, right?"

Her breath hitches when she understands my meaning. The skin stretches over her neck as she arches into me, and her pulse beats erratically.

"I guess so," she nearly whimpers.

Gently, I place my lips on hers. It's a quick kiss. Chaste almost, but we need to talk about one more thing first.

"It could be a few weeks, Saylor. I have no idea how long things will take in California, even with hiring other people to pack for me."

"I figured it would," she says in a daze, and when she stares at my lips, my cock nudges my zipper.

"Did you?" I ask gently. "Do you also know that I am coming back no matter how long it takes?"

The passage in her book about waiting for me breaks my heart whenever I think about it. I don't, for one minute, ever want her feeling like that again. The pain she wrote about? It crushed her, and it torments me that it did.

"I'll empty a drawer for you," she says cheekily.

Arching one brow, I wait for her smile to break free. "One drawer? How generous of you."

"You'll have to earn the other ones." She moves slowly at first, away from me and placing her feet on the floor. I allow it because I'm ready for what happens next.

She takes off running to the bedroom, but I catch her before she reaches the door.

"Earn it, hmm?"

She nods and shivers in my arms.

I pull her body tightly against mine and tilt her head to the left to kiss her neck. My breath hits her skin, making it warm and damp, and I don't stop until goosebumps pebble in my wake.

"I have a few ways I can do that, and none of them involve clothes." My hands fall to her T-shirt, and it's over her head before I finish speaking. Then I turn her in my arms so we're chest to chest and crowd her until her legs hit the bed.

"Oh, Saylor," I say reverently as I lay her on the sheets. "How many ways can I make you come tonight?" She bites her bottom lip, and the sight of her rips a groan from my throat. "I'm going to lick, nip, mark, and defile every inch of your pretty body so when I leave tomorrow, you'll remember who you belong to and who belongs to you."

"Okay. Okay," she pants. "That…That's a good start."

My laughter starts in my belly and works its way up my chest, and when it releases from my mouth, I swear I'm ten pounds lighter.

"I'll show you a good start. A good middle and a good ending." I don't wait for a response. I join her on the bed and get to work—earning my keep.

CHAPTER 30

SAYLOR

*W*hen Dante touches me, my body comes alive like shooting stars. I don't feel weird or empty. With him, I'm just me.

With him, I remember all the ways I used to be and all the ways I want to be again. He's a secret door between my heart and mind. Somehow, he pulls them together to make me whole again.

"Stay with me, Saylor," he demands, then trails kisses down my sternum, removing the rest of my clothing as he goes.

"I am," I whimper. He takes a nipple between his teeth and flicks it with his tongue, then releases it with a pop that tingles in my core.

"You're not, but you will be." He lifts onto his forearms and studies my face. "What's going on in your head, Sayls?"

I'm really starting to miss the days when tears weren't my default. "Us," I say honestly. "How you make me feel."

His smile is a balm to wounds that haven't closed. "How do I make you feel, sweetheart?" His gaze never leaves mine, but his fingers roam lazily down my center.

"Alive." I gasp when he circles my clit, but my admission has him halting his assault on my lady parts.

"Alive? Explain."

I try and fail to swallow past the lump in my throat. It's cemented in place and refusing to budge.

"Tell me," he coaxes in his deep, silvery voice.

How do I explain something I'm only now recognizing? Wanting to reach for my necklace, I drop my gaze to my fingers that flex against the sheets. Instead of grasping for the security of my pendant, I wrestle with my emotions—not to lock them away in a bottle, but to organize them so I can explain what's happening in my mind.

Dante is as patient as ever. The love he showers me with gives me strength because I know he's there waiting for me. With a deep breath, I try to explain the reality of me—of what I've lived with.

"I've spent so long feeling broken, so many years disconnecting from the world so it wouldn't hurt as much when I lost someone or something. It's overwhelming."

He straddles my legs and wraps his hands around my scalp, cradling me.

"What's overwhelming?" he pleads. His cock hangs heavy against my hip. It's so distracting that I stare at the ceiling to focus. "Look at me."

I blink feverishly, trying to make sense of everything rushing through me. How do I put into words something that's so wholly encompassing that not even my old hurts and fears are reaching me right now?

"What's overwhelming?" he asks again.

"Feeling so much after actively blocking my feelings for so long." Embarrassed, I lower my lashes, but I can't move away because he has control of my face.

"Give me more, Saylor."

His hip shifts, and the thick head of his shaft slides

through my lower lips. I gasp and arch my back, but I don't break away from his gaze.

That's where I find my answers. In his eyes, I find myself.

"It was so much easier to retreat from the world and teach myself to avoid feelings in an effort to protect myself. Happy, sad, and everything in between became muted until they felt like a shadow in my life. Then you came home, and you injected me with all the emotions I'd pushed away. You see everything in vivid color, and you suck all the gray from my life until I'm blinded by every color of the rainbow. And it—it scares me because those shadows are always there, on the periphery, trying to drain those colors."

He tenderly wipes at the skin above my cheekbones when moisture pools there, then he kisses the tears away before they can fall.

"It's terrifying, Dante. Never knowing if today is the day the darkness wins. When all I saw were shadows, I knew what to expect. Now every day is different, and I'm scared of the unknown. What if…" I blink, trying to clear my vision, and this time the tears slide down my cheeks. "What happens if I can't fight the shadows one day?"

Dante cradles me like I'm precious but not like I'm fragile, and the distinction matters more than he'll ever know.

He lowers his face until his cheek rests against mine, inhaling me like I'm his first taste of oxygen. "Then I'll turn on every light, open every shade, flood this place with sunshine until those shadows crawl back into the hell they were created in. I'm not scared of your secrets or your shadows, Sayls. In your darkest days, I'll be the light that pierces your storm. Your pain is my pain."

He rocks against my pussy.

"Your joy is my joy."

His lips hover over mine, and he feeds me hope through

311

his kiss. Our breaths mingle like our lives should have always been.

"Your love and fears and dreams? They're all mine too." His voice has taken on a husky edge that makes goosebumps race across my flesh.

Dante releases my face with one hand and uses it to hitch my thigh up to my chest, then he notches his cock at my opening, and the brightest of rainbows explodes in my vision. He rocks in shallow thrusts until his tip teases me open.

"I'll research and learn everything I can," he says. "I promise that the next time you feel broken or empty, alone or overwhelmed, I will be here to hold your hand. To remind you who you are and what you mean to me."

His cock slips inside. Deeper and deeper until he's fully seated, moving agonizingly slowly so every delicious inch of him marks me as his.

"I'm not perfect either. But we're a team. When I push too hard to fix things that are not my job or my responsibility, you'll pull me back to reality."

The next thrust of his hips steals my breath.

"We fit together in every way, Saylor. Your body was made for mine." He picks up speed until my breasts bounce with each movement. "Your heart is the missing piece of my life. Your mind and your sass challenge me in every way."

"Dante," I breathe. Perspiration glistens on my skin. The moment is so intense, not only because my body is primed for a mind-numbing orgasm, but because he's reached inside my fears and massaged the knots from them until everything I am is at his mercy.

"I know, baby. Fuck," he grunts. "When you're over-whelmed, I'll carry some of the burden." His thrusts intensify after each declaration, making it hard to breathe. "When you're sad, I'll pick you up. When you're happy, I'll thank my lucky stars. But no matter where you are, I'll always meet you there."

His words, the purest form of love, and the way his body glides over mine like it's been programmed just for me, bleed together into one all-consuming sensation. And those colors we were talking about? They set off fireworks behind my closed lashes as my body writhes and convulses in the most intense orgasm I've ever had.

"Jesus. Fucking. Christ," he groans. His muscles coil beneath my fingers, but all I can see, all I can feel, is blinding, soul-crushing love. "Damn it, Saylor. Stop trying to push me out." He means physically, but I hear it as a warning for emotional detachment too. Dante slams into me, then grinds his hips against my pelvis, and a new orgasm builds before the last one has even ended.

"It's too much. It's too…"

"I've always got you, Sayls." His voice is ragged against my ear, and I wiggle my body, trying desperately to nuzzle closer. "I need you to come again. I want your walls to milk my cock, and your pussy imprinted on every ridge of my dick. I need all of you."

He was always a dirty talker, but this is rougher, more desperate than I've ever heard him, and I remember with blinding clarity that he needs to know we're real too.

"I love you, Dante. I love you. I love you. I love you," I chant like a promise, a vow, a commitment for life. And then I shatter below him, because no matter how many pieces I break into, he'll keep each one safe, then hand them to me one by one while I put myself back together again.

He comes with a roar that doesn't sound human, and it rattles the windows. It's agony and regret. It's hope and promises. It's love that's finally allowed to be set free. And I take it all. When he collapses on top of me, two bodies coated in each other, I silently build one wall against the shadows.

One day at a time, this man guides me from the path I was lost on for far too long. And he helps me feel like I can finally take the reins of my life and live with purpose. Live with light. Live with so much love it makes even the sassy side of me happy.

"I love you, Saylor," he says sleepily. "None of this will be easy, but we'll get through it together."

I drag my fingertip over his skin. D. A. N.T. E. Over and over again, but when I trace his name this time, it's not a way to survive what my mind is fighting. No, this time, when I do it, it's a promise to live fully for him, for me, for us, because I deserve the happy ending.

I'm the creator of my story, and I'll write it word by word.

I gasp when a fully formed idea finally sinks its claws into my consciousness and doesn't slip away into the ether. Dante slides off me, and even though he keeps his arm draped over my middle, he's asleep in seconds.

I wait until his even breaths indicate he's drifted off completely, then I slip from the bed, tiptoe to my office, open a new file, and take back control of my career—one word at a time.

"Hi," I say breathlessly. I'm not sure how many times my phone rang, but it finally pierced my concentration, and I dove for it, because that ringtone was set for only one person.

"Hi," Dante says reverently.

"Are you home?"

"No, Sayls, I'm not home."

His voice sounds strange, but he recovers quickly. Did I say something wrong?

The call drops and less than ten seconds pass before he calls back on FaceTime.

I don't have my glasses on, so I squint at the screen. "If you're not home, where are you?"

"A house in the hills. Wherever you are is home, Saylor."

What is this squishy feeling crawling up my neck?

"Uncomfortable?" Dante smirks into the phone.

"No," I say, knowing it's a lie.

"Okay." His chuckle makes me inhale sharply because I miss that sound already. "We'll work on naming your emotions when I get home."

"I write emotions, Dante. I can name them." Somehow sass feels safer with so much distance between us. Is it fair? No. Can I help it? Also, no.

"I read a book on the plane," he says, changing the subject.

"Oh, yeah? About what?" I ask with a frown.

"Depression and anxiety."

"Real gripping literature there." My chest tickles like it's being attacked by butterfly kisses.

"It is," he says seriously. "And I learned a lot."

Those butterflies become skin-eating vultures, and I'm clasping my pendant before my brain catches up with the movement.

"Like what?" He's the only man, the only person who could ever tame my sass with a single expression, and he does it now.

"Well, I learned about disassociation. It's not only depression and anxiety you deal with. Is it?"

I openly gape at him. "My therapist didn't explicitly say that I have a dissociative disorder, only that it's a result of trauma and that all three are closely related, but the difference is, I chose this. I did this to myself so I could control something when the dark days threatened to take everything from me. I taught myself not to let things in. It's not a secret,

Dante. Anyone who's seen me the last six years could clearly tell I've done everything possible to avoid everyone because of the messy emotions people always evoke."

"But I haven't seen you. I don't know anything about anything, and I'm trying to understand. I want to be there for you. To do that, I need to know these things, Saylor." He sounds pissed, but I don't want to fight with him.

Besides, he's right.

"I don't talk about these things very often. And we keep getting hit with one disaster after another. I'm doing the best I can here." I sound defensive and bitchy, so I take a deep breath. I'm lifting my hand to my ear when I abruptly change directions.

There's something about Dante unearthing my secrets that makes me work harder to address them.

"I'm sorry," he says, softening his tone. "I'm on edge here without you. And Trent has been here at least once."

Alarm makes my ears ring. "Why do you say that?"

His lips curl at the corners. "I'm sort of particular about sofa cushions. And when I got here, they were all messed up like someone had slept on them, so I checked the security footage. He went through my home office too, which means he also went through the one at Ascendancy."

"Did he take anything? What does he want?"

Dante leans back and rests his head on the back of the sofa. He lifts the phone so I'm looking down at him.

He's so freaking beautiful. Half of his face is hidden in shadow, but it turns his features into a work of art. His thick brows lift as I stare at him, and heat creeps up my neck. I was so lost in staring at him that I forgot to listen.

"Oh, crap. What did you say?"

"I said it doesn't matter what Trent wants. And now I'm telling you that I miss you, but this time it's different. This time I know I'm going back to you, and it makes me so angry that I'm wasting time here when I could be there, holding you."

"You'll be home soon."

"Not soon enough," he grumbles.

"What's your plan?"

He sighs, and it's so heavy I swear it kisses my face from across the country. "Tomorrow, I'm going in to talk to my employees. I'll figure out what kind of packages I can offer them. I have a pretty good idea of who betrayed me, and I have a program working through our servers now that will give me confirmation. I'll turn that over to the police."

"I'm sorry you have to do that."

His smile is sad, and obviously for my benefit because it shows off the dimple that I love.

"Dante?"

"Hmm?" Lines of exhaustion appear on his face that I hadn't noticed before.

"Are you sure this is what you want to do? You worked so hard to build that company into what it is today. You want to just give it all up?"

"Saylor." It sounds like a scolding, and I suppress a grin. "I promised myself a long time ago that if I ever got the chance to love you again, that's the only thing that would matter. And honestly, selling lies for misbehaving celebrities was never my goal. It happened because I was too heartsick to figure out what I did want."

My palms itch, but I don't clench my fists.

"I'm not heartsick anymore, sweetheart. And those misbehaving celebrities paid a pretty penny for me to rehab their image, so now I'll have the chance to figure out what else I want in my life. But my life begins and ends with you, so the sooner I get home, the sooner we can get our HEA."

I raise my brow, but a snigger escapes anyway. "HEA? Have you also been researching romance terms?"

"You know I did. And I've got to tell you, there's a lot I'm willing to try, but RH isn't one of them."

I laugh so hard my stomach cramps. "You're not into a reverse harem story?"

"No, you misunderstand. I'll read the shit out of that, especially if you write it, but there's not a chance in hell I'll share you with anyone. Ever." His tone has dropped dangerously low, and I swallow past the nerves.

"Never?" I squeak.

His eyes darken, and I swear his gaze teases every nerve ending in my body.

"I'll give you anything you want, but no, I'll never share you." His expression is hard, and his lips press into a thin line. Oh shit. Now I've done it. He's angry, and I can't help but find it funny.

"Well, that's good," I wheeze, sucking in laughter. "I've never been very good at sharing either." My entire body melts into my chair, and I press my thighs together. "I wrote a sexting scene today," I blurt.

Dante's face morphs immediately from borderline anger to white-hot need.

"Tell me more," he groans.

Using my notebook, I fan my face. I don't even stop when he chuckles.

"This is going to be a long couple of weeks," I mutter.

"It is," he agrees. "But I can't wait to be on the receiving end of your sexual prowess you've kept hidden from me."

I glare at him, trying to figure out if he's serious. When he stares back with an unreadable expression, my body tingles in anticipation. Our time apart will be as explosive as our time together these last few weeks.

"Let's play a game, Sayls."

"Now?"

"Starting now, and it'll end when I get home."

"What kind of game?"

"I'm going to test your sexting skills." I begin shaking my head before he finishes the sentence, but he's grinning so broadly that his face might be splitting in two. "The goal is to make the other person so hot they finish themselves off. The person with the most self-induced orgasms…"

"What?"

"You heard me. Whoever orgasms the most loses."

"Loses?" Okay, for an author, I've totally forgotten how words work.

"Yup. And the winner gets a reward when I get home. However he sees fit."

It takes me a minute to compute his words, then competition makes my fingers twitch. "Fine. When she wins, the reward will be epic."

His smile is a promise of things to come. "Game on, Saylor. I'm going to own that body when I get home, in every"—he lowers his voice—"delicious way I can think of. I'll give you material for the next ten books."

I open my mouth, but nothing comes out.

"Goodnight, Sayls. I love you."

He hangs up, leaving me frustrated, on edge, and more determined than ever to win this game.

Dante Thompson's ass is mine!

CHAPTER 31

DANTE

"What?" I bark into the phone.

"Things going that well, huh?" Grady's amused voice hits my ear like a slap to the face.

"No. Nothing's going well." Wait. Why is he calling me? "Is Saylor okay? Poppy?"

"Everyone is fine," he says, cutting off my list of concerns.

I scowl into the receiver. "Then why are you calling my office?"

"Because you're not answering your cell, dickhead." Well, there's the grump who doesn't want to be called a friend.

Lifting papers and files and whatever else has been stacked here today, I find my phone at the bottom of the pile. Dead.

I barely contain a groan. That's what happens when you sleep in your office.

"I'm leaving Sassy's," he says, breaking the silence and putting me instantly on edge.

"And?"

"And she told me about your game."

My face grows hot, and my jaw nearly hits the floor. What the hell, Saylor?

"Not the details, thank God." He sounds a little queasy, and I chuckle. "For future reference, that girl has no filter."

"Okay, good to know. And? Don't draw this out on my account, Grady. It's not like I don't have years' worth of work to do in a few days' time."

"I just wanted to say that whatever game your fucked-up mind came up with, it's working. I've never seen her so…"

"So, what?"

"Energized."

Maybe she's having more orgasms than she's admitting. The thought makes my cock jump to attention.

"Yeah?"

"Yeah," he grumbles. "But she's also writing faster than I've ever seen her. You've been gone a week, and she's a quarter of the way through a new book already."

This has me sitting up straighter. "How is that possible?" Worry deflates my erection faster than ice water.

"I don't know, Thompson, but her fingers fly across the keyboard. She said something about chasing Meghan Quinn's daily word count. I don't even know what the fuck that means. But she's okay. She's eating, which is a good sign. She could do with a shower, but that's probably a side effect of being in the zone more than anything else. It wouldn't be the first time she's lost track of time. She's fucking weird when she's on a deadline."

I don't like the thought of her sitting in her office for so long that she forgets about basic grooming. And I especially don't like that Grady knows intimate details about her process.

"Don't go getting all jealous. Get over yourself and accept that some things will take time to learn."

"Whatever, Grady. What else?"

"That's it. I told her I was calling you, by the way. I'm not going behind her back, but I'm proud of her, and I thought you'd want to know."

I do. And as much as I hate admitting he's right, he is. And for the first time, I can appreciate his loyalty to my girl. We've lost a lot of time and changed a lot these past six years, but we have a lifetime to make up for it.

"Thank you for checking on her," I say. "Are the vultures still outside?"

"Yes," he grunts. "But considering she has a garden hose attached to the kitchen sink, I'd say she's pushing them back when she's overwhelmed by it. But whatever she's doing, they seem to love her."

Of course she's protecting herself, and for once, the media is loving her prickly attitude.

"I asked her not to take her midnight walks while I was gone," I say. "I don't even know what path she takes." Still, it was an asshole request. I don't want to be someone who dictates her life, but people do stupid shit, and I'd lose my mind if I wasn't positive she was safe.

He sighs heavily. "She never lets anyone accompany her. The few times I tried to follow her she hid behind a tree and threw pinecones at me when I walked by." He's quiet for a minute, and I hear him shuffling papers. "I think she's too scared because of the crowd, but she's going outside. Adam and I take turns dropping off burgers when we shut down the brewery, and she's always on the back deck staring at the stars."

That piece of information eases some of the worry that's taken up residence in my heart. The deck is better than that dock I want to destroy with my bare hands. "Thanks, Grady. How're Lena and Poppy?"

The silence pings all the nervous energy surrounding me. Did the call drop?

I'm about to dial him back when he speaks. "They're good."

"Grady?"

"They're good," he repeats. "Lena is excited about the salon. Did she tell you she started the process for her Connecticut cosmetology license?"

"She did." I smirk at how uncomfortable he sounds talking about her.

"Did you find that asshole brother of yours?"

That wipes the smile right off my face. "No," I growl. "But I will."

"Have you seen the news?"

Pinching the bridge of my nose, I lean back against my chair. "Yeah. So far, no one from Kingston Corp has commented."

"What do you know about Shannon's fiancé, Blake?"

His question surprises me. I would have thought he knew more about him than me. At least now.

"He was a good guy when I knew him. Nothing like his father, as far as I could tell. You haven't met him over the years?"

Grady grunts in that caveman way that he has. How he ever wore a suit and tie every day boggles my mind.

"No," he says. "As far as I know, he never set foot in Hope Hollow again after the funerals."

"He said he would help Saylor and Ainsley. Did he abandon them?" My pulse gains a jagged edge to it. I always assumed they had him in their corner. It's what eased some of my worry on the bad days.

"Financially, he did everything he said he'd do. But he's never been around in any other way."

My jaw clenches. Maybe I misjudged the guy. Once a Kingston, always a Kingston.

"Grady? Why are you asking? What aren't you telling me?"

"Nothing," he says distractedly. "I'm covering my bases."

"What kind of base could Blake be?"

Three beats of silence fill our space before he says, "An unpredictable one. Companies like Kingston Corp all operate in the same way. They'll make a statement eventually, and when they do, we need to be prepared for every possible scenario."

"Would they really throw the girls to the proverbial wolves?"

"I'm not putting anything past anyone these days," he says. "Listen. Everything is good here, but Lena's on edge over Trent. Shut those doors and get home. Our girls need you."

He hangs up before I process his words—*our girls*.

Well, shit. Tossing my pen on the desk, I plug in my phone, and after a minute, it lights up with notifications. I scroll by them all until a text from Saylor pops up.

I stand and shut my office door. The place cleared out quickly after I told them I was shutting down Ascendancy, but there are still a few stragglers, and seeing me after I got a text from Saylor would not be considered workplace-safe.

My girl is fucking dirty, and I love it.

Once the door is locked, I practically run back to my desk.

Saylor: How do you feel about hand necklaces?

Saylor: This arrived in the mail today.

Saylor: Picture sent.

Holy shit. Is that a dildo?

Saylor: Strictly for research purposes, of course.

Saylor: Have you ever watched anal porn? That does not look comfortable.

My suit pants instantly become way too tight. I can't even read the rest of her messages. I hit call on the video message and wait for her to pick up.

"Hello," she sing-songs in a very un-Saylor-like way. She's really pulling out all the stops to win our game. It has taken every ounce of willpower I possess not to nut in my jeans every time we talk.

"Saylor," I growl.

"Yes," she drawls, then props the phone up in front of her. She's sitting at her desk, and her fingers fly across her keyboard.

It momentarily distracts me. "I like watching you work." It slips from my lips, but it's the truth, and I love the sexy flush that creeps along her collarbone.

"Yeah?" she asks. She's a fucking siren, and I'm entranced by the lure of her song.

It reminds me why I'm calling.

"Are you watching porn?"

She shrugs. "Research." She smirks, and my memory chooses that moment to remind me how sexy those lips were wrapped around my cock.

"Show me," I demand.

Her startled expression pleases me more than it should.

"What?"

"Show me the video you were watching."

She's shaking her head no, but her chest heaves—she can't hide the fact that she's turned on.

"How wet did you get watching it, Saylor?"

Her throat works to swallow, and I imagine filling it with my dick.

"Did you picture me doing all those dirty things to you, sweet girl?"

She doesn't answer, but she doesn't have to. Her eyes are hooded, and she wets her lips like she can already taste me.

I will never get enough of her.

Saylor stares through the screen with a war raging behind her mask. Will she tell me the truth about picturing us in the porno, or will she fib?

"No," she says defiantly. "I did not imagine you fucking me. I fingered myself to it, picturing you on your knees watching me."

Just like that, she turned the tables on me. The triumph shines in her irises like the goddamn vixen she is.

"Show me," I growl, then watch with sick fascination as her breath hitches and her face flames.

"Now?"

"Right. Now. Save your work, Saylor."

Her panic flares, and she chews on the inside of her cheek. She always saves her files the second she removes her fingers from the keyboard, even though the program saves itself every few minutes.

I watch her head tilt back and forth while she waits for confirmation that her manuscript is safe in the drive. As soon as her face perks up, I take over again.

"What are you wearing, Saylor?" It's a stupid question. Now that Grady pointed it out, the same shirt she's been wearing for two days is obvious. Her cheeks flush crimson when she realizes it, and she fidgets with something on her desk.

"Oh, Sayls. You've been fully immersed in your world, and now it'll be my mission to make you so dirty every day that you're forced to take care of yourself."

"I do take care of myself," she says grumpily, then crosses her arms over her chest to prove her point. "It's not unusual for an author to get lost in her craft. I write when the characters tell me to write."

"And you listen so well," I say with a low groan, "but I'm going to make you so wet you'll have no choice but to shower."

Defiance shines brightly in her squinty-eyed scowl, but it's how she bites on her bottom lip that gives her away.

"Take off your clothes."

She glares at me. "You first."

Standing, I hit the remote on my desk that pulls the blinds in my office closed and changes the glass, separating me from the rest of the office to opaque. Then I slowly remove one article of clothing at a time.

When I'm fully naked, I sit in my chair and wait expectantly.

"You're serious?" she croaks.

"Deadly."

She huffs, then stands. There's a slight tremble in her fingers as she pulls the shirt over her head.

"You don't have a bra on," I accuse.

"No."

"Wasn't Grady just there?"

She crosses her arms over her chest. "I had a sweatshirt on, you big baby."

"Say that again and watch what happens when I get home."

"Promises, promises," she taunts while removing her shorts.

Tension winds through the muscles in my back, up through my shoulders, and into my neck, so I stretch left to right trying to find some relief, but I coil like a snake when Saylor tosses her shorts to the floor.

"For fuck's sake, Saylor. No panties either?"

She sits down in her chair without answering. Her tits bounce with the movement, and my pulse turns molten beneath my skin.

"Put your legs up on your desk. Straddle your phone."

"Dante."

I stare without blinking until she lifts one leg, then the other.

My mouth goes dry and when I speak, my voice breaks, giving away my need. "Move your phone back. Show me everything."

She complies, and her pussy comes into view.

"Jesus, Saylor. You're already dripping."

"I've been writing about sex all day. What do you expect?"

That sassy little mouth has never looked sweeter.

"I expect you to show me how you touched yourself to porn today."

"I didn't…"

That's a flat-out lie. I arch a brow.

"I didn't…much."

"What does that mean?"

"It means Grady showed up at the worst freaking time."

The arm of my desk chair cracks under the pressure of my hands. "He what?"

What the hell is she doing to me?

"Oh, don't get your panties in a twist," she says, waving her hand like you'd shoo a fly. "I was locked in my office. I was dressed before I answered the door."

"Saylor," I growl. "That means you were flushed when you went out there. Your cheeks turn a delicious shade of pink when you're aroused, and you can't keep your hands out of your hair. So he not only saw you flushed, but he saw you with fuck-me hair. Were you biting your lip too? Were they swollen like when I devour you? Were you dripping because you weren't wearing fucking panties?"

"Dante," she whimpers.

"Does that turn you on, Sayls? Knowing how unhinged you're making me?"

She nods through her torment. She's seconds away from sliding those delicate fingers over her clit that I'm sure is glistening with her need.

My cock jerks against my stomach like it can reach her through the screen.

"Touch yourself, baby. Show me how wet you are."

Her hand moves so fast it's a blur on the screen. One finger slips inside her channel, and I groan, palming my cock as she rides her hand.

"Show me," I breathe.

She smiles and lifts her finger to the camera, turning it this way and that to reveal the evidence of her arousal.

"Suck it."

She hesitates for half a second before drawing her finger into her mouth and sucking it clean.

I tug harshly on my dick, losing myself in the moment. I slip my hand over the crown and pump into my fist like a lonely teenager on prom night.

"Make yourself come," I tell her.

"You—You first." Stubborn. So, stubborn.

Picking up my phone, I angle it to reveal every throbbing inch of me. I'm swollen and purple and so damn ready to explode. She watches while biting her lip as I drag my hand over the soft skin covering my hardness. I'm rougher than I'd normally like, but I'm so on edge that I need the spike of pain that leads to exceptional pleasure.

"Oh, God," she moans. Her finger flutters across her clit, and I've never been so jealous of a digit in all of my life.

"If I were there, that would be my tongue. But I wouldn't

stop at your clit. I'd lick you from hole to hole until both were so wet, you'd be begging me to fuck you everywhere."

"Dante," she cries.

"Has anyone taken your ass before?" A possessive growl ignites deep in my throat.

"You—" She gasps. "You know they haven't."

"Who do you belong to?" I pump my palm roughly over my shaft, up and around my head, then back to my base. I won't last long.

"You."

"Who do I belong to?"

"Me," she moans, and the first few tremors in her legs and stomach shake her body.

"Come for me, Sayls. Come now."

To my utter shock and delight, she listens, and before she's finished crying out my name, come shoots from my tip and lands on my thigh.

Saylor blinks multiple times before she lifts the phone closer to her face. "That doesn't count because we both came."

That surprises a laugh out of me. She's a competitor to the end, and I need to get home to my girl.

CHAPTER 32

SAYLOR

*T*here's a deafening roar from outside, and I leap from my chair then spin in place while my mind searches for safety. I press a hand to my chest like I can calm the harsh reactions that way.

The reporters are here, from gossip sites to cable news stations, but they've never been that loud. Over the last week, they've become background noise to my writing, but this is so disruptive it broke my concentration.

I startle again at a loud knock on my back door and my heart thunders in my chest. Grady and Lena have keys, and no one else comes by until after dark.

"Sassy? It's Blake," a loud baritone calls over the noise.

What?

My feet eat up the distance in a few steps, and I'm taking the stairs two at a time before my brain kicks in.

Wait. What if it's not really him?

"Prove that you're Blake," I call through the closed door.

"Mr. Pox." His answer sucks the air from my lungs, suffocating me with memories as I slowly unlock the door.

Mr. Pox was Shannon's stuffed animal she'd had since she was a baby. I'd demanded we bury her and her son with it.

My hands shake harder than my body as I slowly open the door and find Blake Kingston, the man I once loved like a brother.

"Blake? What are you doing here?"

"Can I come in?"

Manners kick in even though my mind is working through murky waters, and I move aside so he can enter, then I follow him up the stairs.

I haven't seen him since he FaceTimed us drunk on the first anniversary of the accident. He'd looked like he was dying then, and it wasn't until sometime later that I understood he probably was. Your heart can still beat long after you stop living.

But today, he's clean-shaven and wearing a suit. His skin is pale but not drawn like last time. He's still sad, but maybe not as haunted.

"Can I sit?"

I'm standing there gaping at him like a fish out of water, but I nod.

He drops into a chair, then hangs his head and holds it in his hands, so I cross the room and silently sink into the chair across from him.

"I'm sorry," he says without lifting his head.

"You're sorry? For what?"

When he lifts his gaze, I'm faced with a physical representation of the pain I've been wearing for so many years.

"I don't go online, Sassy. I don't watch the news. I don't even talk to anyone. I had no idea this had gotten out until a friend showed up on my doorstep to kick my ass."

He drags a hand through his hair, and I do a double take when some sparkles float to the floor in front of him. Is he shedding pixie dust? My lips curl up in surprise. "Are you wearing glitter?"

His expression shuts down so fast I almost laugh. "Fucking friends," he mutters. "It doesn't matter. While I appreciate he showed up, my friend has the sense of humor of a ten-year-old girl. Hence the glitter." When I don't say anything, he says, "He basically threw glitter at me for having my head up my ass. Don't ask. It'll never make sense to anyone but him."

He scans my home with an expression of nostalgia and regret. "Have you been trapped in here because of them?"

I shrug, still shocked that he's sitting in my living room.

"I'm writing," I explain.

"What happened with your publisher?"

The moment is surreal, sort of reminiscent of staring at a ghost. Just like when I was a kid, I sink into my chair and spill my guts to my older sister's fiancé.

I tell him everything. Once I open my mouth, our conversation becomes the most exhaustive therapy session I've ever had. I've always believed he was the only one who would ever truly understand me, and as one word spills into the next, I know I'm right. My voice is raw by the end and matches the sadness in his.

"I'm so sorry," he says when I fall silent. "I felt like a piece of me died right along with them, but I should have been here for you. Shannon would have wanted that."

He runs a rough hand through his hair, leaving it standing every which way before he speaks again. "I've spent so many years filled with nothing but hatred. She wouldn't like the man I've become. Sometimes I think I did die with them, Sass, in every way that matters, except my body kept breathing."

He puts voice to the pain that's been haunting my every breath.

"You lost a lot that day," I say.

I lost my sister, but he lost everyone.

"So did you, kid. But I was an adult. I should have been here for you. You'd barely graduated college. You girls were the only family I wanted, but I couldn't be here and not see Shannon everywhere."

A gunshot to the chest would have hit more subtly than his words. "That's why I pushed Dante away."

"We've made a mess of things, haven't we?" His chuckle is forced, but at least he's trying. "We have to do better, kid. Shannon would kick our asses if she saw us now."

That makes me laugh, but it's messy and tear-stained. "Is that why you're here?" I ask.

"It sped things up. I've been trying to pull myself together for about a year. But after seeing everything that's happening to you that I could have prevented if I'd asked for help after Shannon died was the final straw. I've said for a long time she would expect more of me, and honestly?" He runs his hands down his thighs. "I expect more of myself too. She was my best friend, you know?"

I nod and blink feverishly.

"But she loved you girls like you were hers, and that makes you mine too. I've been a shit big brother, Sass. But I'd like to help if you'll let me."

An internal shudder causes a tremor in my voice. "I haven't been living either, Blake. Everything hurt too much. But I'm trying now. And you're right, Shannon would want you to be the man she fell in love with, not someone waiting for his turn to die."

His wounded face guts me. In it is guilt, anger, and something else I don't quite recognize.

"I'm taking back control of my life one day at a time, and that starts with getting the reporters off your back. And…"

His Adam's apple bobs in his throat. "It means saying a proper goodbye to them."

I freeze in my chair. "Have you not been to the cemetery?"

I understand every ounce of pain that crosses his face. "I tried, Sass. I did. But no. Today will be the first time."

The blood drains from my head.

"Are you okay?" he asks.

"Blake. Um. When, well, when we buried them, I couldn't leave him blank." Recognition crosses his face. "I couldn't do it. I needed him to know I was talking to him."

"The baby?" he asks, so quietly I fear I imagined it.

I nod. "We named him Rayne because Shan—"

"She loved the rain." I've never heard a more raw version of pain as I do in his words. It cuts a fresh hole in my heart. "It's perfect, Sassy, thank you. I'm sorry I wasn't brave enough to do it back then."

Grief hits everyone differently, and I never held how he handled his pain against him. I can't deny it would have been easier for us all if we'd been together, but I doubt I would have allowed it either.

"Can you stay a while?" I ask. He doesn't need forgiveness from me. He needs what I need—acceptance.

The muscles in his shoulders relax, and he shrugs out of his suit jacket. "I can."

We sit and talk for a few hours. He explains how he'll give a statement and ask for privacy, but by returning to the land of the living, he thinks the media will follow him to New York and give me a reprieve.

We talk about Dante, and even though he's pissed, he understands I didn't give him a choice.

He tells me how he'll visit Ainsley next week, and he's meeting with his brother at their company because even though he walked away, his brother never gave up on him.

335

And we laugh. It's hard at first, but the longer we talk, the more he helps me relive the happy memories.

By the time the sun sets, we're both emotionally exhausted but spiritually settled for the first time in years.

"I'm going to be a better person, Sass," he says as the night comes to an end. "I hope you'll allow me to be the big brother I should have been."

I have no tears left to spill and no more words to say, so I do the thing I've mostly avoided for years. I hug him.

"I'm so sorry, Shan," he whispers above my head, but I stay silent because he's still searching for closure, and if this gives it to him, I'm happy to be a part of it. "Is Dante taking care of his brother?" he asks when I pull away.

"Yeah. He's trying."

"Can I help with that?"

I shake my head. "I think it's one of those demons he has to slay himself or he'll never be able to shake it."

"I understand that. But Malimar I can do something about," he says with a broad smile.

"What do you mean?"

"Sassy," he drawls, pointing a finger in my direction and reminding me of the playful man he used to be. "I may not have been utilizing my family connections to punish myself for my father's sins, but that doesn't mean they aren't at my disposal. Noah is running Kingston Corp now and is even more ruthless than I was. He can tear Malimar's empire apart piece by shitty piece if I ask him to."

When I was a kid, I had no clue who Blake or his family were. To me, he was just my sister's boyfriend who treated her well and was always nice to me. The power he came from never occurred to me until his father ran Shannon off the road because they had threatened to elope and she didn't fit into the Kingston mold. She died because some angry, enti- tled old man thought he could dictate how someone else lived their life. That's the unfairness of it all because Shannon didn't fit the mold—she created it.

The Blake I grew up with ate SpaghettiOs out of a can and helped me with homework. But the Blake standing before me now is hardened by experience, bound by duty, and out to take back his life.

When I stay silent, he says, "And I'm asking him to do it, Sass. By Monday morning Malimar will experience the pain he's been causing."

"Blake." I'm not sure what I want, but he's patient and allows me to work through it. "I don't want Malimar to hurt anyone else the way he's come after me, but..."

"But you need to fight your own battle too," he guesses, and I nod. "Okay. I get that. We'll start the process of dismantling his organization, but your fight is yours. If you need me for anything, I'll be around this time."

I nod because my throat is dry and scratchy, like I've pulled all my emotions of the last six years through it with thorns attached. I appreciate that he'll help others not fall victim to Malimar, but I'm even more grateful that he trusts me enough to fix my own problems.

"I need about thirty minutes to make a statement down there. Then..." He rubs his palms on his thighs again. "Would you like to come to the cemetery with me?"

I remember the first time I went alone. I cried myself to sleep in the grass with my hands sunk in the ground like if I dug my nails in deep enough, I could bring them back to me, and I don't wish that on anyone.

He'll have to make that arduous trip someday, but not today. Today we take the first step to taking back our lives together.

CHAPTER 33

DANTE

"*T*hese daily phone calls are beginning to feel like friendship, Grady. You'd better be careful..."

"Did you see the news?"

Words catch in my throat, and I toss the clothes I was packing to the floor, put Grady on speaker, and open a web browser on my laptop.

I don't even have to search for it. It's the top hit on everything from Google to Page Six.

The Kingston Heir Returns.

I click on the first one and lights dance in my vision. An older version of the man who treated me like a little brother as a teenager stands in front of Saylor's home, telling the world how he lost his fiancée and his unborn son, and that his father was to blame for it all.

He keeps it short and to the point. He doesn't take questions. By all measures, it's the perfect public relations response.

But he has the same thing haunting his eyes that Saylor does—sadness.

"When was this?" I ask, searching for time stamps, but

they range from one to three hours ago as every media outlet picks it up.

"At least a couple of hours ago," Grady says. "Have you heard from her?" The inflection in his tone sets the hair on my arms on end.

"Why do you ask like that? Where is she?"

"I'm not sure, but she's not home and isn't answering her phone."

If Blake did something to upset her, to cause her harm when I'm not there to hold her, I don't care what his pedigree is. I'll kill him.

"Grady..."

"I know. I'm sorry, but I know. We're looking for her."

"Did you call the hospital? Did you talk to Ainsley?" My heart is grasping for any explanation for where she would have gone. Where the hell does she go when she walks alone?

"Her car is still in the garage, so she hasn't gone far..."

He doesn't finish his thought because we both know where it leads.

"The lake."

"Sassy isn't stupid, Dante. She's lived by the lake for years and has never gone in."

"Except when I scared her with my words," I say, repeating her accusation from the first day I went home.

"Adam and Harrison are in the boat." A fear I've never known tries to cut off my airways. "She's not out there, Dante. It's just a..."

"Then where the fuck is she, Grady? I know she doesn't go in the lake, but she did fall in recently. She can be clumsy, but she hasn't even gone on a walk in the dark for weeks. Not with all the assholes hounding her house."

"Dante."

"And what the hell was Blake doing at her house in the first place?"

"Dante."

"What if he upset her and she—"

"For fuck's sake, Dante. Shut the hell up for a second."

The velocity of his tone stuns me into silence. "Kingston got the media to back off. Mrs. Walker said she only sees one random one wandering through town now. My best guess is he showed up to make sure she was okay, gave his talk, and went home. She's most likely walking somewhere to work through her thoughts. But I didn't want you seeing it and freaking out when you couldn't get ahold of her."

"Screw this." I hiss out a breath. "Thank you. But screw this. I'm done being away from her. There's literally nothing Trent can do to us now. Nothing. He's put all our shit out there, and we survived." I hope. "I'm coming home, and he can burn in hell for all I care."

"You don't mean that."

"Fuck off, Grady."

"Stop fucking swearing at me. If you didn't care about the asshole, you wouldn't have been diddling around this whole time."

"Fu—"

"Don't interrupt me. I didn't say it's a bad thing. He's your family. I get it. But don't say you don't care because everything you've done to this point proves otherwise."

"Fine. But I'm done trying to fix people who don't try to fix themselves."

"I learned the hard way, Dante. You can't fix people, only things. You'll do good to remember that. Lena is dropping Poppy off with Mrs. Walker, and we'll tag team all her favorite spots."

He's melancholy when he speaks. There's so much he keeps locked away, but even with all his secrets, he's quickly become a trusted friend.

"Thank you, Grady. Listen, all I was saying is, if I have to choose between Saylor and Trent, I'll choose her every fucking time."

Dark, maniacal laughter rings out from the front of my house.

"What was that?" Grady asks. He heard it and is on alert too. But I know that laugh.

Trent.

There's some shuffling in the hallway, and then Trent enters my room and props himself up against the wall as the door silently swings beside him. I've never seen him so disheveled. His shirt is wrinkled like he's slept in it for days, and the neatly trimmed scruff he prefers is an unkept mess. His jeans are no better, and he's missing a shoe.

I scan his body from top to bottom and hate what I find. His eyes are listless and unseeing. And the worst part is, he's leaning against the door because he can't hold himself up.

"Dante?" Grady asks. I'd forgotten he was still on the phone.

I open my mouth to answer when the glint of metal has me clenching my jaw tight. Trent holds a gun haphazardly in his hand, and it's pointed at the picture on the other side of my bed.

The shot rings out, but it doesn't sound like you hear in the movies. It's not a pop or a bang. It's like someone crashing cymbals together over your ears in quick succession, and even when they stop, the sound lingers, disorients, and makes your eyes sting.

My ears ring, making it impossible to understand whatever Trent's saying. I blink and shake my head, but nothing unmutes the world.

The phone is still in my hand. Take care of her. Protect her. Tell her I love her. It all mixes with the bell in my head, but I can't bring myself to say it.

I don't want to admit I'll never hold her again, but the

way Trent stares at me with disgust and rage, I resign myself to the situation my brother has put me in. It'll take more than a miracle for me to walk out of here alive, but that doesn't mean I'll go down without a fight.

"Find her for me. Please."

"Dante!" Grady's voice almost pierces the haze in my head, but Trent's lips are moving, and he makes a twirling motion with the gun in his hand. He's telling me to hang up.

"Take care of her, Grady."

I hang up, stare at my brother, and pray to the gods above for a miracle.

Time feels like it's moving backward. Grady will have called the police by now, so I try to keep Trent talking until they arrive. It's harder than it should be with my ears still ringing, but it's my only chance of survival.

"It was supposed to be you and me. That's what you said." Trent's words bleed together, and the menacing void slowly consuming him into nothingness claws at my sense of duty. "But then she had to get in the way. Then that baby I didn't want. Now, after all this time, you take back the whore who threw you away. You chose that slut over your own flesh and blood," he roars. His temper ignites, and he loses his balance.

My fists flex at his derogatory remarks, but he isn't making any sense. None of our issues had anything to do with Saylor until he brought her into it.

I watch warily, reasonably sure I could take him, but I won't risk getting shot—not yet. Not when he's so volatile.

"Everything would have been fine if you'd only listened to me. Now? Now we're going to lose everything. Everything," he cries. "And you don't even care. You're throwing away millions of dollars to spite me. You're a coward."

"I'm not the one who ruined things, Trent." I keep my tone even, but my words are barbed with wire. "If you'd stayed clean, we would have had the world at our feet. But you couldn't do it. Not for yourself, not for me, and not for a little girl who thinks you hung the sun."

"She loves you more than me." He's back to being petulant, and that seems safer than volatile.

"I'm there for her, Trent. If you'd only show up, you'd see how much she loves you, but you don't give her the chance."

"Liar," he seethes. "Lena loves you more. The media loves you more. Even my own kid loves you more. No wonder you're the one that he kept."

Our father has always been Trent's bargaining chip. He's used my guilt against me for the last time, though.

I don't take the bait.

"How much do you owe this time, Trent?"

He lifts the gun, and I'm quick to cover my ears before he shoots at the pictures on the wall. White-hot fury sizzles and cracks in my veins. He shot at a photo of Poppy this time.

"It doesn't matter," he says, sliding down the wall. He bends his knees and rests his forearms on them. The gun is pointed carelessly at me. "All the clients are gone. There's nothing left to sell. You let every client walk free."

"How much, Trent?"

"One point one," he says like it's twenty bucks.

"One point one million?" I clarify.

He shrugs, and it brings the gun up an inch. I'm painfully aware that if it goes off, I'm dead.

"I didn't mean to party again."

"You didn't mean to snort a line of coke? Explain that to me," I say dryly while mentally counting the minutes away.

How long will it take for the police to arrive?

"Brendan Lake got that role that should have been mine. I worked hard for that role. It should have been mine."

My heart sits heavy in my chest because Trent always has an excuse. But this time he's right. He did work hard for that role, and if Brendan weren't a Lake, Trent would have gotten it. Still, losing a role doesn't mean you snort your life away.

"Then I lost the next role too. You were working with that football player at the time. You didn't even notice."

"You can't blame me for your fall, Trent. I was building a future for our family. You could have worked in the office with me. You could have pulled your weight, but you weren't ready to give up the spotlight even if the spotlight turned on you years ago."

The gun fires, and it comes dangerously close to my foot this time, but he doesn't flinch. Is he even aware that he almost fucking shot me?

Where are the police?

Sweat trickles down my spine as reality hits me. What if I never see Saylor again? I promised her I was coming back. I promised her.

"Trent," I say through clenched teeth. "I promised Saylor I was coming back. I never break my promises. If you make a liar out of me, so help me God, I will haunt you the rest of your goddamn days."

"Good thing my days are numbered then," he laughs darkly.

A flash of movement behind him draws my attention, and intrinsically I know I'm supposed to keep him talking. "What about Olivia? She's barely twenty, Trent. How did she get wrapped up in this?"

He scoffs and waves the gun like a Fourth of July sparkler. "She's so fucking dumb," he slurs. "I told her this was all your plan to get her face out there and that if she played it perfectly, movie roles would roll on in. But she didn't like my Poppy story so she tucked tail. She's home in Ohio or Nebraska or some shit."

"So it's not only your family's lives you didn't mind ruining?"

His lips curl into a sneer. "We were never family, Dante."

"Is that why you're doing this then? What the fuck did I ever do to you? What do you think you'll get out of this?"

"I was supposed to get three million dollars," he roars. "If you'd just sold when I told you to, I wouldn't have had to do it, but no. You and your fucking high horse."

"Three million from who?" My molars ache from clenching them so hard.

"They said all I had to do was cause a scandal so big that all your clients left you." His dark laughter sends a shiver down my spine. "Can you believe I finally did something right, and they went back on their word? They gave me nothing, Dante. Nothing. They're just like you."

"Who, Trent? Who are you talking about?"

The gun dangles from his finger. "Playmore," he says with a careless shrug.

He lifts his dark, unfocused gaze to mine. The door beside him snaps against the wall as men in black raid the room, and a final shot rings out. Trent's horror-stricken face slowly fades until everything goes black.

CHAPTER 34

SAYLOR

*B*lake sits hunched over the flowers we placed by Shannon's name and the candy I set by Rayne's. I always bring him candy. I don't know why, but I would have spoiled him in life, so...well, I just do.

We've been here so long my ass went numb an hour ago, but I won't rush Blake. Losing Shannon broke me. I can't begin to fathom his level of pain.

I can't even compare it to losing Dante because that was of my own making. However misguided I was, I'm able to have my second chance. Blake's chance was ripped from him, and I'm not sure his heart will ever recover.

The chill of a summer night and the dew seeping into my clothes make my teeth chatter, but I sit quietly and talk to my sister in my head. I tell her about Dante and my new fears. I tell her about my mistakes, though I'm sure she's been following the drama of my life like her favorite reality show, waiting for me to get my head out of my ass.

I chuckle silently at that. Would Shannon have been able to let go of mothering us and treat us like siblings if she hadn't been taken from us so soon?

I bet if I asked Blake, he'd laugh in my face. She was always going to be our sister-mom.

Eventually, he stands, and when he turns, his face is puffy from crying—no, not crying, but emitting your heart and soul through two tiny tear ducts.

Did he ever allow himself to grieve? Staring up at him now, I fear the answer is no.

"Do you come here a lot?" His voice is so raw it sparks new pain in my chest.

"Most days, at night, after I've finished writing. I didn't always, but coming by myself gave me a sense of privacy, like I could speak more freely."

"What kind of a monster does it make me that this is the first time I've been able to visit?"

I stand and brush off my shorts. "Not a monster, Blake. A man who experienced a loss no man should ever have to live through. And honestly, they're not there anymore." I point to their gravestones. "This is for us, not them. Sure, their bodies are laid to rest here, but what made them *them* is here, in our hearts and minds. They're in our memories and in photos. They're with us whenever we need them. I have to believe that. It's the only thing that gets me through the sleepless nights, even now."

"I wish I'd been strong enough to grieve with you girls." The way he calls us girls makes him sound seventy, not nearly forty.

I shrug him off. There were years when I wish he'd been here too, but I've always understood why he couldn't be. If Shannon were alive now, we could pass as triplets.

"We all handled the grief in different ways," I say. "But there's no right or wrong way to do it. We did what we had to in order to survive. That's all any of us could do. But I'm glad you're back. It's like having a piece of her with me again."

Emotion swims in his eyes. "She would be so proud of you, you know that, right? All she ever wanted was to raise you to be good humans—kind people with loving hearts. She used to say that every night like a prayer. She convinced herself she was messing you both up, but I hope she can see you now, Sass. I hope wherever she is, she's smiling."

My cheeks burn with new tear tracks. I didn't realize how much I needed that information—that she didn't regret giving up so much for us.

Blake pulls me into a hug, and the grief that's been tied to my neck for years folds itself up and neatly tucks itself away into a corner of my heart. I'll always carry it with me, but now it doesn't seem like it's all I'll ever feel.

For the first time since my sister died and I pushed Dante away, my heart is totally and completely free.

"Do you want to get a hot chocolate or something?" he asks, and I laugh.

"You do remember that I was twenty-two the last time you saw me, right? Not four?"

He wraps an arm around my shoulder. A wave of nostalgia washes over me, and I don't pull away.

"I finally understand what Shannon meant when she said you'll always be her babies."

I chuckle roughly. It sounds more like a bark, but my heart smiles at the memory. Blake is smiling too.

"We're going to be okay, Blake."

"I hope so, Sass. Otherwise, Shannon will be waiting at Heaven's gates to give me hell."

We both laugh into the silent night. It's freeing in a new way, and somehow, I know that Shannon sent Blake to me today—he's the sign I've been waiting for.

"Okay, no hot cocoa," he says. I can hear the humor in his voice, and it sounds like a relief. "How about a—"

"Sassy?" Grady's voice calls out.

"Sass?" Lena's voice hits me from another direction.

What the hell?

I turn toward Grady's voice because he sounds closer, and I spot him in the moonlight as he rounds the corner.

Even with the distance and nothing but moonlight, fear siphons the air from my lungs when his face comes into focus. Something's very wrong. Lena runs from the opposite direction, and her tears sparkle on her cheeks like painful glitter.

They meet in the middle, then sprint toward me as one, and my lungs collapse before they get halfway. I sink to my knees while Blake attempts to hold me up. But I'm dead weight. I've seen those expressions before.

How many times can a person's heart break before there's nothing left to keep them alive?

"HAVE YOU GOTTEN ANY UPDATES?" Grady whispers from the front of the plane.

Poppy is tucked into his side, fast asleep, while Lena rests in the bedroom.

I've never been on a private plane before, but the Kingston jet is even nicer than something you'd see in the movies.

Why would they need a gold K in the center of everything, though? I bet it's real gold too. I guess I never noticed how rich Blake was because he never acted rich.

What would acting rich even look like? A snort escapes my nose and tickles my throat, drawing worried expressions from the three musketeers.

Grady, Blake, and Ainsley stand with their heads together. They think they're whispering, but they're not. Poppy must be exhausted to sleep through their racket.

"Are they going to let her in?" Ainsley asks. "They won't tell me anything because I'm not family."

"I have an idea," Blake says. He always had a lot of ideas—ideas for dinner, for movies, for day trips. He got creative because Shannon wouldn't let him spend more than she could afford, even if he was paying for everything. Now I understand why she put limits on him. This plane is ridiculous.

I mentally laugh. But then, maybe everything's in my head. I'm not sure I've spoken since the cemetery.

Ainsley catches me watching them and walks down the aisle with a blanket. I'm shaking, but I'm not cold. I don't even feel it. I don't actually feel anything at all.

"Sweetie, you're in shock. Everything will be okay, though. I promise."

She can't promise that, but she says it anyway. Why do people always say that? And why do they say *I'm sorry for your loss*? How do you respond to that? *Thank you* is messed up. Are we thanking them for our loss? Thanking them for acknowledging our loss? We're aware that we had a loss. What does saying sorry after they're dead do?

It's a stupid thing to say.

You know what else is stupid? When people ask what we need in these situations. Like, bitch, I need them not to be dead. I need them to be here. I need to breathe, so stop asking stupid questions to fill the silence because it makes *you* uncomfortable.

"Sassy?" My sister's worried face lowers to mine. "Can I put an IV in you? My supervisor gave me supplies from the hospital to keep you hydrated. You've lost a lot of fluid, and you haven't slept."

I scan my arms and legs. Did I injure myself?

She lifts her palm to my cheek. "Your tears, Sass. You

haven't stopped crying, and you haven't consumed anything in hours. You need fluids and nutrition."

I haven't? I lift both hands to my cheeks and pull the moisture away with my fingertips to inspect it.

Huh. So strange.

Ainsley pulls gently on my arm, and I hand it over. I watch as she deftly prepares my skin. I don't particularly care for needles, but she's so fast, I blink and it's done.

She's a good doctor.

Did Blake tell her that Shannon would be proud of her too? She needs that. I had a full-on meltdown after she died, but Ainsley did everything privately, quietly, lost in her own shadows.

"There, all done," she says, fastening the last piece of medical tape. "It'll make you feel better." I stare at her blankly. "Well, not better, but it—it'll help."

Does she know that she's crying too?

She kisses my cheek. She's so freaking warm. Maybe she's getting sick. She spends so much time at the hospital, it wouldn't surprise me. Hospitals are germ factories.

Dante is in the hospital.

We're heading to the hospital.

We're in Blake's family's private plane.

We might not make it in time.

For years, all I had was time. Now I'm acutely aware that it's slipping through my fingers, and there's not a single thing I can do about it.

Grady squats in front of me. Jesus. When did he start moving like a panther? He's still cradling Poppy with one arm like she weighs nothing. Why the hell doesn't he lay her down? Isn't she getting heavy?

"Sassy?"

I blink, but I don't even know if my expression changes. Everything is blissfully numb.

"Sass," he says again. "Ainsley grabbed all the pills from your bathroom. She said one of them is a sleeping pill. Will you take it for us? You need sleep so you can be there for Dante when we land. Okay?"

I blink twice, and he sighs, but Ainsley reappears a second later and sticks a pill in my mouth. I tip my head back when she holds water to my lips. Then I stare at my sister and best friend and wait for the darkness to consume me.

CHAPTER 35

SAYLOR

*B*lake slips a ring on my finger as soon as we get in the car. How sad will it be if the only time I wear a wedding band is when my dead sister's fiancé puts one on me?

"Sassy, when we get to the hospital, tell them you're Dante's wife, okay?"

I nod. Will that ever be true?

There are a lot of unspoken conversations happening in the silence around me, but I'm thankful that all I hear are the tires hitting the pavement below us. Whoosh. Whoosh. Whoosh.

"If Dante makes it through surgery, he's going to teach me to swim," I say like a decree.

Everyone in the car swallows in unison. It's a strange symphony of sounds.

Ainsley is holding my hand and squeezes it tightly. "That's a great idea, sweetie."

I nod. "It is. It's a great idea."

Blake's phone rings, and he speaks in hushed tones when he answers it. He's sitting up front with our driver, and

Ainsley is next to me, while Grady, Poppy, and Lena take up the third row.

"How did you fit back there?" I ask without turning around.

Grady's heavy hand lands on my shoulder. The weight of it is comforting. "I'm sitting sideways, Sass."

"Huh."

"They eloped," Blake says. "I don't give a flying fuck what the rules say. If you want to receive another cent in donations from my family, you will do everything I asked before we arrive in"—he lifts his arm, and his watch glints in the early morning sunlight—"ten minutes." It's not an expensive watch, and it certainly doesn't fit with whatever custom suit he's wearing, but he still wears it.

Shannon gave it to him for their last Christmas together. She was embarrassed because we found it at a secondhand shop, but the face was beautiful—an antique. We all thought it was perfect.

"You still wear her watch."

He turns slowly and nods. "It's how I keep them with me until it's our time to meet again."

"If Dante dies, what will I keep with me?"

No one answers. It's not a fair question.

I lean my head against the window and close my eyes.

∼

"Bullet ricocheted."

"Accident."

"Surgery."

"Internal bleeding."

"The next three days are critical."

"Can I see him?" I ask. I'm standing in the middle of a

circle where everyone else is a giant, and I'm a kid trying to sit at the grown-up's table.

The doctor looks at Blake, then back at me. "Of course, Mrs. Thompson. We don't normally allow—"

"Take her to her husband," Blake interrupts.

"Right. Of course."

"What are you? The mafia?" Grady mutters.

"Worse," Blake says. "I'm a Kingston."

"Here's your phone, Sass." Ainsley pushes it into my hand. "We'll be right here. Right. Here. If you need anything at all. Okay?"

I finally take in the scene around me. Grady has an arm around Lena, who holds an abnormally still Poppy. Blake stands like a sentinel. Then there's Ainsley. Who watches out for her?

"I'll keep an eye on Ainsley, okay?" Blake promises, and I allow the doctor to take me by the arm and lead me down the hallway.

Antiseptic hits my nostrils, and a wave of nausea washes over me. An overhead fluorescent bulb flickers like an old-school horror movie, and I suppose that's fitting. This is the stuff my nightmares are made of.

Why does everything beep in hospitals?

"Mrs. Thompson?" the worried doctor says while gently grasping my arm. Shit. How many times has he said my name? "This must be terrifying, so I want to prepare you. He's lost a lot of blood. The bullet—"

"Is he going to die?" It's a little surprising how steady my voice sounds.

The doctor's face softens. Is Ainsley going to deliver news like this? How the hell will she be able to do it?

"It's too soon to tell, I'm sorry. We'd like him to gain consciousness within seventy-two hours, though."

"And if he doesn't?"

The doctor places a hand on my shoulder I think he means to be comforting, but it makes my skin crawl like there are millions of spiders feasting on my arm hair.

"If he doesn't, the rate of survival is severely lowered. I'm sorry, Mrs. Thompson. We're giving him the very best care."

Translation, even our best isn't a guarantee.

The doctor opens the door, and I step inside.

Beep. Beep. Beep.

I stand immobile at the foot of his bed as a nurse shuffles around him.

"Talk to him, dear. Let him know you're here. Give him something to reach for."

"Reach for?" My voice cracks for the first time since I was plucked from the graveyard.

"Those doctors all have their stuff to say, and they're not wrong, but I've been doing this a long time. Thirty-three years, to be exact, and I've seen some stuff in my day that even the most skilled surgeon couldn't explain."

"You think he needs a miracle?" I'm going to break down in front of this stranger.

"I think he needs you. Come on. I'll get you set up. I'm Alice, by the way." She leads me to a recliner near the head of the bed. "You must have some heavy pull around here. I haven't seen anyone move this fast since the president landed here fifteen years ago. They didn't even move this fast for an honest-to-goodness prince."

She keeps talking, but I only hear half of it.

"What's your name, hon?"

"Saylor." I don't recognize my voice. It's hollow and flat.

"Take a seat and get comfortable. I'll bring you some ginger ale, crackers, and a warm blanket." Alice places a hand over mine. "Talk to him, Saylor. I believe in my heart that he can hear you. He's strong, and he's young. Let him hear you, and tell him you're waiting for him. Love is the best medicine, after all."

Her brown eyes smile down at me. They're the kind of eyes that are always smiling too. The wrinkles that line her face show years of happiness.

"But what do I say?" Another wall falls with the next tear.

"Tell him a story. One where the boy gets the girl in the end, and they live happily ever after."

Tell him a story.

Tell him a story.

So I do. I start with the first time we officially met in speech and debate class. I'd been successfully avoiding him for weeks because anyone that pretty was not to be trusted.

Mr. Henderson calls off two more names, and my armpits start to sweat. Not the cute-girl-in-yoga-class kind of sweat, but the weird-kid-on-the-wrestling-team-who-walks-around-wearing-plastic-bags-so-he-makes-the-lower-weight-class kind of sweat.

I'm drenched.

Two more names.

There are four of us left. No. No. No. Mr. Henderson, do not do this to me.

"Julia and Cassie. Okay. That's it. These will be your partners all semester..."

"What about us?" The new kid and I say at the same time.

He sounds calm and relaxed, while I sound like a chicken about to have her head cut off.

Mr. Henderson pinches the bridge of his nose like he always does when he has to deal with me. Every time I enter his classroom, he hopes I'm Ainsley.

"I would have thought that obvious, Miss Greer." Despite new kid and me both asking the question, I'm the one he answers. "There are two of you left. Meet your partner, Miss Greer. I'm sure Mr. Thompson will handle the course load just fine."

"Mr. Thompson?" My voice is pinched. Great. Now I'm getting sick on top of everything else.

"Dante." A rich, husky voice tickles the hair at the base of my neck. "It's nice to finally meet you, Saylor."

"Actually it's, Sass..." My name dies on my lips as I spin to answer and run right into him. He has the bluest blue eyes I've ever seen, and they dance with stories and trouble I want to fall into. I forget how to speak.

This is why I've avoided him. This is why I run in the opposite direction every single time he comes near.

Dante Thompson is the only person in the world who can leave me speechless.

"What about us?" I have no idea why I say it, but when I do, he graces me with a dimple I can't look away from.

"What about us, Sayls? We're just getting started."

Trouble.

I am in trouble.

"This is no exaggeration," Alice says to Grady and Ainsley somewhere behind me. "She's been talking for two days straight. She hasn't slept, or if she has, she's kept on talking, and she hasn't eaten. I did get her to drink some ginger ale, but that was only because she lost her voice. And do you know what that girl did?"

"She kept talking because she believes he heard the words anyway," my sister says.

"Yes!" Alice is totally distraught, but she doesn't need to be. I'll stop talking when Dante wakes up. Because he will wake up—he will. "I'm worried it's my fault," she whispers. "I'm the one who told her to tell him a story."

"No, Alice," Grady says gently. "She's the most stubborn woman I've ever met."

This makes me crack a smile. "Do you hear them talking about me like that?" I say into Dante's ear. "The nerve of them."

He smiles. Dante freaking smiles. I scream so loudly, poor Alice almost has a heart attack.

"He smiled. Dante smiled. I told him a secret, and he smiled."

Alice and Ainsley wear matching expressions I don't like at all.

"What?" I demand. "I know what I saw."

"I'm sure you did," my sister consoles while Alice rounds the bed and checks Dante for signs of change.

"I did," I say with less conviction.

"Sometimes the body has reflexes, Sass."

"No. Stop it. I saw it. I did."

"We're going on thirty hours with no change…"

"Shut up. Shut the hell up and get out. All of you. Out. Now. I saw what I saw, and I will sit here telling him our story until we get the happily ever after we deserve."

"Sass," Grady says softly.

"Out." I'm close to hysterical, so I pull myself together with every ounce of self-control I possess. "Just go, please." I turn my back on my family and climb in bed next to Dante.

Screw what the doctors say—what anyone says. I know what I know, and I know that he promised to come back. I'm holding him to it.

I lie on my side so I don't touch his wound or wires and return to our story.

"Part Two," I say. "College. When Saylor showed up to her dorm room freshman year, she was surprised to find it already full of a hundred different kinds of poppy flowers. Okay," I say, willing him to do it again—to do anything again. "This part I made up, but if you'd like to chime in and correct me at any time, you're welcome to." I stare and pray, then pray some more, but nothing changes.

So, I talk.

LENA CRIES SOFTLY in the corner. "It's been four days."

Don't cry, Lena, for fuck's sake. Not in here. I'm trying to wake him up. You have to be more patient.

I raise my voice to drown them out. "Saylor held her book in her hands. Fear and hope were two sides of the same coin, but she'd been dying a little more each day. And she knew if she released this book into the world, it could change everything. She didn't know if Dante would still want her, and that was the most painful truth she'd ever had to face."

CHAPTER 36

DANTE

"She didn't know if Dante would still want her, and that was the most painful truth she'd ever had to face."

"How could you ever think that?" I flinch. Jesus, did I get shot in the ears? Why did that sound like a garbage disposal?

Saylor's body jerks beside me, and I try desperately to blink, but my eyelids are weighed down, and I must be using sandpaper for contacts.

"Oh my God," Saylor whispers.

"Just. A sec…"

"Oh my God," she screams. "Oh. Oh. Oh. Get someone. Get someone quick. Get them here now."

"Sayls, wait…"

"Oh my God," Ainsley cries.

"Did he? Did he just?" Fucking Grady.

Christ. Is the entire town of Hope Hollow here?

Finally, my eyes follow a basic command and open. I'm flooded with light and snap them closed again.

"Turn off the lights," Saylor barks.

"No, give me a minute," I say, but it sounds like I'm chewing on bark.

Chaos erupts around me as doctors filter in, giving commands and touching machines.

"I need everyone to clear the room," a young doctor says while reading a chart, and I grimace. That was a mistake. Saylor moves before I can say anything to stop her.

"If you tell me to leave this room one more time, I will cut out your tongue myself. Do I make myself clear?"

The doctor pales, as one would when threatened with such a gruesome crime, but Blake steps in.

Where the hell did he come from?

"She stays," Blake says with an air of authority that no one, not even the doctor, questions. "Also, fair warning, she's been up for at least three days, maybe four. Tread lightly."

"Okay," the doctor says, "but we do need her to move back so we can examine him."

Sassy Saylor is in full force today. No matter what Grady, Lena, or Ainsley try, she refuses to leave the room.

While the doctors poke, prod, and ask me questions for close to an hour, Saylor climbs into the recliner and falls asleep.

It's hours before she even twitches. Doctors come and go. I go for scans and tests. Our family takes turns checking on us. And all the while, she doesn't move a muscle.

"I knew the girl could tell a story, but talking for nearly four damn days straight is a new record," Grady whispers.

It's hard, but I finally turn away from her. Grady sits in a small chair on my other side. "You look like shit," I say. And I'm not just giving him a hard time. He truly looks like shit. I might be better off than him, and I'm the one who got shot.

"Yeah," he says, running his hand through his hair. "I've heard that a lot today."

"Something going on?" I ask, even though the pain meds kick in, and I stifle a yawn.

"Lena's pretty upset. She's not sure what she should tell Poppy." He scratches at his beard like it's irritating him.

"Shit. I haven't really had time to process any of this."

Grady nods thoughtfully, but he's staring at Saylor. "She never gave up hope."

"Stubborn," I say with a crooked smile.

When his gaze cuts back to me, there's a crack in his armor. The emotion he hides behind a wall of barbed wire is bubbling to the surface.

"How are they?" I ask, steering us back to Lena and my niece.

"I don't know," he says in a rush. "Lena's so stubborn, and I—she's kind of a mess over the Trent thing. The relationship with her parents is…strained. And what do you tell a four-year-old?"

Until this moment, I hadn't even thought about my brother. I wait for the guilt to come, but it never does. "Where is he?"

"In custody, but the charges haven't been filed yet. Blake found out he was so high that he should have OD'd."

"I tried to get him clean," I say.

"That's what brothers do." Grady's tone changes and his gaze is distant for a split second before he blinks it all away. "But you can't help those who don't help themselves. Sometimes you have to cut people out of your life for your sake and theirs."

"We won't have a relationship, don't worry about that. He almost tore me away from her." I turn my head to study Saylor. "I'll never forgive that."

"And he shot you." Grady chuckles.

"That too," I say darkly.

"I've never shot anyone." This has me returning my attention to him.

"You offering to be my fill-in brother?" I smirk, but I'm fighting another yawn.

"Why do you have to make everything so fucking weird?" he asks, scratching his head and glancing around the room.

"Well, are you?"

"No, I'm just saying I'm glad you didn't die, is all. Jesus. The girls will be here in the morning, and then, unless you need them, I'll take them home."

"Home?" I ask, hitching my brow when he doesn't answer right away.

"Yes. Home—to Connecticut. You'll be here for a while, and this place has too many ghosts. We ah—we're staying at her parents' house, but Lena's more comfortable in Hope Hollow. So hurry up and get better so you can get your ass home too."

He holds out his hand, and I take it, then pull him in for a side hug even though it pulls at every damn stitch in my body.

"Thanks, Grady. For everything." I don't have to say anything else. He gets the deeper meaning. Thank you for being there for Saylor. Thank you for helping with Lena and Poppy. Thank you for being a friend when I needed it most.

CHAPTER 37

SAYLOR

"*W*hat are you doing?" I'm not sure whose voice just came out of my mouth. It's a mix of my sister when she found me on the roof the first time, and Grady when he found out Lilly's boyfriend was buying condoms.

In short, I sound hysterical, and my body reacts accordingly.

"Jesus, Sayls. You scared the shit out of me," Dante says like this is my fault.

"Well, what are you doing?" The decibels of my voice may have dropped a bit, but my tone is still a cross between pissed off and too close to heart attack for my liking.

"I'm only going to sit on the sofa. I'm fine. The doctor said I can move around more now."

Dropping the bags full of groceries on the foyer floor, I dart across the room as anger rises with each step.

"Stand down, Oscar. I'm fine. I promise."

"Fine? You're fine? You were shot in the chest four weeks ago, Dante. That is not fine. That's near death. That's four days I thought you were gone. Four weeks is not enough time and—"

"Saylor."

I hate when he uses that tone on me. The one my body responds to even when my mind wants to stay angry.

"What?" I growl.

"Come here," he says gently, then lowers himself to the sofa and places the laptop he was holding onto the coffee table.

I hate this house. We're still in LA because his doctors didn't think it was safe for him to fly with a collapsed lung—not to mention the bullet they had to dig out of his heart. Well, maybe not his heart, but close e-damn-nough.

"Come here." He beckons again, and this time I do. I march to the sofa with my arms crossed, my brows furrowed, and my lips pursed.

His laugh makes me angrier.

"This isn't funny, Dante. You almost died."

He nods, and his face falls solemn for half a second. "Almost, sweetheart, but I didn't. I'm here. I'm doing physical therapy, respiratory therapy, and all the other therapies you signed me up for. You were terrified, Sayls. I get that, but you need to remember that I'm going to be fine."

"I almost lost you." My lip trembles, and I jut it out in protest.

This is a conversation that won't end because I can't seem to let it go. I fixate on the what-ifs, and every time I see the scar healing on his chest, marring his skin, my body instantly falls into panic mode.

"But you didn't because I promised you I was coming back. It will take more than a stupid bullet hole to keep me from you."

I drop carefully onto the sofa beside him, and he wraps his arm around my shoulder. I try not to lean on him too much, but he's not having it. He tugs me into his side until there's not an inch of space between us.

"I can't wait to go home," I mutter as a chill tickles my spine. "I hate it here."

"Oh, Sayls. We'll go home as soon as we can."

Dante was released from the hospital last week, and we came back to his house that was already mostly packed up, but I refused to come here alone. The blood had been cleaned from the bedroom, but I couldn't do it, and I still won't step foot in that room.

"Trent called again," Dante says, holding me a bit tighter because every other time he's told me that Trent called, I stalked away from the room.

Someone somewhere dropped the ball, and Trent is out on bail. I've barely slept since we got the call.

I stay silent.

"I answered this time," he says gently, and my body goes rigor mortis still. Even my thoughts are morbid these days.

"He said he's giving Lena sole custody—or at least he's filling out the paperwork."

I focus on my breathing, and he tucks my hair behind my ear, but I bury my face deeper into his chest to hide my tears.

I've only felt hate this powerful one other time, and it was for Blake's father. It's a hate that burrows into your heart and will never let go. There will never be a second chance for Trent with me.

Dante sighs, then rubs my back in slow circles. "He's trying to get help but admits he might be a lost cause. He doesn't have the will to fight, and it's…"

"It's hurting you that you can't fix it for him."

"Yes," he says in a throaty voice. "If he keeps going the way he is, he won't live to see forty. But I can't allow him to ruin those I love and I—I told him so."

"What did he say?" I'm almost scared of the answer.

"He said—goodbye."

"Do you think…"

"I'm not sure what to think, Sayls. But I've made peace with that goodbye. I spent six years of my life trying to save him from himself. I couldn't do it. He either will, or…"

"Or he won't," I finish for him. Sitting up, I take his face in my hands. "Are you okay? With everything?"

"He's going to live in my mind like my own personal failure. I can't help that. I want so badly to help him, even now, but he's no longer my priority, not if I want his sobriety more than he does, so I let him go. I hope and pray he gets his life together, but I'm also preparing for a phone call someday asking me to identify a body."

"He's an adult, Dante. He was never your responsibility."

"No," he says, pressing my face to the side of his chest that isn't scarred. "But I wanted him to be. He's my brother, and our lives could have been so different with other choices. But I'm also aware that I can't fix this for him." He shrugs and releases a shallow breath since he's still working on his lung capacity. "I've let him go."

There's pain in those four words, but he squeezes me a little more tightly, and I hold on with all my strength.

"You are my future, Saylor. You and Poppy and Lena. Even the Reids and all our nosy neighbors. Walking away from what hurts us is hard. It's painful, but sometimes, we understand why it has to be done."

He could be talking about Trent, or he could be talking about us six years ago. Two totally different situations, but I imagine the pain is a similar one.

"I'm sorry you had to make that choice," I say solemnly.

"Me too."

We sit in the sterile room, and I breathe him in.

"I heard from Grady today," he says.

I tilt my head and lean into him. "You did? What did he say?"

One corner of his mouth lifts, flashing that dimple at me. "Well, Blake is a little scarier than we gave him credit for."

The tension winding up my neck tightens its hold. "Why do you say that?"

"Apparently, Grady got a call this morning, since you listed him as your lawyer."

I sit up fully now, and my fingers find my necklace while I wait for him to continue.

"And?" I finally blurt when Dante just freaking smiles at me.

"And it seems Malimar Media is under investigation for a laundry list of offenses, so they're dumping weight. His publishing and recording companies are offering their talent a chance to purchase their rights back—below market value."

My hands ball into fists.

"Why are you angry? This is good news," Dante says. The confusion on his face would be laughable if I weren't so irritated.

"It is good news," I fume. "Except I told Blake I wanted to fix my career myself—all by myself. This is— He went—"

"You're so stinking stubborn." Dante chuckles.

My mouth falls open in outrage, but before I lay into him, he kisses the side of my head.

"You wrote your story your way, Saylor. You will still self-publish it and own every second of the process. You did fix your career. This is just speeding things up, removing road-blocks, and allowing you to start fresh as the CEO of your life and career. I'm sure he didn't do it to go behind your back. He said he was going after Malimar, and this is probably a natural progression of things."

"Damn it, Blake," I grumble again. "Seriously, though. What are you doing out here? You're supposed to be in bed, so don't try to distract me with Trent and Blake. You're still in trouble here."

He rolls his eyes. "I'm only on bedrest because you say so. Even the doctors said it's good for me to be up and moving around. Bed rest isn't going to help my lung recover."

God, I hate when he's right.

"And I came out here because the Wi-Fi in the guest room sucks. I was taking more of those classes on self-publishing."

I groan. Writing I can do. It's everything else I'll struggle with. "I'm pretty sure my old editor will work with me on the side, and I found a new cover designer who seems amazing. It's the other stuff I don't get."

He grins. I frown. It seems to be a pattern with us.

"What?" I demand.

"You're stuck with me for life, you know that, right?" His smile almost touches his ears.

"Yes," I say, dragging out the word with suspicion.

"And we're a team, right?"

I nod while my mind races to figure out where he's going with this.

"Well, I've been doing some research on indie authors."

"And? Can you spit it out before I have to change my shirt? My armpits are sweating again, and it's your fault."

Dante chuckles but points to a file on the table, and I can't help it. I fan myself, then grab the file.

Each paper has information on various authors and their businesses.

"What's this?"

"Well, Saylor, it seems all the highly successful indie authors have a team behind them. Usually, a spouse who runs the business while the other writes the words."

"What does that have to do with me?"

"You write the words."

"Yes," I say with an overly dramatic eye roll.

"Well, the other stuff I can do. The ads. The marketing. None of it is too different from what I did at AI, there are simply nuances I need to learn. Instead of having celebrities as clients, I'll alter my business plan for authors."

My throat is itchy, and my heart is beating too quickly. This might be excitement, but my mind hasn't caught up yet.

"You want to be a publisher?"

His entire face lights up.

"We'll start with you and go from there. I have a few clients who want to stay with me even if I'm in Connecticut, so that'll give us some income while we build your empire."

I study his face. He wants this for me. For us. And it makes me love him so much more.

"There's only one problem with that," I say snootily so I can watch him frown.

"What's that?"

"It's our empire we're building. Not mine."

I swear I've never seen a face beam more brightly than his.

"Our empire. Our future. Together. That's a plan I can get on board with, Sayls. Now get over here and kiss me like you mean it."

I twist on the couch and reach for his sweatpants. "Like I mean it?" I ask as I palm his thickening erection.

"Saylor," he growls through clenched teeth. "That's not…"

I rub my palm up and down his length. "Kiss you like I mean it, huh?"

"You sexy little minx," he hisses when I squeeze him hard.

The next thing I know, I'm flipped onto my back, and he hovers over me. "You're injured," I gasp.

"And you're mine."

I swallow down the well of emotion those three words create every time and nod. "I'm yours. And you're mine." I groan when he lowers his weight onto me.

"I told you if we fell into bed, we would fall into forever. This is forever with me, sweetheart. In life. In love. In business. In my heart. And in our bed. You. Are. Mine."

A ray of sunshine bursts through my smile, because his is the only thing I've ever wanted to be.

CHAPTER 38

DANTE

"About damn time you made it home," Grady grumbles, but his eyes shine when he offers me his hand.

It's been seven weeks since I was shot, and we finally got the okay to fly home a few days ago with the promise of continuing with therapy here.

"Happy to be here, Grady. It's been a long road."

He nods and takes a suitcase from Saylor's hand.

"You didn't have to pick us up," Saylor says, hugging him breezily. "We could have rented a car."

"Not happening, Sass." Grady walks ahead of us, and Saylor winks at me.

"Is there something different about him?" I whisper.

Saylor frowns and nods. "He's not as—I don't know. Grumpy?"

"I can hear you assholes. You know that, right?"

Saylor and I laugh, and I squeeze her hand. He honestly doesn't sound much like an asshole anymore.

"The girls were too anxious to see you. They're in the car," he says, and I detect a hint of insecurity in his tone.

I've FaceTimed with Lena and Poppy every day. They're still happily living in Grady's apartment, and he's helping renovate the salon. The sale will close next month, making Lena an official business owner. And Poppy has made so many friends that her birthday party this year will require at least two cakes.

But I don't know what's been happening between Grady and Lena, and my gut says it's something.

The windows roll down as soon as they spot us, and Poppy's ear-piercing screech turns heads a mile away.

I've never been away from her for this long before, and my heart trips over itself seeing her now. Her arms and legs are all waving at me from the confines of her car seat, and my heart thunders in my chest.

I love that little girl so much, and I hope now she can keep her wide-eyed innocence a little longer.

"Gwody, gets me outta here. Unca! Unca! Sassy!" All her words jumble into a mash-up that makes me laugh.

We pick up the pace, and I open her car door a second later. I wrap her in the biggest hug I can around the giant frame of her car seat.

"I missed you the mostest, Lollipop."

"Na ah. I missted you, Unca." Her voice breaks, and tears slip down her chubby little face.

"Aw, princess. Don't cry. I'm sorry I was away so long."

She wipes her nose with the back of her hand. "I wub you, Unca."

My throat closes, so I kiss her forehead and climb over her to the middle seat. Saylor slides in on the other side, and I sit between my two best girls while Grady loads our suitcases into the trunk.

"We missed you. Obviously," Lena says from the front seat. Her smile is shy, but the dark circles under her eyes are missing.

Grady has been helping her deal with the legal side of Trent's rights as Poppy's father. He's put her in touch with friends who specialize in family law anyway, and I'm grateful. It's been extremely stressful for her, and she needed someone on her side.

It shifts something inside me to see her like this. And I probably have Grady to thank for that too.

"You look good, Lena. Happy, too."

She turns her head with shining eyes. "I am, Dante. I'm —good."

Grady opens the driver's side door and climbs in. His large frame eats up any extra air, and I lean back in my seat. Poppy reaches for me and holds one hand, and I reach over to grab Saylor's with my other one.

When I'm settled, I'm shocked to find Grady has also reached across the console and holds Lena's delicate hand in his large one.

My mouth hangs open, and I find Grady glaring at me in the rearview mirror, daring me to say something.

"So," I say, dragging out the word, and he frowns with a warning. "It's been a wild couple of months. For everyone, it seems."

Lena's shoulders stiffen, and I almost laugh when she tries to pull her hand from Grady's and he tightens his hold. Her face turns a shade of crimson that makes me chuckle, but she doesn't turn to me, so I lean forward between them like an annoying little brother.

"So, guys. Seems like there's a story here. Care to share it with the class?" It sounds like I'm laughing at them, but I'm not. I'm happy for them, and especially for Poppy.

There's no doubt in my mind Grady would be a better father figure than my brother has ever been.

"No," Grady growls, and I laugh when Poppy growls back at him.

"I calls him Papa Bear 'cause he's so gwowly," Poppy says with a sunshiny smile.

I laugh out loud when the tips of Grady's ears turn red.

"So…" I prod, but Saylor pulls me back.

"Someday," Grady says with a little less gravel in his tone. "Right now, it's a story just for us."

Lena's shoulders shrink like she wants to melt right into her seat, but she doesn't refute what he said.

When I place a hand on her shoulder, she jumps, Grady growls, and so does Poppy. Love consumes me. "You're happy, Lena?"

This time, she turns to me, but Papa Bear still doesn't let go of her hand. Her eyes are swimming, but there's an ease about her that's never been there in all the time I've known her.

"I am, Dante." She swallows hard and a tear slips down her cheek when she drops her gaze to Poppy.

"Damn it, Dante," Grady mutters. He releases Lena's hand, then swipes the tear away. "Don't make her cry. I— Just don't do it."

My heart pretty much explodes right then.

I squeeze Lena's shoulder, then lean back in my seat. "I'm happy if you're happy, Lena. But it is a story I'll want to hear someday soon."

"Stinking nosy ass… You wanted a family, Dante. Well, now you've got one. A big, annoying, nosy one. Be happy and leave it at that." Grady's tirade fades away as Poppy regales us with everything she's done while we were away.

My gaze occasionally drifts to the front seat, but Grady's right. This is my family—the one I've always wanted. And I've never felt more at peace.

WE PULL up to the old craftsman-style home, and a sense of déjà vu washes over me. I rolled into this town a few months ago, full of anxiety and fear. This time, when I step out of the car and see the sign for Pleasure Bound Bookshop swinging in the breeze, I feel nothing but pure joy.

I stand, rooted in nearly the same spot as that first day, and allow all the changes to wash over me. There's been pain, and tears, and laughter, and so much love I could never explain it in a million years.

Poppy darts past me with a squeal of delight, while Saylor and Lena laugh and walk up the path to the house. But my gaze keeps snagging on the boarded-up building to the left of Saylor's.

"It's been like that a long time," Grady says, stopping beside me with a suitcase in each hand because I'm still not allowed to carry anything over fifteen pounds.

I stare at the second story, then let my gaze wander down the old brick exterior to where there were once large glass-plate windows in the front, and my mind instantly conjures our future.

"Do you know who owns it?" I ask.

"Yup." Grady rocks back on his heels, giving nothing away.

Tilting my head to the left, I find him staring at me with wry amusement in his smirk. "Care to share anything about who it belongs to or if I could persuade them to sell?"

Nothing changes in his expression except for one tiny muscle twitch in his cheek. "It's supposed to stay in the family, but the owners have had no use for it."

"Shit," I mumble.

"But," he says, and I swear I can hear a grin in his words. "Since families are expanding and all that, they'd probably allow some liberties—for the right people."

I turn to face him full-on. "You own the damn building, don't you?"

His smirk is answer enough, but he shrugs and opens his mouth anyway. "Not only me. Adam, Harrison, and Lilly too. Well, Lilly will when she turns twenty-four. Our grandparents owned a bakery there years ago, but none of us could figure out what to do with the place because new businesses haven't exactly been clamoring to move in. Not with the issues Faith Falls has had next door."

Saylor told me the entire town of Faith Falls is struggling, and the poverty rates are double what they are in Hope Hollow or Chance Lake. For a community that seems to care for one another, it shocks me that an entire population would be left out to dry.

"We're trying to rehab it," Grady says, as if reading my mind. "There are new businesses in Chance Lake that will bring in more jobs, more opportunities. The brewery is doing outreach there too, but it's a slow process."

"It's good that you're trying," I say.

"It is," he says gruffly. "So, the building. What were you thinking?"

"Well, the first floor might be the perfect place for a bookstore if someone wanted to take back their home. And the second floor is the perfect size to build a publishing empire and maybe help with some PR problems on the side."

Grady nods hesitantly. "Hear me out, okay? Kate is a pain in the ass, but I've seen what she's done for Sassy's career. It might be something to think about if you're building an empire. She's ruthless, don't get me wrong, but she loves Saylor and Ainsley like sisters."

Internally, I groan, but nod because I've been thinking the same thing. "We're on the same page. I sent her some preliminary plans last night to gauge her interest."

"You're going to do this for real, huh?"

"Yeah. Saylor's the only dream I've ever wanted. Now that I have her, I'll spend all my time making her dreams come true. I'm not afraid of hard work, and she has the talent. Plus," I say with a waggle of my brows, "if we're working together, I'll see her more."

Grady chuckles while shaking his head. "Yeah, remember that when she's biting your head off. You wanted this."

That makes my smile grow. "I can't wait."

He claps me on the back, then drags the suitcases toward the house. When he reaches the stairs, he calls over his shoulder, "Welcome home, Dante. You may have brought a metric ton of baggage with you, but you've unpacked it better than I would have ever imagined. She's lucky to have you."

My eyes sting. I don't need Grady Reid's approval, but I'd be lying if I said it didn't slam into me like something I've been waiting for.

Pulling out my phone, I snap a picture of the building next door. It'll be a before picture for our office when it's done. Then I follow Grady inside, more than ready to start my happily ever after.

CHAPTER 39

SAYLOR

Labor Day Weekend

"*S*assy!" Poppy squeals my name, and I curse whoever gave her sugar already. I'm not sure how this kid is so freaking happy all the freaking time, but she is, and sugar makes it worse.

I won't admit it to anyone, but she has softened me a little. Instead of buying the Bomb Pops that taste like dirty socks and vomit for the bookstore's Labor Day contribution, I got the sugar-infused, sickly sweet regular ones. I did it for Poppy but told everyone else it was an accident.

I have a reputation to uphold, after all.

"What's up, squirt?" I ask as she slides across my kitchen floor wearing a bright yellow bathing suit with a pink skirt and hat. She's also holding inflatable pink tubes in various sizes, and this little girl is suddenly making me wish I'd doubled up on my deodorant today.

"Come on. Come. On. Sassy. We is waiting for you."

Crossing my arms, I dig in my heels. "Who is waiting for me?"

"Ever-we-body," she says with an eye roll I fear she learned from me.

Dante's laugh fills the kitchen before his big head rounds the corner. "Lollipop. You were supposed to let me tell her."

"You is too slow, Unca. Come. On. Sassy. Come. On."

I glare at Dante, wearing a bathing suit with hot pink inflatable floaties around his forearms. Then he holds up a pink bikini, and I debate making a run for the bathroom and locking myself in.

Dante's face shines with happiness, but I'm already shaking my head no.

"Lollipop, go downstairs and tell Grody we'll be a few minutes, okay?"

Poppy shrugs her shoulders, hands me the pink floaties, then dances her little body down the stairs.

"No," I say when he takes a step forward. "No," I repeat when he keeps coming for me.

When he's inches away, he turns me in his arms and guides me to the window that overlooks my backyard and the lake.

"What the hell is that?"

Attached to my dock is an inflatable unicorn that must be ten feet wide and at least as tall. It's ginormous. And rainbow-colored.

But that's not all. Grady is wearing pink swim trunks with yellow floaties cutting off the circulation to his forearms. By the way he keeps tugging them down, I'm sure he's hoping they'll pop.

Adam and Harrison are dressed the same way, except Harrison has a smaller version of the unicorn wrapped around his middle.

Cassie, Ainsley, and Lena are all wearing suits that match the one in Dante's hands, and every kid, adult, and dog has some version of a swim floaty attached to their body.

"What the hell is this?" I wish my voice carried more sass, but I'm not sure if I'm scared, touched, or just completely flabbergasted—and that confusion shows in the bewilderment in my tone.

"Impromptu barbeque, Saylor." Dante's chest rubs against my shoulders when he shrugs, but he keeps his arms wrapped around my middle like he's afraid I'll make a run for it.

"Why is there so much freaking pink? And why is everyone dressed like a toddler at a splash pad?"

"Because you told everyone that if I lived, I would teach you how to swim."

No, I didn't. I wouldn't. I couldn't. Wait—mother freaking hellfire. I might have.

"Relax, Sayls. We aren't going in over your head. And I'll hold you the entire time. Today we're going to float."

"Float?" It comes out like a dog's squeaky toy.

"Mm-hmm. And all those people who love you want to float with you, show you it's not scary, and be there if you need them."

"Don't you think this would have been better in private? What if I freak the hell out?"

He chuckles. "Maybe, but they showed up for you and brought all your favorite foods to bribe you with."

"All of them?" There's no way that's true.

"All of them," he confirms.

"No way."

He nods and kisses my shoulder, and his lips curl against my skin.

"Lobster," I say like the little snot that I am.

"Grady."

"Figures. Coconut cream pie," I challenge.

"Harrison."

Freaking friends.

"Potato salad." Dante's hot breath hits my shoulder like he's about to speak, but I cut him off. "Made with Miracle Whip, not mayonnaise."

His laughter vibrates against my spine. "Ainsley took care of that."

"Hot dogs?" I ask meekly.

"Everything, Saylor. Now, are you going to stand here all day quizzing me on your favorite foods, or will you change into this flimsy fucking excuse for a swimsuit?"

"You didn't buy it?"

He shakes his head with a scowl. "Cassie was in charge of them, and that will never happen again."

Of course she was in charge. "Why was anyone in charge of them? Why did we all have to match? And why aren't they red, white, and blue?"

His face softens, and for a moment, I'd swear he was nervous. Color me intrigued. He glances away, takes a deep breath, then turns back to me with a shrug. "You try telling Cassie to wear anything with red on it. And..." He hesitates, and I melt at his sheepish expression. "I wanted a family picture."

My mouth hangs open, and the hairs on my arms stand on end. I shift my focus from him to the chaos unfolding in the yard, then back to him. "You wanted a family picture? With all of them?"

He nods. "Don't make fun of me. Grady's done enough of that already."

"I..." I blink, trying to clear my thoughts. "I wasn't going to make fun of you. I—I like that idea."

His face morphs into surprise when I take the suit from his fingers and walk to our bedroom. My legs shake, and my heart races, but I want to do this. I want to do it for him, and I want to do it for my sister. But most importantly, I want to do it for myself.

I don't remember the last time I wore a swimsuit, and seeing myself in one now seems like a new beginning even if my fears are clawing through my skin, telling me this is a bad idea.

A knock on the door makes me jump. "Sayls? You okay in there?"

Crap. A quick peek at my phone tells me twenty minutes have passed. Shaking out my hands, I cross the room and open the door to find Dante leaning against the frame like he has all the time in the world.

His eyes smolder when they land on my exposed flesh. "I'm going to kill Cassie," he murmurs. "But you're so beautiful my sweet, sassy Saylor girl."

My body temperature rises, and a flush creeps over my body.

"Ready?" he asks.

"No," I say honestly.

"Trust me, Sayls. Always, always trust me."

"Like this, Sassy. Like this," Poppy says from the other side of the dock. She's floating on her back kicking water all over Lena's face.

Freaking hell.

"It's okay," Dante says. "Listen to me. All you have to do is lean back. I'll hold you up until you get your balance. It's a trust fall, Saylor, and I'll always catch you."

How many times has this man said that to me? Hundreds? And how many times has he let me fall? Zero.

My entire body shakes, and I might be the world's biggest jerk because everyone I love stands in waist-deep water in a circle around me while I scowl at them.

"This is a lot of pressure," I mutter.

Every person moves back, making our weird circle twice as big.

"They're here for you. They want you to know you're not alone. Nothing will happen because we're all here to keep you safe," Dante says with a quick kiss to my lips.

"Why does everyone have to care so freaking much?" My sass is exponentially harsher when I'm scared, and right now, I'm terrified.

"Lie back," he says again with a chuckle. When his hand lands in the middle of my back, I try. How the hell do you lie down in water?

One foot comes up with a toe pointed at the sky, and my arms splash wildly in the water. Well, isn't that the most graceful thing you've ever seen? Embarrassment heats my cheeks.

"You've got this, Sassy!" Harrison yells from somewhere, and I flip him the bird.

"Try again," Dante says in an even tone. "This time I'm going to help you."

His hand inches higher on my back, then he leans down to put one under my knees, and suddenly I'm horizontal and staring at a cloudless sky.

Panic makes my arms flail, but Dante holds me steady. "You're okay, Sayls. You're doing great."

My ears sink below the surface, and I fight to keep my face from sinking while Dante holds the rest of me suspended in the water.

"It'll take a few minutes to get comfortable. Try to relax. You won't go under while I've got you."

"Yay, Sassy!" Poppy shouts, but it's muted with my ears submerged. My hip rests against Dante's chest and he slowly moves his hands up and down my back and legs, but I don't go under.

After an eternity, my body succumbs to the weightlessness of the water, and a slow grin creeps onto my face without my permission.

How many times did I watch Shannon out here doing this? She loved to float. I don't actually ever remember her swimming. But she would float until her sunscreen expired and she'd have to reapply.

Water laps at my toes, and I shiver when I float into a cold patch of water.

Look at me now, Shannon!

My lip trembles, and it's not water lapping my face but tears rolling down my cheeks.

"I'm so proud of you Sayls. You're doing it." Dante's words fling me back into the here and now. His hands are no longer on me. "Don't panic. You're doing fine. I'm right here. You're not going under."

"You promised not to let me go," I scream.

"I promised not to let you go *under*, and you're not."

Semantics. Freaking asshat.

I sit up to tell him so, and my body jackknifes when I suddenly sink. I don't even fully get my head wet before Dante pulls me up again.

He holds me to his chest and spins me around in the water.

I'm still crying when I spot the ring of people around us wearing teary smiles like I saved a baby turtle or something.

But the more faces I see, the harder I cry. It wasn't a baby turtle I saved. It was myself.

"I'm so proud of you. So incredibly proud. Do you want to try again?"

I can't believe I'm saying yes, but I nod, and he beams his rays of sunshine at me. I scowl in return, for old times' sake.

EPILOGUE

Dante

"She's going to wear that bathing suit like a trophy, isn't she?" Grady asks, slipping into the chair next to me.

Turning my head, I find Saylor standing with Ainsley and Blake. It's been a couple of weeks since her first swim lesson, and he's right. She wears that sorry excuse for a suit every chance she gets, and the unseasonably warm weather today is her excuse.

She's still not a great swimmer, but she can doggy paddle and hold her head above water, and that's all she really cares to do. She loves to float, and I tied a raft to the dock so she doesn't drift too far away.

"She's proud of herself," I say with a chuckle.

"I am too," he says.

Together, we scan the wild little family we call ours, and the tiny pain I've always carried in my chest eases. This is what family is supposed to be like.

Harrison infiltrates Saylor's little circle and whispers

something to Ainsley. She stiffens and turns a red that flares like the waning sun.

"What's going on with them?" I ask.

Grady's shrug is a little aggressive. "Fuck if I know. I've never seen him like that with anyone, but Ainsley's not his usual type. She's…"

"What?"

"Mature," he laughs. "She's not a one-night stand, and I made sure he knew that, but man, is he persistent."

On the other side of the fire pit, Cassie and James hiss at each other in not-so-hushed tones. "Mark my words," I say. "Those two will either kill each other or fall in bed together, but either way, there will be hellfire."

Grady chuckles, but it's distracted and, following his line of sight, I see why. Lena stands, rocking Poppy, who sprawls over her mom like dead weight. She swam for four straight hours today.

"I'll be…"

I shoo him away. "Go."

They've both asked me to mind my own business, so I do —for now. And I'm trying, but I think I caught the nosy fucker bug that comes with living in a small town because I really want their story.

James drops into Grady's vacated chair as Harrison sits on my other side. The two of them expel matching sighs, and I know we're about to hit guy-talk hard. Thankfully, we're interrupted when Saylor wraps her arms around my neck.

"Blake is heading out. Want to say goodbye?"

I twist in my chair so I can take her hand. "He wasn't here long. Everything okay?"

She shrugs. "Yeah, he's heading to their Boston office. Something about going undercover in his own company to spy on his cousin. He hasn't told me all the details yet, but it's going to make a fabulous book."

That makes me laugh. My girl can turn everyone's life into a story and make it good.

"Gentlemen," I say to Harrison and James, then excuse myself to shake hands with Blake.

Sadness washes over me every time I'm with this man. He's still grieving, and I'm crushed to find he still carries such heavy pain, but he hides it behind so many layers of hate that I fear no one will ever be able to penetrate his walls.

"So, Boston?" I ask as we approach.

He nods. Gone are his expensive suits and clean-shaven face. Now he'd fit right in at Three Brothers Brewing, and it makes me wish he'd taken Saylor's offer to stay a while.

"My cousin's a prick, and my brother, Noah, has convinced me he's mistreating our executives, if not blatantly stealing from us. Noah has more incentive to check up on him now that his fiancée's best friend is working there." He clasps his hands tightly and mumbles, "Fucking complications." Then he sighs and inclines his head in my direction. "I can't believe I agreed to his asinine plan, but I owe him for ghosting him and our company for so long."

Saylor's beyond happy he's rejoining the living, but I'm curious what it will take to get him to move on—or who it will take.

"It'll be an adventure," Saylor says with a grin that makes my heart stop. "And make sure you keep me posted so I can add it to a book. It'll be a bestseller for sure."

Blake stares at her for a beat too long, and my chest aches for the guy. Sometimes Saylor's expressions are a spitting image of Shannon's. I don't blame him for staying away, but I'm glad he's forcing himself to live.

"I will," he says gruffly, then hugs her.

I offer him my hand, and he attempts a smile. I told him this morning that I was planning to propose to Saylor. I'm not sure why. It's not like I was asking his permission, but if

Shannon were alive, I would have asked for hers, so it felt right.

When he said Shannon would be happy for us, it was all the confirmation I needed. Now, how the hell do I do it?

"I'll be back soon," Blake says.

I believe him. Now that he's back in Saylor and Ainsley's life, he realizes he needs them as much as they need him. They'll never get Shannon back, but together, they'll keep her memory alive.

Music plays softly from a nearby speaker, and I take Saylor's hand when Blake is out of view. "Dance with me?"

"We haven't danced in a long time," she says.

Does she remember our last dance? It's a memory I replayed often. "I haven't danced with anyone else."

She pulls back to check my expression for the truth.

"Sayls, the last time we danced was on your front porch, the day I told you I would marry you someday. There wasn't a dance worth ruining that memory for me."

Her chin wobbles, but when I tug her into my body, all feels right with the world.

"I am, you know."

"Hmm?" she says, and it vibrates against my chest.

"Going to marry you."

"Someday." She smiles against my T-shirt.

"Yes," I say begrudgingly. "Someday. But only because I don't have a ring yet."

Her back expands sharply against my palm, and I chuckle.

"But someday soon, my sweet and sassy Saylor girl, you will be mine."

She nods, and her fists twist into the back of my shirt. "Mio amato," she murmurs, and I've never heard a more beautiful song in all my life.

"I'M GOING to ask her to marry me, and soon," I announce as Grady, Harrison, Adam, James, and Lena help me clean up the backyard.

Everyone keeps moving as if I didn't just drop a bomb.

"I'm serious," I say when no one acknowledges me. "I'm going to buy a ring. Tomorrow."

Lena pats my chest and dumps a bucket of water on the fire.

"What?" I ask, more than a little annoyed that everyone isn't shocked or happy, or, well, anything. "I am."

"Jesus, Dante. Everyone is aware that you'll propose. That's not a question. We're worried about what kind of bullshit you'll drag us into to make it happen," Grady says.

"What do you mean?"

"Dude, you can't just ask a girl to marry you anymore. It's a whole thing now. You have to plan, and there's grand gestures and shit," Harrison says, walking behind me with folding chairs in each hand.

"What?"

"Don't listen to them," Lena says gently. "Ask her from your heart. Whatever makes sense. Make it personal to the two of you."

"It's a lot of pressure," James adds while folding one of the tables we carried out for food.

"It is?"

"I would lean heavily on Lena's advice here, Dante." Adam pushes his glasses up his nose with nothing but pure concentration on his face. "None of us are married, and whatever they say they've probably learned from reality TV."

I sink into an abandoned Adirondack chair. "There has to be a grand gesture?"

"You're here, Dante. That was the grand gesture," Adam says, picking up an abandoned paper plate. "You showed up here without knowing if she'd spit in your face, set you on fire, or still be in love with you. Honestly, the odds were not in your favor, and you showed up anyway. The proposal only needs to come from your heart."

"Yeah, but the ring has to be perfect," Harrison yells from across the yard. I stand to tell him to shut the hell up before he wakes Saylor, but Grady beats me to it with a hard smack to the back of his head.

"Saylor doesn't wear a lot of jewelry," Lena says. "And what she does wear holds a lot of sentimental value for her. It doesn't have to be the biggest or flashiest ring, but it has to be the right ring—for her."

All of a sudden, the three burgers I ate tonight are trying to make a comeback.

"Oh, for fuck's sake," Grady mutters, dropping heavily into the chair next to me. "You know Sassy. She doesn't give a flying fuck about any of that. It's you she cares about. You she loves. She'd marry you with a stupid ring that turns her finger green if that's what you gave her. Don't beat yourself up over this. When you find the right ring, you'll know."

His words shifted while he was speaking, and I wonder for the hundredth time what happened with his ex-fiancée. Did he pick out the perfect ring? Will he pick out a better one for Lena? Because there's no doubt in my mind, they're heading to the altar, but I don't ever want Lena to be second-best anything.

It's a conversation we'll have soon, and judging by how Grady shifts next to me, he's not looking forward to it.

"You'll be fine," he says gruffly, then stands and grabs a bag of trash on his way by.

Moments later, Grady steps onto the porch carrying a sleeping Poppy. He tips his head to me, then he leads Lena down the stairs and around the house. The rest of our guests follow shortly behind them while I stay staring at the stars.

How do I make you mine, my sweet and sassy Saylor girl?

Saylor

"Are you sure this is a good idea?" I ask for the hundredth time as Poppy spins in circles around us.

"We'll only be gone for an hour," Dante promises.

Doesn't he know how many catastrophes can happen in an hour? What if she falls down the stairs or cuts her finger open, trying to peel an apple? Do four-year-olds peel apples? What if she falls off the toilet and hits her head or eats laundry soap? That's a thing. I saw it on the news. I would never have eaten a soap pod, but kids today are different.

"Saylor?"

I frown at Dante. Obviously, he's said my name a few times, but I'm not sure if I'm bitchy or scared yet, so he gets the frown.

"One hour. Lena will sign her paperwork for the salon, and I'll sign the lease for next door. Grady has it all ready for us. One hour."

"What if I'm not ready?"

"You are."

"What if something happens and I don't know how to handle it?"

"You will, and we'll have our phones," Lena says gently.

"Aren't you afraid I'm going to break your baby?" I can tell they want to laugh at me, and the only reason they don't is because fear is escaping through my pores and it shines brightly on my clammy face. If my words hadn't alerted them to the fact that I'm completely terrified, the fanning of my armpits would have.

"No, Saylor. I'm not afraid you'll break my four-year-old. You've spent plenty of time with her. I trust you. You need to trust yourself."

"I ate pudding for breakfast," I blurt. "That's not a responsible thing for a babysitter to do."

Lena leans in to hug me. "I gave her Fruity Pebbles for breakfast. It's basically the same thing."

Oh my God. It's not the same. Fruity Pebbles brought up an entire generation of kids. My sister Shannon would eat an entire box in one sitting.

"But…"

"You've got this," Dante says, shutting down my next protest with a kiss that's far too chaste to calm my nerves.

"Poppy packed some crafts for you to do," Lena says, then kisses the little girl holding up a hot pink sparkly bag. "We won't be gone long."

Crafts? Who the hell does she think I am? Martha motherfucking Stewart?

"Sassy! Come on. I've gots a special thing for us." How the heck does this kid move so fast? She already has my hand in hers and is dragging me toward the coffee table. "Auntie Ainsley said you wub pictures."

This whirlwind of a little girl dumps out the entire contents of the bag and stickers, photo frames, pictures, and glitter cover every inch of the table.

So. Much. Glitter.

This will be worse than getting sand in your butt crack at the ocean. This shit will get into every nook and cranny but never leave.

Poppy plops down onto the floor and tilts her head expectantly. There's no way to say no to this little girl. I honestly thought I would be immune to her charms. But I seem to be the worst culprit for giving in. Saying yes to ice cream at ten in the morning is much easier than dealing with tears at that God-forsaken time of day.

Dante doesn't seem to agree.

Little eyes that remind me so much of him peer up at me expectantly, and begrudgingly, I sit beside her.

I'm not sure how I feel about having kids yet. But Poppy has so much Thompson in her, it makes me think of Dante. Would our kids have his features? His coloring?

"Okay, squirt. You've got me here. What are we doing?"

She waggles a finger at me with a smile to let me know that she's not a squirt, but she doesn't mind if I call her one. It's our thing now. I kind of like that we have a thing.

She stares at me until I can't hold in my laughter any longer, then she goes back to her task. I swear she does it on purpose too. She stares at me long enough that I crack. And I do—every single time.

My chest gets hot and tingly, and I shake out my hands instead of clawing at my heart like I want to.

This kid is like bacteria. But the good kind of bacteria, I guess. The kind that helps your gut, not the kind that gives you massive diarrhea.

Lena would probably not appreciate that analogy, but it makes me laugh.

"What's so funny, Auntie?"

Damn it, Poppy. She catches me off guard every time she calls me auntie, and it traps all the air in my lungs.

"Nothing. Just. You're kind of all right, squirt."

"You wub me. It's okay. I wub me too. I's a funny girl." She picks up a pile of pictures and spreads them out in front of us. This kid has enough confidence for the entire freaking state, and I hope she never loses it.

"You are a funny girl, squirt. And you're right. I do love you."

She grins like she tricked me into saying it, and I shrug. Then she hands me some pictures. I hadn't paid attention until now, and something warm and uncomfortable takes up residence in my stomach.

Pictures of my sisters and me. Pictures of Dante and me in high school. Pictures. So many pictures of my life.

"Where did you get these?" My voice sounds funny, like I'm forcing the words through a straw.

"Unca and Mommy gots them for us. Unca wubs pictures, but you don't got any here and it makes me sad."

"Pictures make you happy?"

"Yup."

"How come?" I can't believe I'm asking a four-year-old a serious question, but my heart rate picks up speed, and I need her answer.

"'Cause pictures show wub."

I stare down at the one in my hand. Shannon, Ainsley, and I sit on the top step of the porch while Dante sits between my legs on the step below us.

Damn it. Poppy's going to make me cry because she's right. This picture is love.

"Where is your pictures?" she asks innocently. I watch as she sticks a purple heart onto a foam frame.

I shrug, but she's too focused on her craft to care. "Um, well, for a while they made me sad."

She whips her little head in my direction so fast her pigtails bounce. Her face is full of concern as she gets up onto her knees and grabs my cheeks with both pudgy hands.

"It's okay to be sad. I can fix it. You need sprinkles." She reaches down, plucks a pink glittery heart from the table, and presses it to my forehead. "There. Per-fix. Happy?"

I swallow hard. The picture in my hand is forgotten when this sweet, innocent face that's mere inches away from my own kisses my cheek. "Yes, squirt. I'm happy now. So, tell me. What do I have to do?"

"We've gots so much work to do." I laugh because exasperation sounds funny on a four-year-old. She hands me some foam picture frames and stickers, already shedding glitter all over the floor. "We're makin' your house happy."

So, I get to work using stickers and glue and so much flipping glitter that I'll never get it off me. But we make my house happy, and that's more than I ever thought I'd have.

∾

Dante

"SHE'S NOT ANSWERING HER TEXTS," I say as I climb into the driver's seat of my SUV. Our meeting with Grady took twice as long as we were expecting.

"I'm sure they're fine, Dante. The last time I spoke to her, she said she couldn't text because she had glitter fingers."

I pause with the key almost in the ignition and openly stare at Lena. "Glitter fingers?" I'm already picturing how much Saylor will hate that, but I love her because she'll do it for Poppy.

Lena smirks. "Lots of glitter. Ainsley dropped off some supplies for their special day together."

Chuckling, I start the car. "It's probably best if we don't tell Saylor where the supplies came from then."

She laughs, then buckles her seat belt with a sigh that has me doing a double take.

"You've done good, Lena." She turns to me with a smile that spreads from ear to ear.

"So have you."

I catch my reflection in the rearview mirror when I pull onto the street, pleased with the man I find there.

"We haven't talked about your living situation," I say. I've tried not to pry, but I want her to know she has options.

"I talked with Grady," she says shyly. "I think for now, we're good where we are. He doesn't mind, and I don't want to uproot Poppy again. It's been a lot of change for her." She's quiet for a minute, but her hands twist like she's contemplating something, and I don't want to push, so I wait for her to continue. "It's been a lot of change for me too."

I reach over and squeeze her hand. "I only asked to make sure you were comfortable. I want what's best for you both, whatever that ends up being."

I pull up to a stop sign in time to witness her cheeks tinting pink, then she turns her face to the window. "Thanks, Dante. We're good."

Giving her hand one more squeeze, I release her and turn onto Saylor's road. "Have you heard from Trent?" I ask gently.

She shakes her head. "Not recently."

I nod because I haven't heard from him either, and it's probably for the best.

"Have you come up with a proposal plan yet?" she asks, and I get it, her need to change the subject. Trent will always be a painful memory for us both.

Now it's my turn to sigh. "No. Nothing seems right. I've been carrying the ring around in my pocket for a month because I'm nervous she'll find it otherwise, but every time she hugs me, I'm afraid she'll feel it."

"You'll know when the time is right."

I pull into the driveway and turn off the car. Lena spoke to Saylor an hour ago when she told her we were running late, but I'm anxious to get home to her.

"The house is standing. I'm sure they did okay." Lena jokes while I walk faster than normal toward the house. "Dante, I'm sure they're fine."

"Yeah, I'm sure they are." But I still take the stairs two at a time.

It's silent when I reach the door at the top. I peer at Lena over my shoulder, but she's totally unfazed.

I open the door to enter, and my heart rate races when the house remains silent.

Lena taps me on the shoulder and points to the sofa where Saylor's toes poke out at the end. I shrug and tiptoe toward her. The air wooshes from my lungs at what I find.

Saylor is fast asleep on her back with one arm bent over her face, while the other one wraps protectively around Poppy, who is passed out on top of her. Poppy may never understand the concept of personal space.

My lip twitches, and my heart leaps into my throat. The two girls who are my entire world are sleeping like peaceful little angels. I lean in closer.

Is that...? Do they...?

I tilt my head toward them and smile when Lena tries to suppress a laugh beside me.

Saylor has a sparkly heart stuck to her face, and glitter covers every inch of them as they sleep. My gaze falls to the coffee table, where an explosion of pink and purple everything is spread out in no specific order.

Lena walks around the sofa and holds up a purple piece of foam with a photo of Saylor and me at an amusement park stuck to it. We were seventeen and eighteen in that picture. She lifts another one, this time pink, and it holds a recent photo of Poppy, me, and Saylor.

I'm shaking my head when her pull calls me to her. Saylor observes me with glassy eyes. She's not grumpy, but she's not necessarily happy either.

It takes me a long time to decipher the expression on her face, but when I do, a sense of calm wrapped in love washes over me—she's content, and in Saylor's world, that's the best kind of way to be.

Lena gently lifts Poppy from Saylor's chest, and a rainbow of sparkles falls to the floor.

Saylor shrugs. "That shit gets everywhere," she whispers.

Then she holds up her right hand. She's pressing her thumb and forefinger together, and her cheeks flush as I watch her. Sitting up slowly, she says, "We accidentally superglued my fingers together."

I openly gape at her. She's not serious. But taking her hand in mine, I chuckle because she really did.

"Nail polish remover," Lena suggests. "I'll take her home."

I kiss Poppy's head.

"Thank you for watching her. It takes a lot to knock her out like this. Maybe you should babysit more often," Lena says with a wicked smile.

I'm pleasantly surprised when Oscar doesn't scowl in reply.

"We kind of had fun. But I could do without all the glitter next time."

Lena laughs, and Poppy stirs. "Wub you, Auntie." Her lashes only flutter for a second, but her words hit Saylor hard, and she bites her trembling lip.

I kiss Lena's cheek and walk her to the stairs. "Congrats," I say. "I'm proud of you, Lena."

She dips her chin to her chest and chokes out a thank you before heading out to her car.

When I hear the clash of wood and metal of our screen door, I turn toward Saylor, who has never looked more beautiful.

"What the hell am I supposed to do about my fingers?"

"Why didn't you try to pry them apart when it first happened?" I ask.

Saylor shrugs like my question is annoying. "Because, hot shot. We were trying to get a stupidly sparkly heart to stick to the foam, so I was squishing the two pieces together for a long time. Then we took the foam frame away, and the corners of my skin wouldn't unstick without tearing me along with it."

I tug her to standing and lead her toward the bathroom. "Let's see what we can do."

Lifting her onto the bathroom counter, I open a drawer and pull out some nail polish remover and a round gauze pad she has next to it.

"We'll probably have to soak it for a few minutes," I say. Then rummage under the sink for a small paper cup. When I find one, I dump the nail polish remover in and place her fingers into the liquid.

"So," I say. "You had fun with Poppy?"

"That girl had a plan, and nothing would deter her."

That's usually the way it is with her.

"But, for the first time in years, she made me want to have pictures around. I want to remember the good stuff, Dante."

"I'm glad, Sayls. And you've made enough frames to line an entire hallway."

"I told you. She had a plan."

I capture her gaze with mine, and even in the shitty lighting of the outdated bathroom, she's the most beautiful woman I've ever seen. Our faces are only inches apart. We're so close I can smell something sugary and sweet on her breath. I can only imagine the junk Poppy coerced her into eating.

"Let's try to pry your fingers apart," I say quietly.

She removes her fingers and with a little effort, they finally peel apart, but she's going to have the glue residue on the pads of her fingers for weeks.

"My hero," she says, batting her lashes like a cartoon pinup.

My throat is thick when I try to speak, and I swallow twice to get words to work. "Always," I grind out.

Her blue eyes sparkle with love and mischief as she stares at me, and I place both hands on her thighs.

"You're amazing, Saylor Greer. I love you so much."

She tilts her head like she's examining me. "You're pretty okay yourself."

My lips curl into a slanted grin. "Just okay?"

She shrugs. "Yeah. I mean, I won't throw you out yet or anything."

"How kind of you," I say dryly. "But what if I don't want you to ever throw me out?"

I say it in jest, but suddenly the ring in my pocket is a living, breathing thing. It pulses against my thigh like a heartbeat, and I clear my throat because this is our time.

"You've got some work to do then," she teases, but the words die on her lips when she looks at my face. Whatever she finds there makes her reach for her necklace and lick her lips.

"The guys said I needed a grand gesture," I say.

"For—For what?"

"But the way I see it, I've been working toward this day since I was fifteen years old."

"What day, Dante?" The tendon in her neck twitches.

"The very first time I saw you was in the hallway. You were on your way to P.E., did you know that?"

She shakes her head and zips her necklace along its chain.

"You were scowling and muttering about changing into gym shorts to walk the track. You were so pissed off, and I was instantly smitten."

"You liked me because I was a scowling, cranky complainer?"

I shake my head. "No, Saylor. I saw your heart that day." She scowls up at me, and it instantly transports me back to that hallway. "The kid you were walking with had terrible asthma and P.E. was a nightmare for him. I learned that day that you grumbled and complained so everyone in that class would focus on you and not that kid."

"Jeffers. His name was Jeffers," she says like she's just remembering him.

"You did it the next day and the one after that too."

"Well, having P.E. five days a week is excessive," she says. Her scowl deepens when she crosses her arms over her chest.

"Then I saw you at lunch. It was a Friday. Pizza day." The memory heats my chest. "Everyone hated the pizza."

"Well," she says with a shit ton of snark, "the cheese fell right off the crust. What do you expect?"

"You brought your lunch every day. You didn't eat the pizza, Saylor. But the kid you ate with every day did."

"She got free lunch. She had to eat it." Her attitude is in prickly emotional-defense mode as she starts to understand the magnitude of how long I've been in love with her.

"And you packed extra food on Fridays to share with her."

"So what?" God, I love this girl. She's always had the biggest heart protected by thorns. "What's your point?"

"My point is you care. You always have. And I've always loved that about you. I think I've loved you since the moment I saw you. And I became ensnared when you hit me with the sharp edge of your tongue. You're strong, Saylor. And smart. You're beautiful and kind even if you hide those pieces from the world. I've always seen them. And I always want them. I want you forever, sweetheart."

Reaching into my pocket, I sink to one knee on the tile floor.

"What are you doing?" Her voice is hoarse, and she starts swinging her feet back and forth against the cabinet.

I take a deep, steadying breath, open the ring box, and stare at her expectantly. "I don't have a grand gesture, Sayls. But I have a lifetime of love and endless patience. I have dreams of a future with you and memories of our past."

A tear slides down her face, and I realize I have a

matching one on mine. Taking her hand, I lace our fingers together.

"We've been through more than our share of heartache, and now I want the forever kind of love with you. I want to wake up with Oscar and go to bed with Sassy. I want to kiss Saylor and love every cranky, sassy, sweet, caring, forgiving side of you."

She uses the back of her hand to wipe her eyes and nose. The dam has broken, and I read everything she's thinking in each tear that falls.

"I want to fall into bed with you at night, knowing it's a forever kind of fall. I need you by my side because you remind me to be the man I always wanted to be. You make me better and stronger and wiser and more loving. You make me me because I was never whole without you. I need you because you're all the pieces I'm missing."

"Dante," she chokes out. A sob escapes, and I release her hand from mine to remove the sapphire and diamond ring from its box.

"Saylor Greer, I've loved you for a lifetime. Please, say you'll be my wife and be my forever."

She's nodding, but no words come out.

"Is that a yes?" I ask.

Tears streak her beautiful face. "Y—Y—Yes," she says, and my heart chooses that moment to dance an Irish jig in my chest.

I jump to my feet and slide the ring onto her finger. She's mine. I don't need the wedding or a certificate to tell me that. Standing here, in our tiny bathroom above her beloved bookstore, I claim her as my happily ever after.

And not even the great Sassy Thompson could have written it better. Or so I thought…

~

BONUS SCENE

Dante

1 year later

"Are you ready?" Kate asks from a desk in the corner. She only visits this office on days we're expecting news, or she feels the need to check up on us, which has been happening more and more lately.

"Yes. No. I don't know." Saylor buries her face in her hands.

Turns out, bringing Kate on board with Sway was the right move. She's helped bring in clients, and I've been able to steer clear of celebrities for the most part. Now we focus on authors and musicians.

"For crying out loud," Kate mumbles. "I didn't work my ass off to get you this deal so you could screw around."

She finagled a pretty epic deal with Holiday House. They publish all of Saylor's paperbacks, while we hold the rights to e-books and audiobooks.

"It's nearly impossible to hit the *New York Times* list as an indie author," Saylor says under her breath.

I stand and wrap my arms around her waist. "You're a hybrid author, so it's very possible you're on that list," I remind her. Turning to Kate I say, "Open it up. We're ready."

"*Trustfall* by Sassy Thompson," she says with a dramatic flair. "Is…" She uses her fingers to drumroll on her desk.

"Knock it off, Kate. Tell me," Saylor demands.

"*Trustfall* is number eighty-seven on the *New York Times* bestsellers list."

Saylor doesn't move, but her chest expands in my arms when she sucks in a long breath before releasing it slowly.

"And you're up to almost twenty thousand reviews already."

This has her walking out of my grasp and running to the computer. "No way," she says. "It took me months and months to get that many reviews on every other book."

"This isn't just a book, Sassy. It's a love story every person can relate to. It's a story of loss and love and regret. You hit every mark with this one, and it's only the beginning." Kate has softened a bit in the last few months. The chip on her shoulder doesn't seem quite as large, but make no mistake, she's still a shark.

"How's that for a wedding present?" I ask with a smile that hurts my cheeks. Our wedding is in three days, and I couldn't have planned this any better. I think Shannon must have pulled some strings from heaven because the immediate success of *Trustfall* is unparalleled.

Saylor looks up from the screen, and I've never seen such pure happiness on anyone. This is how she was always meant to be. The girl who lives in fairytales and writes their happily ever afters.

"This is what happens when you believe in love," I say.

She nods and looks back at the computer, and I sit at my desk, soaking in everything we've accomplished this year.

The office on the top floor of the abandoned building was our first project, and once we started, we didn't stop.

The door swings open, and Grady walks in. "The house won't be ready by Saturday," he says, sinking into a guest chair. It sucks, but I knew it wouldn't be. We've hit one too many snags over there, and we haven't even broken ground on the new bookstore yet.

"Grady," Saylor squeals when she finds him sitting in the office. "We did it! We hit the *New York Times* list."

He stands so abruptly that his chair tips over.

It causes an instant flashback to my meeting with Trent over a year and a half ago when he did the same thing.

This time, the outcome is a happy one. Grady wraps Saylor in a hug and swings her around the room, while I stand and pick up the chair. My gaze snags on Trent's picture in the corner of the room. It's of him and Poppy. My chest thunders like it always does, and I send up a silent prayer for him.

Saylor slips in under my arm, and I realize I've been standing here staring at it.

"He's trying," she whispers. She'll probably never forgive my brother, but she understands what family means to me. It's a strange dichotomy she lives with when it comes to him, but love is all about compromises, and we're compromising daily.

"I know," I say, kissing the top of her head. And I do believe he is. He's been at an inpatient facility for the last six months, and contact hasn't been allowed. After he called to tell us where he was, it's been nothing but silence.

"You both ready for your Jack and Jill parties?"

"No," Saylor says adamantly. "He can do whatever he

wants, but I am not going out the night before a boatload of people will be staring at me."

Our wedding has caused a little bit of tension. Saylor categorically does not want to be the center of attention. What she doesn't know is we all planned the day with her in mind. The ceremony will only be her, me, Grady, Lena, Ainsley, Blake, and Poppy. Everyone else will arrive for the reception.

I've kept it a secret because I know I'll need a wild card when it comes to her.

"Yeah, I know what Harrison says, but I'm not going out either," I say.

"Thank God," Grady grumbles. "The last thing I want to do is pick up drunk people from my barroom floor." He sounds grumpy, but I also know Grady would have done it if a party was what we wanted.

"Okay. I'm out of here," Kate says. "I'll see you all Saturday."

Kate is not a hugger, so she gives a two-finger salute and walks out of the office. Grady follows behind.

"I've got some stuff to do," he explains. And then it's just Saylor and I, alone in the office.

She turns in my arms. "We did it."

"Of course we did, Sayls. I told you, it's only up from here."

She nods and rests her cheek against my chest as we sway like we're dancing. "In a few days, we'll dance as husband and wife," I say.

"Or," she lifts to kiss my cheek, "we'll be dancing as wife and husband."

I chuckle and shake my head. "Nothing will ever be easy with you, will it?"

"What would be the fun in that?"

"You're right." I lean down to kiss her lips. "I wouldn't

change a thing about you. Not now, not ever."

"Remember you said that. I've heard pregnancy and menopause are real relationship testers."

I stop swaying. We haven't discussed children.

"Do you..." I pause to lick my lips. "Are kids something you want?"

Her hand clasps her pendant, but unlike a year and a half ago, she doesn't shut down, and she doesn't swing it harshly on the chain. She takes a minute to compose her thoughts. "I don't know, honestly. I think I do. I know if I have children, I want them to have your eyes, but I'd be a liar if I said I wasn't scared about what a pregnancy would do to my mental health, or what my medications would do to a baby."

I lead her to the sofa in the corner and sit her down next to me.

"All we need to focus on now is if children are a possibility. Worrying about meds and all those fears is a 'future us' point that we'll address when we're ready. Do you want kids someday?"

"Do you?" Saylor will always have an instinct to flee, to deflect and hide. But she comes around much more quickly these days.

"I do," I reply. "But not at your expense. There are a lot of ways to make a family. When and if we're ready, we'll find the one that works for us."

Her shoulders relax in relief. "That sounds like a good plan."

"It is," I agree. "Let's get home. We're going to need all the sleep we can get over the next couple of days."

Saylor groans as she slips into her winter coat. She really has had to deal with the brunt of the wedding planning. Ainsley and Lena would accept nothing less.

"Can't you tell them I'm sick until Saturday?"

"They wouldn't buy it for a second."

We walk down the stairs, across the snow-covered lawn, and through the construction zone that will eventually be our new home.

"This is a mess," she says, walking toward the back of the house.

"Yup. But it's our mess."

Her smile cuts straight to my heart. I reach around her to open the door, and we walk up to our apartment together, like it was always meant to be.

∼

Saylor

New Year's Eve

"I hope he's kidding." The growl in my words rumbles my chest as I peek around the curtain. Why on earth did Dante approve all this—this fluff? They've turned the glass-enclosed gazebo that's normally a restaurant into a wedding venue any princess would covet.

I'm not a princess, but the room is exploding with poppies, and it causes a strange fluttering in my chest. It makes me a little nauseous, so I pull the curtains closed.

"Why all the fairy lights?" I ask my sister, who has made it a point to avoid me all day.

"Because they're beautiful and they'll be absolutely amazing in the pictures."

"Where is everyone? Didn't we invite like a hundred people to this thing?"

"We did," Dante says from the other side of the curtain.

"What are you doing?" Panic causes my voice to rise. "We can't see each other before the wedding. It's bad luck, and I don't need any more bad luck."

"We won't have bad luck," he says calmly. "But I knew you were going to have a meltdown, so I came to tell you something."

"What?" I ask, crossing my arms over my chest.

"Don't bite your lip like that," Ainsley scolds. "You'll ruin your makeup."

I could give a rat's ass about my makeup, but I release my lip so she doesn't have a hissy fit.

"Saylor." Dante's smooth voice filters through the heavy velvet curtain meant to keep the cold breeze from hitting the restaurant. "Are you nervous?"

My lips purse, and Ainsley makes an uncomfortable noise in the back of her throat.

"Yes." I probably surprise them both by answering honestly.

Dante's hand parts the curtain, but he keeps his gaze averted. He simply reaches for my hand. The second our skin touches, my heart rate slows.

"I knew you would be. That's why the only people who will be here for the ceremony are us, your sister, Lena, Blake, Grady, and Poppy. Everyone else will arrive an hour later for the party."

The news makes me lightheaded. "Why the heck didn't you tell me that before?"

He squeezes my hand, and his laughter hits me right in the gut. "Because. If I'd told you sooner, you would have bargained and bartered to keep everyone from coming to the reception."

Crap. He's right. That's what I did with the ceremony, but I didn't know I'd won that fight. If I had, I would have absolutely started working on the reception.

"Are you calmer?" he asks. I turn to ask Ainsley something, but only catch the flowing fabric of her dress as she rounds the corner.

411

"I guess so."

"I love you, my sweet and sassy Saylor girl."

"I love you too."

"Are we ready?" Blake asks, making me jump.

"I'll see you in a minute," Dante says, releasing my hand.

Blake steps up beside me and holds up a small box.

"What's this?" I ask.

"A family heirloom," he says with a shrug. "Shannon would have worn them, so I thought that maybe you would like to. She would have handed them down to you today. That's how it works in my family."

"You're not supposed to make me cry, asshole."

He opens the jewelry box, and beautiful blue stones in the shape of flowers sparkle up at me. "You're stronger than that, Sassy. You're stronger than anyone I've ever known, and I'm so proud of you for fighting for your happy ending."

Blake lifts one earring out and hands it to me. While I'm putting it on, I ask, "What about you? Are you finding your happy ending?"

He turns his head like he's searching for someone. "Some-times I think it finds you," he says but doesn't elaborate. He hands me the other earring, and I study him.

"Are you happy?" I ask. The shadows that haunt him have all but vanished over the last few months, and he isn't carrying his grief like a calling card anymore.

"I'm—trying."

I wrap my arms around him. "Promise me that you'll keep trying, Blake. That's all we can do, keep trying every day."

He pats my back when music begins to play. "Are you ready?"

Ainsley, Lena, and Poppy slip in front of us, and Poppy is already throwing sparkly flowers everywhere. I'm pretty sure we'll be paying an extra cleanup fee for all her glitter, but watching her face, I know it'll be worth it.

Lena goes next, and I peek through a crack in the curtain. Grady wipes away a tear next to Dante, which causes them both to reach for a tissue.

This, us, we're Dante's family.

Ainsley kisses me quickly on the cheek. *I love you*, she says without ever speaking a word, then walks down the aisle. That's something else I have back, the weird twin language I'd blocked for so long.

And then it's our turn.

Blake parts the curtain and my breath catches. Freaking Ainsley was right. With my family standing and staring at me, it's goddamn beautiful in here.

We reach the wall of windows that face the frozen lake, and Blake hands me off to Dante. "Take care of her," he says through a cloud of emotion.

"Always," Dante agrees.

Then we turn to the reverend, and our ceremony begins.

It lasts exactly seven minutes because six minutes standing in front of people was my previous record. It was my only request for this shindig, and when he announces us husband and wife, Dante kisses the ever-living fear right out of me.

"Where's Blake?" my sister asks. I'm in the corner fanning my armpits and really wishing I'd worn men's deodorant today. I've never danced so much in my entire life.

"Oh, Ains, he couldn't find you, and he had to leave early. I don't know for sure, but I think he might be seeing someone." I stop fanning my armpits and stare at my sister with an open mouth. Her lipstick is smudged, and she very clearly has been kissing someone. "Where have you been, missy?"

She sees that I'm focused on her lips, and she immediately

tries to clean up, but then Harrison walks around the corner and bumps into us and my smile nearly breaks my face.

"Hello, Harrison. You're very...handsome." He tilts his chin and clutches his heart like the charmer he is, right up until I say, "My sister's lipstick is a good look on you." His face falls, and he turns a little green while trying to make eye contact with her.

Ainsley pinches her lips and eyes closed while I laugh. "It's not— It's the first— Oh, just shut up, Sassy."

This has me standing up straighter, but it doesn't erase my smile. It's been a long time since she told me to shut up, and strangely, I like it.

I hug her in apology. "I'm not judging, Ains. But I do want to hear all about it."

She sighs but agrees. I don't get to prod them any further though because Poppy crashes into me next.

I bend down to pick her up, and the excessive amount of lace and tulle at the bottom of my dress gets caught in my hands. When cool air hits my legs, I know I'm probably flashing everyone right now, but Poppy is squishing my cheeks. This is serious.

"Tell Papa Bear I is stayin' here. I isn't tired, and I wanna dance."

Grady groans when he finds me holding her. One-on-one, he might win against us. But when we team up, he's a goner.

"Grady Reid. There's no way you're trying to take my new niece away from my party, are you? You do realize I only get one wedding. I know you wouldn't try to ruin our fun before it's over."

"It's almost midnight, and she's five," he says through clenched teeth.

"What do you think, squirt?"

Her face lights up like a Christmas tree. "I thinks we daance." She wiggles, and I put her down. Poppy is a slippery little thing, and she runs right through Grady's legs.

"Thanks for nothing," he mutters. Then his shoulders slump as he admits defeat. "You look really nice, Sassy. And happier than I've seen you in a long time."

My chin quivers because so does he. "We've done pretty well for ourselves. From the ashes of death and betrayal, we rise to shine like the motherfucking rock stars we are."

He chokes on his laugh. "How much have you had to drink?"

"A lot," I say with a grin. "Like *a lot* a lot."

"Got it. Let's get you some water."

"Already on it, big guy." I point at Dante clearing a path with two bottles of water in his hands.

When he arrives at our sides, he pushes one bottle at me, and Grady laughs. "Good luck," he says to Dante, then goes off into the crowd, presumably to find a little girl who is a master at hide and seek.

"Are you having fun?" Dante asks with a smirk. I hope whatever he finds in my expression tells him I am because this is the best day of my life—even with the twinkling fairy lights.

"Shannon loved this place. I'm glad we chose it."

"Me too." He lifts my hands, reminding me to drink. "I think everyone is having fun."

"Well." I laugh and spill water on the floor. "Everyone except Cassie and James."

Dante turns his head and finds them in the corner, their faces only inches apart. "I bet you twenty orgasms he kisses her or she kisses him tonight and it changes everything."

I squint, trying to figure out what he's talking about, but the squinting only makes me see two of them.

"No way," I say. "Cassie's ready to claw his throat out. There's no way she would kiss him."

415

"So it's a bet, then. Your money is on Cassie, and mine is on James?"

"Oh yeah. You're going down, buddy."

He pulls me into his side, and we take in those around us. Harrison is smirking at Ainsley, who pretends to ignore him. Grady dances with Poppy on his hip and Lena in his arms while keeping close tabs on Lilly and Kai.

Even the members of Sexy Scenes and Sips sit in the corner, smiling at all the happiness.

"You're killing me in this dress, Saylor."

Startled by Dante's whispered admission, I peer into his eyes to find them burning hot with need.

I swallow the frog in my throat.

"Yeah? You're not too bad yourself." And he's not. I've never seen a man own a tux so thoroughly before.

"We are out of here at twelve-oh-one and you can start on the twenty orgasms you're going to owe me on the way home."

"Forget it. There's no way Cassie kisses him, but I'm willing to leave right after midnight so you can start on the orgasms you'll owe me."

"Ten, nine, eight," Harrison counts down, and Dante leads me to the center of the dance floor. "Six, five, four."

"Watch Cassie and James, sweetheart, because after they kiss, you won't see another thing until we're in the back of the car."

"One," Harrison cries out like he's about to meet Santa for the first time.

There are cheers and kisses happening all around me. We watch for half a second as Cassie and James collide. I'm not sure which one of them moved first, but there's no denying they're kissing.

"Winner," Dante growls in my ear. Then his lips land on mine in the most possessive, soul-affirming kiss I've ever had. His kiss reaches my heart and makes all my fears, hopes, dreams, and promises of forever, ours.

"We're leaving," he says against my lips.

"But—But who won?"

He pulls back with a smile that makes my core spasm. "Isn't it obvious?" I shake my head. "We're the winner, Sayls."

"No, I mean with Cassie and James. They collided like football players. How do we know who kissed who first?"

Dante shrugs as the fairy lights above us shimmer like stars. "We both win. They crashed into each other. That means we each get ten orgasms, and the rules say they all must happen tonight."

"T—Tonight?" I croak.

"Tonight. Say goodbye, Saylor."

At some point, a crowd surrounded us. "Goodbye, Saylor?"

He laughs and then tosses me over his shoulder. Someone throws a blanket around me before he hits the velvet curtains, and I lift my head to witness the love in the room one more time.

Every single person stands with tears in their eyes and love in their hearts. For me. For us. A single tear slides down my face because I know I could have missed out on all of it.

Thank God Dante is even more stubborn than I am.

I lift my hand to my lips and blow everyone kisses. "I love you all. Even when I hate everything else, I love you."

Everyone laughs, and Poppy throws more glitter-covered flowers in our direction.

We leave our wedding the way we were always meant to —surrounded by life, love, and covered in all the things that shine, because what shines also helps fight the darkness.

And I'm ready for a lifetime of happy.

ACKNOWLEDGMENTS

My family: Thank you for letting the dogs outside when they bark. Thank you for understanding that my weird hours are for a reason. Thank you for being patient while I figured my new world out. Everything I do, and everything I am, is for you.

Rhon: Thank you for understanding all my authorly quirks and luving me anyway. Thank you for standing tall as my protector when I don't feel strong enough to do it myself. I appreciate everything you do.

Beth: I freaking LUV you. That is all. And I miss you. Thank you for always being my biggest fan.

Team TWSS: The amazing team of unicorn publishers. Thank you for continuing to believe in me and constantly telling me to stop trying to take a back seat. I'm stronger, and braver, and more confident because of you all.

Brynne: Thank you for talking through this story with me. I think you'll be very proud that I followed your advice of "Kill him a little." So readers, blame the tears on Brynne this time.

Kathryn: You shiny ray of happiness. I would not have made it through edits without your support and commiseration. Thank you for being the friend everyone needs.

Lucy: Everything goes our way. Thank you for supporting me and guiding me in all things self-help. You are truly a rock star.

Marissa: Thank you for being my travel companion, my emotional support person, and my fill-in PA.

Joyce & Tammy: I would not make it through these books without your daily support. Thank you for always being a safe space for me.

Team Avery: Phew. This is the group who keeps the crap from hitting the fan. The women of #teamAvery help me spread luv and kindness like glitter every single day. When I said I wanted to build my brand on kindness, these ladies showed up with glitter in their pockets and luv in their hearts. Thank you for always being in my corner.

Streat and ARC Teams: Thank you for everything you do, from recommending my books to leaving your honest reviews. Everything you do matters more than you could ever know, and I appreciate all the time, effort, and luv you put into helping me.

The Luv Club: Thank you for being my safe space. In a world full of keyboard warriors, you keep my little piece of the internet safe, luving, and kind to all. You make my world a better place. xo

Beta Readers: Well, this one was a doozy, wasn't it? Never again will I send you a draft before I'm ready (that's draft number seven, by the way!) Thank you for wading through the dumpster to find the diamond.

Sensitivity Readers: My heart feels forever connected to yours. Thank you for sharing your raw, emotional stories with me, and then ensuring I represented us all with kindness and respect.

My Readers: I wouldn't have acknowledgments to write without you. Whether this is the first book you've read by me or your twelfth, I appreciate the time you've spent with my words. Thank you for your support and luv. I couldn't do this without you.

Kari March Designs: I'm not sure how you do it, but you bring my stories to life in beautiful color every single time. Thank you for your talents.

HEA Author Services: Even though developmental edits make me want to crawl under the porch and bury my head in the dirt, I see the value and trust your insight, so thank you for pushing me to be my best. Jess: Thank you for opening your calendar and for talking me off the cliff not once, not twice, but three times with this book, and for going the extra mile to make sure all the edits worked with my excessively empathetic self. You'll never know how much I appreciate your hard work, and especially your patience every time FB dings with a message from me.

GET TO KNOW AVERY!

Hello, Luvs!

Want to hang out with me? I'm in The Luv Club every day sharing my chaos, my mess, my life. Pop in to say hi, meet the other luvables, and stay a while. It's the happiest, kindest, messiest, most inclusive group on the internet and I'd LUV to see you there!

https://geni.us/AverysLUVclub

ALSO BY AVERY MAXWELL

Standalone Romance:

Without A Hitch

Your Last First Kiss

Falling Into Forever